W9-BQL-849

Praise for *Midnight Is the Darkest Hour*

"Ashley Winstead shows her versatility and virtuosity as an author in this dark, eerie, and completely enchanting book about friendship, love, and vengeance. *Midnight Is the Darkest Hour* is as creepy as it gets—and a tearjerker to boot! I loved every minute of it."

—Mary Kubica, *New York Times* bestselling author of *Just the Nicest Couple*

"*Where the Crawdads Sing* meets *Twilight* meets *Thelma and Louise* in this brilliantly realized, totally original thriller. Absolutely sensational—I couldn't put it down."

—Clare Mackintosh, *New York Times* bestselling author

"Dark and lyrical, Ashley Winstead turns her talent toward the Deep South in her latest, *Midnight Is the Darkest Hour*. A compelling story about the occult, evil, and the ways religious fundamentalism can overtake reason, it's also a story about loyalty, friendship and what connects us all at our deepest roots. Once again, Ashley Winstead spins a tale that is equal parts disturbing and redemptive. (And when you're done reading, please message me so we can talk about that ending!)"

—Julie Clark, *New York Times* bestselling author of *The Lies I Tell* and *The Last Flight*

"A Gothic tale that blurs the line between good and evil, love and revenge, and the inherent desire to please our parents while simultaneously struggling to find ourselves. *Midnight Is the Darkest Hour* is unique and unnerving from beginning to end."

—Stacy Willingham, *New York Times* bestselling author of *All the Dangerous Things* and *A Flicker in the Dark*

"Woe unto the preacher's daughter, or at least that's what you might think navigating the dark and broody twists of Ashley Winstead's spellbinding latest, *Midnight Is the Darkest Hour*. Prepare yourself (if you can) for serpents of the Deep South gospel slithering into a beautifully rendered *Twilight* fever dream—like all of Ashley's incredible books, you won't be able to turn the pages fast enough."

—Vanessa Lillie, bestselling author of *Little Voices* and *Blood Sisters*

"Ashley Winstead does it again! Making the hairs at the back of your neck prickle while mesmerizing you with prose so rich that you want to dive into this novel with both feet, Winstead delivers another yet multilayered thriller so nuanced and intricately woven that you absolutely cannot help but race to the end."

—Amanda Jayatissa, author of *You're Invited*

"A dark, sultry fever dream of a novel, *Midnight Is the Darkest Hour* is a powerful examination of love, girlhood, and religion. With lush, gorgeous writing and dynamic characterization, Ashley Winstead carefully dismantles the corrupted hierarchy that has ruled a God-fearing small town and unleashes the trapped scream of being a young woman in the world. This haunting, twisting story will stay with you long after the last page."

—Laurie Elizabeth Flynn, author of *The Girls Are All So Nice Here*

"An utter triumph, *Midnight Is the Darkest Hour* is Ashley Winstead's most dazzling thriller to date. This is a one-sitting binge read, so cancel all plans and prepare to become completely obsessed with Ruth and Everett and the darkly magical world of Bottom Springs, Louisiana. *Twilight* meets *True Blood* meets Colleen Hoover in this completely original, explosive suspense where every line is a poem and every chapter a lyrical symphony. I could not put this book down and haven't been so wholly captured by a story in this way in years."

—May Cobb, author of *A Likeable Woman* and *The Hunting Wives*

"*Midnight Is the Darkest Hour* is a lush, immersive ode to the wildness and violence at the hidden heart of teenage girlhood. The sharp-toothed answer to every fairy tale that warns girls to stay out of the woods…because what if we like what we find? Ashley Winstead has at once crafted an incisive critique of fundamentalism and one of the most unforgettable love stories I've ever read, dressed as a thriller that surprises at every turn."

—Katie Gutierrez, bestselling author of *More Than You'll Ever Know*

Praise for *The Last Housewife*

"A dark, twisted tale of feminism and patriarchy, Ashley Winstead has given us a gripping story about a cult and the ways in which women became psychologically bound, while at the same time exploring themes of power and redemption. Timely and terrifying, *The Last Housewife* will haunt your dreams and change the way you view the world."

—Julie Clark, *New York Times* bestselling author of *The Last Flight* and *The Lies I Tell*

"It's not every day I finish a novel and decide right then and there that the author is now an auto-buy. While I was anticipating a great story from Winstead, I wasn't expecting to inhale her new book in one breathless read. *The Last Housewife* is a propulsive, unputdownable thriller with a dark, beating heart. It chilled me to the bone, and I'm still recovering. Ashley Winstead, I bow down."

—Jennifer Hillier, author of the bestselling *Little Secrets*

"A stunning, disturbing thriller that will have your mind and heart racing. *The Last Housewife* is a clever, twisty, unnerving ride through feminism, patriarchy, and power, and it had me gasping for air."

—Samantha Downing, international bestselling author of *For Your Own Good*

"Provocative and downright terrifying, *The Last Housewife* feels ripped from the headlines as it explores the dark world of a violent, misogynist cult in a New York college town. Winstead deftly tackles the complicated issues of gender, coercion, and agency while crafting an edge-of-your-seat, action-packed thriller!"

—Wendy Walker, international bestselling author of *All Is Not Forgotten* and *Don't Look for Me*

"Ashley Winstead takes her reader into the heart of darkness—and brilliantly reveals the tender, human part hidden in those shadows. Propulsive, smart, and chilling, *The Last Housewife* confirms what *In My Dreams I Hold a Knife* promised: no one writes thrillers like Ashley Winstead."

—Alison Wisdom, author of *The Burning Season*

"The total package—fearless, disruptive, and gripping. Ashley Winstead's talent is astounding. One of the best books I've read this year."

—Eliza Jane Brazier, author of *Good Rich People*

"Only fifty shades of gray? Please. Ashley Winstead's *The Last Housewife* is a technicolor rainbow, provocative and unflinching in its brilliant portrayal of female desire, male violence, and the unsettling link between them. A disturbingly sexy thrill ride that does more than 'twist'—it explodes off the page, confronting dark truths about women in the patriarchy and forging weapons of resistance from the flames. You don't read *The Last Housewife*. You face it down."

—Amy Gentry, bestselling author of *Good as Gone*, *Last Woman Standing*, and *Bad Habits*

"*The Last Housewife* is a seductive, provocative work of literature steeped in a mystery, that kept me turning page after page."

—Yasmin Angoe, bestselling author of the critically acclaimed *Her Name Is Knight*

Praise for *In My Dreams I Hold a Knife*

"Deeply drawn characters and masterful storytelling come together to create an addictive and riveting psychological thriller. Put this one at the very top of your 2021 reading list."

—Liv Constantine, international bestselling author of *The Last Mrs. Parrish*

"Tense, twisty, and packed with shocks, Ashley Winstead's assured debut dares to ask how much we can trust those we know best—including ourselves. A terrific read!"

—Riley Sager, *New York Times* bestselling author of *Home Before Dark*

"Nostalgic and sinister, *In My Dreams I Hold a Knife* whisks the reader back to college. Glory days, unbreakable friendships, all-night parties, and a belief that the best in life is ahead of you. But ten years after the murder of one of the East House Seven, the unbreakable bonds may be hiding fractured secrets of a group bound not by loyalty but by fear. Twisty and compulsively readable, *In My Dreams I Hold a Knife* will have you turning pages late into the night, not just to figure out who murdered beloved Heather Shelby, but to see whether friendships forged under fire can ever be resurrected again."

—Julie Clark, *New York Times* bestselling author of *The Last Flight* and *The Lies I Tell*

"Fans of *The Secret History*, Ruth Ware, and Andrea Bartz will devour this dark academic thriller with an addictive locked-room mystery at its core. An astonishingly sure-footed debut, *In My Dreams I Hold a Knife* is the definition of compulsive reading. The last page will give you nightmares."

—Amy Gentry, bestselling author of *Good as Gone*, *Last Woman Standing*, and *Bad Habits*

"Beautiful writing, juicy secrets, complex female characters, and drumbeat suspense—what more could you want from a debut thriller?"

—Andrea Bartz, bestselling author of *The Lost Night* and *The Herd*

"An unsolved murder, dark secrets, and dysfunctional college days, all wrapped up in a twisty plot that will keep you flipping pages."

—Darby Kane, #1 international bestselling author of *Pretty Little Wife*

"With its compelling puzzle-box structure and delightfully ruthless cast of characters, this twisty dark academia thriller will have you flipping pages like you're pulling an all-nighter to cram for a final. *In My Dreams I Hold a Knife* is required reading for fans of Donna Tartt's *The Secret History* and Amy Gentry's *Bad Habits*."

—Layne Fargo, author of *They Never Learn*

"Looking for an eerie campus setting? This chilling suspense novel has murder, friendship, and defiance when six people return to their college reunion a decade after one of their close friends was murdered."

—*Parade Magazine*

"[A] captivating debut... Winstead does an expert job keeping the reader guessing whodunit. Suspense fans will eagerly await her next."

—*Publishers Weekly*

"A twisty, dark puzzle... Fans of books such as *The Girl on the Train* and *Gone Girl* will find this book captivating, as will anyone who enjoys being led down a winding, frightening path. Highly recommended."

—*New York Journal of Books*

"Packed with intrigue, scandal, and enough twists and turns to match Donna Tartt's *The Secret History*, this is a solid psychological-thriller debut."

—*Booklist*

"Ashley Winstead's mordant debut novel is the latest entry in the budding subgenre of 'dark academia,' where the crime narrative takes place on a college campus... At its heart, Winstead's novel examines what it means to covet the lives of others, no matter the cost."

—*New York Times*

Also by Ashley Winstead

In My Dreams I Hold a Knife

The Last Housewife

Fool Me Once

The Boyfriend Candidate

Midnight *is the* Darkest Hour

a novel

ASHLEY WINSTEAD

Cover art and design by Erin Fitzsimmons/Sourcebooks
Cover photo © Grant Tandy/Shutterstock
Internal design by Laura Boren/Sourcebooks

Published by Sourcebooks Landmark, an imprint of Sourcebooks
P.O. Box 4410, Naperville, Illinois 60567-4410
(630) 961-3900
sourcebooks.com

Cataloging-in-Publication Data is on file with the Library of Congress.

Printed and bound in the United States of America.
LSC 10 9 8 7 6 5 4 3 2 1

For Russell, who said I did not have to be good

Content warnings: religious fundamentalism, substance abuse, ableism, colonialism, familial violence, sexual violence, child abuse, murder.

1

NOW

Five hours and forty-six minutes after a trapper pulls the skull from the depths of Starry Swamp, shaking sludge and Spanish moss out of its eye sockets, the entire town of Bottom Springs, Louisiana—all five-thousand-two-hundred-twenty-nine Christian souls and the small handful of Godless heathens—has heard the news. *Once again,* they whisper, *a person has been claimed by the swamp.*

But days later, Sheriff Thomas Theriot holds a press conference. Sheriff Thomas Theriot has not held a press conference once in his thirty years of service to the law. In Bottom Springs, there's never been a need. So this morning, when he stands outside his office with the reporter from the *Trufayette Town Talk*, flanked by his two deputies, the entire town comes to see it. There have been people lost to the swamp for as long as there have been people living in Bottom Springs, but this press conference means something's different. Even the ones who weren't waiting for it—who haven't, like me, lain awake every night anticipating this moment—are drawn out like a spell from the Dollar General and Piggly Wiggly and Old Man Jonas's Bait & Tackle Shop.

They gather in close quarters on Main Street, some nearly hovering, the better to hear. They know Sheriff Thomas Theriot as Tom, or simply the sheriff. But today he stands unusually rigid in his law enforcement regalia, his mud-brown uniform with its pins and patches. He carries an air of authority that makes him feel like a stranger. Like some big-city cop, not our small-town, small-time sheriff.

"Good morning and thank you for coming," he booms, kicking things off with a gesture of politeness, which is our way. That and the thickness of his accent is a comfort, a reassurance that despite his strangely formal stance, he is still one of us. "I'm afraid I have troubling news to share today."

Unease ripples through the crowd. This is Southern Baptist country, and people are prone to unease, apocalyptic and overly associative, seeing holy warnings in the smallest of things, like the pattern sugar makes when spilled across a counter. My father is where you'd expect him, in the middle of the crowd, the tallest person here, thick, tanned, and already gleaming in his cuffed white dress shirt. As the sheriff speaks, the hands of the townsfolk find my father, until he looks like a massive sun radiating spokes of people. They lay their palms on his shoulders and forearms as if he is an anchor, his holiness a shield to protect them from the coming news. I cannot recall ever touching or being touched by my father that gently.

I watch from the back, alone and invisible as always. An ominous feeling seeps through my veins like silty black mud. It has been seeping since the moment I heard whispers about the skull from Nissa, my colleague at the town library.

"June seventeenth, at approximately 4:32 p.m.," the sheriff says, "while one of my deputies was responding to a vandalism issue in Starry Swamp—"

He stops when the crowd titters, heads whipping to one another, eyes flashing. We haven't heard this part of the story. Like everyone else, I frown. Vandalism in the swamp?

The sheriff raises his voice and continues. "A trapper reported he'd found human remains in the water, caught up in one of his nets."

Murmurs erupt from the throng. They know this information, but there's something about hearing it from a man in uniform, with a carefully stoic face, that feels weighted. It hits me, too, like a punch to the gut. Those with their hands on my father tighten them, gripping him for support. Near the edge of the crowd, gray-haired Mrs. Autin, the town tailor, sways on her feet.

"What kind of remains?" Old Man Jonas calls. "How many pieces?" There are stains on his overalls from a morning spent packing bait. Some *tsk* at the indelicate question, but it's Old Man Jonas, so he will be forgiven.

Sheriff Theriot holds out his hands for quiet. "I'm sorry to say the trapper pulled a human skull out of the swamp. As of now, that's all we've been able to recover."

A head with no body. People turn to gape at each other, wanting to see their horror mirrored. But not me. In the farthest reaches of the crowd, I am silent and dry-eyed. Dry as kindling, in fact. I alone know that whatever information the sheriff holds, he holds it like a lit match poised over my head.

"It was lucky we happened to be there responding to the vandalism," the sheriff adds, almost as an afterthought, the Louisiana storyteller in him cropping up despite the somber moment. "Trapper said he might've thrown it back in the water if he hadn't spotted the law 'round the bend."

A thousand threads of fate, then, weaving together to pull the skull out of the dark water and into the light. A thousand things conspiring for this day to come to pass. *What are the odds?* my mind whispers, and though I've instructed myself to remain blank of mind, of all the things I could be thinking, at least it's probably the safest. My father is only feet away, which means the Holy Spirit is here in this town square, listening.

"It was God's will," someone calls, and the crowd murmurs its assent. Some of them have started swaying, moving to a message from the Creator only they can hear, like they're back in church.

The *Town Talk* reporter clears his throat. "Is it your opinion someone got lost out there? Or are we talking about another alligator attack like the one last year?"

My body is incandescent with fear. *Be a gator.*

For the first time, exhaustion carves the sheriff's face. "Yesterday we received word from the coroner in Forsythe that the skull belongs to a male, aged twenty-five to fifty. And the fracturing on the bone is consistent with blunt-force trauma."

The crowd goes silent. My heart pounds so fast I want to crack my sternum and release it.

"The skull's been bashed in," the sheriff clarifies, his drawl deepening. "This man did not die by gators. He was the victim of a brutal beating. I'm here today to announce we're opening the parish's first homicide investigation in twenty years."

There's a strangled cry as gray-haired Mrs. Autin succumbs, falling to her knees. Some townsfolk rush to pull her up, but the rest devolve into chaos. They shout, imploring the sheriff for more information, imploring my father to intervene. A woman carrying a small child on her hip, who I know only as one of the Fortenot Fishing wives, starts to weep.

Homicide investigation. Those were the words I was waiting for. Inside me, the fire catches and erupts. No one can see it, but I'm standing in the middle of Main Street, burning alive.

The flames of Hell have finally reached me like my father always warned.

"Calm down," the sheriff booms, his voice rising above the fray. "I need you to listen." The two deputies flanking him—old Roy McClaren and young Barry Holt—straighten and finger the sticks at their belts as if they might jump into the crowd to force everyone's silence. Barry's troubled gaze searches faces until he finally lands on mine. He gives me a grim, tight-lipped smile. I have no idea what expression I make back. My body is on fire and I can feel nothing else.

"This is all the information we have," says the sheriff, voice still straining. "We'll update you as soon as we identify the victim. In the meantime, I need any and all information you might have about the homicide. If you know something—*anything*—tell us. We'll follow every lead. Consider this a plea." His gaze skims the crowd until it stops at my father. They hold each other's eyes. A darkness passes over the sheriff's face. "And I must also ask for your prayers. Evil has come to Bottom Springs."

The crowd explodes at this, one of the older women wailing. The sheriff and his deputies turn their backs and stride into their office, trailed by the reporter. In their absence, my father takes command, lifting his arms to the heavens. I can see only the back of his head, his coal-black, slicked-back hair, the dark sweat staining his dress shirt, but I've seen this gesture enough times to know what expression he's wearing.

"Let us pray," he shouts, "for the soul of this poor murdered man." He staggers down to his knees in the middle of the street. Like a contagion, the people around him fall, too, a movement that ripples until the whole crowd is braced against the ground. "May God reveal the wicked soul responsible for this gruesome act, the soul who has betrayed God's holiest commandment." The crowd raises their arms like he does, tilting their heads to the sky, imploring their Creator. "May Christ deliver us from the demon who walks among us even now!"

I cannot be here. Cannot watch them prostrate themselves before my father, cannot contain the grief threatening to erupt. I turn and flee, moving as quickly as I dare, knowing I cannot draw attention. I need to get home to my garden, to my refuge, where I can think.

I'm digging up weeds in my backyard, skin filmed with dirt and sweat, when I feel the change: the air thickens, becoming so heavy and warm I can close my eyes and sink into it like into bathwater. The wild green of the forest at the edge of my yard gives itself over to the heat in one great big exhalation. I smell verdant herb in the air, can practically taste it on my tongue, spicy and mineral. In that moment, all around me, spring shudders into summer.

I still instinctively, clutching the trowel. My eyes find the horizon, a spark lighting in my chest. He used to come every year on the first true day of summer. Every year except the last.

Deep in my bones, I can feel it. He will come with dusk.

Time passes in a blur, until I find myself sitting barefoot at my kitchen table, watching the tree branches dance outside the window. The sheer curtains are twisting as the breeze blows through the screen, and it ruffles my white dress. My hair is wet from the shower and combed back from my forehead like my mother used to do when I was a child. Moisture from the shower still clings to my skin, and the white cotton sticks. I want to pull it from me, but outside my front door, the wind chime tangles, a soft silver melody, and I rise to my feet.

The promise of a summer storm hangs thick in the air outside the screen door. The sun is fighting death, reaching out with grasping fingers of orange and rose against the falling twilight. When I push open the screen door, there's a sharp glimmer of light, and there he is, standing on my porch like the wild has conjured him.

He's grinning the same grin he used to give me when we were teens.

Fitting, because although he's grown more solid and slightly taller, he's never really aged. The grin is lazy and confident, with a wickedness he would never dare show anyone else. He's a head taller than me, and his skin is too lustrous, too milky white for a boy born and raised here in Bottom Springs, where the sun beats unrelentingly most of the year. Instead of tanned and freckled like mine, his skin glows like a pearl, like trapped moonlight. His hair is dark and tangled and his eyes are darker, the kind of dark that sucks you in. When I was younger, I used to draw him with my charcoal pencils, trying to capture the flinty sharpness of his cheekbones, how they knife down, pulling your eyes to the fullness of his lips. But I could never get him right. Every picture I drew made him look otherworldly and menacing, halfway feral. In those pictures you could almost see why so many around here call him the Devil's son.

He's letting me take him in, that grin showing off the sharp points of his canines, his smile echoing in his eyes. He leans against the wooden doorframe, shoulder to the peeling paint, and looks at me, too, starting with my bare feet and traveling up until he meets my eyes. Between his look and the pressing heat, it's like the world is reaching out to touch me with phantom caresses.

My pain has called him, surely. Called and pulled him here.

"Ruth." His nostrils flare, as if catching a scent. "Something's wrong. Your house smells different. Tell me, quick—are you safe?"

"No." I remain still, fingernails digging into the door, carving half-moons. My voice is thick. "Listen to me. It's finally happened. They found him in the swamp."

2

JUNE, SEVENTEEN YEARS OLD

I was seventeen when I went on my first date, much later than the other girls. Since courting for marriage is one of the only forms of entertainment we've got down here in Bottom Springs, and bored girls in small towns are inclined toward entertainment, we tend to start quick. But late or not, it was a miracle I had a date at all. For one thing, my father is Pastor James Cornier, preacher at Holy Fire Born Again and spiritual leader to every soul in Trufayette Parish, minus the handful of Godless heathens. Not many boys want to date a preacher's daughter, and rightfully so. After all, in a town like ours, it's best to keep your vices—your underage drinking and late-night fumbling in the back seat—as far from prying eyes as possible.

But mostly it was a miracle because of who I am all on my own. If you were to ask around about Miss Ruth Cornier, you'd hear the same story: Miss Ruth Cornier, they'd tell you, is a good God-fearing girl, not a lick of trouble, raised by two upstanding, cane-wielding pillars of the community. But intensely shy to the point of muteness, to the point of not being able to function when spoken to, a girl who grows red-faced and stuttering upon too forward a glance. A wisp of a girl, someone who haunts the background of photographs, unlikely to look a boy in the eyes, let alone date one.

And they were right. I *was* shy. But mostly I was lonely. While everyone respected my parents, they also feared them—especially my father, who held the power to damn sinners to Hell and used it frequently. My mother held a different kind of power: she was nearly as quiet as I was, at least in public. But in private her judgment was harsh, her tongue legendary, her whisper campaigns the kind that saw entire families shunned from potlucks and Sunday services over a single member's wrongdoing.

If anyone in Bottom Springs assumed life inside the Cornier house was different—that within the private walls of our two-story clapboard, the three of us shared a special familial intimacy, that my parents granted me a leniency and tenderness they gave no one else, the kind of loving indulgence a mother might give a naughty child who's snagged a sucker from the grocery store—they would be wrong. There were moments of tenderness when I was young, evenings when my father would allow me to rest my head on his knee while he read, mornings when my mother's fingers would soften and slow as they combed through my hair, but these were fleeting moments, dandelion seeds in my palm, lost the second I stopped clutching. For the most part there was no one my parents watched closer than me, looking for any hint of immorality or wantonness. And when they found one, there was no person on earth they would send to Hell quicker, Hell being twelve lashes with my father's rattan cane, followed by a week locked inside my bedroom.

It was therefore wise to be a wisp. Even if my severe quietness meant that at school, I was as unpopular and friendless as poor Samuel Landry, whose Tourette's syndrome made him a target for the crueler students, and Everett Duncan, whose ratty clothes, intense stare, and stubborn refusal to answer questions when called upon made it clear he was following in the footsteps of his ne'er-do-well father, one of the town's chief church-shirkers. But it hardly mattered that no one invited me to drink Coors Light out in Starry Swamp on Saturdays. My whole life, I'd tried in timid overtures to find other people I could relate to, someone to call a friend, but I'd always failed. In such a small town, the pickings were slim. I wasn't my parents' kind of girl, not on the inside, but I wasn't anyone else's, either.

So instead of friendships, I cultivated quiet rebellions. Most came in the form of books. At Sacred Surrender High School, the library was tightly controlled by the church elders. It contained no suggestive books, no books that glorified sins like rebelling against one's parents or sex before marriage. But most of all, it contained no occult. No boy or girl wizards or tales of monsters or werewolf love stories. The occult was a particular sticking point with my father. Because around here, the only belief system that had ever competed with religion was superstition; the only things parishioners had ever feared as much as God were the evils said to roam around us.

In fairness, Bottom Springs does look like the Creator had built it with the otherworldly in mind. Though I have only our neighboring towns to compare to, Forsythe and Trouville to the east and Houma to the north, I've always felt Bottom Springs must be the most beautiful place on earth. Here at the tip of Louisiana, it's as if the sky and swamp and wild green trees know Holy Fire demands we lead staid, ascetic lives and try to make up for it, giving us all the splendor and decadence we aren't supposed to want. Sunrises and sunsets are riots of color, the gulf sapphire blue, the black swamp laced with velvet-green lily pads, tall trees almost floating out of the depths. Trees everywhere, in fact: bending over dirt roads and bracing the shore and thick as a wall of sentries in the woods, dripping with Spanish moss. All this beauty stirs the soul, making one feel the pinprick presence of another order: God, perhaps, but maybe also something darker, secret beings with lives that unfold in the slivers between trees, whose slitted eyes blink open at night in the depths of the swamp, yellow and ancient as alligators'.

One story in particular has haunted Bottom Springs for as long as anyone can remember. It tells of a creature whose true name is so hoary and evil that men's minds can't contain it, and so we call him the Low Man. Cursed to remain trapped in Bottom Springs by men who practiced spiritual magics now long forgotten, the Low Man slumbers for all eternity in the deep, dark heart of the swamp, in a place no trapper or hunter has ever set foot. Every few years, the story goes, he wakes and rises from his underwater tomb to roam Bottom Springs, searching for a way out, seeking to be let loose upon the world in order to devour it.

Furious at his imprisonment, the Low Man settles for devouring us instead. He takes the shape of a beautiful man, a trap for sinners as seductive as a coral snake's bright rings. The Low Man can see into your heart, see your true wickedness, and once he's marked you, whether it's hours, days, or years later, one night he will slip in through your window. He'll sink his fangs into your neck like a rough kiss and feast—not only on your body, dismembering the cage that contains you, but on your soul. There is no Heaven or Hell waiting for those slaughtered by the Low Man. Only the worst fate of all, which is nothingness, which is to be reduced to a sparkless, nerveless thing, a bag of flesh that rots and stinks and then ceases to exist.

While the myth of the Low Man had fallen out of regular mention by the time I grew up, men still told stories after they'd had a few too many Wild Turkeys at the Blue Moon bar, describing how they'd seen him slip into the shadows between houses when they were young, felt his cold presence when they ventured too deep into the swamp. Children still checked the locks on their windows before they went to bed and stared hard at any man with a face too close to beautiful. And the threat of something old and hungry in the swamp lent an extra sense of thrill to the parties teenagers threw there. Once, I'd wondered which scared the people of Bottom Springs more: the Low Man or the Devil.

This, of course, was a problem for my father, who felt God should have the monopoly on fear. So the school library was tightly restricted, youths' minds protected, and that meant it was no place for me. But in the *town* library—a small brick building off Main Street with a roof steepled like a church—sometimes an illicit book would find its way in. One of my greatest blessings was that the library was perpetually underfunded. Without a healthy budget, it relied on donations, often cardboard boxes stuffed with bent paperbacks and the occasional stray T-shirt meant for Goodwill. Even more occasionally, parishioners would forget to scour through their stacks to take out anything damning. By the time I turned fourteen, I'd gotten my hands on a Danielle Steel and the second and fifth Percy Jacksons that way, all haphazardly pulled out of donation boxes and stuck onto the shelves.

While the librarians were sometimes careless, I was always alert, books being my only lifeline. I was as hungry for stories as the Low Man was for souls, devouring every book that wasn't a spiritual, each one proof another world existed outside the one I knew. I believe at one point, I'd read every book available in town. I used to smile at how misguided my father was, thinking the classics he allowed—*Wuthering Heights* and *Great Expectations* and *The Age of Innocence*—had nothing to teach about rebellion. I learned to question and rage and self-immolate over love alongside Heathcliff and Pip and Newland Archer.

And then I found *Twilight*.

The copy was wedged into a shelf of spy novels. It was a miracle I happened to spot it. A miracle I had the courage to take it to the farthest corner of the library and read it in the shadows, chapter by chapter, returning day after day since I could never check it out. It was the ultimate contraband: a story both occult *and* romantic, and meant for girls like me. In Bella, I found a mirror. We were both shy and overlooked, with the smallest of lives, hemmed in by circumstances outside our control. And in the vampire Edward, I found everything I'd ever wanted in a man. He loved Bella with single-minded devotion, a self-effacing passion beyond anything a human man was capable of. That's in turn how I loved him. I read the novel five times in the span of a month, then spent months after fruitlessly searching the stacks for the sequel teased at the end. Eventually, I committed the crime of shoving the book in my backpack and bringing it home. At the time, it was the worst thing I'd ever done. The night I stole it, I woke at midnight in a cold sweat, sure the Low Man or at least my father would come hunting for me.

Twilight was the bridge to my second rebellion: an obsession with the kind of love my father rarely talked about in church. The kind where you felt all the overwhelming awe you were supposed to feel for Jesus, but for another person. It fascinated me. Though I prayed to God every night and believed he was listening, I'd never felt particularly close. I'd never felt close to another person, either. And of the two connections, I wished for the person more. Ruth Cornier, the preacher's daughter, coveted a boy's love more than God's. That was another secret I hid in my muteness.

I found *Twilight* at fourteen. By the time I was seventeen, there was no girl in the world more willing to be consumed by love. I even had a favorite daydream. My hair—long, wavy, and copper—was the one thing about me worth attention. It was unprecedented in our family, mine alone. I used to imagine a boy combing his hands through it, letting the curls loop around his fingers like rings, binding us together. He would whisper that it was beautiful—not me, necessarily, not my round, freckled face, but my hair. And then he would kiss me. I told myself if life could just give me that—one moment to feel lovely, a single, perfect kiss—I would never ask for more.

So the Sunday a new face cropped up in the pews, I took notice.

3

JUNE, SEVENTEEN YEARS OLD

He was short but handsome, with sandy hair, brown eyes, and deeply tanned skin that told me he worked for one of the construction crews that used to come through Bottom Springs back when Forsythe, the bigger town to our east, was going through a growth spurt. Later this suspicion was confirmed by gossip. Over the course of many Sundays, I learned his name was Renard Michaels and he was seven years my elder at the age of twenty-four. I watched and watched him, but I would have gone my whole life without uttering a word—except one Sunday he turned his head in the middle of my father's lecture and caught me staring. I yanked my gaze away and stared in silent horror at my Bible for the rest of service. When I finally stepped outside after church, he was lingering with the last of the parishioners on the wide front lawn.

He caught my eye over their shoulders and smiled. One of his front teeth was turned slightly inward, and I must have stared again, because he ambled over. "I'm Renard," he said, sticking his thumbs in his pockets. He wore tight jeans and work boots with a collared shirt. "What's your name, Red?"

If he didn't know my name, he didn't know I was the preacher's daughter. "Ruth," I said, managing to speak around my shyness. Omitting anything more.

"I got you this." He pulled a strawberry hard candy from his pocket, its wrapper drawn to mimic the seeds and stem of the fruit. My mother and I placed these candies in little wicker baskets outside the doors to the nave for parishioners to take on their way out. He held it up. "Here."

I blinked at his hand. "It's for you."

That produced another glimpse of his strange tooth as he smiled. "It's just a candy. Won't bite."

We held eyes until it was too much to bear. "Okay," I said, dropping my gaze to the grass. "Thank you."

Renard placed the candy in my hand. Before he pulled away, his pointer finger stroked down my palm. Just for a millisecond, a breath's worth of time, but it froze me in place. Long after he'd ambled away, I stayed rooted there, clutching the small strawberry. I never could bring myself to unwrap it.

After that, he found me every Sunday. His job in Forsythe would take a few months to complete, he said, and then he'd be on to the next town, wherever in Louisiana his company took him. He liked Bottom Springs because it was cheaper than Forsythe and—he said this with a smile that made my cheeks burn—the place was full of pretty girls. He was so easy to talk to that he wore me down. I opened up, little by little, until eventually I wondered if I was really so shy after all.

The three most important things to know about Renard were that, first, he loved his mother, who he called Momma. She lived back in Breaux Bridge, where he was born. He loved her so much he wore a gold chain with the word *Momma* in script letters around his neck, even though it tangled in his chest hair. Second, he was an avid trapper, working all week with the single aim of getting to the weekend, when he could escape into the swamp and check his traps. And lastly, there was nothing he was prouder of than his truck, a shiny red behemoth. It was far too expensive for a man who lived in the aging Courtyard apartments and carried one of those prepaid plastic cell phones. He finally told me he'd bought the truck with a payout after he'd gotten injured at a job site, lucking out that the owner was eager to avoid insurance with a chunk of cash.

No one had ever talked to me as much as Renard did. Like I was normal, too. The rush was so intoxicating that he could've told me any story and I would've found it fascinating. Half of what I heard when he talked was the drumming of my own heartbeat in my ears, anyway.

One ordinary Sunday, so like the others there was nothing to warn me, Renard marched up after the service and asked if I'd like to go parking at Starry Swamp with him. I was surprised he knew about it. The swamp was where my classmates went to drink and make out. At least that's what I'd heard, listening to gossip at lunch tables. They called it Starry Swamp because at night, the water was so black it turned into a mirror, reflecting the sky above. Wading through it was supposed to be like swimming through the stars. I'd never seen it for myself. I wasn't allowed outside at night.

So when Renard asked me, biting his lip, I thought, *My first date, and I'm going to be kissed in a wild green place, like the meadow where Edward kisses Bella.* I'd nodded, unable to speak, and Renard had grinned. "This Friday, then."

When Friday afternoon came, he picked me up where he instructed, two streets down from my house. He didn't say why, but I knew it was because he'd discovered I was seventeen and the preacher's daughter, and we were a secret. But everything in my life worth having was. When we got to the edge of Starry Swamp, he didn't pull off where everyone else did, at a vast clearing far from the water, where the soil was drier. "Somewhere more private," he'd explained at my look, and once again I heard the unspoken meaning: somewhere no one would catch us. He was twenty-four and I was seventeen; he was a handsome, churchgoing bachelor and I was a wisp. I was lucky to be with him, even hidden in the swamp.

I'd nodded, too nervous thinking about what being kissed would feel like, after all this time imagining it. My palms were so sweaty I had to wipe them against my dress. We drove deeper and deeper in until we came to a small clearing in the trees. Renard parked and cut the engine. The trees ringing us were so thick that all I could see beyond was darkness.

He spread a blanket on the muddy grass and pulled me toward him. I knew what was coming and closed my eyes. With my sight gone, I could hear the buzz saw of the insects and low throat-singing of the frogs and whistle of the wind, all of it intensifying as Renard pressed his lips to mine.

I was being kissed. But it was not like I'd imagined. His lips were rough and calloused and they fumbled over mine, urgent from the start, wanting something I didn't know how to give. I didn't know what to do with my hands. Somewhere in the distance a bird shrieked—a high, clear burst of warning—and Renard solved the problem of my hands by pulling me tighter against him. His lips kept moving so insistently that it occurred to me I needn't do anything at all. He wasn't waiting for my response.

He pressed me down against the blanket and followed the wild pounding of my heart with his mouth, kissing down my neck to my chest, tugging at my dress to taste more skin. I made a noise of surprise, startled by the quickness with which he moved, remembering Bella's first kiss, the paragraphs devoted to the way Edward had held her, touched her softly. Renard's scratchy hands were moving under my skirt. I pulled back and said, "Wait," breathless and urgent, but he didn't. He only grunted "Relax, Red," in that thick honey accent, the words curling with impatience. Hands and mouth roving, pinning my shoulders with his weight even as I tried to roll free: at first hesitantly, unsure of myself, then frantically, panic kicking in.

It wasn't like *Twilight*. It was everything my father had warned. I beat at Renard, trying to twist free as dusk fell around us, pastel blue. We were alone this deep into the swamp. The frogs kept singing, the bugs kept whirring. Nothing cared that I was trapped in the coffin of his arms, drowning in fear. The earth was as indifferent as Renard was, the man who hadn't, it turned out, seen anything in me beyond a girl who was naive and desperate, willing to be quieter than the others.

Just as I was breaking in the grass, Renard made a choked sound and heaved off me, struck by something large and dark. I rolled away, sobbing in pure shock—then scrambled to my feet when I saw what saved me. It was Everett Duncan who straddled Renard between his thighs, trying and failing to catch hold of his arms. Everett was dressed in black as always, dark waders and a cheap thrift-store T-shirt full of holes. There was a water bottle dropped nearby, still rolling past the wet corpse of a large, fat nutria, the river rats that thrived 'round here. *He'd been hunting*. The thought came to me clearly amid the shock.

Renard managed to get a hand free and landed a blow across Everett's cheek, so hard his head snapped to the side and I got a clear view of his face. Once a year for as long as I could remember, one girl or another would overlook the stink of loneliness and anger surrounding Everett, the bruises blooming around his eyes that caused snickers about bar fights, the accusations that he was a goth and a freak, drawn in by the power of that face. It never mattered which girl tried: everyone was icily rebuffed, one after another, while the rest of the school watched and laughed.

We'd sat next to each other in classrooms for years, Cornier and Duncan, alphabetical destiny. But in all that time he'd only spoken to me once of his own volition, the first year of high school, right after I'd discovered *Twilight* and carried it everywhere in my backpack. I'd been walking down the hall when a group of football players, roughhousing and not looking, slammed into me, knocking me off my feet and scattering the contents of my bag. They hadn't even stopped to apologize, like I was invisible. That was common enough, but that day it had stung.

As I'd scrambled on my hands and knees, searching frantically for *Twilight*, dark boots had appeared in my line of sight. Everett, of all people, had crouched down and extended the beat-up paperback with a single word: "Here." In the flash before I looked away, breathing thanks, I saw his lip was busted and scabbing over, an old wound on its way to healing. He wrested me to my feet with one cool hand and then kept walking, expression unchanged. An unrippled pond.

And now here he was, grappling on the grass with the man who wanted to hurt me. As I watched, the tide turned. Renard, who had thirty pounds on Everett easy, managed to flip him over and crush his hands around his throat.

"You weird fucking *kid*," Renard yelled, striking Everett so hard he made a sucking sound, desperate for air. His arms flailed, trying and failing to gain purchase against Renard's chest, just like mine had.

"Stop it!" I screamed, as Renard hit Everett again, his face nearly purple with rage. Bested by a teenage boy without a weapon, and me escaping, the whole plan shot to hell. In the transparency of his fury, I saw clear to Renard's soul, to the truth he'd hidden from me every Sunday: deep down, he was rotten.

"You're going to kill him!" I shouted. Everett was trapped, his arms starting to still, his eerily beautiful face turning blue from lack of oxygen. My heart burst open in my chest, certain he would die. And in my desperation I turned into my own kind of roving creature, dropping to my hands and knees in the grass, fumbling through tree roots and bushes, all the under-places you weren't supposed to poke. I seized upon a rock as smooth as an egg and as big as a summer melon.

All understanding faded except for one truth: Everett Duncan had tried to save me, and I could not let him be harmed. I ran back to the blanket where Renard loomed over him, squeezing Everett's neck with both hands, and didn't think a second more before I brought the rock down over his head. He jerked to the side and it didn't seem enough, so I brought it down again, letting loose a sob, the impact jarring my wrists. And then I couldn't stop until I lifted the rock to hit him once more and Renard slumped over on the blanket, blood leaking from his head.

I froze.

Everett scrambled to his feet, breathing hoarsely, and we stood there, him in black and me in white, two chests heaving, both of us splattered with blood. An eternity passed until I whispered, "I didn't mean to."

"Shh." He put a finger in the air, as if testing the wind. Immediately, I stilled—except for my heart, which was still pumping, pushing my chest tight against the neckline of my dress. The whole melody of the swamp opened to me then, the creeping crawling things rustling the leaves and the water dripping from the branches and the birds calling overhead. In the middle of it, faintly, was a thin sucking noise, the sound of a man struggling to breathe.

"He's still alive," Everett said, and I startled. I'd forgotten the way his voice sounded, deep but also lilting. He looked at me and I cringed, waiting for his revulsion. It would be what I deserved. I was going to burn for what I'd done. I would never enter Heaven.

But instead of disgust, tenderness flooded Everett's face. I'd never seen such an expression on him in the years we'd orbited each other. Out of everything, it was what brought chills to my skin, tiny hairs raising like antennae on high alert.

"Give me that," he said, and held out his hand. He was looking at the rock.

Mutely, I handed it over. My arms were too light without the weight and I shook them. Everett crouched beside Renard and stared at him a moment—thinking what, I couldn't fathom—then bent and whispered in his ear, too low for me to catch. Renard's eyes were shut, but at the whisper he gurgled. Then Everett smashed the rock to his temple, one quick hard stroke, and Renard was utterly quiet.

"He was suffering," Everett said softly. "Like an animal in a trap." He set the rock on the blanket and rose, swaying a little.

He'd shown Renard mercy. I searched his face as he steadied himself. "Do you need to go to Blanchard?" The hospital was at the farthest edge of town, and I had no way of getting there, but Everett looked like he needed it.

He jerked his head. "No. I'm used to it. Besides, they'll ask how it happened."

Our eyes met. And that's when the weight of it truly hit me: I'd killed a man. Or Everett had. Or both of us together, the shared sin staining our hands the same as the blood. I dropped to my knees in the grass.

"Ruth." Everett gripped my shoulders. "Not now, okay? Later. Now we have to get rid of him."

I looked up at him from where I knelt, too far gone to wonder at his touch. Despite everything, his dark eyes were clear and calm.

"Stay here while I get an ax. I think my father has one in his shed. At least a knife."

"You were hunting in the swamp." I looked at the dead river rat, my words coming out faded and distant. "And you didn't bring a knife?"

He squeezed my shoulder. "Don't move. I'll be fast."

He was gone before I could beg him not to leave me alone with Renard, and I tumbled forward on the blanket. In my shock, time must've warped, thirty minutes compressed into five, because he was back too quickly, tugging me up, holding an ax.

I climbed to my feet and joined Everett where he stood, staring down at Renard's body, at the bloody mess of his head. The chill calm of shock seized me then, emptying me of feeling. The first man I'd kissed had turned out to be no Edward.

Everett's words were cool. "We've got to do it fast, before nightfall. That's when the swamp is hungriest."

"Are you sure?" I asked. "About any of this?"

"We'll put him in the swamp, and tie the rock and blanket to him. The gators will find him quick and eat it all. No one will ever know. You'll be safe."

Across the empty space, he held out his hand. After a moment, I took it. "Don't be afraid," he said. And with our fingers twined together, with the twilight falling, I wasn't.

We chopped Renard's body into pieces we could carry to the edge of the water and walked those pieces in up to our knees. Then we waited at the tree line until the smooth placid surface of the water thrashed—quick as lightning, once, twice, water roiling—and then he was gone. It was almost peaceful. We left his truck where it was parked. Everett said that when they found it, they would think Renard had gone off hunting or exploring in the swamp, confident he was enough of a rough-and-tumble Louisiana woodsman to survive.

No one knew about our date, by Renard's own design. His cheap plastic cell phone had no tracking device. And there was no such thing as DNA testing in a parish poor as ours, with a sheriff's department of three men. Especially not for a man just passing through, an itinerant construction worker. The very things I hated about life in small, backward Bottom Springs would be the things that saved me.

It happened just like Everett said. News of Renard's disappearance in the swamp, when it eventually hit, barely made a ripple. Too many other men had died in the untamable wild for the town to be anything but used to it. My father used Renard to start a sermon about hubris one Sunday morning, and after that he faded from town lips. Days of waiting in terror for someone to knock on my door turned into months of quiet disbelief and then years of tentative acceptance, the monotony of so many ordinary days burying this one extraordinary one. Finally, the strangest thing happened: a small part of me started to believe, deep in the furthest reaches of my heart, that maybe what we'd done wasn't really so bad. I didn't know whether that was my voice whispering or the Devil's, but either way, it soothed me.

One thing did change after that day—the most important that had ever happened to me. My third and mightiest rebellion. I might've lost part of myself in Starry Swamp, might've floated my childhood right off into the dark water with Renard, but in exchange, I got Everett. He appeared outside my window the next day at dusk, waiting for me at the edge of my lawn. After that, he came every day like clockwork. We became inseparable. To everyone's astonishment, he became the friend I'd always dreamed of, except he was real, alive and vital, not trapped inside a book.

We never, in all the years since, spoke the name Renard Michaels again.

4

NOW

Everett straightens against my doorframe, voice dangerously low. "What do you mean, they found him?"

"Not out here." I push the screen open wider, but he stays stock-still. "Come in." I'm being paranoid, but I can't help it. Finally, Everett heaves himself off the doorframe and follows me inside.

I lead him to my small kitchen with its open window, twilight breeze still blowing the curtains. Just like my run-down Datsun, which soft-hearted Old Man Jonas gifted me out of pity when I turned eighteen and couldn't afford anything else, everything in this house is in need of repair. It's a tiny cottage far from town, right on the edge where the woods turn thick, the only house for miles. I have to collect my mail at the post office because Mr. Broussard, the mailman, won't come out here. Too alone, he says, too near the dark woods. But I rent this house with my own money and live here by myself. Those are things to cherish.

Everett scans as he walks. "You got new curtains."

Though we have far more pressing topics to discuss, the small talk is a relief. A temporary stay from the guillotine drop of my news. "The old ones tore. I sewed those myself."

He raises his eyebrows. "New books?"

"So many." *Two years' worth, since you didn't come.* I nod toward the bookshelf. "A ton you'll love."

We move into my living room, with the old floral couch I found at a garage sale and my towering bookcase. Everett has curled on that couch a thousand times, reading beside me late into the night. But now he keeps his distance, resting his hand on the spine of the couch, oddly formal. When he looks at me, I see he's waiting.

So I tell him everything: the trapper, the skull, the blunt-force trauma. The fact that it's only a matter of time before they put the pieces together and say Renard's name out loud. I didn't think Everett's face could grow any paler, but by the time I'm finished, it's managed.

He swallows. "I know this seems bad, Ruth, but we'll think of a plan. There has to be something."

For some reason, it's Everett's hope that breaks me. For the first time since hearing the news, my eyes sting hot with tears. "We're going to get caught. We're going to be arrested and spend the rest of our lives in prison, unless they electrocute us. Either way, we're going to burn in Hell. There's no getting around it."

He shakes his head, dark hair tumbling. "It was self-defense. Renard was hurting you, and he was going to kill me. We did it to save our lives."

"But we covered it up. We thought they'd never find him, but they *did*. And now the whole town's talking. Eventually someone's going to remember some detail that will lead to us. There's nothing we can do."

"There's always something we can do. I promise, I'll figure it out." Everett stops, pressing his palms to his head. "I just...can't think straight right now. The smell is driving me crazy. Ruth, tell me why your house smells like a man before I go insane."

A startled laugh breaks from me. Of all the things to be thinking about right now. Besides, it's been days since Barry was here, and I can't smell a trace of him. Everett's nose is even better than I remembered. I look at him, so rattled, and feel a surge of anger. If anyone owes anyone answers, it's Everett owing me.

"After all this time, *that's* where you want to start?"

His dark lashes blink faster. My heart skips into a complicated rhythm.

"You're not allowed to ask about my house until you explain why you didn't come home last summer. Where were you? Why didn't you at least warn me?" My voice climbs too high. "I was worried, Ever."

Worried. What a small, weak word. It can't possibly contain what I felt last summer when the seasons shifted and he didn't appear. It was the first time he hadn't returned since he'd moved away from Bottom Springs. The first time he'd let me down since we were seventeen. I'd lain awake all night, letting it sink in that he'd finally wised up and realized he was better off without this place, me included. I'd cried so hard and long I'd imagined the salt carving great tracks down my cheeks, like it did to rocks over eons.

Everett's mouth quirks. His strangeness is legendary in Bottom Springs, but I suspect no one but me knows what playful expressions it can take. "I don't own a cell phone or a computer." He raises his eyebrows. "Should I have trained pigeons to find you?" He's trying to make light of it, distract me. But the sight of him teasing only makes the place where my heart broke and scabbed over ache worse.

"I didn't know if I'd ever see you again," I say quietly. He straightens at my tone. Here we are, facing an imminent threat from the sheriff, and *this* is the subject I'm stuck on, the thing that hurts most.

"I know." Ever leans against the couch. "I can't tell you why I didn't come. Please just trust me that I had to stay away. I should've stayed this summer, too, but I'm weak. I missed you. And now, with everything happening…it's good I came."

"Don't ever say you shouldn't come. You can't leave me here to fend for myself." One of the best things about me and Everett has always been that we can say whatever we're thinking, total honesty, even if it makes us look silly or greedy or weak. That's the upside of being the pastor's daughter and the Devil's son, two outcasts who became friends the way we did. From the start, nothing has been off-limits.

His dark eyes are full of regret. "I really am sorry for making you worry."

I study him, feeling the weight of the secret he won't tell me. I could try to keep my anger going. I could tell him how last summer I'd been so sad I stopped going to work, stopped reading, even stopped getting out of bed, until my parents showed up to pray over my body, convinced something unholy was trapped in my head. I could try to make him suffer like he's made me. But the truth is, my heart is a fickle betrayer. Despite everything—the fear and panic and stress—the simple sight of him makes happiness spill through me, slow and sweet as honey. Against all reason, a small part of me believes what he said: that with him here, somehow it will be okay.

Everett exhales, long and deep. "Will you tell me who he is now? The man whose scent is in your house."

I can think of no way to avoid it, so I rest a hand on the wall for support. "I couldn't call you. I didn't know where you lived because it's always changing. What could I have thought other than you'd left me? It was either that or you were dead." I take a step toward him, then stop. "You have no idea how lonely I was."

Ever hears the pleading tone in my voice. His eyes meet mine.

"You know what my parents are like. How they push."

He stays silent, but the corners of his mouth turn down like he's starting to feel sick.

"A year without you and I caved, Ever. I let them set me up."

His voice is rough. "With who?"

I take a deep breath.

His dark eyes flash like he already knows.

"Barry."

"Barry *Holt*?"

"I know he was never our favorite—"

"Not our favorite? Ruthie, he's an asshole."

"He never did anything. He was just oblivious, part of the football crowd. But he was a kid back then. It was high school. People change."

Everett braces a hand against his mouth, which is what he does whenever he has trouble processing. It's as familiar to me as my own tics. His eyes cast around the room, like he can't stand to look at me. "Is it serious?"

I bite the inside of my mouth. Ever has to understand that the thought of being without him made me feel like a kid again, trapped in those awful years before we became friends. The loneliness had been so powerful I would've done anything to stanch it. Even say yes to my parents, who'd been trying to marry me off since the day I turned eighteen. Without Everett around, I'd been too tired to keep beating them back.

I'm struggling to find the words, but it turns out my silence is enough.

A look of panic flashes across Everett's face, so vivid I'm halfway reaching for him before he schools his expression. His next words are directed at the wall. "First Renard and now Barry. I don't come back for *one* summer, and the whole world falls apart."

"Nothing's official yet," I say, trying to soften it. "He hasn't proposed."

Ever still won't look at me. He presses his hands to his mouth again, his distress palpable. "*One* summer, Ruthie." He's trying to keep his voice low, but it comes out choked. "I thought you and I were supposed to—" He cuts himself off. Then he shakes his head and pushes away from the couch, away from me, striding out of the living room. My screen door rattles as he shoves through it.

One night when we were seventeen, after we'd escaped Ever's father and mine, escaped the whole miserable town, we'd charged deep into the woods, running until we were out of breath. We'd stretched out together, looking up at the stars through the trees, and he'd said, "Promise me it'll be you and me forever." I'd promised, the stars my witness. We would never give ourselves over. Never let them win. It would be the two of us always, safe in the secret world we'd created for ourselves. It was the kind of vow a person made when they were young, still reeling from discovering the world was hard and cruel. But for years, our promise had such a hold over me. I used to float past other people, barely registering them, ignoring their stares, their whispers that my oddness, while excusable in childhood, was becoming uncomfortable as I grew into a woman. I had Everett, so I didn't need them. Even if I was trapped in Bottom Springs, I was free.

That's what his disappearance took from me. Without Everett, there was no more safe, secret universe. I'd been shoved back into the world where things and people outside us mattered. He'd escaped, but I was stuck here and always would be. So of course I knew dating Barry Holt meant breaking our promise—but I thought Everett had broken it first.

"Wait!" I yell, shoving my feet into Keds and flying after him, laces whipping my ankles. Everett's making his way to his car, an old black convertible he rebuilt after high school, tweaking it until it ran as fast and smooth as he does.

"I can't be inside your house." He hops in the car, not bothering with the door. "All of it together is too much. I need to think."

I wrest his door open and climb into the passenger seat. He turns to me, glaring, but I fasten the seat belt and look resolutely ahead. "I know where you're going and I want to come."

He's quiet for a long time while I stare out the windshield, refusing to look at him out of fear that if I do, he'll kick me out. The wind blows my hair over my face until I can't see, but I remain stubbornly still. Finally, I hear his soft sigh and then he shoves his key in the ignition, roaring the engine. Ever slings an arm over the back of my seat and takes off, gunning backward down the road.

5

NOW

There's a place in the woods near my house he showed me years ago. It's one of the sacred spots no one else in Bottom Springs knows about, because it turns out no one else can comb through the wild quite like Everett can, a skill born from necessity. When he pulls up and cuts the engine, tires settling in the grass, we get out and step inside the thicket without speaking, as synchronized as birds in the wind.

Eventually the tall, skinny pines give way to a small clearing, and in the middle is a tree that towers above the others. It reaches out with a hundred snaking arms, some of them bent low to the ground. We call it the Medusa, because long ago, Everett and I decided we would give our love to villains. We know all too well how easy it is to become one when you're misunderstood. Our love is a corrective measure.

Ever leaps onto the Medusa's lowest branch and extends a hand. I take it and feel him shoulder my weight until I'm light as a feather. Then we're off, climbing. Maybe it's childish to climb trees at twenty-three years old. My parents and Barry would certainly say so. But joys are few and far between in this life, so I can hardly bring myself to feel guilty. Besides, Everett's expression is already calming. I can feel the forest settling me, too.

"If you won't tell me why you didn't come last summer, will you at least tell me where you were?" I find a curved branch and pull myself up. My white dress is useless for this kind of climbing: already filthy and with no protection for my knees. But there are more important things to focus on, like getting information.

Above me, he catches hold of a branch and pulls himself up. "I heard the mechanic in Trouville passed away and they had no one else, so I moved. That's where I've been the last year. It's a bigger town. There's more work for me." Everett's a mechanic like his father. It turns out that even if you hate your family, you still inherit from them. But unlike his father, who planted his garage here in Bottom Springs, Ever's an itinerant mechanic, unable to commit to any town for more than a few months at a time. I've never been able to get to the bottom of his restlessness.

He's made it safely to the branch above, so he turns and grips my hands, helping me climb the rest of the way. Perched on the same branch, he leans back against the Medusa's trunk and I lean toward him, still holding his hands for balance. "Do you think you'll stay, then? Is Trouville the one?"

He shrugs and looks away. "I like it. But it doesn't feel like home." He nods up at the next branch and releases my hands. We like to go high enough to get a clear view of the forest. "One more, I think."

I follow after him, trying to gain purchase on the slippery bark.

"You stuck?"

I shake my head and wedge my foot into a cranny, forcing my way up. "It's actually easier today. No books." The Medusa's branches are so wide and smooth you can lay stretched out on them like a couch. We used to spend days up here reading. One of the most thrilling discoveries I made about Everett after we got close is that he loves books as much as I do. I never would've guessed with the disinterested way he acted in school. But then again, the way I've acted has shielded a great many things about me, too.

"All clear," he says when I reach the final branch. I shimmy around the tree trunk, then settle against it, breathing a sigh of relief.

"Look," he says, pointing. From this high up we can see for a mile. It's getting dark, summer dusk long but not eternal, the leaves so shaded they're almost blue. A flock of starlings swoops low, circling in intricate patterns. We listen to the wind through the branches, to the crickets starting to chirp. This is where I belong. Alone in nature with him.

It's what I'll miss most when they send us to prison.

As if he can read my mind, Everett cups his mouth and howls into the forest, a deep and melancholy sound. I startle even though I'm used to it, and the flock of starlings breaks apart like a wrenched wishbone, birds streaking in different directions.

People at church used to swear they could hear werewolves howling in the woods at night, and it used to make me smile to know the truth, that we were what frightened them. Now, I don't smile. Everett's howl sounds too close to the feelings in my chest.

"Do you love him?" he asks suddenly.

The question surprises me, but I don't have to ask who he means. "I think so," I say softly. I don't add that my heart has always been hungry to love, so maybe it isn't such a surprise. Everett already knows.

He nods and moves his gaze far into the forest. I study his face. His dramatic cheekbones are not small-town Louisiana cheekbones. Nothing about his profile is. It's too stark, too lovely. The kind of beauty that sinks ships and ruins lives, though that's probably a line I lifted from a book. He hated it when I asked what it's like to look the way he does. I meant beautiful, but he said I made him sound like an alien. The truth is, I've always thought he might be.

He doesn't look at me when he speaks, keeping his voice deceptively light. "Did you even want me to come back? Now that you have him..."

"Of course I did." The words are thick in my throat. "You're my best friend. Always."

He's quiet for so long. Only the sounds of the forest stretch between us.

"Okay," he says finally. He smiles, but I can tell it's forced. "If he makes you happy, then okay."

I let out my held breath. "We can ask Barry for details about the investigation. He's bad at keeping secrets."

Everett frowns. "Why would we ask him?"

Barry was only a year ahead of us in school, but sometimes I forget Everett hasn't kept up with everyone like I have, on account of his moving away. "Barry's a deputy now. He's part of the investigation."

Ever freezes. "What?"

I chip the tree bark with my nail. "He joined the sheriff's office after old Beau Linnet retired. There's still only three of them. Barry's the rookie."

Everett sits ramrod straight. "Ruth. What the hell are you playing at, dating a cop?"

"It gives us an advantage." I kick his dangling legs, but he doesn't smile. "You remember how Barry likes to talk. Being with him is a protection."

The last rays of the sun slip over the horizon. The air shifts into deep purple, the effect like being plunged underwater. The woods at night scare most people, but I haven't been scared of any wild places, not for years. Maybe it's because of Everett, or maybe my instinct for danger is broken.

Ever slides closer, until our dangling feet touch, then closer still. Our knees hit, and he wraps his legs around mine, locking us together.

"Don't worry," I start to say, but fall quiet when he places his hands on either side of my face. He didn't used to like touching. Not before me. After me—with me—he can't stop, like he's making up for lost time.

"Ruth." His dark eyes cast such a spell that I can't look away. In their depths he says a thousand things he would never say out loud. "You know I'll always protect you."

"I know." In an instant, I see that bloody rock, smooth as an egg and big as a summer melon, coming down to meet Renard's head.

Yes, Everett will always protect me. And I will protect him. Some days that's what I'm most afraid of.

"But you're right," he says. "If we're going to come up with a plan, we need to know as much as possible." Everett still holds my face between his hands. "After the press conference today, the whole town will be gossiping about this. Do you think Barry will join them?"

I nod. "He can never resist."

"Then we need to go and listen."

I grimace. Because we both know exactly where the people of Bottom Springs go to talk.

6

NOW

The moment we pull up in front of the Blue Moon bar, the summer storm finally arrives in all its thundering, sheet-rain glory. We're soaked the instant we run from Everett's car, and by the time we burst through the heavy oak front door, we're flinging water and half in shock at the cold. Unfortunately, our arrival draws every eye in the bar.

The Blue Moon is packed tighter than I've ever seen it. As expected, the whole town—at least everyone willing to set foot in a den of sin—has gathered to talk about the homicide. Even if Everett and I weren't soaked, even if we weren't both making a rare appearance, they would stare simply to see us together. The town's oddest pair. People in Bottom Springs stare no matter where we go, though we've been best friends for six years now. I know it's mostly about Ever and the lore surrounding his father, but sometimes it makes me resentful, like I only blinked into existence the moment he and I became friends.

"Don't worry about the eyes," Everett murmurs. He points to the only empty booth left in the bar, in a distant corner. "How's that?"

The Blue Moon is a dark, dingy hole-in-the-wall, lit by dim red lights that give it the feel of a country bordello, but it's also an institution. The place has been remarkably resilient over the years, considering Bottom

Springs is God's country and the Blue Moon is a breeding ground for sin, as my father likes to say. I've always wondered why he's never run it out of town. Typically, I avoid this place for a laundry list of reasons. First, because no matter how old I get, in the town's eyes, I'll always be the reverend's girl. Second, because the Blue Moon attracts people, and the older I get, the less I like those. And third, because the people who come here most often are the ones I'm specifically trying to avoid. Like Lila LeBlanc, former cheerleader, sitting in front of us on a barstool, looking Everett and me up and down with an almost prurient curiosity.

"You sit," Everett says. "I'll get drinks." He doesn't need to ask what I want because I rarely drink, and when I do, the only thing I can tolerate is Boone's Farm strawberry wine cooler, which the bar doesn't carry. No, tonight, our drinks are props.

I slide into the empty booth, red vinyl slippery against my damp dress, and Everett pushes into the only empty space at the bar. Remy the bartender eyes him warily. Everyone in Bottom Springs eyes Everett warily, but I don't exactly blame Remy for it, given Everett is the son of the town's worst drunk. Thankfully, Remy doesn't give Everett any trouble, just takes his order without comment and turns to someone else.

"Everett Duncan, while I live and breathe." Even from here, I can hear Lila. She leans as far as she can in Everett's direction. The women surrounding her—a lot of them Fortenot Fishing wives I recognize from church—go quiet to listen. "It's been forever since I saw your face." Lila's own face is unchanged from high school, wide-set and youthful except for the lines under her eyes, the kind particular to mothers of young children, exhaustion no concealer can hide.

I try to remember if Lila was one of the girls who'd tried to win Everett's attention back in high school but can't recall. She seems ready to do it now, though. Although the fishing wives are eyeing her, she plows ahead. "What brings you back to town?"

Everett turns from the bar, holding two beers by their slim necks. "Oh, you know." He shakes his rain-wet hair and grins at me. "This and that."

Lila follows Everett's grin to me, and her mouth twists like she's sucking a lemon.

She and I have a complicated history. We're the same age, but she grew up pretty and well liked, the star in church musicals, until she got pregnant out of wedlock and her life was derailed. My mother was vicious behind the scenes, and my father devoted a whole month's lectures to the dangers of the fallen woman, a spotlight that humiliated the LeBlanc family until they finally got the hint to leave. Lila had been quickly married off to an older man from Forsythe who was supposedly the father—though people continued to whisper other, more scandalous names—and eventually her family started coming back to church. Still, rumors keep spreading about how often Lila can be found at the Blue Moon bar in the company of men who aren't her husband.

It's amazing how closely women are watched in Bottom Springs. It makes me think once again that my invisibility has been a protection.

I give her an uneasy nod as Everett plunks our beers on the table and scoots in next to me. She doesn't nod back. She's staring at us, completely arrested, like we're a puzzle she can't figure out.

"What's her deal?" Everett asks in a low voice.

I break Lila's gaze and reach for a beer. "I don't know." Maybe Lila hates me because she can sense my guilt over her treatment and interprets it as pity. Or maybe, somehow, she can sense I've committed a sin far worse than hers and have never been punished.

"Good old Bottom Springs," Everett says, knocking my knee. The fact that he's sitting so close to me that our legs and elbows touch might be another reason people are staring. But touching is just Everett's compulsion. Ever since he discovered physical closeness could be safe, that it didn't always come with a sting, it's been hard to reel him in.

I roll my eyes at his comment, though. This is what Everett does now. He comes back and acts like a tourist. It's the biggest thing that's changed about him since he left. My whole life I've tried to look at Bottom Springs like an anthropologist observing a foreign land, wanting the illusion of distance. But Everett's the one who actually achieved it. All the cruelty, the backwardness—he can laugh it off now because he's just passing through. Except I don't think that's an option for either of us anymore. Not with the investigation. Now everything is a threat we must take seriously.

I scan the bar. "I don't see Barry yet."

"Hey, Everett." From a nearby table, Gerald Theriot smirks at us. Gerald is Sheriff Theriot's nephew and a Fortenot Fishing captain, a tall, wiry man whose skin is prematurely leathery from spending so much time out in the gulf. "Planning on getting in any fights tonight? Should I tell my boys to gird their loins?" The men around him, his crew, laugh.

It turned out the rumors that circulated when we were teens about Everett getting into bar fights were true. Everett *was* always in and out of the Blue Moon. But the reason was one no one in our high school could've guessed: night after night, Ever came to pick up his dad from the bar after he'd gotten too drunk to see straight. On more than one occasion, before he fell unconscious, Mr. Duncan managed to piss someone off so bad they were willing to take up the matter with his son.

For Everett, walking into the Blue Moon used to mean walking into a viper's nest. A place people waited to hurt you; a place where you nevertheless had to go. When he finally told me this, Everett said he was proud that he mostly walked away with nothing more than a black eye. I'd told him next time, he should just let his father rot, and he'd responded that it was funny what you could see for other people that you couldn't for yourself.

Now I shoot him a warning look, but he's one step ahead. "I think you're safe tonight," he says, tipping his beer at Gerald. His unwillingness to be baited bores the table of men, and they go back to ignoring us.

I start to say something to Everett, but he touches my arm and nods in the direction of the booth next to us. I strain and catch the end of a sentence.

"And wouldn't you know," a shrill voice whispers. "She told me what the vandalism was."

Everett and I glance at each other, then lean closer.

"Vandalism—that's what the sheriff was investigating when they found the skull, right?" An older woman's voice.

"Why anyone sets foot in that swamp is beyond me," whispers a third. "It's a death trap. What'd you hear?"

"You're never going to believe it." The shrill voice nearly trembles—with fear or anticipation, I can't tell. "There was evidence of *witchcraft*."

I frown at Everett, but he looks as confused as me.

One of the women sucks in a breath. "What kind of evidence?"

The heavy door to the Blue Moon bangs open, stealing my attention. Barry strides in, still wearing his deputy's uniform. Instantly, the crowd at the bar shouts to him and swallows him up. I glance at Everett, suddenly nervous. I've never seen the two of them in the same room before, not even in high school, and I don't know how it will go. "It's not too late to leave."

Ever nods in the direction of the bar. "I think it is."

Someone has clearly whispered I'm here, because Barry leans back from the bar, beer in hand, eyes searching. When he sees me, they widen in surprise. Then he notices Everett, and the pleasantness falls from his face. He launches from the bar.

"Incoming," Ever mutters.

Barry strides up, wearing a plastered-on grin. He takes off his deputy's cap and rustles his mop of brown hair. "Ruth, what are you doing here?"

It feels like the whole bar's watching. "I haven't seen much of you the last few days." I try to speak loudly, so everyone can hear. "What with the investigation. Thought I'd surprise you. Plus, look who came to visit."

Barry leans down and pecks me on the cheek. When he rises, he directs his affable grin at Everett. Barry looks like I'd always imagined Heathcliff would—short and stocky, with longish brown hair and a thick, square jaw. But he has none of Heathcliff's broodiness. He, like Lila, grew up in the sun, with his football career and perfect church attendance and easygoing smile. The way *atta boys* and *yes, sirs* roll off his tongue makes everyone love him, including my parents. "Well, well, well. Look what the cat dragged in."

The women at the booth next to us titter. The tables have turned, and now they're spying on us.

Ever glances at me. I give him the slightest nod, and he sticks out his hand. "Nice to see you again, Barrett."

Barry chuckles and grips his hand. Their forearms flex as they each squeeze tight. "Please. Barrett Holt's my daddy. It's good to see ya, ol' boy. Wasn't sure we'd ever catch you here again. Figured you had more exciting places to be than little ol' Bottom Springs." He shares a knowing grin with Gerald and his table.

"Ruth's still here," Everett says as they release each other. "That's reason enough."

"Sure, sure." Barry chuffs my cheek. "Tell you what, why don't I join you." He glances between me and Ever, trying not to let his displeasure show over how close we're sitting. I swallow. I need to smooth things over.

"Please, sit." I gesture to the other side of the table. "We've been dying for you to get here. You must be exhausted from the investigation."

He drops into the seat with a sigh. "It's been a long week, I'll tell you what."

Gerald shoves his chair back and stands. "You talking homicide?"

"Oh yeah," Barry groans, with what seems like overperformed resignation. "What else? We got more news this afternoon."

"Well, in that case," Gerald says, hunching down next to Barry in the booth. "I'm all ears."

There's a mad scramble as another one of Gerald's fishing crew members scoots in next to Gerald—now there's three grown men squished into their side of the booth—and the women in the booth next to ours climb to their knees to peer over the partition. Even more people scoot their tables and chairs close to ours. One woman looks ready to claim the third seat on Everett's and my side of the booth, then glances at Everett and thinks better, settling for a chair instead.

"Is it true you found witchcraft in the swamp?" asks one of the women hanging over the partition. It's the one with the shrill voice.

Every eye is on Barry. He sighs and takes a long swig of beer, drawing out the wait. "We got the call a few days ago from Hardy Tullis—you know, that crazy fella that tries to wrestle gators?"

Everyone murmurs.

"Well, he said there were symbols carved into all these trees out in the swamp. At first, Sheriff said to ignore him, on account of his being Crazy Hardy. But eventually I decided to check, and it's a good thing I did. Otherwise we never woulda found the skull. Anyway, sure enough, there they were. The same symbol, carved into a dozen trees. Most hair-raising thing you ever seen. I swear I started praying the minute I saw it."

"What kind of symbol?" Gerald asks.

I glance at Everett. He's playing like he's not interested, slowly tearing the logo from his bottle, unwinding the paper delicately, like it's a sash from a woman's dress he's unraveling.

"Spooky Satanic stuff," Barry says, and chills race up my arms. "A circle with two horns, one on top, one on bottom. Sign of the Beast."

A jolt of recognition hits me as whispers of *Satan* spread like a hissing echo through the bar. Everett leans forward. "The horns—did they look like crescent moons?"

I swallow hard as people turn to stare at him. It's clear they're not surprised Everett Duncan knows to ask such a question, and of course, neither am I. Suddenly I wonder if we're doing more harm than good being out in public.

Barry bristles. "The sheriff said they're horns. He's seen this thing before. An old witchcraft symbol, he said. Has to do with the Low Man."

"My God," whimpers one of the women in the booth beside us. The older woman next to her elbows her. "Don't take God's name in vain!"

"The Low Man," Gerald repeats, sounding shell-shocked. "Sweet Jesus." He takes a fortifying swig of beer. No one admonishes him for taking the Lord's name. The bar is quiet. Chilled.

"You better saw down those trees right quick," says one of Gerald's fishing crew, and there's a murmur of agreement. "Better yet, torch 'em."

Two crescent moons resting on a circle, their barbed ends pointing out like horns. I don't know the symbol—but I've seen others like it, years ago, painted in blood. My voice comes out too high. "Do you have any idea who did it?"

Barry looks at me and smiles. "Aw, look. I done scared poor Ruth. I swear, y'all, sometimes I think she's just a teenage girl at heart." He shares his grin with the table. "Scared a' everything."

"Actually." Ever's voice is deadpan. "I doubt there's a single thing on God's green earth that could scare Ruth Cornier. God's earth or the Devil's."

"Hey now." Barry shifts uncomfortably, eyeing Gerald. "No need to talk like that. Devil's earth and all."

For some reason—maybe it's sitting next to Everett—I feel a rare stir of courage. "He's right, though. I'm not scared. And what's so embarrassing about being a teenage girl?"

"Every teenage girl I've met has been the scariest creature on the planet," Everett says. "I'd put them up against the Low Man any day."

I smile at him. I'm not sure if he means that as a compliment for me or a dig at the girls we went to high school with, like Lila over there, but either way, I like it. And just like that, we're back in our private world. Despite everything, hope lights in me that our friendship can be revived. However, as much as we're enjoying ourselves, our exchange has won us no fans in this crowd. Quite the opposite. People are giving each other charged looks around the table. We've never been good at fitting in, even when we try.

"Well, excuse me," Barry says. "I didn't realize Everett Duncan was the patron saint of teenage girls."

His comment breaks the tension, winning laughter. Encouraged, Barry turns to me. "I also didn't realize I was going to have the pleasure of attending the Ruth and Everett Variety Show. Your momma warned me 'bout it, too. But it's different seeing it up close."

His words make my stomach sink. "You talked to my mother today?"

"I had to go to your folks' house to deliver my report to the reverend. Just got back. That's why I was late to the bar." He winks at Gerald and the boys. "By the way, your momma says don't be late to Bible study tomorrow."

Somehow my parents already know Everett's in town.

"I thought the sheriff was your boss," says Everett, taking a swig of beer. "Not James Cornier."

If there's one thing you don't do around Barry, it's insult my father. "He is," Barry says darkly. "But don't act like you don't know everything that happens in this town runs through the reverend. You ain't been gone that long, Columbine."

A hushed silence fills the bar.

"Barry," I say sharply. "Don't."

"It's okay." Everett's talking to me, not Barry. "Don't worry." He nudges my knee. "I don't care."

Even though Everett's the one who's been insulted and I'm only defending him, people glare at us so hard I can feel the heat from their stares. Women aren't supposed to talk sharply to their men, especially in public. I don't know if this rule is Southern Baptist or southern Louisiana in origin, or if those two cultures are so intertwined here in Bottom Springs that they've become inseparable. Either way, my father says a woman's place is one step behind her husband, serving as his most faithful lieutenant, and as such, public contradiction is betrayal. "'Let your women keep their silence,'" he likes to say, which is a line from Timothy.

Yet another reason I don't come to the Blue Moon: I'm bound to endanger myself.

But to everyone's surprise, Barry doesn't admonish me. Instead, he groans and dips his head. "Ruth's right." He directs his words to Everett. "I'm sorry. That was un-Christian. It's the stress. No offense intended."

"None taken," Everett says, and I'm probably the only person here who believes him.

Gerald clears his throat. "You and my uncle find out anything else 'bout the skull?" He gestures round the bar. "You've got all of us here racking our brains trying to come up with information. Sad to say, there've been a fair number of folks who took off or disappeared these past years. Kinda hard to remember anything suspicious."

"You know," Barry says, settling back. He looks glad to be back in the spotlight for the right reasons. "We did learn something critical."

The bar hushes, the air charging. Every hair on my body pricks to attention. This is it.

Everett goes still. "What, you figure out who the skull belongs to or something?"

I'm amazed at how cool his voice sounds. How benignly curious.

Barry nods. "We got the results back this afternoon. A match on dental records." He glances around. "I'm really not supposed to say before the sheriff."

"Tell us," pleads the woman who opted for a chair over sitting next to Everett. "We're going to find out eventually. This just gives us more time to think."

Barry eyes Gerald and the Fortenot Fishing crew. "All right, then. But I need y'all to brace yourselves. You're not going to like it."

For six years Everett and I have avoided speaking Renard's name. Willing him away, keeping his spirit locked in whatever dark hell he was sent to after we killed him. Now I'm going to hear his name again, and like an invocation, it'll call his spirit back. There will be hell on earth.

Barry takes a breath to speak. *Renard*, the darkness whispers, like a spell curling out of Barry's mouth.

"The skull's Fred Fortenot's." Barry shakes his head. "Can you believe it?"

Gasps erupt around the bar, loudest from Gerald and the Fortenot Fishing crew, Fred's former employees. Even the people who'd remained at the counter now get up to join us, sensing something big has happened. Fred's name leaps from table to table.

For a moment, all I feel is strangely hollow. Where Renard's name should be, there's an impostor. "Fred Fortenot," I echo. My voice is hoarse. "I thought he died in a boat accident. Lost in the gulf."

I grew up my whole life next door to the Fortenots: Fred; his wife, Mary; and their daughter, Beth. Fred founded Fortenot Fishing, which by God's grace has grown into one of the biggest commercial fishing companies in southern Louisiana, employing more than half this town, sending hundreds of men out into boats to trawl the gulf for shrimp and red snapper. Gerald Theriot and a big chunk of the people in this bar worked for Fred or were married to people who did. Fred had been one of the most respected men in Bottom Springs, a church elder and one of my father's closest friends. When he disappeared three years ago, Fortenot Fishing suspended work for a month to join the sheriff in searching the gulf. All they recovered was Fred's personal skiff. The whole town had gathered for a vigil on Main Street to mourn the man lost to the same sea that had given him his livelihood. Everyone except Fred's wife and daughter.

How is it Fred in the swamp, and not Renard? It doesn't make sense.

"We assumed that's how Fred died when we found his boat," Barry says, "but forensics says his body's in the swamp. And he didn't die by accident. Someone beat the living shi—" He glances at me. "Sorry. I forgot, delicate ears."

Gerald and the other Fortenot Fishing captains still haven't uttered a word. For once, their shock is too great.

"That's hard to hear," Everett says, still calm. He has to be in shock like I am, but doing a better job of hiding it. I should be relieved—Holy Father, I should be *ecstatic*—but I can't accept the idea that we've dodged a bullet. Something still feels terribly wrong.

"The sheriff's planning on announcing it tomorrow," Barry says and, to my surprise, reaches across the table to take my hands. I'm so rigid he has to yank them, but he does, persistent. The way his fingers circle my wrists feels like handcuffs sliding on.

I can't shake the feeling I should be going to prison.

"Don't worry, Ruth." Barry rubs the thin skin where my pulse beats in my wrists, and Everett looks down. "You don't have to be scared. Whoever did this, we're gonna find him, and he's gonna fry."

"You can find him," Gerald says darkly. "But you won't have a body left to fry. I'm going to take that man apart just like he did to Fred."

The conversation erupts around us, vows of vengeance and whispers of horror from voices thick with alcohol. Under the table, Everett bumps my knee again. When I glance at him, he raises a dark eyebrow in question. Inviting me back into our secret universe, just him and me.

At his look, I realize why I'm not relieved, despite our narrow escape. Because Fred Fortenot was murdered and disposed of in the exact same manner, in the exact same place, as the man we killed years before him. Which means there's another killer in Bottom Springs.

A copycat.

Does someone know what we did? I wish we were alone so I could ask Ever. I want to read the reassurance on his face, hear him say, *We'll figure it out.*

For the first time, I can't tune out the world. It presses its fingers around my throat, suffocating: Gerald's face, purple with rage; the voices clamoring over each other to be heard; the animal smell of too many close-pressed bodies mingling with the sour tang of beer.

Could the person who killed Fred be in this very room? Are they watching Everett and me, swirling ice cubes in their glass, smiling to see us sweat?

Have we escaped one noose only to find our necks in another?

Ever leans so close his lips brush my hair. "It's okay, Ruth," he whispers. "Don't you see? You're safe."

Goose bumps ripple over my arms. He's wrong. This discovery isn't a reprieve. We've entered some dark game I don't understand. Our secret is a wound, a vulnerability. We're bleeding in the water, and there's a predator circling, so cunning I never saw it coming.

Safe is the last thing we are.

7

JUNE, SEVENTEEN YEARS OLD

Every day after we fed Renard to the swamp, I watched for Everett to appear at the edge of my property—and when he did, I followed him into the wild. Over time, through forest, mud, and meadow, I learned to move as smoothly as he did, to sight birds swooping through trees, discern different types of bog flowers. In a million years, I never would've guessed that the first time I'd fall in love, it would be with the earth itself. The pure, sweet smell of trees after rain. The sucking squelch of mud under my boots. The sound of leaves shaken so furiously by the wind that they rang like bells. Most intoxicating of all, the way my body felt moving through it, confident and alive.

At night we stayed out as late as we dared. My mother always told me night was when the world became the Devil's playground. But Everett showed me the opposite. At midnight, when every shred of light seeped from the world and it hung at the pinnacle of darkness, the creatures of the forest woke and soared and sang. So did I. Under the protective spell of the dark, I became a wolf, howling with Everett, exploring, traipsing through the swampland unafraid. Midnight Ruth was my boldest self, too precious for sunlight.

Eventually my parents discovered what I was doing and were

incensed. They tried everything to stop me. But there was no threat or punishment that would make me give up Everett. When my father screamed, spittle flying, when he told me Everett was a corrupter with a tar-black soul, sent by the Devil to debase me, I let his words tumble past. When he caught me sneaking home and struck me with the cane until my back bent, I let the pain sink in and flow out. I have no idea where the bravery came from, why their disapproval didn't trigger the same debilitating fear it always had. Perhaps it was simply that I could sense, even in the beginning of our friendship, that Everett was a lifeline I'd better hold on to.

One day I came downstairs for breakfast wearing my sneakers, planning to meet Everett after, and found my parents sitting side by side at the kitchen table. That was bad enough, but when I saw what was on the table, my stomach seized. Two thick envelopes, torn open. My admissions results from Louisiana Tech and LSU, the two schools in the state with the strongest English programs and cheapest tuition. The two I'd secretly applied to. If I could just get accepted, I'd reasoned, I could come up with a plan to pay so I wouldn't have to ask my parents for money, and then I'd stand a chance of convincing them.

Graduation was now a week away. I'd been waiting for these letters all spring.

"You went behind our backs," said my mother in her quietest voice, which was also her most dangerous. My father and she were fire and ice—and like Robert Frost said, when it came to destruction, either was nice and would suffice. She flicked the letters with her bony fingers. "How dare you make plans without us, like we're nothing? Your parents who raised you?"

"I was going to tell you—"

"Don't interrupt your mother," my father boomed. The great James Cornier was thick and towering, larger than life, with a sonorous voice, square teeth, and wild chest hair that curled from the tops of his dress shirts. The dark giant to my mother's pale sprite. When he rocked forward, the entire table quaked. "Where's your judgment, Ruth? These places are Sodom incarnate."

"That's not true." Desperation pitched my voice higher. "They're places for learning. That's all I want to do." Books were my refuge; the idea of devoting my life to them was a dream that had carried me through every day in Bottom Springs.

"Learn what?" My father was flummoxed. "You can learn everything you need to be God's servant here."

"'A woman should learn in quietness and full submission,'" said my mother. "Timothy 2:11."

"That's what you're doing in this house. We're teaching you everything the Bible says you need: how to love your future husband and children, how to be self-controlled, how to submit to God's will." My father shook his head. "The need for worldly education is a lie told by the government, Ruth. We appease them as we must, but enough is enough. I won't let your head become clouded."

"'Charm is deceitful, and beauty is vain, but a woman who fears the Lord is to be praised,'" my mother quoted. Her white-blond hair, as stripped of color as mine was full of it, swished over her shoulders. "I know those books you read when you think we're not looking give you airs. But you're almost a woman now, Ruth Cornier. It's time to stop being vain and childish and grow up."

They weren't supposed to ambush me. I was supposed to find the letters in the mailbox and, if they contained good news, present my case methodically, persuasively. I'd win them over and then I'd escape to a city where no one watched or whispered, where Renard Michael's bloody face didn't haunt me around every corner.

I took a deep breath and dared to meet my father's eyes. "The cost won't be a burden, I swear." I kept my voice subdued, the way he liked it. "I'll take out loans and work a part-time job, if you'll just sign the paperwork." He was my legal guardian; without his signature, I couldn't access anything. "Please, Daddy."

The thought that I could lose the one shining light at the end of my tunnel was suddenly too much to bear. Instead of keeping calm, I made a fatal mistake. I fell to my knees and placed my head in my father's lap, willing him to see me as his daughter, to feel a spark of tenderness that could sway his heart. The words tumbled out: "I want to see the world. I want to learn and have a career." My voice cracked. "*Please*. I'll suffocate if I don't leave."

I knew the moment I looked up that I'd revealed too much. Given my parents a glimpse of the real me, the emotions I'd hidden. It was a line I could never uncross.

My father jerked his knee away and I fell back against the kitchen floor.

"It's that boy, isn't it?" my mother hissed. "He's in your ear. Getting you to want things you have no business wanting."

My heart felt as if it were physically breaking. They were going to blame Everett and kill two birds with one stone. I scrambled to my feet. "This has nothing to do with him. I've wanted to go to college my whole life."

"You're not leaving Bottom Springs." My father's words were heavy and final. "You're a Cornier. You will set an example."

"*Please.*" My legs trembled as I gripped the table. "Don't take this away. It's all I've lived for."

One of my greatest weaknesses has always been that sometimes grief and fear can grip me so completely that I lose control. I could feel it happening then, that old demon clawing: the shortness of breath, a pounding heart, the sense that I was spiraling and couldn't stop.

"Do you see now?" My mother turned to my father as if they were picking up a conversation they'd started long before. "She's hysterical. God demands we intervene."

I willed in air. If they were going to call the elders to lay hands on me, I'd run.

"Your mother's right." My father crossed his arms. "It's time we take you to the doctor."

I gaped. "You said they're for the weak, for people without the moral fiber to connect with God."

"You *are* the weak," he said. "And you've been masking it for years, haven't you? But your momma and I've seen it. Our only child, a deviant. Well, God calls us to face down the Devil even when he's inside our own home."

My heart pounded. I couldn't let them touch me.

"Listen to me," my father commanded, and that's when the switch flipped. I had the sudden sensation of being pinned down, unable to breathe. I'd do anything to escape. I lunged for the letters and bolted down the hall, ignoring my parents' shouts, then burst from the front door and streaked across the lawn.

As I shot around the street corner, there was Everett, making his way to my house. He stopped short but I kept running, clutching my letters, not even stopping when I got close enough to register his fresh black eye.

"Ruth," he called, amazed. "What's happening?"

I blew past him, then felt him chasing me as I charged down the street. I took the turnoff to the woods, cutting through neighbors' lawns, running hard enough to keep myself from thinking. Trees appeared in the distance and I plunged into them.

After another minute of exertion, I fell against the trunk of a pine, gasping. Soon Everett was beside me, his face flushed. He braced a hand on the tree near my shoulder. "What the hell's going on?"

I shook my head. My muscles burned. Sweat plastered my hair to my forehead. When I'd gulped enough air, I managed to say, "Panic attack." I'd never told anyone—I didn't even know for sure. I'd read a book with a character who had them, and it had been like a lightbulb going off. I'd diagnosed myself.

"What'd your parents do?" Everett asked, and I didn't stop to wonder how he knew.

I pushed the letters against his chest. "I'm not going to college."

He smoothed the papers and scanned them. "Funny, because it looks like you are."

"They said no."

Everett wiped his face with the hem of his T-shirt, exposing his muscled stomach. I jerked my gaze away. "Who cares what they said? You're almost eighteen. Go anyway."

I flushed. "With what money? I don't even have a checking account. I need them to sign for a loan." I shouldn't have to explain to Everett. He should know as well as anyone that money was destiny.

He laughed—it startled me enough that I glanced up. "What?"

"These people. If they can't trap you one way, they just find another." He looked back at the letters. "A thousand to confirm your spot, huh?"

I leaned against the tree, letting the bark bite into my back. It was getting easier to breathe. "Might as well be a million. I have the same chance of coming up with it."

"There's a community college out in Saint Lafitte, you know. That's only an hour away. It's not LSU, but it's something. Won't cost you a thousand to register, neither. Maybe you could work a little after graduation, save up, then apply." Everett's eyes traveled from my clenched hands up to my face. He wore that tender look again, the one that had alarmed me the first time I saw it. "I've sat next to you in class for years. You of all people should be going to college."

"Are you going?" Under my dress, sweat was drying on my skin, cooling it. I rubbed my arms, trying to ignore the fact that even the hint that he'd paid attention to me made me feel strangely light. "To community college?"

He scrubbed his neck. "Maybe. I don't know. I've got some things to work out first."

I studied his face. The question slipped out. "Do you really get in bar fights like people say?"

Everett's eyes narrowed. For years I'd tried not to look too closely at his face. For a thousand reasons, it had seemed too dangerous. Now that we were becoming friends, I kept discovering things that took me by surprise. Like how his eyes were impossibly dark, yet sparkled with flecks of brown, like little stars. The dark bruise around his eye did nothing to diminish the effect.

"Never mind the black eye," he said quickly. "I found something."

He fished in his pocket and pulled out something that glinted—Renard's *Momma* necklace. It was streaked with dirt and something darker—blood.

A chill washed through me. "Where'd you get that?" Talk of Renard's disappearance was fading, but if anyone saw this necklace in Everett's possession, distinctly Renard's and covered in blood, we'd be in grave trouble.

"I found it in the clearing." Everett watched for my reaction.

He meant the clearing where we'd killed Renard. "Why did you go back?" Returning to the scene of the crime seemed the most suspicious thing he could've done. In books, it was what killers did when they wanted to soak in the glory of their crimes.

He shrugged. "I was hunting, and the clearing's close to a burrow. There's reliable game there."

"You were hunting when you found me, too." I'd seen the dead animal he dropped. "Why do you hunt so much?"

He looked past me. "I have to eat."

"Doesn't your father buy groceries?" Mr. Duncan, who ran the garage on the other side of town, was someone I crossed the street to avoid. Even from far away, you could feel the dark miasma of anger that ringed him. Churchgoers whispered he'd sold his soul to the Devil and was now his emissary, a rumor strengthened by the fact that he and Everett had never once stepped foot inside the church. Some whispered they'd burst into flames if they tried. But Mr. Duncan's garage seemed busy despite the rumors—there were always cars there—which meant there had to be at least enough money to eat.

Everett's words were clipped. "Like I said."

He clearly wanted to change the subject, so I gestured to the necklace. "We have to get rid of it, right?"

He nodded. "I thought you might want to do the honors. All things considered."

He watched me calmly, like it wasn't revolutionary that someone had thought of me—not as background filler, not as the mute daughter of Pastor Cornier, but as a person, with thoughts and feelings as complex as anger and a desire for revenge.

All I could manage was a weak "How?"

"Come on." He turned to face the deep woods, the one place we hadn't yet ventured. "I'll show you." He glanced back. "Unless you need to go home?"

All of my life, my mother warned that the Louisiana deep woods were no place for children, especially girls. There were wolves and bears. Venomous snakes and frogs spotted like leopards and spiders as big as your fist. No well-worn paths to guide you out of the maze of trees. In the deep woods, I was prey.

But right now, nowhere was as dangerous as home.

"Show me the way," I said.

8

JUNE, SEVENTEEN YEARS OLD

After we'd hiked for an hour, Everett stopped. "This is the place."

I looked around, my breathing labored from keeping pace with him. As far as I could tell, there was nothing special here. The ground was nice and flat, clear of tree roots, but… "Is that trash?"

Everett bent and grabbed the plastic bag, shaking it so I could see inside. There were bright wrappers, the kind on processed food from the gas station. There was rarely trash in the woods or the swamp. Too few people ventured in.

"I don't know why," he said, "but this spot is popular with drifters. It's not even close to the highway." He looked around and shrugged. "Maybe it feels sheltered. Either way, I've seen people camp here."

I studied him. "You really are always outside, aren't you?" That was another one of the rumors at school: Everett Duncan was a Satanist freak with ripped-up clothes and an antisocial personality, practically a feral animal, always lurking in the swamp or woods.

His laugh was harsh. Usually, Everett was stoic. Every day when I met him on my lawn, he asked benign questions in an even tone: *How are you doing? How's your homework going?* I knew he did it to calm me, make me feel like even after what happened with Renard, normal life was possible. I'd gotten used to him being unflappable. This pained laughter was a crack in his armor. It made him seem human, and I wanted more.

"What's that laugh for?" I asked, trying to goad him.

His expression turned disdainful. "Where else should I be? In church, with your father? At home, with mine? Should I join the football team or the yearbook so I can make memories I'll treasure forever?" He was breathing hard. "I'd rather take the gators."

I looked at him. And grinned.

"Why are you making that face?"

"I can't believe you would dare critique Sacred Surrender. All those innocent, learned scholars, just trying to drink life to the lees." I felt a tug of embarrassment quoting Tennyson, who we'd just read in English class. You weren't supposed to care so much about your homework that you memorized it. But the chink in Everett's armor was too inviting. He was being himself, so maybe I could, too.

Everett's mouth curved into a smile. The sharpness of his canines was still new to me, so I couldn't help but stare. "'How dull it is to pause.'" The words rolled off his tongue. "'To make an end. To rust unburnished, not to shine in use. As though to breathe were life.'"

"So he does do his homework."

"And she talks. Surprise, surprise."

We grinned at each other. When Everett finally pulled his gaze away, his smile still hung in the air, like the afterimage of sunlight that stays glowing long after you close your eyes.

"Let's start the fire," he said, and dropped to the dirt.

I joined him, brushing back pine needles until I saw what he was looking for: burn marks scoured deep into the earth. "You're not supposed to light fires out here because it's a burn hazard," he said. "But people do it anyway."

He nudged the bag of trash. "If the sheriff or anyone ever stumbles on this place and they see someone's been setting fires, ours will be unrecognizable from the campers.'"

"You're burying our fire in theirs, like a needle in a haystack."

He dropped Renard's necklace into my palm. I straightened the chain gingerly, like it was a relic. Then Everett gathered the pine needles back in a pile and pulled a lighter from his pocket, thumbing up a flame, and set the needles smoking. We sat back and watched as they caught frond by frond. The fire was small but hungry; soon the whole pile was ablaze. The heat flushed my face. I pressed a finger to my cheek and felt the spot of cool like an island in a sea of lava.

"Do you want to put it in now?" he asked. "I think it's ready."

I hooked the necklace and let it dangle over the fire until it got too hot. Then I released it. It fell, shimmering, into the center of the pit.

"Now we'll see how much he really loved his mother," Everett said. "If it's real gold, it won't burn."

I had a sudden vision of Joan of Arc, tied to a stake and going up in flames. It was an image that had haunted me since I was a child, like Christ on his cross with his rivers of blood. "You're betting it's not."

"Fake gold is iron and aluminum. They have a lower burning point." At my look, Everett shrugged. "I help in my dad's garage. I've learned things."

I watched the necklace closely. The answer was important. How much had Renard loved his mother? Enough to redeem him, and damn us? A moral judgment hung in the balance.

"Look," Everett said. *Momma* was blackening at the edges, the little *a* starting to curl. His voice was dry. "Guess he didn't love her that much after all."

"Don't say that." The words came out harsh. "Just because someone can't afford something doesn't tell you what kind of person they are."

It wasn't just me and college I was talking about, it was my fear that

I'd be trapped here and years from now when people passed me, they'd see a woman like everyone else, not the Ruth Cornier who'd tried to escape. I also felt an urge to protect Renard's mother, to keep her son's love for her true. I didn't know anything about the woman except she was out there somewhere, grieving the loss of her child. The son we'd taken.

"People's money might not tell you who they are, but their actions do." Everett was looking at me with the oddest expression. "You'd defend the man who hurt you?"

I looked away. My eyes were pricking and I didn't want him to see. "No one is all bad. I refuse to believe it."

"Says the reverend's daughter about her would-be rapist."

I flinched.

"Do you want to say something, then?"

The change was abrupt enough to make my head snap. "What sort of thing?"

Everett shrugged. "I don't know. Whatever's in your head. You can be the preacher."

I looked into the crackling flames, where Renard's heart darkened and burned, and was surprised to find I did want to say something. But I didn't have words of my own. So, like I'd done my whole life, I leaned on others.

"'I am part of all that I have met,'" I recited softly. "'Yet all experience is an arch through which gleams that untraveled world. Whose margin fades—'" I looked up from the fire to Everett, who watched me closely. "'Whose margin fades for ever and forever when I move.'"

A smile ghosted his lips. "For ever and forever. Amen."

The fire popped. I looked at him. "That day in the swamp. You held my hand."

His lashes fluttered. "Did I? I don't remember."

I hadn't wanted to be touched since. The Sunday after, my mother had come into my room with a floral pin for my hair. I'd shrunk against the wall, but she'd insisted. So I'd stood rigid in front of my mirror, and as she tugged and scraped the tines against my scalp, I'd remembered my daydream: a boy's fingers moving gently through my hair. My eyes had filled with tears.

But for some reason, Everett was different. I kept thinking about the way his hand gripped mine that day at the swamp.

Now he looked down at my side. "I don't normally like to..."

"It's okay," I said softly. "No problem."

He looked into the fire, pale skin turning the lightest shade of rose. Then he took my hand, his skin remarkably cold for a summer's day, and laced his fingers between mine. He examined our locked hands with an indecipherable expression.

"What are you thinking?"

"Nothing." He swallowed. "You give a good funeral, is all. Do mine one day?"

I squeezed his hand. "Be serious."

"I am. I think we should be friends."

"I thought we already were."

We sat in silence, warmed by the fire, until the necklace was close to disappearing.

"'That which we are, we are,'" Everett murmured, sounding strangely resigned. "Tennyson was right about that. No escape."

We watched the last piece of Renard Michaels blacken into ash, flakes as thin as feathers, and then float into the sky. Everett stood and reached a hand to help me up. We smothered the fire, gray smoke curling, and left, combing carefully back through the forest.

By the time we spotted the tall-grass meadow waving in front of us, my mind was pleasantly absent, drifting somewhere in the clouds. "For ever and forever," I murmured. "Ever, forever, amen."

He turned over his shoulder with an amused smile, and then his eyes hooked down to my feet. "Ruth, no, *wait*—"

But it was too late. The moment I looked down and saw the copperhead, its beautiful body red and brown like the leaves, it was already rising, its slitted eyes like twin slashes from a knife. It struck, sinking fangs into my inner thigh. I screamed, the pain like being stabbed, and the snake lit away so fast it looked like it was gliding over the earth. I crumpled to the ground as Everett flew past me, chasing the snake. When I cried out again, clutching my leg, he stiffened and rushed back.

"It's going to be okay," he promised. "Can I touch you?"

I nodded, sobbing, feeling slippery blood roll down my leg from the puncture wounds. Two thin streams, like bloody tears, staining my blue dress.

Everett scooped me in his arms and took off. Even clutching me, he was surprisingly fast, blowing through the meadow grass like a meteor. When we were a hundred yards from the trees, he jerked to a stop and laid me on the ground.

"What are you doing?" I cried, cupping my wound.

"Do you trust me?" He bent over my thigh, one of his hands still cradling my head. He looked down at the bite, dark eyes burning, and pulled out a pocketknife. Flipped the blade up.

Did I trust him? It seemed not the right word for what I felt: both imprecise and not quite strong enough.

I drew a deep breath. "Yes."

At the word, he spread my legs in the grass, lifting the thin cotton of my dress. "Bite down," he instructed, and placed two cool fingers against my lips. I didn't know what he meant until he drew the tip of the blade across my thigh, opening the wound with a strong, sure cut. I bit down on instinct, tasting the salt of his skin as tears flooded my eyes.

I could hear my father's voice: this was punishment for my sins.

Suddenly Everett pressed his mouth to the inside of my thigh and sucked. I lifted off the ground, gasping, with his fingers in my mouth. The sensation was unlike any I'd ever felt. Nerves lit electric through my body.

He drew away and spit a mouthful of blood into the grass. My blood was smeared over his face, crimson and deadly. If anyone saw him like this, bent over me dripping red, they would shoot him dead. But before I could think, he fastened his mouth over my thigh again, and I felt that warm sucking pressure. He gripped my leg and pulled it closer, pressing his lips harder to my skin, the movement desperate, like he had a raw thirst and I was the only thing in the world that could quench it.

The panic faded as something new built inside me. A hot pulsing, in rhythm with the blood pumping through my veins. I closed my eyes, tipped my head back, and dug my fingers into the warm, dry dirt. All thoughts of punishment fled. There was only Everett's mouth on me. Like a blade of grass, I was rooted in the meadow, unburdened by shame and simply—unbearably—alive.

Everett withdrew from my leg and spit once more. I opened my eyes, trying to gain control over my breathing.

"That should help," he panted, wiping his mouth on his T-shirt. His teeth were stained red. "But we need to get you to the hospital for anti-venin. I don't have a working car. I need to take you back home."

I nodded, still breathless, lost to the pulsing even as it waned.

"I'm going to pick you up again. Is that okay?"

"No one asks for permission." The pain and strange pleasure had transformed my brain into a fog. Thoughts were hard to hold on to.

"I'm taking that as a yes," he said, and heaved me up. We made our way out of the meadow and back into my parents' neighborhood, cutting across lawns. My house loomed menacingly in the distance.

"I changed my mind," I breathed. "I don't want to go back." Our house had been freshly painted and now gleamed unblemished white, an upgrade my mother had insisted on even though vanity was an affront to God. "Please, Ever."

He stopped, gazing down at me, looking torn. Just then, at the house next to ours, Fred Fortenot ambled out of his front door. He was large and tan like my father and wore his blond hair slicked back like him, too. They could be brothers. Fred stopped and bent over a flower bush. Quickly, he stomped on a small lizard running through the mulch.

"I can bring you to Fred," Everett said. "Fred can drive you to Blanchard instead of your parents, and that way—"

"*No.*" My heart thundered against my rib cage. "Not him. Please, Everett, don't let him see us."

He studied me, dark eyes narrowing. Our faces were so close our noses brushed. "Why are you scared of Fred?"

"Take me home after all," I whispered. "Just leave me on the porch so they don't catch you."

Everett rested his forehead against mine and took a deep breath. Then he ducked past Fred's and brought me to my parents', laying me outside their front door.

"I ran away today to avoid the hospital." I grit my teeth. "It's just like you said. One way or another, they always get you in the end."

"One of these days," Everett said softly, close to my ear, "someone's going to get them back." And before I could respond, he jabbed the doorbell and gave me one last look before he ran.

My mother opened the front door and screamed.

9

JUNE, SEVENTEEN YEARS OLD

Night fell eerily orange as I lay in bed, staring at the ceiling. Although some distant voice of reason, buried under layers of fog, said it was impossible, my ceiling swirled with constellations, glittering stars that spun and tilted exactly the way science books said they did, meteors that shot with fiery plumes from one corner of my bedroom to the other. I was watching it all when I heard three sharp raps against my window.

I swung off the bed and crept over. Everett sat on the other side of my second-story windowpane, his face glowing reddish-orange. Quickly, I unlocked the window and heaved it up. Everett climbed inside, bringing balmy air and the scent of night-flowering jessamine from the garden.

"Blood moon tonight," he said by way of greeting. He kept one hand hidden behind his back. "Have you seen it?"

I'd been grounded to my room since getting back from the hospital. I leaned out the window and gasped. The moon was full and vivid red—it looked like it was on fire. "It's like the prophecy," I breathed. "From the Book of Joel. 'The sun shall be turned into darkness, and the moon into blood, before the great and terrible day of the Lord.'"

Everett grinned. "You should see the town. They're buying all the dry goods out of Piggy Wiggly, convinced it's the apocalypse. I'm not sure how elbow pasta's going to save them from the Rapture, but maybe be glad you're locked inside."

I glanced down at the grass below. "How did you get up here?" My voice came out low and dreamy.

Ever frowned at me. "There's a trellis running up your house. Practically a ladder."

"Ah." I smiled at the image of Everett scaling my house like a jungle gym, then had to lean against my desk when the same thought made me dizzy.

He stepped forward, frown deepening. "What happened at the hospital?" Gently, he took my elbow. "Here, why don't you sit down."

I let him usher me to my bed. "They know we were together in the woods."

"Who?"

"My parents. There was no getting around it when the doctor mentioned someone had cut my snakebite and sucked the venom out."

Everett said nothing. He looked very beautiful standing there in the red moonlight. Tall, with dark hair falling every which way. Even the bruise that ringed his eye seemed a delicate decoration, the swelling gone down since this morning. I kept the thoughts to myself.

"The doctor called it an old hunter's trick," I said, trying to distract myself. "He said it's not supposed to work. But he could hardly find a trace of venom in me." I laughed. "You really stumped him."

Ever didn't laugh. "But he still gave you the antivenin, right? And something for the pain?"

I nodded. Moving my head felt like dragging it through mud.

Everett studied me. I was wearing an old, faded nightshirt and shorts that barely peeked out underneath, but for some reason, I didn't feel ashamed. "Is that why you're acting so strange? Because of the pain meds?"

My head was too heavy to hold up. I dropped back onto my bed. "After the doctor left, the psychiatrist came in. The one my parents wanted me to see. I was already in the hospital, so I was trapped."

I couldn't see Everett but felt him draw nearer. "What did the psychiatrist say?"

"He asked a lot of questions. How often I felt unhappy. If I was aware my overactive imagination and emotions were hurting my parents, if I felt ashamed when I became hysterical, if I believed people were out to get me, if I had the urge to run away." I shook my head. "It was exhausting."

"That's not fair." Everett's sharp voice came from above me. "If you feel like people are out to get you, it's because they are. You're seeing clearly. Hysteria's the only sane response to this town."

I watched the stars glitter on my ceiling. "He gave my dad a prescription. I don't know what, but something has to be wrong with me. They gave me one of the pills, and I've felt..." I searched for the right word. "So foggy, ever since."

"Ruth." Everett ran a hand over my arm, fingers skimming my skin, and the touch sharpened my focus. His worried face appeared in my line of sight. "Don't take any more of those. Even if your parents force you, I don't know, throw them up or something. This doesn't feel right."

I shrugged. "The pain's gone, though. And I stopped feeling guilty..." I let my voice trail off, not willing to risk calling Renard's ghost into the room.

Everett's fingers trailed to my shoulder. Goose bumps followed in their wake. "Pain is how you know you're alive, Ruth. It's not something you should bury."

I struggled to sit up. "You haven't even told me why you're here."

His intense stare remained fixed on me. "I wanted to check on you. And give you this." Everett pulled his hand from behind his back, presenting a dead copperhead, the tail coiled around his forearm. The snake's slitted eyes were open, glassy and unseeing.

If it wasn't for the medicine muffling my feelings, turning them cotton-ball soft, I think I would've screamed. Instead, I leaned closer, morbidly curious. I studied the leaflike pattern of its scales. "Is this the snake that bit me?"

He nodded. "I went back and found him while you were in the hospital. Now you don't have to worry when we go back to the woods."

He held the snake higher, presenting it like a trophy.

"An eye for an eye," I murmured. I searched myself. "It's strange. But I think it does make me feel safer. Thank you."

He lowered his hand. "You should always feel safe, Ruth. I'll make sure of it."

I looked out the window at the blood moon. Every part of tonight was surreal; reality twisted on its side. I was half-convinced I was dreaming. "Let's go outside," I said. If this was a dream, I could do anything.

Ever eyed me. "Are you sure you can manage?"

I floated to the window and leaned out. Apocalypse or not, the sky was a splendor. The red-orange light and the eerie quiet made my neighborhood feel like another, more peaceful place. "Yes. I want to be outside. Not trapped in here."

"Okay then, Rapunzel. Let's climb to the roof. That'll be the best view."

I turned to him.

"It'll be just like climbing a tree."

Slowly, I shook my head.

"You've never climbed a *tree*?"

"You climbed through my window holding a dead snake, and I'm the strange one?" I raised my eyebrows. After a moment, his face cracked into a smile.

"Fair enough," he allowed. "I guess that means you don't want it?"

I bit my lip. "No, thank you. But if you throw it in the garden, it'll scare my mother."

His smile turned wolfish. He crossed to the window and dropped the dead snake matter-of-factly into the flower bed. Then he glanced at me. "Come on. I'll help you up."

Everett turned out to be right about the trellis: it was almost as good as a ladder. We climbed it slowly, then made our way across the roof, me in front and Everett behind, his hands hovering over my waist, ready to grab me if my feet slid on the shingles. Halfway across I looked back and found him concentrating intensely on my feet. "What?" he asked when he caught me. But I only smiled and kept moving.

Finally, we came to the edge of the roof and sat with our legs dangling over the side, the whole bloody landscape sweeping before us. "I know it's supposed to be scary," I said. "But it feels more like a fairy tale."

"The Bible is a fairy tale."

From up here, Bottom Springs seemed smaller and more manageable, less like it could hurt me. I felt a surge of affection—for my hometown or my heretical friend, I couldn't tell. "Promise me you won't say those sorts of things to other people. And don't ever bring them snakes."

"I know. But it's you."

I closed my eyes to soak in the feeling of being a *you*—and swayed, hands slipping on the shingles.

"Careful," Everett said, gripping my arm. "Lean against me if you're having trouble."

For a boy who'd been reluctant to hold my hand earlier today, this seemed a leap. My heart rate climbed, a small echo of the way it pounded in the meadow when his mouth closed over my thigh. I scooted until our legs touched and leaned my head against his shoulder. Everett wrapped an arm around me. He smelled green and mineral, like the woods.

"Will you show me how to climb trees? I like the way the world looks from high up."

He squeezed my arm, which I took to mean yes. We sat in contemplative silence until he said, "Ruth?"

"Hmm?"

"Can I ask you something, and will you tell me the truth?"

I tilted my head to face him. In the moonlight, his black eye looked like a shadow spreading over his face. "Of course." I didn't think it was possible for me to lie right now, thanks to the pill.

He looked into the distance. "Why wouldn't you let me bring you to Fred Fortenot?"

A chill stole over me despite the balmy air. "I'm not supposed to tell anyone. I promised my parents."

His mouth quirked. "If it helps, I've been told I'm a nobody."

I kicked his dangling foot, then blinked at the square of cotton taped over the fang marks on my thigh. Fear coiled inside me. I remembered vividly the night Beth, Fred's daughter, came home late from a party. Beth was a year younger than me. Growing up as neighbors, she'd been one of the first people I'd tried to befriend. But ultimately we were too different: though she was naturally quiet like me, Beth was obsessed with being popular.

As we grew up, I watched her slowly become friends with the football players and cheerleaders. She wasn't pretty like Lila LeBlanc or naturally charismatic, but her father was the boss of Fortenot Fishing, and that made her important. The night she tried to sneak in, she was wearing a scandalously short skirt with a frayed hemline, like she'd cut it herself. I could tell the moment I spotted her through my bedroom window that she'd had too much to drink. Though her father was as strict as mine, I wasn't surprised to see it: Beth would've done anything to fit in.

"One night last year I watched Beth sneak in." I cleared my throat.

"She must've thought her parents were asleep, but I could see her dad in the kitchen, waiting in the dark. I waved to get her attention, but she didn't see me." I took a deep breath. "The moment she stepped inside, he found her and started yelling."

I would never forget the image: tall, beloved Fred Fortenot towering over his small daughter in her short skirt, his face red, veins ropy in his forehead. I couldn't hear his shouting, but I could feel it. I knew in my gut violence was coming—it was an instinct, or maybe the look on Fred's face was close to my father's right before he took out his cane. Either way, I watched it unfold through the window like a horror movie.

"She must've said something to him that made him really mad, because..." I waited for the lump in my throat to clear. "He started choking her." Beth had sunk to the floor so fast it was almost astonishing. But he was very large, after all. She was a doll in his hands.

Everett went rigid. "He hurt his own daughter?"

Now that I'd started, the secret poured from me. "She was sobbing on the floor, but he hit her anyway. Over and over. His hands were all over her..."

Everett's body grew so tense it practically hummed. I looked at his black eye and was about to ask about it when he said, tersely, "What did you do?"

I took a deep breath. "I ran and woke my parents. My dad went over to Fred's house, but I don't know what happened after that because they closed all the blinds."

I'd come to the part of the story I was truly not supposed to reveal. I swallowed thickly, the words stuck in my throat. It was amazing how embodied obedience was. Amazing how, even though sometimes I thought I hated my parents, their commandments still wormed their way so deep into my subconscious that obeying them was more muscle memory than choice. That had to be the worst kind of prison—the one whose bars were buried under your skin, invisible cages around your heart and mind.

Getting the words out felt like pushing through a heavy door. "Two nights later...when Fred went out...Mrs. Fortenot came to our house, crying. We didn't have the front door locked, and she just burst in." The sound of the door banging against the wall had cracked like thunder through the house. "My parents were in the living room. She fell at my father's feet and begged him to help her and Beth escape, said they needed our mercy. He tried to shush her, but she only got louder, telling him Fred had been hurting Beth for years and it was only getting worse. She was grateful my family had finally witnessed it. Now my parents would believe her and help."

"But Beth and Mrs. Fortenot are still here." Everett's face was unreadable. "They never left."

"My father told her she was breaking her covenant with God, airing her husband's business. And in front of a child, too." I'd never forget Mrs. Fortenot's face when she turned and saw me in the kitchen, frozen and watching. There'd been shame in her face. But underneath the shame was desperation, an instinct to survive. She'd looked at me, then kept on begging.

"My parents made me go to my room, but before I did, I heard my father say Scripture commanded Mrs. Fortenot to submit to her husband the same as unto the Lord. She had to have faith in him, like she had faith in Christ. Eventually Mrs. Fortenot went home, and my parents told me I wasn't allowed to speak about what I'd seen. It would be a mercy to Mrs. Fortenot to hide that she'd betrayed her family. I tried to talk to Beth about it at school, but she practically shoved me away." The look of horror on her face when she'd realized I knew. "Now she won't speak to me at all. And the blinds at their house stay closed."

Everett took a deep breath. "They can't be allowed to keep doing this."

I leaned so I could look at him more clearly. "They?"

"Fred Fortenot. Your father. Mine." He jerked his hand out at the neighborhood, the bloodred lawns stretching in front of bloodred houses. "All the men who run this town, who are getting fat and rich being cruel while everyone sings their praises. I *hate* them, Ruth." His voice thickened. "I hate them so much I can't keep it inside anymore."

His words shocked me into silence. I'd never heard anyone speak like that. It was more than complaining about school or Bottom Springs's smallness. Everett's words were a transgression, his visceral anger mixing with the red moonlight to form black magic, words capable of changing perspectives, opening doors. It felt in that moment that we really were glimpsing the beginning of the end. The waning of one world, the dawn of the next.

"They hurt people and they take things—" His voice grew ragged. "Things you can never get back."

"Who took from you?" But Ever was already shaking his head, so I changed direction. "What do we do about it?"

Slowly, as silence stretched around my question, the stiffness left Everett's body, melting into the night. He leaned back, bracing himself against the roof with his hands, and looked at me. A shiver ran the length of my body. The fog cleared from my mind and the night revealed itself with sudden sharpness: the sounds in nearby woods not melodic but the triumphant baying of predators, the houses on the street not peaceful but too still, like corpses, painted lurid bloody red by a moon with pockmarks, its face not a jewel but a network of pits and bruises.

"There are people in this town," Ever said quietly, "who get away with bad things. People who face no consequences."

He held me pinned with his eyes. And as I stared back, I saw him with a sudden sharpness, too. Saw beyond his outer strength to his fragility, this boy who had been bruised, both in ways I could see and some I was beginning to suspect. His anger was a life raft, keeping him afloat.

But I could be a life raft, too. I could help him like he'd helped me.

Slowly, shingles scraping my thighs, I slid over the roof until I fit against his side again. Everett leaned his head to rest on mine. On my leg, next to my bandage, our hands met, fingers lacing together, the same as they had in front of the fire.

"One day," Everett whispered, "there's going to be real justice."

10

NOW

Caught you," says Nissa, and I nearly jump out of my skin.

She steps up behind me and rests a hand on my shoulder, metal bracelets jangling. "I told you if you kept reading that spooky stuff, you'd regret it."

I shove my notebook into my lap, heart thundering, and manage to squeak, "What?"

Nissa points at the book on the circulation desk. "'Tell-Tale Heart,' huh? You got something you want to get off your chest?"

For a second, I simply blink at the Edgar Allan Poe collection, which is cracked open to the beginning of "The Tell-Tale Heart." I'd grabbed the text at random to shield my notebook, where I was writing every question we needed answered now that the skull in the swamp had turned out to be Fred's. I'd figured if I was stuck at work and couldn't talk to Everett, the least I could do was strategize. The fact that my cover-up turned out to be Poe seems a damning detail.

"I don't blame you for being on edge," Nissa continues. "We all are, with a killer on the loose." She shivers, wrapping her peach cardigan tighter. Nissa Guidry's personality shines through in the bright colors she wears, a beautiful complement to her rich dark skin and glossy curls, and in her special way of walking, which I privately call sashaying. If she wasn't such an excellent librarian, she could've been a performer. Nissa has natural stage presence. She's been my sole colleague for a year, ever since she and her doctor husband, Elijah, moved here from Baton Rouge after Elijah got an offer at Blanchard Hospital, which employs the other half of town not employed by the Fortenot Fishing Company. According to Nissa, it had been worth quitting her beloved job as a research librarian at LSU so her husband could fulfill his dream of working in rural medicine.

I once asked how she could possibly stand living and working here after experiencing city life and a real library. To my surprise, she'd said Bottom Springs was paradise on earth, postcard-perfect with its little Main Street, a town untouched by modernity and the encroachment of big businesses like Walmart, small enough to know your neighbors, beauty everywhere you looked. Hearing the admiration in Nissa's voice had pierced my heart, as if her inability to see this town the way I did was a betrayal. But even so, before her, I'd worked with crotchety old Mrs. Dupre, who died of a stroke two days after she retired, so I'm grateful to have Nissa.

It's 9:00 a.m. and we're alone. Not that we'd tell anyone, but sometimes whole days go by without a single patron. On those days, Nissa and I entertain ourselves—or, rather, she entertains me, and I play willing audience member. Our topics range from books to town gossip, which Nissa somehow gets faster and fresher than anyone, despite being a newcomer.

"That man of yours tell you anything new about the case?" she asks now. "I almost keeled over when I heard the skull was Fred Fortenot's. Of all people. Fred was almost as big in this town as your daddy. Apparently Fortenot Fishing is at a standstill over the news."

"Barry hasn't told me anything." I twist my fingers under the desk. Barry drove me home last night, a thing I couldn't avoid even if all I wanted was to be alone with Everett so we could discuss Fred and the second killer, what our next move should be. The fact that Ever doesn't own a phone and I have to work today seems akin to cosmic torture.

I notice Nissa is hovering instead of sitting. "You going somewhere?"

She roots around in her cardigan pocket. "I heard Barry found a symbol carved in the swamp."

Of course she did. She's a magnet for information.

"A circle with two crescent moons," I confirm. "Heard it too."

To my surprise, she produces a folded-up napkin from her pocket and smooths it. "Like this?"

It's a drawing of the symbol in blue ink. "Yeah," I say quietly. "That's it." There are so many things I need to talk to Everett about.

"Perfect." She spins on her heel and beelines to one of our biggest sections: state and local history.

I swivel in my chair. "What are you doing?"

She stops at a bookshelf and bends over, pulling out two massive tomes. Hefting them, she heads back to the desk.

"A couple weeks ago I was doing my sweep for any un-Christian material. Weeding out anything that might've slipped in through the donation box, like your daddy asked."

I flush. I am the secret cause of this particular precaution.

"And I found these." Nissa slides the books onto the desk: *Coastal Louisiana: An Arcane History of Your Backyard* and *Modern Wicca in the South.*

"You *kept* them?"

It's Nissa's turn to flush. "A little history's not going to hurt nobody."

I suppress a smile. Like me, Nissa is a book eater. Except her passion is nonfiction, histories of things that really happened, while I need fiction to escape.

"The point is, I remembered these books when I heard about the symbol."

I reach for *An Arcane History of Your Backyard*. "Really? There's information about the symbol in here?" If she's right, and I've had it sitting at my fingertips all these years...what a fool I've been.

"There might be." Nissa grips my shoulders, her eyes wide with excitement. "Do you know what this means, Ruth?"

I shake my head.

Her thousand-watt grin lights up her face. "It's time for a good old-fashioned research project."

Her enthusiasm is contagious. "The best part of any investigation—"

"Is the part with the books," she finishes, and drops into the chair beside me. Nissa taps the cover of *An Arcane History*. "I've been fascinated by the history of southern Louisiana all my life." Her words come faster, charged with passion. "At LSU, we were starting to see more research come out on precolonial history from indigenous scholars. What I wouldn't give to still have access to those archives—" She stops herself, biting her lip. "Anyway, one of the things that interested me most was evidence that southern Louisiana used to be a sanctuary for people escaping religious persecution."

"Like the Pilgrims fleeing England?"

"Oh no, honey. I'm talking about people who held beliefs Protestants *and* Catholics considered so profane that even being associated with them was enough to get you killed. Something about this area made it a haven for the outlandish and eerie. The truly heretical."

Bottom Springs: a place that looked like it had been created with the otherworldly in mind.

"The kind of beliefs that might be linked to the symbol in the woods," I guess.

"Mm-hmm." Nissa opens *Modern Wicca*. "Hopefully we'll find something."

We sit reading side by side as the minutes tick by, the only sound

Nissa's hum of contentment. I scan *An Arcane History*. Its pages on Bottom Springs are scant, but it does outline Trufayette Parish's bloody history, how years before France sold Louisiana to the fledgling United States, European colonizers arrived on the coast of southern Louisiana and began a campaign of terror against the Chitimacha people, until they'd killed or driven most of them away. After that, control over the area had passed back and forth between the French and Spanish—even between Catholics and Protestants of the same country—but the fighting was no less deadly, massacres over who controlled Bottom Springs's precious access to the gulf. Though I know this history, it still pains me to remember how deeply our soil is soaked in blood.

What's new is a chapter titled "French Intra-Religious Wars." Like Nissa said, it seems Europeans fleeing religious persecution were drawn to southeast Louisiana, particularly those from France. But, according to the book, the promise of freedom in the New World was a ruse. A group of mystics called Les Voyants, who escaped the guillotine in France, built a strong reputation in New Orleans only to be hunted down and beheaded by traveling Catholic priests. Another group of French exiles called Le Culte de la Lune, who practiced an offshoot of Catholicism that worshipped the Virgin Mary, settled in what's now Forsythe.

I have to read this part twice. "Above all," I whisper aloud, "Le Culte de la Lune worshipped a goddess known as the Queen Mother, believed to be a reimagining of Mary the Virgin, a deity responsible for all creation, symbolized by the moon. Catholic in origin but pagan in practice, Le Culte de la Lune performed rituals to ensure the earth's continued balance. Light and dark, summer and winter, genesis and destruction, they believed all must be held in harmony."

I keep going, scanning the page. "To achieve balance, Le Culte de la Lune's ceremonies could involve bloodletting and animal sacrifice. Adherents often dressed in animal pelts, emphasizing their place in the natural world, and their matriarchs wore antler crowns, meant to invoke the image of the Queen Mother. Catholic settlers in the eighteenth century who reported visions of Satan haunting the woods are now believed to have sighted Le Culte de la Lune." I wince as I read the last line: "While Le Culte de la Lune managed to persist longer in the New World than many other persecuted groups, eventually they too were hunted to extinction."

I close the book and swallow hard.

"I've got something," Nissa says, and splays out *Modern Wicca* on the desk, pointing to a black-and-white photo of a group of men and women standing in a clearing ringed by trees. They're wearing dated clothes and giving the camera apprehensive smiles, as if unsure they want their picture taken. The caption reads: *Trufayette Parish Wiccan circle, photographed 1985.*

"Wiccans *here*?"

"Look at the trees," Nissa urges.

I squint until I realize the trees surrounding the clearing are covered in carvings: so many symbols my eyes swim, like the trees have been transformed into living books. And there, among them, is the circle with twin moons.

I look at Nissa with wide eyes.

"I *knew* I'd seen it," she says triumphantly.

Scanning the paragraphs accompanying the photo, a sentence leaps out at me: "In the late twentieth century, southeastern Louisiana is home to many practicing circles, including Le Culte de la Lune (pictured l.), a richness that reflects the area's history as a religious sanctuary." Excitedly, I shove my book at Nissa. "I just read about them. But this says they were hunted to extinction."

I wait with bated breath while Nissa reads. Finally, she looks up and raises an eyebrow. "I think those tricky heathens survived. And now they call themselves Wiccans."

"Wiccans here in Bottom Springs," I murmur. "As recently as 1985." Pieces of a puzzle I've been working on for years appear in my mind. I need to talk to Everett.

"Your daddy probably wiped them out as his first order of business," Nissa says blithely. "Exodus 22:18: 'We shall not suffer a witch to live.'"

I tense. Nissa is as close to a friend as I have in this town, so sometimes I forget she's a devout Christian, the first in church every Sunday.

"Many terrible things done in the name of God," she adds, still scanning the book, and I relax.

"Anything in here about what the symbol means?" I clutch *Modern Wicca*. "People are guessing it calls forth the Low Man. Do you think they're right?"

Legend says the Low Man was trapped in the swamp by men who practiced spiritual magics now long forgotten. Could that refer to Le Culte de la Lune? Is the Low Man myth rooted in actual history?

Nissa scoffs. "This town. For such God-fearing folk, it shocks me what nonsense captures them. I don't know what the symbol means, other than it clearly comes from Le Culte de la Lune, according to that picture. I'm going to put in a request to my friends at LSU."

Relief floods me. If the carvings and Fred's murder *are* related—there's no evidence they are, but still—the more information I have, the better. "Don't forget our other question," I remind her.

She blinks at me.

I clear my throat, pushing away thoughts of Ever. "If Le Culte de la Lune still exists, who are they, and why are they carving these symbols all of a sudden?"

Nissa is practically buzzing. "I'll do an internet deep dive, but if the answers aren't there, I bet they're in LSU's Louisiana Heritage Archive. They have materials on old languages and symbology."

"I'll comb through old newspapers," I offer. "Bottom Springs used to have its own, the *Bugle,* and we have copies on microfilm. Maybe something about Le Culte de la Lune has cropped up before."

Nissa rubs her hands together so fast she's liable to start a fire. "Look at us—the librarian dream team. The sheriff asked for all hands on deck, and boy, are we giving it to him."

Though I'm halfway to standing, I freeze. "You're planning to show the sheriff what we find?"

She stacks our history books. "Someone's got to help. You know some people are going around whispering Fred was murdered by the Low Man? If we can show this town how useful libraries can be, maybe people will actually start coming in. Plus, don't you want to help solve a crime? We'll be like CSI: Bottom Springs." Nissa chuckles to herself.

"I don't think the sheriff—" I start to say, but the sound of the front door scraping open and Nissa's look of surprise stop me.

"Well, I'll be!" she calls. "If it isn't the man himself. I think we must've conjured you."

Stomach dropping, I turn to see Sheriff Theriot tugging his belt higher on his hips as he makes his way to us.

"Well, ain't that a coincidence, Mrs. Guidry." The sheriff gives her a smile, but his eyes flick to me. With every step he takes toward the circulation desk, I can feel the old demon trying to take over, making my heart pound, air hard to come by.

The library is supposed to be my sanctuary—hallowed ground. It feels wrong for the sheriff to step foot in here.

The skull isn't Renard's, I remind myself. *You aren't guilty.*

Sheriff Theriot tips his hat. "Morning, Ruth. Barry says the Duncan boy's in town. I tell you what, must be nice to have a visitor."

"Yes." I can barely hear the word over the blood pounding in my ears.

The sheriff turns to Nissa with an apologetic smile. "Do you mind if I talk to Ruth alone? Shouldn't take more than a few minutes."

"Of course," Nissa says, almost tripping over herself to pick up our books and scoot away. Before she leaves, she gives me a warning look I easily interpret: *Don't you spill the beans about Le Culte de la Lune and steal my glory.*

Once Nissa is tucked safely in the back office, I'm alone with the sheriff. He leans casually against the circulation desk. "You can go ahead and retake your seat."

Only then do I realize I'm still half-standing. I drop obediently into the chair. "How can I help you, Sheriff?"

"I'm sure you've heard the remains pulled out of Starry Swamp belong to Fred Fortenot?"

"Yes, sir." It's difficult to keep eye contact, but I force myself. The sheriff has a thick mustache the same mud-brown as his shirt, and I allow my eyes to rest there. "Terrible."

"Tragic," he agrees. "You were close to the Fortenots, weren't you? Being neighbors and all."

I shift uncomfortably. His unblinking eyes feel like a spotlight. "I wouldn't say close. But we were neighbors. Have you told Mrs. Fortenot and Beth the news?"

He clears his throat. "We're still working on tracking them down, actually. Any idea where they are?"

I shake my head. Even if I knew, I wouldn't say. I owe those women that much.

He sighs. "Well, that makes your insight even more critical. Let me ask you, Ruth: in all your years living next door to the Fortenots, did you ever see anything unusual?"

"Unusual?" *Like Fred Fortenot choking out his daughter on the kitchen floor?*

"Anyone coming by and making threatening remarks. A stranger lurking, maybe—someone you didn't recognize from church." He squints at me. “Do you recall anything suspicious? Even if it happened a while ago, I’d like to know.”

“Have you talked to my parents?”

His gaze slips away. “I’m asking you.”

There’s something about the way he won’t meet my eyes. Why, out of all the leads he could be chasing, all the people he could be talking to—men who were actually close to Fred—is Sheriff Theriot talking to me?

“I’m sorry, Sheriff.” I speak as calmly as I can. “I can’t recall anything out of the ordinary.”

“Ruth, I need you to think real hard.” He folds his arms over his chest and frowns. “Are you sure you can’t think of anyone who might’ve wanted to hurt Fred? Anyone who bore him ill will? Not a single person? Let me remind you, now is not the time to protect anyone.”

“No, sir,” I say smoothly, and this time it isn’t a lie.

I don’t know a single person. I know so many.

11

JUNE, EIGHTEEN YEARS OLD

It was the brightest, clearest day of summer—so naturally, Everett and I were spending it reading.

"Pass the lemonade?" he asked without taking his eyes off his book. He lay splayed next to me on the dock in red swim trunks and a faded T-shirt, one arm behind his head. He was reading a book of poems by Frank O'Hara, who Ever said was cool, ironic, and playful, attributes that were hard to come by around here. There was nothing Ever liked better than poetry. I brought him volume after volume from the library, but couldn't keep up with his appetite.

The sun was high in the sky, baking us both. Sweat had gathered in small lakes under my knees, and I could see small drops glistening on Ever's forehead. The air was thick with brine from the gulf water. This was our favorite spot to sunbathe: an old, abandoned dock in an inlet that rarely saw visitors, far from Main Street and the bustling docks of the Fortenot Fishing Company.

I was lush and spoiled off a full year of Everett's friendship. We were together through all seasons, but at our best in summer, our most alive when spring growth turned overripe, dizzy and fecund; when the air burst with so much hot, sticky life that you knew it was unsustainable, and fall would have to come and temper it soon. But for now, the days were long, sunlight bleeding into late hours, and when it finally vanished, we had our new world in the dark.

I rolled my eyes at Everett's request even as I set down my book and leaned to pick up the jug of lemonade from my house. The ice-cold condensation spilled down the sides and dripped onto my dress, the coolness a relief against my toasted skin. "Suddenly you're not capable of walking three feet?"

Ever shrugged. "You're closer." He took the jug with both hands and tipped his head back, pouring lemonade straight into his mouth.

For a moment I was arrested by the sight of his Adam's apple moving in his throat, his pale skin somehow unaffected by the sun. The way the curve of his neck swooped into his shoulders, which were broader this year, and his biceps, more pronounced. Then I shook myself and smacked him on the arm. "Animal. You're not supposed to drink straight from the jug."

He set it down and wiped his mouth with the back of his hand. "How else am I supposed to drink it?"

I twisted to the plastic cups I'd stolen from my parents' kitchen and thrust one at him. "With these."

"Oh. Oops." Ever's grin, if anything, grew brighter. "What's this about, anyway?" He grabbed for the book I was reading but I was faster, snatching it away.

He cocked his head. "*Leviathan* by Thomas Hobbes?"

"It's famous. They're reading it in Intro to Political Philosophy at LSU. I looked it up on the computer at the library."

He scratched his head. "You do remember we graduated last year, right? There's no need to assign yourself homework."

I stretched out on my side, facing him. "Actually, I had an idea. Since I can't go to college, I'm bringing college to me. Classes are mostly reading, right? Well, I have a whole library full of books. All I have to do is look up the syllabi and read along. I'm calling it my independent study." I beamed at him.

He gave me a doubtful look.

"It'll work. Watch." I opened *Leviathan*. "Hobbes says humans are selfish brutes by nature. Back in the day, when we didn't want people to keep going around killing each other, we had to agree to certain rules. That's why we have kings. We agree to obey the king's rules, and in return he protects us. It's called a social contract. Any thoughts?"

Ever didn't say anything. He just kept looking at me in that disapproving way. I shielded my eyes against the sun. "What? I need a political science credit for my English degree."

"You should've left when we graduated and never looked back."

I flinched. When he'd said this to me a year ago, it had been a balm. Now it stung. "You know that wasn't an option." I nudged him with my toe. "Besides, look at us. I'm working at the library and can read whatever I want, and you're going to have enough money from the garage to get your own place soon. No more torture at Sacred Surrender." My parents had even stopped trying to punish me for being friends with Everett—satisfied, I guessed, with the bigger win of keeping me home.

I threw my arms out at the clear sky and the blue-green gulf. "I know this isn't what we always hoped for, but it's not bad, right? Couldn't you be happy?"

One day, as soon as he saved enough money, Ever wouldn't need his father or the garage. And despite our vows to never abandon each other, I was afraid the pull of freedom would be too strong to resist. Ever looked at me a beat too long; my stomach dropped. Then he said softly, "I could."

"Good." I swallowed my relief. His eyes shifted over my shoulder and he lunged around me before I had time to react.

"You might be an adult now," he whooped, snatching the copy of *Twilight* I'd brought. "But some things never change."

"Hey!" I shouted, but Ever leapt to his feet. I scrambled to mine, snatching at the book he held just out of reach. "If you drop it in the water, I will *never* forgive you!"

"Philosophy and a vampire romance," Everett laughed. "You're a weird one, Ruth Cornier."

I leapt unsuccessfully for the book again, cursing myself for growing comfortable enough with Everett to tell him about *Twilight*.

"Ruth and her one true love, Edward Cullen. The only man who will ever possess her heart." The look on Everett's face was so wicked I could think of nothing to do except pull my dress over my head and toss it on the dock. Ever froze at the sight of me in my bathing suit—the first two-piece I'd ever owned, purchased secretly with my library money. Yellow, with tiny white daisies.

I held out my hand. Wordlessly, Everett gave me the book. "Thank you," I said primly. "Now take off your shirt."

He blinked. In the year we'd been friends, even when we went swimming, he'd never taken off his shirt. I didn't know why or what had gotten into me to ask him. After a moment of charged silence, Ever grabbed his collar and pulled his shirt over his head.

There was nothing to do but look. His chest was moonlight-pale, which I'd expected, and carved with muscle, which I hadn't. My gaze snagged on the scars: a handful of jagged lines across his stomach and a quarter-sized circle over his heart, the ugly red of old burnt skin.

"What are those from?" I asked, but Everett made a scoffing sound. "You know, you didn't have to get naked just to shut me up." That wicked grin, revealing his sharp canines—a smile he only showed me—split his face.

It was a provocation, a distraction, and it worked.

I pressed both palms to Everett's chest and—relishing his shock—pushed him into the water. Then I set *Twilight* safely on my towel and took a running leap, shrieking as I jumped in after him.

The gulf water sucked me down, warm and salty, until the air in my lungs tugged me back up. I broke the surface, laughing, and whipped around, looking for Ever.

Ever wasn't there.

12

JUNE, EIGHTEEN YEARS OLD

I scanned the dock. No Ever there or on the shore. He should've surfaced by now. A fist squeezed my heart. I tried to see through the waves before they lifted me, but it was—

There. Under the surface, in a patch of darker, cooler water, a flash of pale skin.

I dove without hesitation, swimming until my hands struck his shoulder. Lungs straining, I dragged him to the surface, gasping for air. Everett's head lolled and I choked back a sob. I'd done this to him—taken him by surprise. Normally Everett was a strong swimmer, but he hadn't been ready.

I'd been too happy, and now God was striking at me.

Using all my strength, I kicked us to the shore and hauled him onto the coarse sand, dark as brown sugar. The waves lapped our feet as I bent over him, breathing hard, and pressed two fingers to his throat. No pulse. I listened for his breath. Nothing.

He looked fragile and beautiful. Still as death.

There was no time to panic. I pressed my palms to Everett's chest and pumped, tilted his face back, pressed my lips to his, and gave him my air.

Again—pump, pump, pump. Hands holding his jaw, lips to his, blowing—

Beneath me, Everett's eyes opened. His mouth stretched into a grin. "Hello, Ruth," he said against my lips and brushed a wet strand of hair from my cheek.

I froze over him, uncomprehending.

He started to laugh.

"Everett Duncan, how *dare* you?" I'd given him all my breath, so I couldn't even yell as loudly as he deserved. He was winded, too, wheezing with laughter. "That is the cruelest joke anyone has ever played on me."

I shoved his shoulders and rolled off him, collapsing on my back in the sand, nearly crying at the storm of anger and relief.

"Oh, don't be mad." Lithe as ever, Everett rolled on top of me, bracing his hands on either side of my head. "I'm sorry."

I said nothing. He dipped his head lower, trying to catch my gaze, his black hair dripping salt water. I jerked my face to the side. "You weren't breathing," I said to the waves. "You didn't have a pulse."

His voice gentled. "I'm sorry, Ruth. Okay? It was a joke." He leaned in so his lips were near my ear. "Don't be mad."

I twisted my head even farther away, the sand biting into my cheek. He'd nearly given me a heart attack.

"Don't be mad," he repeated, squeezing my shoulders. I felt the slightest pressure of teeth against my skin, and whipped my head to look.

Everett was biting my bicep. My mouth dropped open.

Wordlessly, his hands grazed down my arms to my elbows. He gripped them, then gently bit my wrist.

I didn't say anything, and his hands slid to my hips. His mouth hovered over my stomach, right below my belly button.

I took a deep breath.

"Don't be mad," he whispered. I could feel the words in the air he exhaled.

His thumbs rubbed my hip bones. Caught and tangled in the bow ties of my bathing suit.

I watched him, transfixed.

Ever looked up at me through his lashes. Slowly, he lowered his mouth and bit me very, very gently, canines pressing into skin.

I lay still. If I moved, even blinked, I felt sure I'd disrupt whatever was happening, this glimpse of the surreal. Ever's mouth was warm on my cold stomach. I could feel the points of his teeth push deeper into my skin. Once, then twice, then the swipe of his tongue.

He lifted his head and rolled off me, falling to his back in the sand. He was breathing fast. We lay there side by side, my eyes wide and unblinking. Finally, he turned to face me. His wet hair fell sideways over his forehead, his eyes darker than the water I'd rescued him from.

"Like your vampire," he said softly.

"You," I whispered, "are the strangest person I've ever met."

He leaned closer. "That's why you should leave Bottom Springs. Go meet some stranger people to put me in perspective."

Above us, a flock of gulls swooped low, wings dipping to ride the wind. "I think the only way I'll make it out of here is if I wake up one day as a bird."

A drop of water slid across his forehead and fell into his lashes. He blinked it away. "A scarlet Ruth-bird."

"If I was a bird, what would you be?"

"Whatever hawk eats birds."

A laugh burst from me. "*What?*"

He grinned. After the water and the sun, his lips were watermelon-red. "To keep the other birds away."

I shook my head.

He bit his lip, which I knew meant he was going to say something silly. "'Having a lemonade with you is even more fun than going to San Sebastian.'"

"You've lost me. Where's San Sebastian?"

"I don't know, actually. It's a line from a Frank O'Hara poem."

"He wrote about lemonade?" I'd pictured Frank O'Hara as a New Yorker in a black beret. "I guess he really is playful."

A small, secret smile curved Everett's mouth. His hand came to rest on top of mine in the sand. Gone were the days he shied from contact. Now I could always count on him to find some way to touch me. "'In the warm Louisiana 4 o'clock light,'" he recited, "'we are drifting back and forth between each other.'"

I rolled my eyes. "Now I know you're making this stuff up. There's no way Frank O'Hara wrote about Louisiana." But still, drifting between each other—that was exactly how it felt with him on the best of days, like today.

The look in Ever's eyes turned weighted. "'I look at you and I would rather'—"

Shuffling footsteps, the sound of someone traveling fast across the sand, made Ever and me startle apart. I scrambled to my feet. He followed suit, only slower. My heart pounded. Who could it be? No one ever came out here.

The man came into sight, squinting. "Ruth? Is that you?" Fred Fortenot stopped in his tracks. A red flush climbed his neck. He was dressed for boating, in long sleeves and deck boots, a black duffel bag slung over a shoulder.

His eyes flicked to Everett and his whole demeanor changed, like a curtain falling. His open mouth snapped shut, eyes narrowing.

"Mr. Fortenot." I tried to push down my nervousness. Whenever I was around Fred, I felt like he'd caught me at something, and now, horror of horrors, he had. For a fleeting moment I wished for one of those hospital pills that made me numb. The ones I lied to my mother about, pretending to swallow every day—and lied to Everett about, pretending I always spit them out. "What are you doing here?"

"What am *I* doing here?" Fred's eyes flicked between me and Ever, and suddenly I realized the picture we made—our disheveled hair, the sand pressed into our skin, my two-piece suit. Fred's face flamed red. "Ruth Cornier, of all the girls." He thrust a finger at me. "Was it you who taught Beth how to be a whore?"

The shock and shame were knee-jerk, immediate and lancing. Tears sprang to my eyes.

"Hey," Everett snarled, and lurched forward. I grabbed his shoulders to hold him back. "Apologize to Ruth and walk away." His voice was nearly shaking. He radiated an intensity beyond any I'd witnessed, even that day in the swamp. Hatred, sure as the day was long.

"Don't act like you have authority over me." Fred's hard eyes glinted. "Look at you. Your father's spitting image. Seducing poor girls who don't know any better. A rotten apple from a rotten tree."

Anger burned bright in Ever's eyes. "Where are you going, Fred?" He jerked his thumb. "The Fortenot Fishing docks are that way." The way he said it was like a veiled threat.

Fred's expression slackened. He and Ever stared at each other for a long, charged moment. Then Fred turned to me. "You should be at home where your daddy can watch you."

"I'm eighteen," I whispered, scared even of this small rebellion.

His eyes roamed my body. The shame was so hot I wanted to carve off my skin wherever he looked—so much exposed in my first bikini. "You may be grown, girl, but you'll always belong to your daddy."

Motorcycles roared from the highway, followed by the gunshot sound of an engine backfiring. Fred tensed, head cutting in the direction of the sound. When he turned back to us, he hitched his duffel higher and thrust a finger at me. "Stay away from him. Mark my words: he's unnatural."

Fred turned his back on us and stalked all the way to the bend in the shore, where he disappeared. His words hung in the air.

"Do you think he's going to a dock on the other side of the inlet?" I forced my voice to come out light. "It's strange, right? I thought his personal dock was next to the Company's."

Everett didn't respond. His eyes were fixed on where Fred had disappeared.

"I hate him," I said.

"Sometimes I think he's right." Ever's voice was hollow. "I am unnatural."

I frowned. Normally Ever was impenetrable, shielded by a suit of armor no one—not the kids at school, or our teachers, or his dad—could crack. His imperviousness to Bottom Springs was a force I depended on. "That's ridiculous. You know you can't take anything Fred says seriously. He's awful."

Ever's eyes cut to me. "Is it still happening? With Beth?"

"Worse." I'd been keeping the secret out of respect to Beth, but I felt compelled to share with Ever now, shake him out of this strange mood. "She's pregnant."

"What?" For once, I'd managed to shock him. "How old is she now?"

"Seventeen. She won't tell anyone who the father is. No matter what Fred or my dad threaten. I heard my parents talking. They think she's protecting some boy she's in love with from school."

"What's going to happen to her?"

I was almost afraid to say it. "They're making her get an abortion."

Everett's eyes grew hard. "I thought that was an unforgivable sin."

"Fred told my parents if she has the baby, the whole town will shun them. It would hurt the Company and the church."

"He *should* be shunned."

"My father said Fred's too important. It would be better if no one knew." It had been a shock to hear.

To my surprise, Everett tipped back his head and laughed. It was almost a cackle, thin and edged with something sharp.

"You're freaking me out."

"The *hypocrisy*." He shook his head, smile lingering. "I guess when you're in charge, you don't have to play by the rules."

"They're God's rules."

"Sure, Ruth." His expression grew pensive. "Do you think one of Fred's friends got Beth pregnant? Or Fred himself? And that's why she won't tell?"

My mouth dropped open. "That's disgusting. Seriously, where is your mind right now?"

Ever looked at me for long enough that I began to feel uncomfortable. Just as I was about to do something—shake his shoulders, walk away and leave him in the sand—he spoke. His voice was strangely gentle. "You'd be surprised how sadistic people are when they know they can get away with it."

"Whoever the father is," he continued, "he might be furious Fred's forcing Beth to get rid of the baby."

"Maybe it's one of the Fortenot fishermen." That was so scandalous it made me wince to say it, but Ever had all but called me naive.

He nodded, taking the idea seriously. "The way Fred's been under-paying them and cutting their hours? Gerald Theriot and his guys are already raising hell. Wouldn't surprise me if one of them seduced Beth just to spite him."

"Where do you hear this stuff?"

Ever shrugged. "The garage. Or the bar when I pick up my dad. Trust me, you'll learn everything you never wanted to know once those guys put down a few whiskeys."

My mind raced. "I didn't realize so many people hated Fred."

"Why don't they just run away?" Ever asked abruptly.

"What—who?"

"Mrs. Fortenot and Beth. Why don't they run away, or kill him in his sleep and be done with it?"

I stood rooted in the sand. "Please tell me that's gallows humor. Because they'd go to *Hell*, Ever. Because it's evil."

He gave me a pointed look. "Not always."

"Yes, always." That was the law of God, written in stone and carried down from the mountain. And the law of man, the Almighty, and the courts weaving together to form an ironclad prohibition, a cage to stay our brutish hands. Ever and I had broken it, and one day, whether by man or God, we would be punished. "I don't understand where all of this is coming from. Why's Fred making you spin out?"

There was a moment of fraught silence, then Ever put his hands over his face and sank into the sand. "Ruth. I need to tell you something. There's this feeling I get…these thoughts, eating at me. I can't tell if they're right or wrong, crazy or natural. But I can't get rid of them."

It was surreal to see Everett like this: vulnerable, armor falling off. I did the only thing I could think of, which was help him put it back on.

"Hey." I crouched. "There's a voice in my head, too."

He didn't move his hands. "There is?"

"Do you know what communion is?"

"Sort of."

"You kneel in front of the pastor and drink grape juice and eat a wafer. It's supposed to represent the blood and body of Christ."

"How vampiric."

"Yeah, well, when I was young, it was my least favorite part of church. You had to kneel in front of my father while the whole church watched and repeat his words back so everyone could hear. When it was my turn, I was always so nervous all I could do was whisper. No matter how frustrated my dad got, I couldn't raise my voice."

His demands, escalating in volume until they were thunder. *This is my body: take it. This is my blood: drink it.*

"Sometimes when I have a hard decision to make, I hear myself whispering the rites: 'You will be saved. You must be good. Be good and be spared the lake of fire.' I don't know what it means that I'm still whispering it even in my own head, but it calms me."

I squinted against the sunlight. Ever's long, elegant fingers still hadn't dropped from his face. "You think I'm crazy."

"No." He cleared his throat. "It's just...the voice in my head, Ruth..." He took a deep breath. "It doesn't whisper to be good."

I let his words wash over me. Like the small waves here at the shore, I sensed they were only a glimpse of what lay out past where I could see, in the dark, unfathomable abyss.

So I made a decision.

I peeled Everett's hands off his face. He watched me warily. "Everett Duncan. You will never say a thing like that again. Not to me or anyone. Do you hear me?" I pressed my fingers to his bare chest, over his scar, his heart, and pretended to turn a key. "Never."

13

NOW

When I leave the library for lunch and spot Sheriff Theriot through the window at the Rosethorn Café, laughing with his nephew, Gerald, and Gerald's fishing crew, I finally realize what I have to do. Standing there rooted to the sidewalk, my brown bag lunch clenched in my hand, watching the sheriff slap Gerald on the shoulder over some joke, the understanding crystallizes: I need to know who killed Fred, for my protection and for Everett's, and I cannot trust the sheriff to find out. Not good ol' boy Tom Theriot, chumming it up over there with his nephew, the same man who got his promotion to captain only *after* Fred's death; or Gerald's crew, who Everett once said had been planning a mutiny while Fred was still alive.

All that motive sitting there at the table, and the sheriff's questioning me. I'd suspected it before, but now I know: I can't trust the sheriff, or Gerald, or frankly anyone in this town. I understand them too well. Absent the true culprit, I know where their eyes will turn, looking for a scapegoat. Same place they've always turned. And that's a problem.

Once again, I must cultivate a small rebellion, provide a corrective measure. But this time it's not illicit books, or an independent study, or a dark mission at the stroke of midnight. This time I must find a murderer.

And I know exactly where to start. A place the sheriff and his deputies would never think to look.

—

Of all the people in this town, perhaps none are more invisible than the Fortenot Fishing wives, women known not even by their names but by their husbands. They live in a neighborhood far from the grand lanes of my parents'. Their modest houses are pressed close together—easier, I suppose, when you need to bring your children over to a neighbor's to be watched, or borrow a cup of sugar, or commiserate over the absence of your husbands, away to the sea once more.

Since I've been as guilty as anyone of overlooking them, I'm surprised when I drive through their neighborhood after work and find it bustling, tree houses and rope swings full of children, shaded porches lined with women in rocking chairs calling to each other as they watch their lawns. And now, sitting at Julie Broussard's kitchen table with a steaming cup of coffee and a thick slice of hummingbird cake, I'm even more surprised by the many sets of curious eyes looking back at me. Between the time I pulled up outside Julie's house and when she settled me here in her kitchen, fussing over whether I took sugar and cream, three other women materialized, presumably pulled off nearby porches by the novelty of my visit.

It may be the most attention my presence has ever warranted.

I wonder for a brief moment if Everett, who always knew things I didn't, could've told me secrets about the Fortenot Fishing wives that would've helped me unlock them. I chose not to beeline to his house after work like originally planned because I was certain he wouldn't approve of me sticking my nose in this investigation. I can almost hear him: *Ruth, what are you* thinking? He doesn't seem to understand that our necks aren't off the chopping block yet. So, absent his intel, my fellow women from the margins and I are forced to sit crammed around this table, blinking at one another, not knowing where to start.

Julie finishes pouring the last cup of coffee and settles at the head of the table. She and her husband, Noah Broussard, have attended Holy Fire for long enough that my father recently rewarded Noah with an usher position, which is how I know of them.

"Miss Ruth," she says uncertainly. "Pardon my asking, because of course it's an honor to have a visit from the reverend's daughter, but what can I do for you?" Julie's my age, maybe a year older, so I bristle at the deference in her voice, the way her cheeks flush pink as she talks. There are toys belonging to a young child strewn all over the house, and her gaze keeps flicking to them. The other fishing wives stare at me raptly, waiting.

"Thank you for having me, Mrs. Broussard." I finger the warm edge of my mug. The intensity of their looking throws me until I decide that for this visit, I'll pretend I'm Jane Austen's young heiress Emma Woodhouse, a woman at ease wherever she goes. I take a deep breath. "I'm sure y'all have heard about Fred Fortenot."

Four sets of eyes around the table grow wider.

"Course we have," says one of the wives, who looks to be roughly six months pregnant. Her hair is braided neatly, but she has dark circles under her eyes. "It's all anyone's talking about." She blushes. "Sorry, I'm Laney. Seen you at church, of course. I—we always sit in the back on account of the kids."

"Right," I say, folding my hands together. "I came to ask about Fred. Some unresolved questions I was hoping you could help with."

My words cause an immediate charge of interest, legible in the way the women's backs straighten.

"No one ever asks us nothing," another woman says. She's so fair she's almost pale as Everett.

The other women nod eagerly, and I stifle a sigh of relief. I'd prepared myself for resistance, a closing of the ranks, since I'm a Fortenot Fishing Company outsider. But it seems the rareness of being consulted is enough to lure these women in.

"Well, that's a shame," I say. "I'm sure you have plenty to offer."

Their faces open like books. I can read their curiosity, their hunger to talk.

"It's kind of a delicate subject." I drop my eyes to the hummingbird cake, all those creamy layers studded with nuts, and think back to Everett's speculation from years ago that whoever got Beth Fortenot pregnant might've been in love with her and furious at Fred for making her give up their baby. Or, in a less romantic theory, maybe Fred finally discovered the father's identity and held the knowledge over his head like a cudgel. Either way, those are two compelling possible motives. Tenuous, yes, but like this cake before me, the possible reasons for Fred's killing are many-layered, and I don't trust the sheriff to attend to all of them.

"I know the men who work at the Company spend a lot of time together off the boats, and y'all have a close community. You probably know a lot about what the Company men get up to in their off time."

So far, they haven't contradicted me, so I swallow. "Do any of you remember if Fred's daughter Beth was involved with a Company man?"

Laney, the pregnant one, gasps. "Beth and one of the fishing boys?"

I scour their faces. Each woman looks scandalized. "I take it you never saw her around?"

Julie shakes her head. "If she had shown up, even at one of the barbecues Coby and her husband like to throw, which are usually pretty open—" She pauses to nod at the brown-skinned woman sitting nearest me around the table, whose face is sharp-boned and delicate. "She would've been shooed away. You don't mess with the boss's kid."

"I never even talked to Beth," Coby says in a surprisingly husky voice. "I only knew her from church."

"So you never..." I take a breath. This is probably immoral, what I'm doing, but I badly need to know the truth. "Heard about Beth getting pregnant?"

The women reel back. Pregnant Laney's mouth actually drops open.

"Never," Julie says, forceful like she's swearing on a Bible. "I wouldn't even believe you, except you're the reverend's daughter."

Coby shifts in her seat, making the wooden back of her chair squeak. "Is that why Beth and Mrs. Fortenot took off right after Fred went missing? We always wondered why they didn't come to his memorial. It was like he went missing, then they did. We thought it seemed so disrespectful. But maybe they were ashamed."

"No, it happened years before Fred went missing." I'd been eighteen when I heard Beth was pregnant, and twenty when Fred disappeared. Two years for the mysterious father to stew in hatred, maybe. But something Coby said stood out. *It was like he went missing, then they did.*

It was also two years for Beth to stew. I used to think I knew why she and her mother had fled as soon as they were free of Fred. But maybe there was more to it...

"It wouldn't have been one of the Company boys who got her pregnant," says the pale woman. Her tone is absolute. "Messing with the boss's daughter would've meant an automatic firing. No one would risk their job like that. Hard to find good work these days."

I tap the end of my fork uneasily. "Did any of you...know anything about the Fortenot family? Like, behind closed doors, how they were?"

The women shake their heads.

"Fred was the big boss," Julie explains. "And he acted like it. Kept his family life private. Didn't invite us over to his house or treat us like peers or nothing. Beth and his wife didn't even acknowledge us at church."

"Like we were beneath them," the pale woman says.

"Betty Lee's son Gentry is around Beth's age." Laney glances at the other women. "He said Beth didn't even talk to any of the Company kids at school."

That matched what I remembered. Beth always had her sights set higher.

So these women never saw Beth hanging around any of the fishermen, and they didn't even know anything was amiss with the Fortenot family. I hold in a sigh. This has been a dead end.

Julie must sense my disappointment, because she says, "Sorry we aren't much help."

"It's okay." I rise from the table. "I should get going, though. I'm expected at my parents' for Bible study."

Julie leaps out of her chair. "Let me cut some cake to take with you."

"Oh, please don't go to any trouble. My mother will have—"

"I insist." Julie is already cutting. "It would be an honor to feed the reverend."

I look down at Laney, Coby, and the pale woman, who are still watching me with interest. On a bold whim, I ask: "Have things gotten better at Fortenot Fishing since Fred's death?"

The question takes them aback. "Better?" Laney frowns.

"I remember a few years back, hearing complaints about extra shifts and not enough pay to make up for it."

Laney still looks confused, but Coby nods. "I know what you're talking about. That was mostly Gerald Theriot and his crew complaining." She cuts a look at the other women. "Remember how they were going on and on about having to do all this side work and not getting paid for it?"

"Oh, right," Laney says. "How could I forget? Gerald made a big stink."

"I think it resolved itself when Fred disappeared," the pale woman adds.

Julie slides a Tupperware full of cake onto the kitchen table, wiping her hands on her skirt. "Gerald basically runs things now, so I guess that means no more side work."

"Side work?"

Julie shrugs. "None of our husbands are in Gerald's crew. Whatever overtime Fred was making them do, our husbands weren't involved."

Laney snorts. "You know what I heard from Betty Lee?" She looks at me. "Betty Lee's husband, Jimmy, is in Gerald's crew. She said sometimes Jimmy didn't even fish. He'd go out on the boat for hours and wouldn't bring anything back."

"What?"

"Yeah, that's right." Laney twists the end of her long braid. "One time Jimmy mentioned going all the way to Mississippi to drop something off."

"Oh, not this again." Coby sighs. "I thought you were done with that foolishness."

"Done with what?" I ask. There's a thick gossipy charge to the air, sweet and dense like molasses.

"I know it's un-Christian to speak ill of the dead," Laney starts, and the pale woman rolls her eyes.

"Oh Lord, here we go."

Laney's undeterred. "But we were *convinced* Fred was running a side business selling illegal fish on the black market."

"We?" Julie scoffs. "Try 'I.'"

"There's lots of critters in the gulf you're not allowed to touch 'cause they're endangered and the like, but people will pay a high price for 'em."

Coby snorts.

"What?" Laney protests. "Why else would Jimmy be told not to look at the boxes?"

"Boxes?" I glance between them. "Is that a normal thing for fishing boats to carry?"

Coby shrugs. "Not when they're fishing, no. But don't listen to Laney. She's got too much time on her hands and watches too many of those Law & Order shows." She snickers. "An illegal fishing ring."

"Y'all are simpleminded," Laney sniffs. "There's a secret dock and everything."

"There is? Where?"

I know immediately I've crossed a line—sounded too sharp, too interested. The women's good-humored smiles disappear.

"I don't know," Laney says, cutting a glance at Julie. "It was just a rumor. Probably nonsense like everyone's sayin.'"

I think of the day Fred stumbled on Everett and me at our secret spot in the inlet, dressed for boating. How cruel and biting he'd been. Like a man with something to hide.

Excitement sizzles in my gut. "Well, I really do have to get going." I tuck in my chair and take off in the direction of the door.

"Miss Ruth," Julie calls, and I freeze, feeling caught.

But she only holds up the Tupperware. "Don't forget this."

"Of course," I say, and double back for it. "My parents will be touched."

"Tell your daddy we loved his sermon on Sunday," the pale woman adds shyly. "Especially that passage from Psalms. The meek shall inherit the earth. Felt that in my heart."

I give her a tight smile. The meek shall inherit something. If I have my way, it will be all of Fred Fortenot's secrets.

I haven't been back to our dock in over a year, not since the summer Everett didn't show. The place is unchanged, like a slice of time preserved in amber. It's twilight when I make it over from Julie Broussard's house, the hummingbird cake tossed on my passenger seat. Twilight's the most beautiful time to be anywhere in Bottom Springs, but especially near the sea. Out past the tall grass and sand and old docks slowly crumbling into the water, the orange sun sinks into the horizon, lighting the waves like God revealing the path to Heaven. I give our old dock a wistful glance as I walk past it, tracing Fred's path from that long-ago day.

It's not until long after I've followed the bend in the shoreline that I see it, nearly hidden by a shroud of tall pampas grass: a boat tied to a dock, and two men I don't recognize carrying cardboard boxes.

Heart skipping, I drop gracelessly to the sand, praying the long stems will be enough to obscure me. The men's work is monotonous. They emerge out of the grass—coming from the distant parking lot, I assume—holding a stack of two boxes each, which means they must be fairly light. They trek down the wide sandy shore and onto the dock, which is in better shape than Everett's and mine, more recently repaired. Finally, they disappear onto the boat. As I watch, twilight turns to night, and suddenly I can barely see my hands in front of me, let alone the men. Luckily, they quickly flick on flashlights, like they're used to this.

I don't know what I was expecting, but I'm deflated by how innocuous this looks, how little I can glean from their methodical motions. Maybe the trick is to get closer...

I wait until both men retreat into the grass and take off, kicking up sand as I streak across the shore. The wooden planks of the dock give under my feet with creaking sounds that make me wince. I have a minute, tops, before the men will return with new stacks of boxes.

As I edge along the boat, the clouds shift. Moonlight illuminates the white paint, making it glow against the pitch-black waves slapping the hull. And there, faintly, are traces of an old logo someone has taken pains to sand off. If I didn't know the image so well, my mind might not have made sense of the faint Fs wrapped around three sharp spears of a trident.

But I do know it: the sign of the Fortenot Fishing Company. Which means Laney was right. The Company is doing something outside official channels, literally in the dark. What was Fred up to? And did it get him killed?

I need to know what's inside those boxes.

Silently cursing myself for the spectacularly bad idea, I place two hands on the railing of the boat and use all my strength to heft myself up and over the side, tumbling onto the dark floor with a grunt I immediately regret.

I need to make my search lightning fast. I stagger to my feet and feel my way around with one hand flat against the wall. I can't see anything and halfway hope I'll walk into a wall of boxes, but there's nothing.

They must be hiding them inside the boat. Of course—if they don't want people to see, that would be smartest.

The boat lifts and falls, buoyed by waves, and I try to keep my balance as I search for an entrance to the inside: a door, hallway, hatch.

My hand collides with a metal handle and I clutch my fingers, silently screaming at the pain. The door has announced itself.

As I reach for it, two glimmers of light catch my attention. I turn. On the shore, twin orbs bob in the dark.

Flashlights.

The dock groans under the men's feet. I was too focused and didn't notice them emerge out of the grass. Now they're practically at the boat, at my back.

How will I escape?

"You hear something?" asks a rough voice with a thick northern accent. I almost jump at how close it is, then inch back slowly, shoulders sliding against the boat, heart thundering so violently I worry they'll hear it.

"Just the waves," says a second voice, colder. "Sea's getting a little rough." He sniggers. "Can't take a country boy out on the water, I see."

"It was a footstep," the first insists, and I hear the horrifying sound of his feet landing on the floor of the boat. *Thump.*

My back hits a cold metal railing. I press one hand to my mouth and the other to my chest, as if to hold my heart still.

"Paranoid," says the cold man. Another thump sounds as he lands in the boat.

"Fuck you. I'm looking."

The clouds have passed back over the moon, snuffing out the light. Behind me, it's so dark I can't see where the sky meets the water—can only hear the waves, a half second of pregnant silence as they lift, then the clap as they crash against boat.

Shoes scuff around the corner as the man who can sense me begins inspecting. There's no more time for paralyzing panic. I can't let them find me. There's only one way out.

I take a big gulp of air, hitch a leg over the railing, and let go.

I fall for longer than expected through the pitch-black air, and in my disorientation I think somehow I'm soaring up instead of hurtling down. It makes the gut punch of the waves an even greater shock, and I'm so surprised by the sudden salty cold that I nearly gasp, releasing the air in my lungs. The inky sky is replaced by the inky water and now I truly cannot tell which way is up or down, if I'm sinking to the ocean floor or floating to the moon, on my way to Heaven or Hell, if there is even any difference between them after all.

14

NOW

In the past few days, I've been a woman who has lied to authorities, who has hardened her resolve into a diamond in her chest, who has thrown herself into the sea, who has crawled, gasping, across the wet sand of the inlet's farthest shore, and now, one day later, I'm a woman getting served breadsticks and Barefoot wine in Bottom Springs's best attempt at an Italian restaurant. Which is also the only restaurant in town.

"She'll have a glass of the bubbles," Barry tells the waitress, an older woman named Jo who used to babysit me.

"It's okay," I murmur, catching Jo's eye. "I don't really drink."

"Actually, why don't you leave the whole bottle?" Barry beams at Jo, exuding that easy confidence that's always fascinated me. "It's going to be a night to celebrate."

Unsurprisingly, Jo sides with Barry. She leaves the bottle on my side of the table. It sweats like a person facing the barrel of a gun.

So far Barry has spent tonight trying valiantly to win my attention, picking me up outside my house in his immaculate Ford F-150, opening doors and sliding out chairs, even taking the single red rose out of the vase on the table and sticking it behind my ear, like a regular Casanova.

He looked so pleased with himself I didn't even make a face when the thorn caught my skin.

Unfortunately for Barry, mentally I'm in two places, and neither are here: the first is the pitch-black water of the gulf, which haunts me, and the second is Ever's house, where I desperately need to be.

But Everett has disappeared. Last night I drove to his house soaking wet, all the way from the inlet, in a frenzy to tell him about the boxes and the fishing boat, willing to take whatever rebuke he'd give me for investigating. But Ever wasn't there—not him or his car. Imagining he'd left me yet again, I'd slid down the side of his house, feeling the beginnings of panic. Then I saw the note taped to his front door, barely visible in the dark.

It said simply, *R—I'll be back.*

I'd leaned my head against his house and laughed until there were tears in my eyes. A note on the door. Not a carrier pigeon, but close.

I still don't know where Everett's gone, or when he'll be back. What I do know is that if Barry hadn't nearly melted down when I suggested we reschedule dinner, I'd be at Ever's house now, waiting.

"Don't you love Rosethorn's breadsticks?" Barry talks as he chews. "Best in Louisiana, guaranteed. Don't even need to leave town."

"They're good," I agree, mentally making a list of things that could be in those cardboard boxes.

Barry brushes his thick brown hair over his forehead. He's worn his hair long and swooped to the side since high school. I can still picture him on the football field taking off his helmet, his hair damp with sweat but otherwise perfectly intact, as he grinned at all the cheering people in the stands.

"Let's toast," he says, holding his champagne flute.

The expectation in his eyes finally captures my attention. I realize Barry's tapping his foot at high speed under the table.

"Okay." I lift my glass. "What to?"

"To us," he says quickly. "To you being my girl."

I resist the urge to raise my eyebrows at his uncharacteristic sentimentality and simply sip my drink. It's syrupy-sweet. The bubbles burn my throat.

Though I haven't thought of *Twilight* in some time, the scene returns to me: Bella and Edward in that restaurant in Port Angeles, Bella circling closer to the truth about him, Edward's plate strangely empty. The secret burning under the surface of their conversation: that she is what he really wants to eat.

"What's the latest on the murder investigation?" I ask, realizing too late I've interrupted Barry midsentence.

He blinks for a second, taken aback. "We've been crawling the swamp for more evidence."

"More pieces of the body?"

Barry cocks his head and studies me. "You know what? I don't really want to talk about what we found. It's dark stuff. That's not what tonight is about."

They found something new. My heartbeat picks up. "Has the sheriff mentioned who he's looking—"

"Shoot." Barry grips the table, shaking his head. "I was gonna wait for dessert to do it, but I'm too nervous." He laughs to himself. "Me, nervous!"

I slowly put down my glass. "Do what?"

It happens so quickly—too quickly to stop. Barry slides out of his seat, pulls a small box from his pants pocket, and drops to a knee.

He opens the box and there it is: a small diamond glinting on a gold band.

Around us, the entire restaurant goes quiet. I feel the weight of a dozen sets of eyes.

I can barely breathe.

"Ruth," Barry says, and although he swore he was nervous, he sounds confident and calm. "I love how big-hearted you are. How devout. How good you've always been, ever since we was kids. You never made any trouble like the rest of us growing up, weren't a loose girl like some others, tryna' trap… Anyway, point is, I shoulda asked you out sooner. I love you and I love your momma and daddy, and we make so much sense together. So…" He's blown these words at me full speed, but now he pauses. "Will you marry me?"

I can feel what I must look like: how wide my eyes, how red my cheeks, how arched my brows. Under all this scrutiny, my hands start to shake. It's not the proposal I dreamed of, not the way I would've chosen to hear these words, and there's this feeling inside me, like I'm in a car speeding off a cliff.

"We've been dating less than a year." My voice comes out a squeak.

He laughs. "Your daddy married your momma after courtin' three months."

"I—"

"If you're worried about your daddy's opinion, don't be, 'cause I got his blessing. He and your momma are real happy about this, Ruth. They're waiting for us back at your house. Soon as we're done with dinner, we're gonna have a little engagement party."

The Rosethorn Café has turned into a fishbowl. No one is moving. They're all waiting. I want to melt into the floor.

"I don't know what to say." I clear my throat. "I didn't see this coming."

Barry shifts on his knee. For the first time, it seems to occur to him that I haven't burst into tears and seized the ring. He glances around the restaurant. "What do you mean? Course it was coming. You're my girl. All you have to do is say yes."

"Can I… Is it all right if I have some time to think about it?"

His expectant smile drops. "Think about it?"

"It's just…I'm not good with surprises."

A red flush creeps over his face. "Are you saying no?"

"No—this has nothing to do with you, I promise. I'm just saying… let me think."

This time Barry takes a longer look at our fellow diners. I can see the embarrassment in his eyes. He picks himself up off the floor and sinks back into his chair. I'm immediately ashamed of myself.

The restaurant explodes with whispers, and Barry's face goes from flushed to tomato. "Is this about Everett?" he hisses.

"What?" His voice has gone from persuasive to angry so fast it takes me a second to catch up.

"Is this because Everett's back? Is there something between you?"

"Of course not. Ever's my best friend. This has nothing to do with him."

"You've been a different person since he got here. Like you're off in la-la land. I swung by your house last night and you weren't even there. Off with him, right?"

"No, I…" But what do I say? That I went to see the Fortenot Fishing wives for reasons I can't reveal, then spied at the inlet?

My inability to provide an alibi makes a look of grim satisfaction creep over Barry's face. "I knew it. Ruth, there's a conversation we need to have that's long overdue. I didn't think it would be a problem, 'cause Everett seemed like he'd hightailed it for good, but he's back now, so I'm going to shoot straight. Your so-called friend's a freak show. You know that, right?"

My cheeks flame. "That's not true. And it's cruel of you to say."

"Cruel of *me*? Do you even know what Everett's daddy got into? How sheltered were you?"

I want to tell Barry he liked that I was sheltered when it made me a good girl, fit to be his wife. But instead I say, "I know he was an alcoholic. But that was Ever's problem more than anyone's. Don't pin that on him."

"His daddy was a Satanist, Ruth."

"Who told you that?"

"*Your* daddy."

"My father has called more people Satanists than I can count. Do you want to know who's a Satanist, according to him? The president of the United States. The man in charge of the ACLU. Librarians who read spooky books to children."

"Your daddy swore on the Bible that Killian Duncan was an honest-to-God Devil worshipper. Seen it with his own eyes. And Everett's just like him. All those things people used to say about him? That he was feral, and violent, and hurt animals? It's all true."

"He *hunted* animals. Plenty of people around here hunt." He needed to eat, I want to add, but don't.

"You just don't want to see it." Barry reaches across the table and places his hand over mine. "On account of your soft heart. But the truth is, he's always been a bad seed and you walk around with these shutters over your eyes when it comes to him. You know he used to get in fights every weekend? Nearly killed someone 'fore he even graduated."

"He had his reasons. I know everything about Ever."

Barry's eyes narrow. His hand slides off mine.

"Because he's my friend," I clarify.

"Everyone thinks you're crazy bein' friends with him."

"I don't care."

"For a woman who needs time to say yes to me, you're plenty quick to defend him."

It throws me because it's true. Once again, the desire to see Everett, to tell him everything that's happened and hear what he thinks, hits me hard.

Barry picks up his glass and chugs the bubbles in one go. When he's done, he wipes his mouth and leans over the table. "Your daddy's grooming me, Ruth. Now that Holy Fire's grown so big and there are so many people comin' to Bottom Springs 'cause of it, he's practically running this town. And he wants me to be next. I'm already part of the family, according to him. So say yes, and let's make it official."

I glance around. Jo, our waitress, hovers by the kitchen, too shy to come over. The rest of the diners still eye us, but their expressions are no longer anticipatory. Now they're hungry. Watching what passes between Barry and me so they can report it all over town. We haven't even ordered yet. This dinner has gone off the rails on the breadstick course.

I rise from my chair. "I'm really sorry, Barry. I promise I'm excited about the ring. I don't mean to fight. I just need some time, and some air."

"We're going to your parents', Ruth. They're expecting us."

"I'm not feeling well."

"You know your daddy suspects Everett used to steal money from the *church*?"

I freeze.

Barry wears the satisfied expression of a man who knows he's got me on the hook. He waits until I've dropped back into my seat before he spreads his hands over the table. "The money was in a safe and everything, but somehow Everett got in. The only way a person could've done that is through black magic."

"Why does my father think it was him?"

Barry gives me an incredulous look. "Who else? Your daddy says Everett was only friends with you for information. He knew the church collected tithes and wanted it for booze or worse. Like father, like son."

I'm silent against the crush of surprise. I've never heard my father accuse Ever of this, and it's a weapon he would've used against me, surely.

"The reverend was thinking of pressing charges a few years back." Barry leans over the table, his face hovering over the empty vase. I remember I'm wearing the rose that belongs there, like some sort of woman in a love poem. I pluck the flower from my hair and drop it on my plate. Barry's eyes linger on the thorn. "That's who you're so devoted to, Ruth." He slams his hand on the table, and I jump. "A *Satanist*."

"No—"

Bam. His hand smacks the wood. "A *criminal*."

I open my mouth to protest, then stop.

Because that accusation is true. In more ways than one.

15

JULY, EIGHTEEN YEARS OLD

Everett folded his arms over his chest and shot me a dubious look. "I think you're really setting yourselves up for disappointment here."

From behind the folding table, I wrapped an arm around Samuel Landry's shoulders and squeezed. "Ye of little faith. The football team makes so much money from these things." I glanced at the empty pavement behind us. We were camped right next to Dale's Country Corner, the only gas station on Main Street. This little concrete lot was where countless school teams had held their car-wash fundraisers, car washes being a town tradition. On past car-wash Saturdays, you could barely drive down Main Street, it got so packed with cars waiting in line. "I heard the football team made *two thousand dollars* last time."

"Even half that would be a godsend," Sam said modestly. He was small for seventeen, with a mop of blond hair and curious eyes that telegraphed intelligence. "I really can't thank you two enough for helping me."

"Are you kidding?" I said, at the same time Ever shrugged and muttered, "It was Ruth's idea."

"You're going to Durham if I have to wash a million cars to get you there," I said, and Sam beamed.

He leaned over the folding table to get a good look at Main Street. I was proud of the table: I'd hung a poster that read, "Send Sam Landry to College! Car Wash: $10. Cause: Priceless," and had even roped Everett into helping me decorate it. "You think they'll start coming soon?" Sam asked.

I followed his gaze. It was a bright, beautiful Saturday, mild for July, and there was ample traffic, people traipsing in and out of the Piggly Wiggy and the bait shop and hairdresser. We'd gotten a few curious glances but no takers. "Any minute now. Adult Bible study just ended, so we're about to see a rush of people."

Samuel Landry had done what no one else in Bottom Springs had ever managed: gotten accepted to Duke University, a school so good it called itself the Harvard of the South. Despite how cruelly kids had always teased him for the tics he couldn't help, calling him stupid and worse, Sam was the best student in the grade below us.

He and I had always been friendly, if not friends, likely on account of our mutual wariness around other people. So when I heard the news that he'd been accepted to Duke and I immediately burst into tears, I didn't know what was wrong with me. It took a full week of misery and several pointed comments from Ever to realize I was heart-sickeningly jealous. Not only did Sam hold my dream of college in his hands, but he'd dared to think bigger than even I'd allowed myself. Bottom Springs had hemmed in my possibilities, but not his.

Of course, I'd felt terribly guilty about my reaction. So when I found out Sam wouldn't be going to Duke after all because his financial aid left him a few thousand short of tuition—Sam's momma was a cashier at the Piggly Wiggly and she'd raised him on a single income—I'd decided the only way to repent was to make sure Sam got to go.

Everett kicked a pebble and it skittered away. "When this all goes to hell, don't say I didn't warn you."

I narrowed my eyes at him. "You didn't even wear your bathing suit like I said. Your jeans are going to get soaked."

Sam laughed—at the idea of a soaked Everett or Everett in a bathing suit, I didn't know. It was obvious Sam was still intimidated by Everett, because he kept shooting nervous glances Everett's way. Sure enough, his laughter cut off abruptly when Ever turned his cool gaze on him.

"Maybe that was the point," Ever drawled. "Get 'em wet so I don't have to wash 'em later."

"Gross."

Ever raised an eyebrow. "We can't all be supermodels in our Vacation Bible School T-shirts."

I looked down at my oversized VBS shirt, with its crucifix wreathed in flowers, and flushed. I'd thought this shirt was the prettiest I owned. "It's a cover-up for my bathing suit. At least I remembered mine." I was wearing my old one-piece under my shirt. After the encounter with Fred, I'd hidden my yellow bikini in the farthest reaches of my dresser. "I'm dressed sensibly."

"Oh!" Ever clutched his heart. "'Is *this* the face that launched a thousand ships?' 'She walks in beauty, like the night.'" He pretended to stagger back. "'Your two great eyes will slay me suddenly; their beauty shakes me, who was once serene.'"

"Great." I rolled my eyes. "Just what we need. Everett's feeling goofy. And that's Marlowe, Byron, and Chaucer, for your information."

Sam looked at me in amazement. "Is he...reciting poetry?"

"Don't encourage him," I warned, opening the empty cashbox. "It's a game we play when we're bored. Ever's never met a poem he didn't like—or, unfortunately, memorize to use as a weapon of annoyance later. For some reason, he won't stop repeating the Chaucer even though *I guess it every time*." The last was directed at Everett.

Sam's astonishment only seemed to grow.

"'Brightness.'" Ever found my eyes. A small smile curved his lips, the kind he wore when he was pushing it. "'Pouring itself out of you, as if you were burning inside.'"

I cleared my throat. "Neruda." Ever knew I liked Neruda. His eyes didn't leave my face. Like twin black holes reordering space and time to pull me in.

"I've got one," Sam said. "'How do I love thee? Let me count the ways.'"

Ever's eyes cut away, and I took a deep breath, as if resurfacing. "Ladies and gentlemen," he whooped. "We have a contender!"

Sam laughed. "Wait, I've got another—"

Down the street, the door to the Rosethorn Café swung open and people began filing out. The post–Bible study crowd. "Hey!" I elbowed Sam. "Big smiles, okay?"

Sam sat straighter in his folding chair and smiled obediently.

I turned to Ever and he rolled his eyes but bared his teeth.

"On second thought," I said. "Maybe just stand a ways behind us."

As the crowd approached, I mustered my courage and waved. "Hi, Mrs. Anderson! Mr. Blanchard!" I waved harder at Herman Blanchard, who'd been my Vacation Bible School teacher growing up. If I talked quickly enough, maybe I could outpace the heat running up my neck.

"Ruth," said Mr. Blanchard warily. He was normally known for his easy nature—it was why children loved him. Right now, he looked like he wanted to turn and flee.

With tight smiles, the group stopped in front of our table. There were different tiers of people in Bottom Springs. You could tell where someone stood by how they were treated in church. The people at the bottom, the Fortenot Fishing wives and their families, and other newer folks who'd moved here for jobs at the Company or Blanchard Hospital sat near the back. They were hardscrabble people who were to be assimilated at Holy Fire, but not treated as bosom friends. The people in the middle, whose families had lived in Bottom Springs for generations, like Old Man Jonas and Mrs. Autin the tailor, were treated with modest respect and affection, sometimes made ushers. While their ties to the town were admirable, their families had never amounted to much. And then there were the people in front of us, who lived in my parents' neighborhood, with jobs that passed for lucrative and respectable families. They were the kind of people my parents kept close. The top echelon.

Mrs. Anderson read the sign on our table. "Send Sam Landry to college, huh?" I sat up straighter. Mrs. Anderson was a friend of my mother who was so under her sway she'd even taken to wearing her hair the same style, dyed platinum blond and cut bluntly at the shoulders. Looking at her, I felt an echo of the same anxiety that surfaced whenever I was home.

She gave her best approximation of a smile. "You three. What an... interesting group."

I knew the subtext: *A troupe of misfits.*

"You're Tia's boy, right?" Mr. Blanchard smiled tightly at Sam. "Only got you for two summers in VBS."

"Yes, sir." Sam ducked his head. "My mom had to work and couldn't always take me."

"A shame," Mr. Blanchard tittered. "Letting worldly matters interfere with the instruction of a young soul."

I could feel, more than hear, Everett's scoff. I knew what he was thinking: Herman Blanchard was the grown son of Augustus Blanchard, owner of Blanchard Hospital. Their family was the richest in town. Herman Blanchard hadn't needed to worry about "worldly matters" a single day in his life.

He could write us a big check, though. I smiled as widely as I could, prepared to make a pitch, but just then Mrs. Anderson frowned at Sam.

"Can you even wash cars, dear? On account of your..." She wiggled her fingers at his head. "Disability."

There was a stretched-taut moment of silence, then Sam said curtly, "Of course I can."

An uncomfortable pall fell over the group. A few of the women shot glances at each other, followed by small, private smiles, a promise of gossip to come.

"Well, unfortunately, we don't have the time," said Mr. Anderson, pulling on his belt. "We'd better bid y'all good luck."

"Wait," I said, shocking everyone, most of all myself. "If you don't have time to get your cars washed, could you at least consider a donation?" I nodded at Sam. "He would be a local legend—the first person from Bottom Springs to attend Duke. He's worked hard for it."

Out of the corner of my eye, I saw Sam's shoulders tense. He was embarrassed I was trying to sell him to these people.

Mr. Anderson cleared his throat. "Uh, the reverend—your daddy. He said y'all would be down here today. But that we shouldn't, uh, encourage you. These colleges, he says they're brainwashing factories, tryin' to teach kids the sky is red even though Christ says it's blue. Your daddy says one day Jesus is going to come in all his wrath to demolish them. So we have to steer y'all away, especially, uh..." He glanced at Sam. "The weakest among you."

"Psalms 82:3," Mr. Blanchard explained, like he was being helpful. "We must defend the weak and the fatherless."

Of course my father had put his sword through my gut even from far away. But it was one thing to do it to me. It was another to do it to Sam.

The Bible study group ambled away. We sat in heavy silence.

"I'm sorry," I said finally. "The next people will be different."

"I'm not," Sam said quietly. "Weak, I mean."

I turned to him. His cheeks were pink, eyes glued to the table. Under it, his foot tapped. "Of course you're not. You were valedictorian of Sacred Surrender. You've made it through seventeen years in this place. And now you're going to be the one who gets away. You're going to go out there and succeed, and one day Bottom Springs will be nothing but a distant memory."

I was feeding him my own dream, measured out in spoonfuls.

Sam gave me an appraising look. "You know, I didn't expect you to be like this. I always thought you were nice, with a better-than-average vocabulary, but still one of them. 'Cause of your parents."

"Heads up," Ever murmured, and I jumped at his voice in my ear. I hadn't even heard him approach. He pointed to a truck rolling down Main, headed our way.

My stomach dropped.

The windows of the truck rolled down. It was packed with kids from school, former football players like Barry Holt and the quarterback Jace Reynolds and cheerleaders like Lila LeBlanc. So many they were squished into the cab and hanging out of the truck bed, clearly on their way to Starry Swamp for a party.

"Look, y'all," Jace called from the driver's seat. The truck slowed to a crawl. "We got ourselves a freak show!"

"They're all gathered in one place," snickered a young cheerleader from the truck bed. "Creepy how they stick together."

"Even freaks need friends," Jace cackled, and the entire truck started laughing. I could see Barry's eyes squeeze shut next to Jace in the cab, Lila's white-toothed grin in the back.

"Good luck with your car wash," the young cheerleader yelled. "Looks like y'all are super busy!"

Lila blew Sam a kiss. "Have fun at Duke!"

They were still laughing when Jace gunned the engine and took off, making the cheerleaders squeal. The truck raced to the stop sign at the end of Main, then peeled around the corner.

The moment they were gone, Sam stood up. "This was a mistake."

"No," I pleaded. "Stay. It's still early. Plenty of time for things to turn around." I looked back at the lot, where I'd stacked our supplies. "I bought these new sponges and this soap that's supposed to be real good for cars, Mr. Dale said. And a fancy windshield cleaner that leaves no spots..." My voice faltered.

I could feel Sam studying me. "Okay," he said quietly, resuming his seat. "A little more time, then."

"I'm out of here," Ever said, kicking one of the empty water buckets.

"What?" I spun in my chair. "You can't go."

He squinted at me, which was code for *You sure about that?*

"If you say I told you so, Ever, I swear..." I sat back in my chair and crossed my arms, feeling his betrayal reverberate. "Where are you even going?"

"Nowhere."

"Of course," I scoffed. "Figures."

"Hold down the fort," he said, and strode away.

After a few minutes of people watching, Sam looked at me out of the corner of his eye. "I heard Everett has to drink blood twice a day to keep his protection against the sun."

"What—"

"I'm *kidding*. Obviously, I don't believe that." The way Sam said it made it sound like "anymore" was missing from the end of his sentence. "It's okay." He nudged me with his elbow. "I was surprised he even helped. I never expected him to last."

And here I'd thought he would.

Two long, miserable hours later, as Sam and I were folding up our table, Ever materialized behind us.

I sucked in a breath. "You need a bell."

He glanced at the unused sponges and dry buckets. "You calling it quits?" He had the nerve to sound surprised.

I dropped my half of the folding table and turned to him, nearly vibrating. "Are you really asking that? The person who left?"

"No one was coming," Sam said, taking pains to sound cheerful. "Figured we might as well close up shop."

"Not a *single* person?"

I ignored the question. "What are you even doing back? Did 'nowhere' get boring?"

It was the maddest I'd been at Everett since we'd become friends, and you could hear it in my voice. He raised an eyebrow, looking amused, which was further infuriating.

"And what are you doing with that bag?" I jerked a hand at the brown grocery bag he was holding. He never went inside the Piggly Wiggly, even for a Coke.

"Can I talk to you?" He nodded toward Dale's Country Corner. "In private?"

"No, thank you."

"Ruth." Ever gripped my forearm. I looked up and found his expression serious. "Please."

The moment we made it to the parking lot behind Dale's, weeds growing through cracks in the pavement, I turned to Ever with my arms crossed. His answering grin derailed me.

"Why are you smiling?"

He nodded at my crossed arms. "I'm glad you trust me."

I felt like I did whenever I read a line in a book that peered into my soul, putting into words a feeling that had, until that moment, lived only vaguely inside my brain. How remarkable for another person to capture your feelings exactly. Though I suspected I knew, I asked, "What do you mean?"

With his free hand, he rubbed my arm. "You're the queen of walking on eggshells. That's why you've always been so quiet. But you're not walking on them with me. You feel safe enough to get mad."

Only Ever could take my anger and bend it into something like affection. I swallowed. "Where'd you go, anyhow?"

He opened the grocery bag. "To get this."

Inside was stuffed with bills—tens, twenties, fives. Not crisp, like from the bank, but bent and wrinkled.

"For Sam," Ever explained. "Since none of these people will let him wash their stupid cars. Think of it as a cruelty tax with seventeen years' interest."

My jaw dropped. Ever watched with a neutral expression, waiting for me to speak.

"How—*where*?"

"Holy Fire." He said it so lightly.

"From my dad's office?" It was where he'd kept the tithe collections since I was young. His office, not the elders', who were technically in charge of the budget. Very few people knew that.

Ever nodded.

"How'd you know it was there?"

His gaze cut away. "Good guess."

"You got all of this from his safe?" My father had installed one in the wall behind his desk, hidden by a large painting of the two unnamed men crucified next to Christ, history's most famous thieves. It was meant as an inside joke and a warning. He trusted that safe so much it was where he kept everything important: car titles, birth certificates, even the deed to our house.

Ever nodded again. His expression said he was being patient with me while I processed.

"How'd you get into it?"

He shrugged. "You could say my father taught me."

I stared down at the stuffed bag. There was so much money. More than I'd ever seen. I inhaled the peculiar scent of cash. What made money smell so good? The paper, the ink, the hands it traveled through—or was this what power smelled like?

"We're going to talk about how you learned to do that later," I promised. "But for now...how much money is this? It looks like hundreds."

"Thousands," Ever corrected.

I blinked up at him. "He said tithing was up at the church, but I never imagined this much."

"That's not even half of what was in the safe."

Holy Fire had grown over the years, from the modest white clapboard my father had inherited to the sprawling complex it was now after two additions, both paid for by congregants. He and the elders were planning yet another expansion to accommodate all the new people who had started showing up, filling every pew. My father was building an empire.

"They really do love him," I said softly, which was nowhere near the important thing to focus on. But faced with this concrete proof of what his congregants were willing to give, I was gutted. Some part of me had been waiting for Bottom Springs to come to my side all these years.

Ever remained silent.

Time seemed to crawl as we stood looking into the bag of money. As the shock of where it came from dissipated, a vision began to form: me slipping the bag under my T-shirt and walking it home, hiding it in the dark space beneath my dresser, where my parents never looked. Sitting at the library desktop, back on LSU's website, but this time, accepting my admission. Packing my things into a suitcase. Leaving Bottom Springs forever.

It was right there in Ever's hands, in all those soft crinkled bills: the life I wanted.

Ever cocked his head. “Whatcha thinking, Ruth?”

Desire was thick in my throat. I couldn’t pull my eyes away.

His voice was silky. “You can have it. You can take it and do whatever you want.”

I reached inside the bag, fingering the bills. Then I looked at the empty car-wash lot. Sam was stacking the buckets. Behind him, people walked past, inspecting him and then looking away.

“No.” I almost choked on it. “I can’t.”

Everett and I locked eyes. “But you,” I said softly, testing the words. “You could use it to finally get out of here.”

Everett looked at me at that moment in a way I’d never been looked at before: like I was a thousand different people he was sorting through, trying to make sense of. His dark eyes searched my face, his voice husky. “Would you come with me? I finally fixed the old convertible. We could race the whole way up Highway 1 and never look back. I could find work in a garage and you could go to school.”

“Yes,” I said hoarsely. “I’d go.”

Questions swirled in his eyes. My heart pounded. We stood on the edge of a cliff.

Ever looked down at the money. And then at Sam, packing up his book bag, his expression despondent now that he thought we weren’t looking. I could feel his decision. Even before he took a deep breath and turned from me, I could feel it in the air and my heart cracked at the loss.

Ever walked over to Sam and presented the money. I would learn later what he said: it was an anonymous donation. A kind soul who wanted no recognition, only to see Sam succeed.

I watched the first tendrils of acceptance push past the doubt on Sam’s face. Then that acceptance turned to joy as he took the bag, looked into it. I wondered if he thought: It’s a miracle, like Pastor Cornier always swore could happen.

Ever slapped him on the shoulder and walked away, cutting off the gushing Sam was trying to do. Before Everett left, he glanced to where I stood, still frozen behind the Country Corner. He nodded, one sharp incline of his chin, and I knew in that moment that what he'd done had been right, that what was lawful and what was just had been two different things today, and we'd chosen correctly.

So yes, Everett and I had done some things I needed to repress. Yes, we were criminals. There was no getting around it.

But I swear to God—to Christ and the Holy Spirit. In the ways that mattered, I always believed we were good.

16

NOW

It's barely light outside when I slip out my front door, screen banging behind me, wielding a pair of gardening shears with blades as big as my forearms. The morning's cool, the sun taking mercy on the flowers in my garden. More mercy than I will show Everett's back door, the one his father broke in a drunken rage and Ever never got repaired. For years it's stood bound with a flimsy padlock, a tempting invitation for home invaders if Bottom Springs had any. Though even if we did, they, like everyone else in town, would probably be too afraid of the Duncan house to rob it.

Actually, I suppose *I'm* the home invader. The thought makes me smile as I take swift steps across my lawn. I'm shirking my duties at the library to head straight to Everett's house and see if he's back—and if not, I plan to break into his back door using these shears and wait for him, however long it takes. There's a killer out there and the Fortenot Fishing Company is hiding something and Barry has proposed, and altogether it makes me feel like a powder keg waiting to explode.

I'm still smiling in a way that can't look wholly sane when I hear the crunch of tires and twist to find the sheriff's familiar brown-and-white Ford Crown ambling down my drive. I still like a rabbit, gripping my gardening shears, too surprised to do anything but watch the car jerk to a halt, a cloud of dust swirling. The sheriff steps out.

"Mornin.'" He tips his hat and adjusts his sunglasses against the glare of the sun. A grin spreads over his face. "Who's in trouble?"

I blink at him. "Sorry?"

He points to the shears. "Those wicked scissors. Who's in trouble?"

My mouth goes dry. "My star jasmine. They're due for a trim."

The sheriff moves toward me in a showy way, taking big steps that make the holstered gun at his side bounce so it's impossible to ignore. "Awful early for gardening."

I swallow the lump in my throat. My long grass, in need of a mowing, pricks my ankles above my Keds. "I thought I'd get it done before work while it's cooler." I frown. "It's awful early for you to be here, Sheriff."

He smiles. Tom Theriot used to have a single gold tooth, the result of an old football injury, but he got it fixed a few years back at some fancy dentist over in Forsythe. Now his smile is pure white. "Thought I'd catch you before work this time." He gestures at my garden. "Go ahead. I can talk while you trim."

With no other choice, I walk stiffly to my jasmine bushes, the sheriff trailing close behind. I begin to cut. Each slash of the blades is satisfying. "If you're here to ask more about Fred, I'm afraid I haven't remembered anything new."

"Actually." The sheriff takes his time with the word, drawing it out. "I'm here on another matter."

I pause midcut. "I see."

"Not sure if Barry's mentioned, but we've been dragging Starry Swamp, searching for more remains. It's hard, nasty work, but we found another piece. Except this one don't belong to Fred. Know how we know?"

I shake my head.

"It's another skull."

It takes all of my willpower not to drop the shears.

"Our best guess is that it belongs to a man named Renard Michaels. Construction worker who passed through here 'bout six years ago, 'fore Fred went missing."

I can hear Ever's voice in my head, clear and ringing: *"Never send to know for whom the bell tolls; it tolls for thee."*

Donne, I whisper back. *As in, we are done and buried.*

I wait for the flames. Renard's name spoken like a spell, his soul unleashed, the devils coming. But there's nothing. Only the sun beating down, the air thick with sweet, cloying jasmine, the buzz of bees. No cosmic reaction, no opening of Hell. The debilitating guilt I expected is nowhere to be found. In its place, curiously, is a ribbon of rebellion: the sheriff stands beside me so imperiously. I want to leave him frustrated, evaded.

I want to best him.

"We're working with a fancy forensics center up in New Orleans now that there's two victims," he continues. I can feel the intensity of his stare but don't meet it. "They say the skull's been in the swamp for 'bout six years, which is around the time Renard's truck was found abandoned in the swamp. That's how we figured it was him. We'll confirm the identity and cause of death soon."

Red blotches appear on my freckled skin, spreading over my arms like a tell.

"Now, Ruth," says the sheriff, startling me into snapping off a long, elegant arm of star jasmine. Its beautiful scent sharpens in death. "I made a mistake going public with Fred and the vandalism in the swamp. I'll own up to that. The town's up in arms about witchcraft and the Low Man, and it's starting to put the screws to our investigation. So we're keeping Renard quiet for now, and I'ma need you to do the same. No stoking this into a furor, you hear?"

I thrust my arms deep into the jasmine bushes to hide the scarlet blotches. Focus on the rhythm of cutting, cutting, cutting, until I realize I need to answer him.

"Of course, Sheriff. I'm very sorry to hear there's another skull." It's too little, too late, but it's something. "It's awful, whoever it turns out to be." I cannot say the name Renard. I will choke.

"Well, Ruth, it's good to hear you say that. Because back when Renard disappeared—you was still in school—we chalked it up to him meeting a bad end on a trapping trip, on account of that's how he used to spend his time. You know trekking out into the swamp ain't for casual fools. We figured he was an outsider, and Starry got 'em. But now that we got two skulls, two signs of blunt-force trauma, our calculation's different. We're looking into some things we didn't look into before."

I chop and chop. The sun has risen high overhead, and there's sweat at my hairline. I want the vines to swallow me like the trees swallowed nymphs in Greek myths. I want to be green and inhuman and at peace.

"Turns out Renard was real close to his momma," says the sheriff. He re-angles so he's standing in front of me, and I have no choice but to look at his face. "Told her a lot. And one of the things he said was that he'd met a nice girl here in Bottom Springs, a preacher's daughter with flamin'-red hair. He actually said that: flamin' red. Ain't that some poetry? It made the detail stick in his momma's head, and she told me all about it when I called 'er up."

I stop cutting, arms still in the bushes. "She's not lying. I did meet Renard at church. Like I meet everybody."

"And what was the nature of your relationship?"

It's going to be okay, I promise myself. All I need to do is say the things I was prepared to say six years ago.

"We didn't have one. We were friendly at church, that's all." I meet his eyes. "You know me. Not much for talking."

The sheriff smiles. "Yes. A modest girl. Miss Ruth, can you think back to where you were six years ago, on the night of Friday, June 1st?"

"That's an awful long time ago, Sheriff."

"Do your best."

"Well...I was never one for going out with friends. Friday nights back then, you could find me home reading." I smile tightly. "You can ask my parents. Hasn't changed much since."

"I see." Sheriff Theriot nods, as if he was expecting that answer. "And speaking a' friends, you're friends with Killian's boy, Everett Duncan, that right?"

He knows I am. He just asked about Everett two days ago. I nod warily.

"He ever mention Renard? Either back then or since?"

It's almost otherworldly how, despite the heat, goose bumps spike on my skin. I clear my throat. "Never."

"When you was bein' friendly with Renard at church, did he ever say anything about spending time at Killian's garage?"

The question is so strange I forget to keep my composure and frown. "No."

The sheriff lifts his sunglasses so I can see his eyes. They're brown and bloodshot, but cunning. "Six years ago. Ain't that about the time you and Everett starting hanging out?"

I step back, shaking the jasmine. "I... Well—"

Something hot and sharp pierces my skin. I gasp, jerking my hands out of the flower bush. A wasp lights up into the sky, buzzing loudly. I've been stung.

Tears prick my eyes at the radiating pain. A red welt is already rising on my forearm, a white gouge mark in the middle.

"Ooh." The sheriff winces. "Nasty. Better get some antihistamine and an ice pack."

I nod, clutching my arm, trying to will my tears away.

"Well, I'll leave you to tend that," he says, turning to walk away. But after a few steps, he swings back and locks eyes with me. "Move careful round dangerous creatures, Miss Ruth. They get cornered and desperate, their first instinct is always going to be to sting you."

17

NOW

Everett Duncan's house is haunted. Though, like his father, supposedly it had potential once. It's not small—bigger than my parents' before all the additions. In the center of the front door is a beautiful stained-glass inset, one of many expensive details that signal once upon a time, someone had big plans for this place. It's as far away from my rental as I could get, but edges up to its own lonely forest just like my house does, forests being easy to come by around here. Behind it, you can see an ocean of pines stretching in an undulating wave.

These days the stained glass is so filthy you can barely discern the colors. There are permanent oil stains on the driveway, and the wild has crept in and run roughshod, sweeping tall grass up the walls and vines over the roof, choking the house so much the gutters are falling off. If I was being romantic, I'd say Everett's house looks like the castle in "Sleeping Beauty" after the thorned plants have held it in their clutches for a thousand years.

But I do not feel romantic. This house is an unhappy place for unhappy people. I've asked Everett a million times why he doesn't just sell it, and a million times he's replied that he can't in good conscience burden someone else with his family's ghosts.

His convertible is in the driveway when I drive up, flooding me with relief. I pull up next to it, leaving the garden shears, and pound on his front door. The pain from the sting on my arm is still white-hot. "Ever," I call. "It's me."

After a moment, the door cracks open. Ever's black hair sticks straight up like he's been electrocuted, though I know it only means he's run his hands through it a million times. He has dark circles under his eyes and leans against the doorframe like he needs it to stay upright. "I thought you had work."

"*That's* what you have to say?" I shoulder in past him, brushing my long hair out of my eyes. The house looks exactly like it did four years ago when his father died. There's the sad, dilapidated couch and worn armchair Killian lived in when he wasn't at the garage, facing the same rabbit-eared TV. Other than the omnipresent half-empty liter of vodka and crumpled Coke can on the side table, Ever hasn't changed a thing. The sight of the room works like a time machine, taking me back to when we were teenagers. I shiver.

"Where've you been? I can't believe you took off on me."

"Left you a note."

"Where, Ever?" I don't have time for evasiveness.

He runs a hand over his face. "I drove to Durham."

I cross my arms, then wince. "You think now's the time to go on vacation?"

He peers at my arm, having clocked my pain. "I didn't go on vacation. I went to see Sam. I've decided to sell this shithole."

This is enough to sidetrack me. Everett Duncan, cutting his last tie to Bottom Springs. Though I've bugged him about selling for years, now that he's actually doing it, I realize I expected him to resist forever. This house is the one piece of insurance I'd clung to when I wondered if he'd ever come back. The news is such a gut punch it takes me a second to process the other part. "Sam as in Sam *Landry*?"

"I needed his help."

Sam had, as I'd predicted, moved out of Bottom Springs and never looked back. He'd graduated top of his class at Duke and was now at Duke Law. I kept track of his accomplishments through his momma, the only other person who felt a similar bittersweet mix of pride and pain at Sam succeeding out there in the world.

Ever takes my arm, twisting it gently. "Wasp?"

"Yes. What did you need Sam for?"

"Ice," Ever says, and tugs me into the kitchen, where he cracks open the old freezer and pulls out a handful of brown-tinged ice.

"Ew."

"You're not drinking it." He presses the ice to my wound and I inhale sharply at the cold.

"What did you need Sam's help for?" I repeat through gritted teeth.

Ever looks at my wound. "Sam's a lawyer—"

"Law student."

"Well, he knows things. More importantly, people. He was able to get me what I needed. Think I spooked him, though. Appearing out of thin air like a ghost."

"Doesn't he study estate law?" Sam was going to manage rich people's money, his momma told me. Help wealthy people like the kind, generous benefactor who'd paid his way to college.

"Yeah, well, I need to make sure everything's taken care of."

Ever's persistent vagueness finally annoys me so much I wrench my arm away. Ice cubes shatter on the kitchen floor. But Ever doesn't say anything; he just walks to the sink and dumps the rest of the ice, then grips the counter with both hands. Staring at his broad back, I think: *Stop being scared and tell him about Barry.* I open my mouth but can't bring myself to do it.

"I can't remember the code to that damn safe," Ever murmurs, staring out the window. "I know it starts with an eight."

I push thoughts of Barry's proposal aside. I'll tell Ever later, when things are less urgent. "Why are you talking about a safe? Focus."

He spins on his heel and blows past me back into the living room, tugging at his hair. "I think a seven is next."

I follow him. "Everett, come on."

He paces in front of the couch. "But the third number I can't get. A nine or a six... I just can't—"

"*Ever*," I say sharply, and seize his T-shirt by the hem. He halts, eyes flicking to my mouth. "Snap out of it. We need to talk about the investigation."

His jaw tightens. "That is what I'm talking about."

I tug his shirt harder. "You don't understand. While you were traipsing around Durham, they found Renard's skull. The sheriff came to see me, asking questions about my relationship with Renard and *you*. He knows we knew each other."

"Shit."

"Exactly. He asked if Renard ever visited your dad's garage. Why would he ask that?"

Everett's silent.

"Now is really not the time to be evasive. If you have something to say, speak."

He looks up at the ceiling, then blows out a breath. "Okay. You're not going to like this, but...Renard used to work for this gang out of Forsythe."

I release his shirt. "What kind of gang?"

"Bike gang that calls itself the Sons of Liberty. Real notorious in certain circles. They move drugs through south Louisiana."

"How do you know that?"

Ever's silent again. Finally, he says, "Because they used my dad's garage for drops."

Surprise locks my limbs. "Your dad worked for them?"

His laugh is throaty. "Ruth, my dad was an alcoholic who could barely finish a repair job unless I stepped in. Where do you think his money actually came from?"

I can barely keep up with all the memories I now have to reconsider. Mr. Duncan was more than just a sadistic drunk; he was a criminal. *Does that change anything?* the voice in my head whispers. "I can't... I don't know what to say."

"You're repulsed," Ever says quietly. Certain of it.

"No. I mean, yes, but—how do you know Renard was involved with the Sons of Liberty too?" Their name feels strange in my mouth.

I know what Ever looks like when he doesn't want to do something, so I know he's forcing himself to look me in the eyes. "Because Renard used to come by the garage all the time. Someone from the Sons of Liberty would drop off a package, Renard would come pick it up, and then the same thing would happen in reverse with the money, except that round my dad got a cut. The garage was a way station. Everyone needs repairs, especially motorcycle riders. They had the perfect excuse to be in and out all hours."

"What kind of drugs?"

"Oxy, mostly. Fentanyl. Meth. Painkillers, Ruth. That's where the money is." Challenge shimmers in his eyes. "This is opioid country. Surely you're aware."

I sidestep his pointed remark. "None of this makes sense. I know for a fact Renard worked construction."

"From what I could tell, he was in deep with the Sons. His construction job probably made him the perfect runner, traveling from place to place all over the state. How do you think he paid for that big ugly truck with the rims?"

Renard and his beloved truck. My voice is dazed. "So you're saying

Renard and your father were involved in a drug ring, but you never said a word. And we were supposed to be best friends."

Ever studies me a moment, then nods. "Ruth—"

That's when it hits me. "You knew Renard before you found us in the swamp. Why did you let me think you two were strangers?"

"I didn't want you to freak out. You were already dealing with the guilt and getting college taken away, then the hospital. I didn't want to add to your stress when it didn't matter anyway." He shakes his head. "And truthfully…I didn't want you to know about my dad and the Sons because you already thought so low of me. You were scared of me before the swamp. I was afraid if I told you the truth, you'd stop being my friend."

"I never thought badly of you, Ever. Only him." A wild thought occurs to me. "Is that why you were there that day? Because of Renard?" Had Ever followed us into the swamp?

"No," he says emphatically. "I was hunting, like I told you. And okay, I spotted Renard's truck. That's why I got within earshot. Normally you see another person when you're hunting, you hightail in the opposite direction. But I saw his stupid truck out there where no one ever goes, and I had to know what he was doing. He was a son of a bitch at the garage and I didn't trust him. So I moved closer, and that's when I heard you. Not even a scream. A whimper."

I turn my back on him, hands sliding over my mouth. Six years, and I'm only now learning the truth about the day that changed my life.

"Talk to me," he urges.

I try to shake off *not even a scream*. Clear my throat. But my voice still comes out hoarse. "This gives the sheriff another connection to trace. Now it's not just my date with Renard; it's your dad's garage. They're going to put it together." It's my turn to start pacing.

"They won't." Everett's voice is the surest I've heard it. "Trust me.

The Sons of Liberty have been running drugs for years and doing worse things, too. If the people in charge wanted to stop them, they would've done it by now. This is a stone they don't want to overturn. We're going to have to force them to look."

I freeze midstride.

"I told you I'd come up with a plan," he says. "What do you think I spent the car ride doing? I know how to throw the sheriff off our scent."

"You didn't even know they found Renard's skull until I just told you."

"It was inevitable. Now, listen. The runners had to leave collateral with my dad. Something valuable they'd lose if they tried to screw the Sons and take off with the drugs or the money. Renard's leverage was the deed to his mom's house. I know because my dad used to give him hell for it, told him he was the world's biggest tool for putting his momma's house on the line instead of his own truck or something."

I think of Renard's *Momma* necklace: that measure of his love, blackening in the fire.

"My dad used to keep the leverage in a safe in the garage. And the man I sold the garage to after he died works for the Sons, too. They're still using the place as a drop site. This man, Earl Hebert, is sharp as a rabbit. More than that, he's lazy. I'd bet a million dollars he hasn't changed a thing in there."

"You want to go find out."

Ever strides to me, pressing his hands together like he's begging. "Hear me out. We can sneak in when Earl's away and look for the safe. I used to watch my dad. If I can remember the code, it'll be easy. But even if I can't, I'll get in."

"Like you got into the safe at the church."

Ever nods, his eyes grave. "You remember how it was back then with my dad—constant warfare. I learned how to steal things from that safe just to piss him off."

I sink onto the couch cushion. It smells musty and sour, but I'm too lost in the magnitude of Everett's bad idea to care. "Absolutely not."

"If we can find that deed, that's something unique and valuable of Renard's. It's at least something with his fingerprints on it. And I know where to find the Sons in Forsythe. We can plant it on them and send an anonymous tip to the sheriff. Then we'll spread rumors Renard was mixed up with the Sons. You know Bottom Springs. It'll spread like wildfire. The sheriff will have no choice but to search them if there's pressure. When he finds the deed on the Sons, boom—there's your suspects and your motive. Drug deal gone wrong."

I shake my head. "We're not doubling down on danger by trying to frame a drug gang for our murder. Do you hear yourself?"

He throws up his hands. "What other options do we have? Remember when we burned Renard's necklace where the drifters made their fires? It's the same thing. The Sons are committing crimes. All we have to do is bury ours in theirs." When I don't say anything, he continues. "I'm trying to save us, Ruth. There's a clear fall guy. Better than clear—*deserving*. This is the best chance we've got."

My throat goes dry. Before I make any decisions, I need answers. "Ever. Did you carve that symbol into the trees? The one they found in the swamp?"

The abrupt change in direction throws him, but only for a second. He shakes his head. "No. I've never seen it before."

"But at the bar, it sounded like you knew—"

"I don't." His voice is firm, final.

Okay, then. I swallow. "There's something else I need to ask you."

His look turns wary.

"While you were gone, I went digging into Fred." I tell Everett everything about the secret dock at the inlet and the men loading the boat with the scraped-off logo. His pale cheeks flush with color when I describe jumping overboard. Before he can give me a hard time, I ask him the question that's burning a hole in my head, the only option that makes sense.

"Do you think it's possible Fred was a drug runner too?"

Ever tenses, eyes dropping to the large rust-red stain on the carpet, a leftover from one of the bad nights. His long, elegant fingers clench into fists.

"Do you think Fred could've done something that pissed off the Sons and made them kill him? I know we're inventing that story about Renard, but could it actually be true for Fred?"

Ever's hands relax.

"Because if they did…if they *are* murderers, and it happens to be Fred they killed and not Renard…" All the pieces light up in my head, guiding me to a single conclusion. "Then they would deserve to be framed."

"If there's one thing I'm certain of," he says softly, "it's that the Sons of Liberty deserve to go down."

"It wouldn't be such a sin, then—your plan. It would be justice, in a way."

Ever's face remains neutral. "You get to decide, Ruth. You tell me what to do."

My own voice in my head, whisper-quiet: *Be good and be spared the lake of fire.*

But what is good here? I picture a scale. On one side: the heart of Renard Michaels, drug runner and would-be rapist. Fred Fortenot, abuser, possible drug runner. The Sons, drug kingpins, maybe murderers. And on the other side: Ever and me, trying to survive. The scale rocks back and forth with indecision.

And then Ever looks at me. And among the brown flecks that look like stars, I see it: fear. It's a look I've seen before, and my response, like then, is automatic.

"Okay," I say. "One last crime to end it."

The scale tips.

18

JANUARY, NINETEEN YEARS OLD

A whole year exploring the deep forest and salty coast and Starry Swamp by foot, being bitten and scraped and burned by the sun, cold, and plant poisons, and still there was one place so foreboding I'd never been willing to go: Everett's house. Where he lived alone with his father, his mother killed giving birth to him, a family history he'd spoken of for the first time only weeks ago, and only in passing, the subject too painful to dwell on. Although my heart had ached to know his loss, a small, selfish part of me had been happy when he told me, honored to be trusted with such an intimate part of him.

Now I stood in front of his house with dread settling like lead in my stomach. He was supposed to meet me at the library after work so we could take a canoe into the swamp, but he hadn't shown. Normally he was predictable as a clock, all the more extraordinary since he didn't own one, not a watch or a cell phone or anything, just seemed to know the time by the angle of the sun and stars. I'd searched for him everywhere: the Blue Moon, the gas station, even my house in case he'd gotten the meeting spot mixed up. But he was nowhere, which meant there was only one place left to look.

I wouldn't have gone—would've simply let Everett stand me up—if it wasn't for my sense that something was wrong. It was a dark, oily suspicion that crept through my veins.

The Duncan house was as bad as you'd expect from the rumors: the garage door was half-open, jugs of antifreeze and rusty tools strewn everywhere, a stained white T-shirt lying limply in an overgrown front lawn. The last person I wanted to face was Mr. Duncan, but his car wasn't in the driveway, and either way, this was Ever, so I needed to be brave.

I knocked on the front door and no one answered.

I knocked again, harder, and the door opened of its own volition.

I toed inside, on high alert, then bit back a gasp. The house was in ruins. The coffee table overturned, a lamp lying shattered on the floor, the carpet streaked with sick yellowish-brown stains I could tell from the smell were liquor. It was ice cold, just as wintry inside as out, and I saw why the next second: the back door hung nearly off the hinges, bent outward at the wrong angle like a broken bone. I could see clear to the hundred naked pines in their backyard.

I drifted into the middle of the living room, unable to wrench my eyes away. A tale of violence was written in every wounded object.

And then I saw Ever.

"No," I cried, and flew to the couch. Everett lay crumpled there, almost hidden among the dark cushions, one of his eyes swollen shut, his beautiful face marred by blood around his mouth and nose.

"Ever," I urged, shaking his shoulders. He startled, his good eye flying open, the look on his face so profoundly afraid that seeing it felt like a stab to the heart.

"Ruth?" he whispered, voice garbled. He shifted and groaned, clutching his left arm.

I could feel the tears in my eyes, warm against the cold leaking in from the door. "What happened? Never mind. Get up, we have to go to the hospital."

"No," he said weakly, the words thick out of his swollen lips. "I'm okay."

"You're *not*. It looks like someone took a hammer to you." I felt nearly hysterical, like I could do anything, pick him up and carry him all the way to Blanchard if I had to.

His good eye fluttered shut. "Wasn't a hammer."

"Please let me take you." I pressed closer to him, trying to share his space, breathe for him, I didn't know—something. "To the hospital and then the sheriff."

"No," he snarled, his one eye flashing open, full of fire. We'd found a squirrel in the swamp once, badly ravaged by a wolf or bobcat, hanging on by a thread, shivering with fear and pain. Ever had bent to pick it up, to take it to old Mr. Wilkes who ran a small clinic, but the squirrel had hissed with all its strength, glaring up at him with the same look Ever was giving me now, a wounded thing fighting for its life. "Not the cops. *Never* the cops. Do you hear me?"

I looked at him and felt the tears fall down my face.

His glare softened. "I'm sorry, Ruth. I just...can't."

"Then let me take care of you." I wiped under my eyes, determined to be useful, then touched the arm he was cradling. "Is it broken?"

Ever shivered. "No. Just pulled out of the joint. I already popped it back in."

I didn't ask how he knew to do that. I just nodded. "I'll be back."

I marveled at how clean and orderly his kitchen was, how unlike the living room, as I collected ice from an empty freezer and a hand towel from a drawer with a single matching oven mitt. My mind raced, picturing Ever here as a kid, cooking and cleaning for himself, keeping the kitchen tidy despite his father. In search of Everett's bedroom, I stumbled into two rooms, the first clearly his father's, empty bottles of vodka and soda cans littering every surface, his bedsheets twisted off the bed. The second room was pristine, like it hadn't been touched in years, a desk with a sewing machine in one corner, books stacked tidily on a bookshelf in another, framed pressed flowers on the wall surrounding a yellowed illustration of the Virgin Mary. I wondered about the room, whether it had been his mother's, then forced myself to turn and keep going.

Everett's room was the smallest and barest, with only a rickety wooden bed covered by threadbare white sheets, the hospital corners a trick Everett had learned to do from me. There was a small stack of books by his bed, all of them volumes I'd brought him from the library, and a small square window high up in the wall that looked out at the sea of naked trees. The whole room smelled like him, like I was standing in the middle of the forest. Ignoring the pain in my heart, I swooped low and tugged Ever's blanket off his bed, then returned to the living room.

He groaned with relief when I tucked the blanket around him, shielding him from the cold, but when I bent low with the ice-filled towel, the look in his eyes froze me.

"What?"

"Lay with me," he whispered. "Please."

It was the invitation I'd been waiting for. He sat up gingerly as I climbed on the couch, then laid him over my lap, his back and head resting on my legs. When we were settled, he took a deep breath and turned to face me, closing his eyes. With a mother dead in childbirth and a father like Killian, had he ever been held? I set about cleaning the blood from his face, touching him as gently as I could, stopping whenever he winced.

As I was finishing, fresh blood caught my eye—lower, on the arm he'd cradled and shielded. Before he could stop me, I lifted it and looked.

Two puncture wounds on his bicep—a bite mark sharp and deep as the one I'd gotten from the copperhead, slowly oozing blood.

"Ruth," Ever said, soft but still a warning.

"Who did this to you?"

His eyes slid away. After a minute of silence, he said, "You already know."

I did, didn't I? I'd suspected Ever's bruises and cuts, his weekly badges of dishonor, could be chalked up to more than the drunks at the Blue Moon. No matter how evasive he was, how dismissive, I should've pushed the issue, forced him to say it out loud.

"Your father," I said hollowly. Mr. Duncan wasn't just a church-shirker or a drunk. For once, the people of Holy Fire had gotten it right. He was a living, breathing monster.

"We got into another argument," Ever said.

"About what?"

He tried to shrug and winced. "He wants me to do something I won't."

I looked at the bruises on his face. "What's so bad it's worth this?"

He laughed—a dark sound. "He doesn't need an excuse anymore." He must've seen the impatience in my face because he added, quickly, "Someone's been missing down at the garage, and he wants me to fill in. That's all."

I frowned. "I thought it was just the two of you at the garage."

Ever didn't say anything.

I tried a different tack. "You need to go to the sheriff."

He closed his eyes. "Never."

I couldn't stop looking at the fang marks. "If you don't do something, one of these days your dad is going to kill you."

He didn't even blink. "This is the way it's always been. I ruined his life when I was born, and now he haunts mine. I killed her, so I'm responsible. I can't leave him, can't turn him in, and I can't make him better. He's my devil to bear."

We watched each other. I didn't know how to refute his logic or argue his mother's death wasn't his fault, or even tell him I understood, that my own father, though practically an angel in this town, was mine to bear, too. But Ever's body chose a path for us. Suddenly, he winced.

"What's wrong?"

"Just—the pain again." He gritted his teeth, eyes squeezed shut. "Do you have your pills with you?"

I felt caught. I didn't speak, unsure what to say.

He bared his teeth. "It hurts."

"Yes," I admitted. "But only because my parents told me to keep them on me." It was a bad lie and I was prepared to keep digging the hole, but he shook his head.

"I don't care right now, Ruth. Please, just give me one. I need this pain to stop."

There was no choice after that. I gave Ever one of the pills whose name I still didn't know, pulled out of the small hidden compartment in my bag, and he settled back in my lap and closed his eyes. Over time I watched his breathing even out, his face relaxing into something close to dreamy.

"We'll talk about the pills later," he murmured, eyes closed. "Don't think I don't have words for you."

Is this what I looked like when I took them—this slow untethering? As Everett floated away from me, I vowed to never take another pill again. Now that I knew he needed taking care of, escaping wasn't a luxury I could afford.

He shifted in my lap, revealing the fang marks again. I stared at them and pictured his father as a giant snake, rearing back against the coffee table and striking lightning fast. The poison from his bite eating its way through Ever's veins.

I bent and put my lips against the wound—only a gentle pressure, nearly a kiss. He tasted like salt and iron, like the minerals in sea water, sand that would harden into rocks and last for eons. That's what I wanted for him: permanence, solidity, the ability to outlast. I kissed the wish into his wound.

His fingers lifted weakly to brush the hair from my face. I looked up to meet his eyes. I could feel his blood drying around my lips, smeared and sticky. I must've looked like some sort of beast. But Ever was arrested, his eyes slowly tracking over my face. A small smile curved his lips. It lingered there until he closed his eyes and fell asleep.

I sat holding him for hours in the cold, not even afraid of Mr. Duncan coming home. In fact, I could think of nothing but Mr. Duncan. I imagined pushing him in front of a car. Beating him while he screamed. Chopping him into pieces and feeding him to the swamp. In that miserable house, with Ever's blood ringing my mouth, I felt an urge for violence the likes of which I'd felt only that day with Renard. Hatred grew in my heart until I burned to do for Ever what he'd done for me—my desire to protect him so intense that in those hours, guarding his broken body, the only words I had for it were *holy passion.*

If Ever had opened his eyes and asked me to do anything then, I would've done it. Anything he asked, I would've been capable of.

Like some sort of beast, surely.

19

NOW

There he is." Everett points, and my eyes skim the twin scars on his arm, perfect circles like a snakebite, before they find what he's pointing at. I press my face closer to the window of the Blue Moon bar.

"The one sitting by himself at the end?" The man in question has long, oily hair in need of a wash and a dark beard so long it brushes his chest. He's bent over a tumbler at the farthest end of Remy's bar, looking like he wished he could fall inside the glass.

"Yep." Ever's expression hardens. "Good old Earl Hebert. He had a lot in common with my father." He turns from the window. "Come on. It's safe to go."

But I can't look away from Earl. "Are you sure we'll have enough time?"

Ever tugs me. "Trust me. He'll be there all night."

In the dreamy dusk light, the old Duncan garage looks like an abandoned relic of some long-lost time, a building you'd see in a documentary about small towns and economic ruin. Or maybe that's just me and my aspiring anthropologist's eye. No matter how run down and disarming it appears, I know this place is secretly insidious, a way station for dangerous men. We cruise past it in Everett's car and park blocks away so no one will be able to recall an old black convertible parked outside.

It's unlikely there will be anyone, though, since we're on the outskirts of Bottom Springs in the middle of backcountry roads shielded by trees that have grown bent over the road like an archway. This remote location, so poorly chosen for a garage hoping to do swift business, is the perfect place for an illicit drop site. There were clues.

I study Ever's face as we trek to the garage. All my life I've prided myself on seeing things clearer than most. Yet I'm starting to realize the depths of my myopia.

Ever gives the lock binding the garage door an experimental tug, but it doesn't give. "Changed this lock. That's okay."

I crouch and squint. "Does that mean we can't get in?"

"There's another way." He rounds the corner and points up at a square window just out of his reach. It's so streaked with dust it's almost fogged. "See that? The lock on it was always broken. I guarantee Earl hasn't fixed it." Ever glances down. "I'm going to lift you, and then I need you to pound on it until it pops open."

"Me?"

He grins his devil's grin. "It's an adventure, Ruthie. Like *The Count of Monte Cristo*. You've gotta get your hands dirty."

"*Monte Cristo*'s a revenge story," I mutter, but let Ever circle his hands around my waist, his grip steady and cool through the fabric of my shirt.

"Ready?"

Thrill sparks in my chest. I nod, and he lifts me until I'm face-to-face with the window.

"You're going to have to hit it hard," he warns, his words tickling my thigh.

I prod at the window, trying to jimmy it open, but it doesn't budge.

"Hard," he insists, and I fist my hands and start to pound.

"*Harder.*"

My heart takes off. I batter the window like it's a locked door imprisoning me inside a burning house. My fists ache but I don't stop, and the truth is, it feels good to hit something. Suddenly the window wrenches inward and my fists sail through empty air.

Ever drops me unceremoniously and inspects my hand. "Good work. No bruising. Now this time, I need you to climb inside and unlock the back door."

I'm still trying to steady my breathing when his hands circle my waist again, the feeling familiar from climbing trees together, and when he lifts me, I grip the windowsill like it's a branch, haul myself up, and—

Tumble inside, straight to the concrete floor. I land with a crack I can feel in every bone.

"You okay?" Ever's voice is muted from outside. "Sounds like you knocked over something heavy."

"Gee, thanks," I mutter, peeling myself off the floor and limping to unlock the back door. My bottom lip throbs. I dart my tongue and taste blood.

Ever's standing outside the door when I open it. He zeros in on my lip. "You're bleeding."

"I know." I wipe my mouth with the back of my hand. "I managed to trip through the window."

Ever musses my hair so it falls over my eyes and I can't see. "You're mad at me."

I bat his hand away. "Let's just find the safe and get out of here."

He salutes me, unnervingly playful given we're in the middle of a break-in, and turns to scan the garage. It's small, lit dimly by dusk light filtering in through the windows, and in a state of disarray I remember from the few times I passed it when it still belonged to Mr. Duncan. It smells almost dizzyingly of gasoline.

The sound of an engine revving cuts through the silence. Ever claps a hand over my mouth the second I open it, and we wait, bodies tensed, as the sound from the car grows louder, and then starts to fade. After a few seconds, the only thing I can hear is my heart drumming in my ears.

Ever withdraws his hand. "Just a random person," he says, but his voice is shaky. "Come on. The safe used to be over here." He strides to a low gunmetal-gray cabinet hiding in the corner of the garage. "See—I *knew* Earl'd keep it. God bless stingy Southern bastards."

I peer over his shoulder. The cabinet door opens to reveal a silver and black safe, rectangular and roughly two feet tall, with an electronic keypad and a large silver handle. Ever hauls it out of the cabinet and I take a few steps back, giving him room.

"You remember your dad's combination?"

"No." He says it nonchalantly, moving to a nearby table to search through the tools.

"Then how do you think you're getting in there?"

"With these." Ever turns, holding a hammer and tire iron. He's got them raised triumphantly, much the way he once held a dead copperhead. "There are subtler ways, but they'd take too much time. With these I don't need two minutes."

I shake my head. "There's no way."

"Watch."

Something—possibly my sanity—breaks as Ever circles the safe with his tools held aloft. I can't help myself; the image is too funny. I start to laugh.

He raises his eyebrows. "Am I witnessing your mental breakdown?"

"You look ridiculous. Like some sort of movie villain."

"Disrespectful, Ruth." He sighs. "Stand back."

I stifle my laughter and step away—and as soon as I do, he jabs the tire iron into the gap behind the door of the safe and strikes it with his hammer, wedging the iron in. With every blow, he wrenches the door forward a little more. Then he drops the hammer with a clang and works the tire iron, putting his whole body into it, the corded muscles of his arms and back straining.

Something strange happens as I watch Everett bend the metal: I remember that he is a man. Strong and solid and formidable. His methodical exertion calls back the image of him taking apart Renard's body, that bloody ax swinging down, violent and steady. It's like I've grown so close to him I've forgotten what he looks like from a distance. But now I remember.

He peels the door of the safe forward like it's the lid on a tuna can, and it swings open. I stand gaping—at the accomplishment and the contents.

"Told ya." He drops the tire iron and wipes his sweaty brow on his shirtsleeve, breathing heavily. "Don't worry. I used the subtler method in your dad's office."

"Ever—the money."

The safe is filled with stacks of bills bound haphazardly by grubby rubber bands.

He crouches in front of it and I follow suit. "Yeah. Most runners give the Sons money as collateral. They make them buy in with more than the value of a shipment so it doesn't make sense to run off. Here, help me clear it out."

Together we pull stacks of money out of the safe and place them neatly on the concrete floor. The last time I saw this much money, Everett was holding it out to me in a grocery bag behind Dale's Country Corner. When it's cleared, all that's left in the safe are a few slips of paper. I pick up one that calls to me—Pepto-Bismol pink.

"A car title." A truck, registered to one Mr. Jebediah Ray.

Ever waves a creamy page. "This one's a boat title."

"Jeez." The next piece of paper looks like it's been ripped out of a notebook. An address in Shreveport, scribbled in pen. I show Ever. "What do you think this is?"

He studies the address for a moment. "Nothing good."

I stare at the paper until I realize. And then I wonder whether whoever lives there knows their lives are collateral, kept hostage in this safe. Goose bumps prickle my arms.

"Bingo." Ever unfolds the last pages, thick and bound by a heavy-duty staple. "I was right. It's still here."

I take the pages and smooth them. Sure enough, it's the deed to a house in Breaux Bridge, where Renard's mother lived. The form details the transfer of ownership from Renard Laurent and Sue Ellen Michaels to Jebediah Ray.

"Wait." I frown, grabbing the car title, then the boat one. "All of these are in Jebediah Ray's name."

"Exactly." Strangely, Ever's beaming. "That's the part that's gonna make this whole plan work. If a runner can't get his hands on enough cash to buy in, the Sons make him transfer ownership of something valuable. That way, if he runs off, the property's already theirs."

"So if you want to escape the Sons, all you lose is whatever you turned over?"

"No. The price for taking off is they hunt you down and kill you. Whatever you turned over is just a tax for the effort."

They hunt you down and kill you. Like I suspect they did to Fred. That's who we're messing with. Stone-cold killers. Professionals.

Ever taps the deed. "This is our proof Renard was mixed up with them. If we send deputies to their place in Forsythe and they catch them cooking *and* find this? Game over."

"But who's this Jebediah Ray?"

He hesitates for a moment, then says, "They call him the Serpent King. He's the leader of the Sons. They wear rattlesnakes on their jackets," he adds, off my dubious look. "It's their club symbol. Something to do with colonial America."

"Like 'Don't tread on me'?"

He snorts. "Exactly. Real patriotic heroes, these guys." Ever scoops the papers and stacks of cash into his shirt, lifting the hem to create a makeshift basket. "Help me get all this."

I seize his wrist. "What are you doing? We came here for the deed."

"And they'll know that if we don't take everything. It's gotta be a full robbery."

Every instinct screams this is wrong, not how the plan's supposed to go. I squeeze his wrist tighter. "You're stealing money from men you just said have no qualms about killing people."

"Don't worry. We're about to make it so they can't go after anyone. Too much attention coming their way."

When I don't move my hand, Ever sighs. "I need you to relax, Ruth. Desperate times, remember? It's them or us."

I imagine Sheriff Theriot's car rolling to a stop outside my house again, except this time he's there to cuff and drag me away through a gauntlet of people that includes my red-faced father, screaming about murder and mortal sins, and the horror-stricken faces of every person in Bottom Springs. My grip on Ever's wrist relaxes.

"All right, then. You take those stacks."

Once we've gathered everything, Ever wrestles the safe back into the gray cabinet and shuts the door. "Earl might not even notice anything's missing for a few days." He grins. "You wanna go back out the way you came?"

I glare at him. While we've been in here, dusk has deepened, and now only shreds of sunlight remain. I can barely make out his face, but his teeth are clear, gleaming white. "Stop having fun with this. What we're doing is seriously messed up."

The teeth come closer and closer until Ever's mouth is near my ear. My heart pounds at his proximity, at his cheek brushing mine, at the fact that it's getting harder to predict him. "Come on, Ruth," he whispers. "Admit it. You're having a *tiny* bit of fun."

There's no heat from his body; what makes me lean into him is more like a magnetic pull. It hits me again, the instinct to tell him about Barry's proposal. But the words stick in my throat. Instead, I whisper, "Not even a drop."

He turns, catching my eyes, and grins wider. "Race you to the car."

I roll my eyes, assuming he means to rile me up, but the second we've got the door locked, Ever takes off.

"Hey," I call, panicked, and suddenly adrenaline hits in one big surge, fireworks exploding in my chest, nerves firing, urging me to action. I take off behind him, one hand clutching my pile of cash, running like I've robbed a bank, like I'm an outlaw, the bane of the West. Bonnie and her Clyde.

Ever's already far ahead, ungodly fast, his laughter trailing behind him, high and ringing. I pump my legs faster, willing my body to match his, and that's when the giddiness hits, the sheer absurdity of fleeing the scene of a crime, the elation of the thick wads in my shirt, the relief of not getting caught, the beauty of all the trees bending over the path, like they're leaning in to watch us foolish creatures streak past.

Laughter bursts from me, and with it, despite the circumstances, comes pure, unbridled joy. *We got the deed, the plan is working, there's hope.*

We flat out sprint the last hundred feet to the car. Ever pops the trunk and we dump the money and papers. He leaps into the driver's seat and holds up a hand for me like I'm some kind of genteel lady, keeping me steady as I hop in. Ever revs the engine and turns his grin on me, a thousand stars in his eyes, moonlit skin glowing as the dusk deepens into night.

He must read something in my face because he shoves the car into drive and takes off so fast, I keel backward.

"Faster," I yell, and he laughs. The car's speedometer soars as we race down the backcountry road, kicking up plumes of dust. There's nobody but us back here, no witnesses but the faint emerging stars, and I'm seized by the urge to *do something*—something else I'd never do.

I climb to my knees in the passenger seat and throw my arms wide, head back, letting the wind whip my hair like a red banner. The trees rush past us, the air thick with the smell of pine needles. Up ahead, fireflies flicker. I'm beyond giddy: the earth is wild and beautiful and I'm alive inside it.

Ever whoops, pressing his foot to the gas, pushing the car even faster. The wind buffets me, lifting me until I'm almost flying. We're teenagers again, radiant and ungovernable. It's night and that's our time. I close my eyes at the crescent moon and howl, a loud, triumphant sound, a sound to announce myself. Ever's laughter beside me is music.

But even now, in my rare freedom, I can't escape the smallest seed of guilt. I'm Ruth Cornier, after all, and I *know* better—really, I do. I know how dangerous it is to climb this high. (I stretch my hands up to the stars regardless.) I know what it means to set yourself up for a fall. (Even still, I breathe deep from the air whipping past.) I have been here before, I have leapt, I have shattered.

I howl again. What do you call it when you know better, but—

20

JUNE, ELEVEN YEARS OLD

I'd never won a single thing in my life until today. I was sure it was coming, sure my name was on the tip of Mr. Blanchard's tongue, the way he kept darting secret glances at me. I sat up straighter, practically buzzing with anticipation as he walked a zigzag route among the desks, bending over students' shoulders to take a look at their poems.

Mr. Blanchard spent a long time bent over mine—so long I'd thought I'd combust from anxiety, the strangeness of having an adult so close I could feel the heat from his skin, the brush of his trouser leg, see the dark, wiry hairs on his hands. I had to sit on my own hands to keep stock-still and rigid like a good student, a good pastor's daughter, a good girl. Luckily, I was well practiced in self-containment. Much better than the other students, who squirmed and yawned and whispered when they weren't supposed to.

I could tell Mr. Blanchard appreciated my rigor. When he was finished reading my poem, he made a low hum of approval in the back of his throat. It was enough to get my hopes up. In regular school I was mostly ignored, quiet and well behaved enough to turn invisible. But here at Vacation Bible School, where the Godly children of Bottom Springs spent their summers, I had a leg up from a lifetime of studying the Bible under my father's watchful eye.

"I've come to a decision," announced Mr. Blanchard, moving to the head of the class. He folded his hands over his stomach, eyes gleaming as he waited for the whispers to cease.

Mr. Herman Blanchard was young as far as teachers went—only twenty-seven—and a study in contradictions. He was short and wore his hair combed over like an old man, despite the fact that he had no bald spots to hide. He dressed in the same outfit every day—ill-fitting khaki trousers and a white short-sleeved button-down—and wore thick glasses that magnified his eyes, making him look perpetually startled. As for his mannerisms, he leaned toward a kind of carefree impishness that estranged him from other adults—I once heard my father say Herman had the demeanor of a man who'd never faced the word no—but endeared him to children.

Herman was the only child of Augustus Blanchard, the rich man on the mountain, or so we called him, since he lived in the biggest house in Bottom Springs at the top of what passed for a hill around here. Augustus was considered a Godly man despite the fact that people rarely saw him. He came down from the mountain once every few months to attend church, where he walked around with a stiff back and refused to speak to anyone but my father. But the fact that Herman was his son, and that he would one day inherit the entirety of the Blanchard Hospital fortune, made him someone other adults were forced to treat with respect.

His eyes swept the classroom, pausing on students who squirmed in their seats, and finally landed on me. I wanted to throw up from an overwhelming mix of terror and delight.

"The winner of our poem contest," Mr. Blanchard trilled, "is Miss Ruth Cornier, who wrote a lovely little ditty about her namesake."

As I'd feared and desired, the eyes of my fellow students turned to me, telegraphing resentment and begrudging admiration. Our assignment from Mr. Blanchard had been to choose a heroic figure from the Bible and write a poem about them. The winner would get a prize worth its weight in gold: a trip with Mr. Blanchard to the newly opened Dairy Queen in Forsythe, rumored to have ice cream treats called Blizzards that were so thick you could turn them upside down and nothing would fall out. With stakes that high, I'd chosen Ruth. I knew her best, having studied her closest out of vain self-interest.

I couldn't believe I'd actually done something someone thought was good.

"Ruth, tell us what makes Ruth so special." The corners of Mr. Blanchard's eyes crinkled at his joke.

"She—" My voice cracked, unused to being used in public, and some of the students glanced at each other with knowing smirks. I struggled to regain myself. "Was known for her kindness."

"Right." He nodded. "But I liked the other part of your poem best. Why do we *really* consider Ruth one of the most important women in the Bible?"

"Because of her loyalty. She followed her mother-in-law, Naomi, into Judah even though she risked her life. Ruth was—" I thought of something I'd heard my father say. "Relentlessly obedient to her elders."

"Excellent." Mr. Blanchard beamed. "And she was rewarded in the end, as we all will be, so long as we too obey our elders, even when it might seem wrong. Ruth, you'll have the pleasure of joining me at Dairy Queen."

I'd just begun to soak in my triumph when he added, "But!"

All eyes jerked back to him.

"There was one other poem that deserved a prize."

My stomach dropped.

Mr. Blanchard turned his beaming face to Lila. "Miss Lila LeBlanc."

The shock sent whispers around the room. Lila, who'd been slumped in her chair with a vacant expression, twisting a finger in her long blond hair, suddenly straightened. She looked as surprised as anyone.

"Who did you write about, Lila?"

She hesitated a moment—then said, in a defiant voice, "Mary Magdalene."

The classroom broke into loud titters. Even at eleven, we knew Mary Magdalene was a whore, not a hero.

"Quiet," Mr. Blanchard shushed. "Now, why did you choose Mary?"

Lila bit her lip. Most of the time she acted confident, but once in a while, her veneer cracked and I got a glimpse of her self-doubt. It made it hard to dislike her, no matter how skewed life seemed in her favor.

"Because even though Mary did bad things in the past," Lila said, "she believed in Jesus more than anyone. She was the first person to see his empty tomb."

"Very clever." Behind his thick lenses, Mr. Blanchard's eyes blinked tremulously. "Mary Magdalene teaches us that it's possible for even great sinners to be redeemed. As long as we repent, there's room for all of us in the Kingdom of Heaven."

I frowned at my clenched fists, hidden underneath my desk. Not only did it sting to share my victory with Lila, but the way Mr. Blanchard talked about sinning was different from my father. Mr. Blanchard made it seem light and easy—make a mistake, repent, and it's erased. According to my father, sinners were owed heavy punishment and got no guarantees.

"Congratulations, Lila. You'll join us at Dairy Queen this afternoon." Mr. Blanchard clapped. "All right, children. Next we're going to talk about Samson and Delilah. Take out your workbooks."

As students sighed and shifted, Lila's eyes met mine from across the room. We rarely spoke to each other, being so different. But we were going to sit together in Mr. Blanchard's green Jaguar all the way to Forsythe, then share the prize of Blizzards. Was she annoyed to be stuck with me? I had no idea how to react.

Suddenly—tentative as the first light at dawn—the corners of Lila's mouth lifted in a smile.

"What clever girls you are," said Mr. Blanchard, holding our hands. "Be sure to keep a tight grip on me. We don't want you getting lost."

"Yes, Mr. Blanchard," said Lila and I in matching singsong. We were on our way to ice cream and on our best behavior.

Lila stole a glance at me as we walked across the church parking lot. I smiled, emboldened by her earlier kindness, and she grinned back.

"I'm going to get a gummy bear *and* Oreo Blizzard," she blurted, as if the information was finally too much to keep inside.

I raised my brows, impressed. "I didn't know you could get more than one topping."

"You can get as many as you want," she chirped. "That's what I heard."

"Hurry up, girls," said Mr. Blanchard, tugging us forward. "We don't want to get caught in traffic."

Lila and I practically scurried to match Mr. Blanchard's purposeful strides. He moved faster than I would've thought possible with his short legs.

"All right," he said, sounding frazzled as he popped open the passenger door of his car. He wiped his brow on his shirtsleeve. "I think both you ladies can fit in the front seat. It'll be our little secret, okay?"

Lila and I giggled.

"Herman Blanchard," boomed a voice, and the three of us startled, spinning in the direction of the sound. Before I could collect my wits, my father was upon us, a bull charging the last few feet across the parking lot. Instinctively, I cowered back, bony shoulders hitting Mr. Blanchard's car. I'd seen my father rage many times, but this time, he was incandescent with fury. His very hair seemed to writhe, the veins in his neck bulging.

"Reverend." Mr. Blanchard's voice trembled. I'd never heard him scared. I had no idea what was happening.

"I *told* you," my father snarled. "Not her. Do you hear me? Never her."

He lunged and seized my arm, pulling me violently off the car. I cried out in pain and Lila gasped, but my father's grip didn't loosen. He stepped toward Mr. Blanchard, and Mr. Blanchard staggered back, almost tripping into the open passenger door.

My father raised his hand in Mr. Blanchard's face. "You so much as look at Ruth again, and I'm going straight to your father. Do you hear me?" Mr. Blanchard's eyes darted around the parking lot, whether searching for help or witnesses, I didn't know. "One more time and Augustus knows."

My father didn't wait for Mr. Blanchard to respond. He stalked away, pulling me with him with such force I thought my arm might pop.

"Please, Daddy." Hot tears ran down my cheeks. "I won the poem contest. Mr. Blanchard was taking us to Dairy Queen. It's not that far away, and I've never won anything before, and Lila—"

"Quiet, Ruth." I felt the command in my bones. "No one asked you to speak."

As he yanked me back to church, I twisted over my shoulder to find Mr. Blanchard already sitting in the driver's seat, his door closed. But Lila stood by the passenger door, still watching me with a storm of emotions passing over her face, among them pity and regret.

I cried hardest to know Lila had witnessed what my father really thought of me, how little I meant, how I didn't deserve one simple pleasure. My heart crumbled as I watched her turn and slide into the passenger seat. The door closed behind her with a smack that echoed across the parking lot, and off they went: Mr. Blanchard and Lila, the lucky one.

21

NOW

The bar emerges out of the trees like a mirage. One minute, there's a thick sea of cypresses on both sides of the road, the air clotted with the smell of bayou vegetation; the next, an army of parked motorcycles guarding a squat brown building with no sign and people everywhere. White men, mostly, sauntering up and down the ramp to the door holding longnecks in smokers' circles around the bikes or bent over the deck railing, spitting chew. With Everett's convertible top down, I can smell the acrid tang of the smoke and hear the pounding music from behind the door, muffled like it's underwater.

"Told you," Ever says quietly, his eyes dark. "Rattlesnakes."

We turn into the dirt lot, earning narrow-eyed stares from those we pass. Ever's right—despite the summer heat, most of the men wear thick leather jackets with coiled rattlesnakes sewn onto the back, raised to strike. So much skin covered in black ink: tattoos running up necks, even carved across cheeks.

We've stepped onto the other side of the law. Entered an outlaw world for people who deal in thievery and death. This isn't a game anymore—we're not stealing from some backcountry garage. We're in Forsythe, on the edge of a dark, deep bayou at the place Ever said we'd find the

Sons of Liberty. I can feel these men's hardness, the violence in the air, their scrutiny sharp as a knife's edge. These people would hurt us and not think twice.

Ever parks. "It's not too late to change your mind."

"No."

"Are you sure?"

I glance behind us. Over the roof of the bar, the setting sun glints through the trees, casting an orange light, eerie and strange, like a portent of trouble.

"No," I repeat, and kick open the door.

All eyes are on us as we walk to the entrance. From somewhere Ever procured a leather jacket, a thing he said he simply "got around," and now he moves with a reckless swagger I struggle to imitate. He looks different with the jacket on, like that alien, distant creature he was before I got to know him. I'm forced to remember he's been outside Bottom Springs for years now, living a life I know nothing about.

A man spits at my feet when we reach the door. A nasty grin splits his face and I look away quickly, heart pounding. The noise behind the door grows louder. Ever grips the handle.

"Don't talk to anybody," he says under his breath. "Don't take anything anyone offers. Try not to make eye contact. Follow my lead."

I nod, so slight it's almost imperceptible, and he yanks open the door.

Dark synth rock rushes at us, a hard, sinister wall of sound. As we move inside, parting the dark, the music snakes inside me, trying to take over my heartbeat. The bar's crowded with tattooed men I glimpse in flashes from the flickering bulbs swinging from the ceiling. There's so much cigarette smoke it acts like a veil, plumes that shield the men we pass until they move and break the illusion. A man to our left lunges, cackling as another man staggers back. Against the walls, the smoke curls around women lined up, dressed in impossibly short skirts like the one I saw on Beth the night she snuck in. Their hair is teased big and their makeup heavy. Some of them stare vacantly. Others won't look up from their feet. All look like they're waiting to be plucked.

I do my best not to make eye contact as I follow Ever to the bar, but it's hard not to stare at the people snorting white powder off their hands and tabletops. Faces in here are sheened with sweat, more than the humidity calls for. Men emerge out of the smoke with dilated pupils, as if seeing ghosts.

"Let's get drinks," Everett says, voice raised over the music. I can barely see him in the flickering lights. "Can't be empty-handed."

"Beer, then," I say, and Ever slides a bill across the counter to the bartender.

When our drinks arrive, I take mine and turn. "Tell me again."

His arm brushes mine as he takes a swig of beer, eyes cast out over the tables. "About ten years older than us. Shaved head with a snake tattoo. Thick, muscular. Long blond beard."

Jebediah Ray: part one of the plan.

I crane my neck, squinting to see. "Come on," Ever says, slapping my shoulder. "Let's move in."

We weave through the smoke, eyeing the men we pass as subtly as possible. I hate that my hands are shaking, so I keep tipping the beer to my mouth, even though I don't like the taste. After a minute of this, the razor's edge of fear dulls. It's when I take my last sip, my bottle light and empty, that I see him. There, in the back of the room at a crowded table, surrounded by men like a king thronged by subjects. Head bare so the first thing I notice is the enormous snake, its mouth open wide across his skull, fangs dripping, sinuous body coiling in a spiral down his neck. His long beard is braided, the end touching his chest, and though he's listening to someone talk, his eyes roam restlessly, the scan of a predator taking stock of his surroundings.

I squeeze Ever's hand and nod.

"Good," Ever murmurs. "Eyes on him, but not obvious. Let's stand over there to stay hidden."

We're walking to join the women on the wall when a man stops in front of Ever, solid as a house, and shoves him. He's large, with long, wild hair trailing down his arms, and a leather vest with nothing underneath. A friend stands behind him, a foot taller, with a raised scar that bisects his face from lip to eyebrow. It looks like a knife wound healed wrong. "Hey," the first man says, raising his chin. "Stranger. We don't know you."

I take a small step back. We're caught.

But Ever doesn't flinch. "Just passing through. Heard this was the place to be."

"Oh yeah?" The man raises his eyebrows. "We don't like people hearing so much about us."

Ever shrugs, casual. "Then tell your friends to stop running their mouths. Heard about y'all all the way out in Trouville."

There's a moment of charged silence as the two Sons glance at each other. Then the taller man says, in a swampland accent so thick it's nearly indecipherable, "Trouville, huh? I reckon we got people out there. Whatchu want then?"

Ever looks around. "Here?"

"You see any five-o?"

To my surprise, Everett slips his hand inside his leather jacket, peeling out a handful of crinkled bills—money from the safe. He slides the bills between his fingers, making them dance. The men's eyes follow. "Whatchu got?"

I bite back a protest. Ever's going off script.

Eyeing the money, the man with the long hair pulls out a plastic bag of white powder from inside his vest. "This shit'll knock you sideways."

I bite the inside of my mouth as Ever nods. "If you say so."

The man yanks back the baggie and wags it just out of Ever's reach. "Don't you want to sample first?"

I shift, trying to communicate *no* without speaking, but it's the long-haired man, not Ever, who notices. As the overhead lights flicker, I watch his hungry gaze travel the length of my body. His tongue darts out to lick his lower lip.

"Sure, I'll try it," says Ever smoothly, standing squarely in front of me and blocking the man's sight. I breathe again the moment his eyes are gone. "Why not?"

The man shakes powder onto his hand and holds it up to Ever with a look of challenge. Before I can figure out how to get him out of this, Ever snorts the powder in one long rip, like he's done it before. It's abrupt, almost violent, and at the same time intimate, the man's hand so close to Ever's face, almost like he's cupping it.

I freeze in horror.

"How 'bout her?" The tall man nods at me, and the long-haired man shakes out another bump.

"Not her choice of poison," says Ever coolly, and before the men can insist, he snorts the second line, then reels back, almost stepping into me.

I press my hands against his shoulders, steadying him though I want to shake him. Our plan is spiraling.

"All right now, boy." The long-haired man wipes his hand against his jeans. "You racking up a tab." He tosses the baggie of powder at Everett's chest. "Least we know you're not a cop."

Ever leans closer and opens his jacket. "Maybe I've got a bigger appetite. What would you say to that?"

The long-haired man's eyes widen, and the tall man whistles, long and low. I can't see what's inside Ever's jacket, but I have a feeling it's the rest of the money from the safe. Enough money to demand their attention.

"Woo!" The long-haired man slaps his hands together. "I'd say you came to the right place, Trouville. You and me 'bout to be good friends." He grins at me over Everett's shoulder. "You too, quiet lady. What I got to do to make you talk?"

Ever snakes his arm around my waist, tucking me into his side. "Like I said, she has particular tastes." He smiles wide, showing off his canines.

The long-haired man laughs. "Fuck, no need to fight over pussy. We got plenty."

"Shoot." The tall man with the scar nudges his friend. "He almost pretty as her when he smiles."

The two crack up. Their grating laughter makes me stand ramrod straight. It's one thing to hear them call me names, but hearing Everett speak their language bristles.

Across the room, Jebediah Ray suddenly stands. That triggers mass movement: the crowd of men ringing him stumble or stagger to their feet, taking last sips of beers, eyeing the women against the wall. Together, they move through the bar, Jebediah the point of the crown.

"It's your lucky day, Trouville." The man with the long hair beckons us. "You didn't have to wait long. Follow us."

We lose ourselves in the crowd making their way out of the bar, Ever's arm still circling my waist. As soon as the two men's backs are turned, I lean in and hiss under my breath, "Who *are* you, with those drugs? And why are you trying to buy more? That's not what we planned."

Ever glances at the men's backs and leans over like he's going to kiss under my ear. "We never would've gotten into Jebediah's place if we'd tried to follow them," he whispers. "We had to be invited. The only way to be invited is to buy big."

I start to reel back, but he cups my jaw, holding me still. "I didn't tell you because I knew what you'd say. But look. It worked."

We burst out of the bar and follow our Sons down the ramp to the motorcycles. The night is pitch-black and frantic with the sounds of croaking frogs, chittering grasshoppers, the bayou on edge. I squash the impulse to run for Everett's car.

He straightens up. "We can follow y'all in my—"

"Stop you right there," the long-haired man says, leaning against a large bike. It's matte black, like it's meant to disappear into the night. "No outside cars." He pats the bike seat. "You want to buy, you ride with us."

Ever glances down at me—a look that lasts only a second, but I read a world of meaning. *Please, we have no choice; everything will be okay*. "Fine," he says to the man. Before he releases me, he whispers, "*Count of Monte Cristo*, remember? Whatever dark lengths."

We mount up on the bikes, Everett behind the long-haired man, me behind the scarred one. My heart beats rapid-fire, straining against my rib cage. Around us, nearly a hundred bikes rev, the noise of the engines like beasts roaring. How have I gotten here?

"Hold tight," the scarred man yells, but I refuse to touch him until the bike thunders to life, the vibrations chattering my teeth, and suddenly we lunge forward. Only then do I fasten my arms around his waist, pressing my cheek to the coiled rattlesnake on his back.

From the back of his bike, Everett finds my eyes. Whatever he's snorted has hit him: his eyes are glassy and unfocused, high cheekbones tinged with pink. For a single charged moment, we stare at each other in dread, and then his motorcycle takes off. Mine roars behind it.

Like a swarm of locusts, the Sons of Liberty explode out of the parking lot onto the dirt road. Wind rips our hair as we charge forward, one large army, a hundred men's war cries filling the night.

22

NOW

Jebediah's compound appears in the distance, lit by floodlights and ringed by bonfires, so thundering toward it feels like racing toward the heart of Hell. When we pull up, there are people camped out everywhere on the wide expanse of yard. We must be on the outermost edge of Forsythe now, where the cops don't patrol, because I can't imagine anyone seeing this massive building crawling with people and not knowing immediately it's a place where bad things happen.

I think of *An Arcane History of Your Backyard*: all those men sailing to this corner of the world to stake their claims and build their castles, ravaging whoever stood in their way. What is it about Louisiana that gives so many men delusions of grandeur? Is it the swampland, the primordial landscape sparking primal urges?

I nearly fall off the bike when the scarred man kicks the stand, my legs weak from squeezing so tight. Immediately, Everett is by my side, gripping my arms.

"Follow me, Trouville," rasps the long-haired man. "We're going inside."

As he leads us across the lawn, I finally see the wisdom of Ever's plan. In my version, where we tracked Jebediah to his home, we had to sneak in undetected. But as buyers, we walk in the front door.

One more crime to end it, I whisper to myself.

"Something's wrong," Ever murmurs, as we step over holes in the grass.

I set my attention on the lawn around me and feel it: a thick unease. From opposite sides of the bonfires blazing around the yard, men eye each other distrustfully.

"Fuck you, then," shouts a bearded man in a rattlesnake jacket, lunging for a man with a cross tattooed on his neck. Two other Sons of Liberty grab the first and hold him back.

The long-haired man leading us snickers. "You picked a dicey time to be here. We got a faction of them country boys from up north here, tryna' to work out a truce."

"Truce?" Ever ventures. "What, you got a mutual enemy or something?"

He grins wide, showing off a silver tooth. "Nah. A common need. We been fightin' over territory for years, but these days our supply chain ain't been the most stable, you feel me? We need options." He shakes his head. "But them pig-fuckers 'bout overstayed they welcome."

Ever and I glance at each other as we snake around one of the bonfires, sparks drifting near our faces. His fingers brush mine and I take his hand. Into the belly of the beast.

Inside the compound is a whole new world, as methodical and organized as the outside was chaotic. The large kitchen we enter runs like a well-oiled machine, leather-jacketed men moving stacks of money and rubber-band-bound bags of weed, pills, and powder across tables, riffing numbers and instructions to one another.

"Wait here," our long-haired Son says, and takes off. As soon as his back's turned, Ever nods.

"Be fast," he whispers, sliding the papers out of his jacket. "Find somewhere to hide it, but don't make it too obvious. And don't get caught."

I nod, heart in my throat. This was always part of the plan: where I step up, and Ever acts as a distraction.

I keep my head down and slip out of the kitchen into a hallway where more people mill. I'd like to hide Renard's deed in as incriminating a spot as possible, a place the deputies will surely look when Ever and I call in our tip. I just have no idea where that is.

Count of Monte Cristo. I can do that—play a part like the Count, suffer indignities for the sake of triumph in the end. I loosen my gait, stumbling a little down the hall, and start opening doors. Most are empty bedrooms, but in one I find a man stretched out on a futon. The moment I swing open the door, he jerks up and grabs the handgun at his side, pointing it at me.

"Oh." I slur, speaking slow despite my pounding heart. "This isn't the bathroom."

The man's eyes are dilated, black pupils eating the white. He stares at me, the barrel of the gun shaking.

"Nah," he says finally, "it's not," and collapses back onto the couch, gun slumping to the floor.

I shut the door quietly and press my back to the wall, heart thumping so hard I actually do feel high. *Keep going. Everything is riding on this.*

A door at the end of the hall opens and a man in a wifebeater walks out, dripping with sweat, sucking in a deep breath before turning the corner. I straighten. Behind him I'd glimpsed a staircase descending into the dark. If I was Jebediah Ray, that's where I'd keep my most incriminating things—hidden in the bowels of my house.

I check to make sure no one's watching and slip inside.

The smell of ammonia is so overpowering I gag and almost turn back. I press a hand over my mouth, forcing myself down the stairs. A large basement stretches before me. Lining the walls are black plastic shelves, the kind you assemble yourself, filled with liters of fluorescent-colored chemicals, stacks of plastic bags, zip ties, and gram scales. In the center of the room are four islands with stove tops, the burners covered in black-bottomed pots. Thankfully, there's no one else here.

I creep closer to read the labels on the liters, despite the fact that I know I need to plant the deed and get out. It's just—this is where the Sons cook. There are no windows, the only light from bulbs hanging from the ceiling, so the place is dim and suffocating. How hot it must get in the daytime, in the thick bayou heat, with all the burners going. Like Hell on earth.

Footsteps shake the ceiling, rustling loose dust that rains down, and I snap out of my morbid fascination. There's a desk scattered with papers in the farthest corner. I beeline to it. If I hide Renard's deed in this cookroom, among those papers, the deputies will surely find it, right? Out of all the rooms in this place, this is where crime is most evident, most concentrated. It will be a magnet for the cops. I feel a strange urge to kiss the deed before filing it away: the potential key to our freedom.

Heavy footsteps pound the floor above me—the sound of people running. The hairs on my arms rise. I shove the deed into a pile of papers, making sure it's covered, and whirl away. I need to get back to Ever as fast as I can.

But my feet catch on something and I fall hard to my knees on the concrete. Muffling a sob, I kick at whatever tripped me, shaking it off my feet, then look to see what it was. An upturned cardboard box. Felled by cardboard.

I don't know where it comes from, but from one second to the next, the rage is there. I'm in this basement, risking my life to avoid prison, just because I happened to kill the man who tried to rape me—*rape* me. The injustice of it makes me choke, and suddenly I'm kicking the boxes, over and over, hot tears spilling down my cheeks.

The boxes slide over the floor, pinwheeling as I kick them, and a small white paper pokes out. I seize it, eager to have something to tear. Then I freeze.

It's the kind of paper you'd find on a notepad, blank except for an address printed at the bottom: 300 Old Highway 1, Bottom Springs, Louisiana 70357. I know that address. Everyone in Bottom Springs knows that address.

Blanchard Hospital.

I stare at the boxes. They're stealing drugs from Blanchard. That's how they're getting their hands on the oxycodone and other painkillers—they're stealing from doctors and patients, from people who need it, only to turn around and feed other people's sicknesses. No wonder the long-haired Son said their supply chain had grown unstable. It couldn't be easy to keep up such large-scale theft under authorities' noses.

A gunshot cracks like thunder, the sound unmistakable, paralyzing me.

All hell breaks loose. Footsteps stampede across the ceiling, followed by shouts and screams that travel through the floorboards.

Everett's up there.

I scramble to my feet and bound up the stairs two at a time. The basement door opens to chaos, people running down the hall and screaming, men charging in the other direction holding shotguns. I barrel toward the kitchen but am shoved by a giant leather-jacketed man with a gun running past. The impact throws me into the wall, making me bite my tongue, but I push off and keep going, streaking into the kitchen.

I spin in frantic circles. The kitchen's been barricaded, tables shoved against the windows. Men are sweeping cash and weed into grocery bags, rushing past with guns held high, crouching by the windows. I can't find Everett in this maelstrom of people.

Something shatters a window, and I scream as glass goes flying. The men start firing, each boom so loud my ears ring. The front door flings open, and men with crosses on their necks start to pour through—the country boys from up north.

I'm standing in the middle of a war, unable to move, panic locking my limbs.

"Ruth!"

Everett. I turn, relief flooding me until I realize he's pointing over my shoulder.

I whip around just as a bald man with a crucifix under his ear levels a gun at me and pulls the trigger.

I'm struck by an incredible force that sends me tumbling to the linoleum. Time dilates: my ears ring, dulling the explosion of gunshots, my vision swimming so all I can make sense of is the pressure of another body lying across me.

"Ruth!" Ever shouts. He's here, in my face, shaking me.

The world tilts. I can't breathe with the wind knocked out of me.

Gunfire thunders rapid-fire. "We have to go." Ever lifts me by the shoulders clean off the floor. That's when I see the rip in his leather jacket, the crimson smear of blood.

Horror cuts through the haze. "You're bleeding," I rasp. "Ever, you're *shot*."

"Run *now*." He yanks me out of the kitchen, and as I turn, I see the man who fired at me reloading.

All reason flees. I drop Ever's hand and together we race through a den, dodging people and overturned furniture, until we burst out the back door into the yard.

It's a hellscape—open battle, lit by bonfire flames. Men shoot at each other from behind cars and fight in the grass, shoving each other's faces in the mud. One Son wields a flaming log like a sword, the ground behind him ablaze, fire quickly spreading.

"Shit." Ever clutches his arm. "Keep going, Ruth. He's right behind us."

God help us. I run so fast my legs and arms feel like they're on fire, but I don't let myself stop. Ever grunts beside me, faster than me but guarding my back, somehow able to do it even though he's shot. He shouldn't be able to move like this injured. I want to believe it's the adrenaline, but when his face was pressed close to mine, I saw his wild pupils. He's under the hold of the drugs.

The sound of a close gunshot makes me turn over my shoulder. The bald man takes aim again. A sob escapes my throat.

"Eyes ahead!" Ever yells, but suddenly there's another gunshot and the man chasing us rocks back like he's been punched. A perfect circle of blood blooms on his chest, and then he's down in the grass.

He's dead.

A hysterical laugh bubbles out of me and my legs give out. I bend over, hands clutching my knees, chest heaving as I try to fill my lungs with air and laugh at the same time.

"Hey." Ever is beside me, rubbing soothing circles on my back. "You're having a panic attack. It's okay; it's understandable. But the bayou's just ahead. Just make it there, and we'll lose them in the water, okay?"

I look up at him—his face flushed pink, beads of sweat glistening along his nose, eyes so round and otherworldly—and shout, "You could've *died*."

"Now's not the time—" He stops, glances back at the compound, and groans. "The bullet just grazed me. I'm going to be fine, Ruth."

"But you didn't know that when you jumped. When you stepped in front of me, you didn't know."

"Listen." Everett crouches, bringing his face level with mine. We're both breathing hard. All the stars in his eyes have been blown out, eclipsed. "I'm never going to let anything happen to you." He squeezes my shoulders. "Which is why you have to trust me when I say we need to keep going."

I want to sink into his eyes—the total darkness of oblivion and peace—but I force myself to stand, recognizing the hot-wire urgency of his words. And the minute I do, the volume on the world turns back up: gunfire and shouting, roaring at full blast.

Ever seizes my arm. "Eyes ahead, Ruth. Go!"

I pull the last dregs of strength from my body and take off.

"Don't stop," shouts Ever from beside me. "Don't let them catch us."

His words trigger an old warning, given to me before I was old enough to understand. That harsh, deep voice comes back: *You must never let them catch you.* Ahead, moonlight glitters on the bayou, and I know in my heart: I would rather drown in it than be caught.

23

AUGUST, THIRTEEN YEARS OLD

Always, the men descended on our house at night. Once every few months, our front door would swing open so fast it cracked into the wall and my father's baritone laugh would boom through the hall, followed by their too-loud voices as they stumbled after him. Shiny faces and unfocused eyes, spills down their shirts, blood scabbed on their knuckles from whatever they'd been up to besides drinking. I was always swept upstairs immediately, so I never found out, but I'd heard my mother refer to these nights as my father's "social hours."

Tonight, the sudden tornado of braying and hooting was the only warning before they poured inside, more men than usual, their presence freezing me at the kitchen sink. I stood listening to their laughter as they made their way to my father's secret liquor cabinet until the water overflowed my cup and spilled down my hands. Hurriedly, I turned off the faucet.

I was wiping my hands on the kitchen towel, planning how to avoid them—a mad dash up the stairs, maybe, or a slink through the shadows—when Augustus Blanchard shuffled into the kitchen, bent stiffly over his cane.

He stopped in his tracks when he saw me. I flushed hot, cheeks burning—caught in my nightshirt by Augustus Blanchard, of all people, who was less a real man than a myth. Before this moment, I'd only seen him in profile. On the rare Sundays Augustus came down from the mountain, I passed the time staring at him while my father lectured, wondering what marvels filled his enormous house.

His lips peeled back in a strange smile, showing too much of his gums. "Miss Ruth Cornier." He had a stentorian voice with only the faintest bit of our drawl, which gave him an air of grandeur. Even now, late at night, he wore a dark three-piece suit with a pocket watch tucked into his vest, the gold chain swinging.

I didn't respond—only thought hard, trying to understand what I was supposed to do. His eyes—green once, maybe, but now discolored with age—narrowed keenly. He took a fat brown cigar and a lighter from inside his jacket and, to my horror, stuck the cigar in his mouth and lit it, puffing out smoke like a fire-breathing dragon.

There was no smoking allowed in our house. But maybe Augustus was above even my mother's authority.

"What do you think of all this ruckus, Ruth?" Augustus puffed on the cigar again, then waved it at the house. The rich scent of tobacco traveled to me.

"It's daddy's social hour," I whispered, and to my surprise, that elicited a great booming laugh.

"Well," he said, settling his great body into a chair at the kitchen table. "Aren't you clever." He patted the table. "Sit. Let's test this mind of yours. I enjoy talking to young ones. Imparting my knowledge. With Herman, he was never..." He let his voice trail off, then patted the table again insistently.

Though I wasn't supposed to be out here and it was the last thing I wanted, the instinct to obey was automatic. My legs dragged me to the table and dropped me in a chair. I watched Augustus carefully, the way a rabbit watches a bobcat. In the window over his shoulder, I could see men filtering into the backyard, the glowing orbs of their cigars like fireflies bobbing in the dark.

"Tell me what you're reading in school," Augustus said, folding a hand over his cane, the top of which was carved in the shape of a bear's head. I'd heard a rumor its glittering red eyes were made of real rubies.

His question took me by surprise. I looked down at the table and answered truthfully. "*Where the Red Fern Grows.*"

"Disgraceful." He puffed his cigar, then waved. "Fluff."

"But..." I lowered my voice. "I'm reading *Little Women* on my own."

I don't know why I said it. Maybe deep down I was vain and proud and wanted Augustus Blanchard to know I was smart. And since I couldn't tell him about the books I'd found in the town library, like the Percy Jacksons, *Little Women* was my safest confession.

"Ah." His bushy eyebrows raised. "A reader, then." He eyed me. "Dangerous quality in a girl."

It was like he could see inside my soul with those cloudy eyes. Silence stretched between us until Augustus knocked ash from his cigar onto the kitchen table. "If you had to sum up the lesson of *Little Women* in one word, what would it be?" He sounded like his son then, like a teacher.

Independence, I thought. "Duty," I said carefully.

He studied me for a long time before his face split into a great gummy smile. "Well, look at you. It seems James has a ticking time bomb on his hands. I do admire a learned woman, Miss Ruth. They're as rare as those exotic birds at the zoo." He cocked his head. "You ever been to that zoo up in New Orleans?"

I shook my head.

"Ah, well. Zoos are places we hold creatures that are better off caged. Kept contained, you hear?"

He was waiting for my response, so I nodded. Unease crept through my belly.

"Are you going to grow up a good girl, Miss Ruth, or are you going to be a threat to your daddy?" His smile grew so wide I could see the dark crescents where his gums were pulling back from his teeth. "He gonna need to cage you?"

Both sets of eyes—Augustus's and the bear's glowing rubies—locked on me. He sucked on his cigar and the end flared, a perfect, quarter-sized circle of fire.

"A good girl," I whispered. For the first time, I longed for the noise of the other men. Someone besides me and Augustus, alone in the house.

He knocked more ash on the table. "I have a secret for you. Do you want to hear?"

I didn't answer.

"Some people, like some animals, belong in cages. I know that better than anyone. Sometimes even good seed bears rotten fruit. Split it open, peer inside, and you'll find nothing but maggots." A feeling seemed to seize him. He smacked the table so hard it rattled and roared, "Through no fault of your own, you hear?"

I cowered back.

"You're a smart girl, Ruth. So I'm going to tell you the truth. Maybe it'll spare your daddy what I wasn't." His voice was thick. In his hand, his cigar burned down. "Men'll do wicked things to a slip like you. They'll take their fill and leave you twisted and broken like a little bird on the side of the road, mark my words. It's in their nature—they can't help themselves. Beasts, all of them. That's the evil your daddy fights against."

I stared at him, hypnotized.

"Your daddy," he repeated, flicking the gold rings on his fingers, "is out there every day fighting the beasts that live inside men's and women's souls. It's a great and holy war, Ruth. The highest mission, trying to contain them, make them docile, sedated. Do you know what life would be like without civilizers like him?"

He was waiting. There would be no relief until I spoke. "No," I whispered.

"Destruction and chaos would reign. Men raping, beating, killing. Women fucking at their whim. Hell on earth."

I went rigid at the curse word, but he continued.

"That's the gift God gave us with his teachings. Religion's the only thing strong enough to tame the beast." His cloudy eyes searched my face. "I want to make sure you understand. You should be very grateful to your daddy. Christ's laws are the only thing standing between you and men's hunger. And let me tell you, that hunger is endless. Perverse and sickening. I've witnessed it firsthand. You be a good girl and stay right here under your daddy's protection."

"Augustus, there you are." My father bounded into the kitchen. Immediately, his expression hardened. "Ruth, why aren't you in your room? You know you aren't allowed down when we have company."

I lit up from the table as fast as I could. "Yes, Daddy. I was only getting water."

He turned apologetic eyes to Augustus. He didn't even blink when Augustus blew out a lazy ring of smoke. "We apologize. She'll be punished if she bothered you."

I didn't flinch—only kept moving. Facing the cane would be worth it to escape.

"Miss Ruth," rumbled Augustus. I turned back, though I dreaded it.

"Better move fast past them men, little bird. Whatever you do, *you must never let them catch you.*" He hissed the last part, and when I startled back, he boomed with laughter, clutching his cane. His laugh followed me as I ran up the stairs and down the hall. Even when I shut the door and hid under the covers, I swear the spirit of Augustus Blanchard snaked up through the floorboards, searching for me, a spectral bear with ruby eyes.

24

NOW

I watch the news, waiting to see Jebediah Ray's compound appear on TV, but there's nothing. No breaking alerts that men have been shot in Forsythe or a suspect in the Renard Michaels case has been found. All this silence despite the tip Ever called in to the sheriff two days ago. I've told myself to stick to my routine, do nothing to arouse suspicion, but it's hard to act normal when the entire town of Bottom Springs has turned into a powder keg, ready to blow.

"Look at them," Nissa says in a low voice as we walk down Main Street. "It's a feeding frenzy."

Main Street is more alive than I've ever seen it—it feels like the entire town is here, huddled in circles outside the Piggly Wiggly, staring distrustfully out the windows of Old Man Jonas's bait shop, running Dale's Country Corner out of gas, like a hurricane is coming. I've seen Bottom Springs on high alert before, seen the rumor mill whirring, but never like this.

"What's happening?" I ask Nissa. We're making our way back to the library from a rare lunch at the Rosethorn Café. She'd asked me to go—a treat, since we both usually saved money by bringing lunch from home—and I'd said yes to pretend there was nothing amiss. Rosethorn had been flooded with people, women packed at tables whispering, men having low, dark conversations. It's hard not to suspect the paranoia inside my head has somehow leaked out, infecting the entire town. I'd spent our lunch hour praying Nissa couldn't see the sweat dampening my dress or my knee bouncing under the table. "Why's everyone so afraid?"

She eyes me. "You haven't heard?"

I shake my head.

"Sometimes I think you must disappear into thin air the moment you leave the library. They found more symbols in the swamp." Her voice lowers. "More of those moon-cult marks."

"Who else could know about Le Culte de la Lune?"

"No idea. And I'm still waiting on those history books from the Louisiana Heritage Archive to arrive. Hopefully they'll tell us what those marks mean." Nissa casts her eyes around the street, looking every bit as paranoid as the people gathered outside. "There's another thing," she whispers. "A big one. They found a second skull."

"What?" Has news about Renard gotten out despite the sheriff's wishes?

She nods. Instinctively, our pace picks up. Now we're hurrying as fast as everyone else down the sidewalk, as though the grim news is nipping at our heels. "Belongs to a man named Renard Michaels, I heard. He passed through town a few years ago." She waves her hand. "You woulda been a kid back then."

I nod. *I was, until I met him.*

"Now that there's two skulls," she continues, voice hushed, "everyone's saying it's proof the Low Man's behind the killings. They say he's risen and hunting. More bodies will come."

"You don't believe that, do you?"

"No," Nissa scoffs, but she doesn't meet my eyes. "The thing is, ever since the sheriff asked the town to think back on Fred, there's been a lot of memories surfacing. Most of them 'bout how he might not've been the man people thought he was."

I'm floored. "What are they saying?"

She speaks quickly, like the words taste bitter. "That Fred might've abused his little girl. The fishing wives have been talking, and it turns out people remember bruises on her. Apparently, this one time, she and her momma disappeared into thin air, then came back a month later, no explanation. There's rumors it was so the girl could..." Nissa clears her throat. "Get rid of a baby."

It seems certain I've done this. My prompting questions to the Fortenot Fishing wives must've planted seeds. Despite the fact that I've betrayed Beth's secrets, I feel a strange wash of relief to have the real Fred Fortenot finally out in the open.

"And," Nissa says, "as if that's not enough, *everyone's* talking 'bout how Renard Michaels was involved with a motorcycle gang out in Forsythe. Real nasty crowd."

This part is Everett. The last phase of our plan: get overheard talking about the Sons of Liberty over drinks at the Blue Moon. Engineer rumors to create pressure on the sheriff to investigate our tip. At least the rumors worked.

"Old Man Jonas says the Low Man came for Fred and Renard because they were secretly bad men, masquerading as good ones. It fits, Ruth. That's all I'm saying."

We're rounding the corner to the library when a voice screams, "I'm going to *kill* you, heathen!" A young boy dressed like Joseph from the Christmas manger streaks past us. I startle, throwing myself flat against the brick wall, as another little boy with a toy gun and an American flag painted on his face gives chase.

"You mind where you're going, young men!" Nissa shakes her head as I peel off the wall, trying to steady my breathing. The sudden shout—for a second, I was back at Jebediah's compound, listening to all those screams.

Nissa clucks. "I plain forgot the Fourth of July festival was today."

The Fourth of July festival, which Ever and I used to privately call the Uncle Sam–Jesus Christ Bonanza, is my father's brainchild, a spectacle celebrating America as the holiest Christian nation on earth. Held in the parking lot of Holy Fire, it's drawn bigger and bigger crowds every year, from Forsythe and beyond—but I can't imagine, given that we just saw most of the town gossiping along Main Street, that attendance was high this year.

My father will be furious.

"Come on," Nissa says, waving me forward. "I need to get back into the AC. We had warm summers in Baton Rouge, mind, but this swampland is hotter than the Devil's armpit."

"Sorry. They rattled me."

She snickers. "Warn me if you've developed a sudden aversion to children. I can always take over story hour. Though heaven knows I don't have it in me to do those voices."

We finish rounding the corner—and there, leaning against the library's locked front door, arms crossed, is Sheriff Theriot.

My stomach drops. What's he doing here? He should be out in Forsythe, busting the Sons of Liberty.

"Afternoon, ladies." The sheriff straightens. "Been out at the Fourth of July festival?"

"Hello, Sheriff." I can tell Nissa's surprised to see him, too. "Actually, we were having lunch at Rosethorn."

He frowns. "Not participating in this recent silly gossip, are you?"

"Oh no," she says smoothly, and that's when I learn Nissa is an excellent liar. "This town can spin a mountain out of a molehill, so I keep to myself."

"Glad to hear it." The sheriff's eyes shift to me, and I school my face into a smile. "Ruth, may I have a moment? Somewhere private?"

Nissa and I glance at each other. I can see the curiosity in her eyes and have to tamp down a bolt of alarm. "Of course."

I bring him to the small office in the back of the library. He surprises me by closing the door and remaining standing, even when I take a seat behind the desk. "Well, Sheriff. Are you here to ask more questions about Renard?"

It seems to rattle him. "Renard? No." He adjusts his belt. "After further investigation, we determined Renard Michael's death was accidental. Like we originally thought. Man was an avid trapper who must've gotten turned around in the swamp and met a dark end."

My mouth actually drops open. I have to snap it shut. Was all that work with the Sons of Liberty for nothing? "But what about what they're saying around town? His involvement with a motorcycle gang?"

The sheriff's face turns scornful. "Hogwash," he growls. "Nothing but ridiculous rumors. This whole town's up in arms for no good reason."

My mind whirs. Ever sent in the tip. The sheriff is aware of the rumors. The last time we talked, he said the evidence in Renard's case pointed to murder. And yet he's calling his death an accident. Did his office not investigate the Sons despite our tip, or did they investigate and miss the deed—and the drugs, guns, and women?

Is Sheriff Theriot really this ignorant?

Our eyes lock from across the room like those of a pair of adversaries. I'm not misreading the tension—the sheriff has come to confront me. But why, if he's dismissing Renard's case?

Twice now, I've felt the law's breath on my neck, and twice the threat has been abruptly pulled away.

"Ruth." The sheriff clasps his hands in front of himself in a show of calm control. "What do you know about Herman Blanchard?"

It seems I won't be able to predict a single turn in this conversation.

"He was my youth pastor, obviously. And my Vacation Bible School teacher. *Everyone's* Vacation Bible School teacher."

"What do you know about his passing, I mean?"

For the first time, I break eye contact, searching my memories. "He died two summers ago, right?"

I look up. The sheriff says nothing.

"A gas leak, if I remember. He was found in his garage."

A tragic accident, everyone had said, though not an uncommon one. Herman Blanchard had never been known as the most street-smart of men…

"The door from Mr. Blanchard's house to his garage was locked from inside the house," says the sheriff. "And the electronic control on his garage door was malfunctioning, making it unable to open."

It takes me a second. "You're saying he was killed?"

The sheriff rolls back on his heels. "You practically grew up at Holy Fire Born Again. How well did you know Herman? Did you ever hear any…disquietin' rumors?"

The question touches a nerve. "Like what?" I fold my hands to match his.

He notes it and clenches his jaw. On the pocket over his heart, the starred sheriff's badge gleams pure gold. I think of the crescent moon symbol in the woods. So many inscrutable talismans I cannot read. "Some things have come to light regarding Fred Fortenot, as you might've heard."

"Oh?" I raise my eyebrows.

The tic in his jaw seizes again. "Some unsavory behavior that escaped the town's attention while he was alive." He raises an eyebrow back at me. "Skipped his neighbors' attention as well, apparently."

"My father was close with Fred. You should ask him." I cock my head. "Come to think of it, Fred was a church elder like you. I remember seeing both of you those nights at our house. Remember those nights? When you used to come over late, drinking and smoking?"

The sheriff glares. I can't decide whether I'm more victorious or terrified to be going toe-to-toe with him. "Back to Herman," he says eventually. Anger edges his voice. "If I recall, he was very close with his students. What do you know about that?"

This question is the challenge he's come to lay before me. I can see it in the way he tenses: this is what he cares about.

"Mr. Blanchard was beloved," I say carefully, "because he went above and beyond what other teachers did. He used to hold these competitions in VBS. The winner would get to go somewhere with him, Dairy Queen or McDonald's. Places children get excited about. But I never got to go."

His eyes flash. "Why not?"

I look at the desk and shrug. "Not much of a winner, I guess."

The sheriff stares at me for a long time before he says, "You know, Ruth, you're different these days. Not the girl I remember."

I say nothing. I recognize the trap.

"Well, I won't take more of your time." He moves to the door. I watch him, glad to be seeing his back.

"Oh, wait." He turns. "One more thing."

"Yes?"

"Everett Duncan—he never went to Vacation Bible School, did he? On account a' his dad."

I was wrong: lulled into a false sense of security, a false sense of superiority. *This* question, delivered so casually, is why the sheriff has come to talk to me. Me, of all people. Because I'm Everett's only friend.

"Right."

"He ever have any dealings with the Blanchard family, to your knowledge? Say anything about Herman or Augustus?"

Slowly, I shake my head, heavy with the weight of the lie. "No, sir. I never once heard the name Blanchard come out of his mouth."

25

JUNE, TWENTY-ONE YEARS OLD

We were inside a fairy tale, the still water of Starry Swamp a black mirror reflecting the night sky, a thousand stars shining on the surface, one great glittering universe above and below. As we glided through the water, caught somewhere between Heaven and earth, I thought about how none of this should be happening. Two summers ago, when we were nineteen, I'd done a great and terrible thing. Gotten involved in something Everett had expressly forbidden me to and made a deal with the Devil. It had caused Everett to move away. Back then, I'd been convinced I'd never see him again. Yet here we were two years later in the lovely dead of night, our canoe parting the stars. It was the surest proof I had that redemption existed.

He rowed, biceps straining under the sleeves of his black shirt, paddles dipping into the water. "'The lights begin to twinkle from the rocks,'" he recited, in time with his movements. "'The long day wanes. The slow moon climbs... Come, my friends, 'tis not too late to seek a newer world.'" Silence hung for a moment, then he asked, "Do you remember that?"

I looked around. The moon was half-shadowed, so the light in the swamp was low. Still, I could see the cypresses rising from the water well enough to duck their branches as we drifted past, push aside the curtains of Spanish moss. It was quiet tonight, the frogs and crickets subdued, only the faintest hooting of owls. As if the swamp shared my melancholy.

"Of course I remember." The muscles in my back stretched as I rowed. "Lord Tennyson, from English class." I would never forget the day Ever recited it. It was the first time I'd felt like I wasn't alone. But that was four years ago, and so much had passed between us since then. "'And though we are not now that strength which in old days moved earth and Heaven,'" I recited quietly, "'that which we are, we are.'"

"You missing our glory days?" The corners of Ever's mouth lifted. "Feeling nostalgic at the ripe old age of twenty-one?"

We navigated a narrow passage between two trees, their low branches dipping into the water like a woman bending over with cupped hands. Moonlight reflected off a pair of slitted eyes resting just above the water. The alligators weren't afraid to come close, though they usually remained still as statues. Only their eyes tracked, waiting.

The branches, the gators, and me. Quiet longing everywhere.

"It's different now that you're only here for the summers," I said.

He grew still at the other end of the boat. I knew talking about it made him uncomfortable. But it was the truth. He'd moved away from me, and now each time he came back, a clock started ticking, counting down our time together. Each minute felt precious. "You're sitting right there," I continued, "and somehow I already miss you."

It was wrong of me to push. It was just… The first summer he'd returned after my terrible sin, I'd simply been happy to see him. But this summer, I was finding it hard to feel grateful for the short amount of time we got together, hard to remind myself *I* was the one who'd caused him to move in the first place, a consequence of my betrayal. This summer, it seemed the more I tried to hold on to Ever, the more he slipped away. And on some nights, like tonight, I found myself haunted by what I couldn't have.

The canoe rounded another corner and the narrow passage opened into a wide bayou, ringed by hardwoods. The half-moon shone a path across the water to our boat.

We stopped rowing and let ourselves drift. Ever leaned over and picked up a bottle of Boone's Farm from the middle of the canoe, untwisted the top, and handed it to me. "You're sad tonight. Here."

"Don't make fun of me."

He nudged me with the bottle. "I'm not. I'm trying to distract you."

I took it, fingers brushing his, and drank, eyes closing. The wine was sweet, more dessert than alcohol, but ever since we were eighteen and Ever stole me a bottle from the Dollar General, I'd loved it.

"Look," he whispered, and I opened my eyes to a blanket of mist rolling over the water, fast and purposeful as a sentient creature. "A warm front must be closing in."

"Here it comes," I said. "Watch out."

I'd no sooner spoken the words than the fog swallowed us. In the dense, wet air, I could only sense Ever as a darkness at the other end of the canoe.

"Ruth." His disembodied voice emerged through the fog. "Did you notice how strange Herman Blanchard acted at the store?"

I leaned and extended the wine, which he found by feeling through the fog. I listened to the sound of his throat working, and when he was done, he laughed. "It continues to surprise me how much I don't hate this stuff."

I settled back into my end of the boat. "Herman has always acted strange around me." While we were picking up the Boone's Farm at the Dollar General—paying this time—we'd turned down an aisle and there he was, carrying a green plastic shopping basket with nothing inside but crayons and strawberry hard candies, the kind we gave out at church. The minute he saw us, he'd turned and fled, not even a hello. "Well," I corrected. "He's been that way since the summer before sixth grade."

"What happened then?"

The fog made it so talking to Ever was like talking to a priest on the other side of one of those Catholic confessionals on TV. I told him how I'd been on the verge of getting to go to Dairy Queen with Herman and Lila LeBlanc until my father roared out of the church and took me away.

"For a long time I was really sad about it. I mean, not about the ice cream. It was more like I realized around then that I'd probably never have a normal life." I could still remember the way Lila had smiled at me, like it was the dawn of something. She'd barely looked at me since. Hadn't even responded when I'd asked how her Blizzard was. Since then, we'd been distant.

"Hmm." It was the kind of nonjudgmental sound Ever specialized in.

"As I got older, I started thinking about how strange my dad's reaction was. He wouldn't talk about it, but I think there was something under the surface I was too young to realize at the time."

The shadow that was Ever was quiet. Finally, he asked, in a thick voice, "What do you think that was?" Wine sloshed as he lifted the bottle.

I sighed and lay back in the canoe, careful not to rock it. My long hair fanned everywhere, even trailing over the sides of the boat, ends dipping in the water. "I think my father secretly hates Herman Blanchard."

Ever didn't respond.

"Herman's weird—no doubt about it. But it's the kind of weird that doesn't register until you're older. Except everyone who *is* older has to treat him with kid gloves because of who his daddy is. I think my dad finally got sick of it."

"Augustus Blanchard," Ever said. "And his sharp bear's cane."

"Sharp?" I thought of it—those ruby eyes and giant fangs. Sharp if it struck you, maybe...

The canoe started rocking, enough so I had to grip the sides. Ever crawled closer.

"Ruth." Now I could see his face. His eyes were urgent.

"You're going to capsize us!"

"Have you ever spent time around Augustus? Did your dad make you?"

"Yeah. He's a church elder, so he used to come over some nights when I was a kid. I talked to him once, but that was it. He used to scare me."

Slowly, the concern bled out of Ever's face. He sank down into the middle of the canoe. "Creature fear."

"What?"

"The animal part of you that senses threats."

I took the Boone's Farm from him, swallowed, and wiped my mouth. "He was creepy, but I used to dream about being a Blanchard anyway. Imagine having that much money." I shook my head. "It's wasted on Herman and Augustus. They never even leave Bottom Springs."

"I don't know." Everett's eyes followed the strands of my hair off the edge of the boat. "There's something to be said for being the biggest beast in the forest. That's power, and it's something people get addicted to. Rots their insides." His voice grew lower, gravelly. "If you know how to look, you can actually watch them transform into monsters over time."

"Like werewolves on a full moon," I joked. "All broken bones and twisted flesh." Ever had been into pulp magazines last summer and I was trying to make light, sensing his darkening mood.

He didn't smile. "Like werewolves," he agreed, and was quiet. I could sense him drifting away to that place I couldn't follow.

"The one time I talked to Augustus," I said, trying to pull him back. "He said he knew what it was like to bear rotten fruit. I didn't understand as a kid, but now I wonder if he was talking about Herman."

"If there's something rotten," Ever said stiffly, his focus returning, "it's in both of them."

I frowned. "What's with all this talk about the Blanchards, anyway?"

He cut his eyes away, so I knew I'd hit something. Then he tapped the side of the canoe. "Did you hear Augustus isn't naming Herman in the will?"

It was a side step, a cheap distraction, but it worked. "You're kidding." Imagine thinking your whole life you'd inherit millions, only to have it taken away. "Who's getting it, then?"

Ever shook his head. "That's the thing. No one knows. I was hoping you'd heard something—from your daddy, maybe."

"I didn't. Where'd you hear it?"

He shrugged. "Around."

"At the Blue Moon?"

He bit his lip. "Yes."

"Ever—"

"I can handle myself, okay? I'm not like him."

The mist was finally clearing, right in time to watch Ever lean in and tuck something soft as satin above my ear. I felt for it and pulled out a flower, marveling at it in the moonlight. Small and pale and star-shaped, with a dark-purple heart. A water hyacinth. I'd learned their name from Ever years ago.

I looked at him in question. He opened his palm to reveal a handful.

"How?"

He pointed to the water. I peered over the boat and gasped. While in the mist, we must've drifted into a floating garden. All around us, delicate hyacinths sat on thick webbed leaves like teacups on saucers.

Fast, clever Everett. He must've plucked them so swiftly in the fog I hadn't noticed.

I tucked the flower back into my hair, and he smiled. "Hold still." He rose to his knees, leaning over me. The boat dipped.

"Careful," I whispered, but I wasn't really thinking anymore. Not with Ever so close, when I could breathe in the air he exhaled. He slid the flowers into my hair gently, one by one, then leaned back and surveyed me, an artist examining his work.

He grinned—and, without warning, touched my temple, pushing his fingers into my hair. The long strands slid like silk between his fingers, falling like a rose-red curtain. A small curl caught around his pinkie and stayed there. My breath caught.

"You look like that painting of Ophelia from your art history class," he whispered. "The red-haired princess lying in the water, covered in flowers."

"By John Everett Millais." Three years ago, when I was still excited about following along with LSU courses and teaching myself since I couldn't go to college, I'd "taken" LSU's Western Art class. The painting had been one of my favorites. Millais had painted Ophelia, Hamlet's would-be bride, singing in the river in the very last moment before she drowned.

"Show-off," Ever teased.

My heart beat so hard I could feel my pulse in every limb. Ever's eyes sank to my throat, lingering where my vein jumped, then he swallowed and looked away—to the floor of the boat, where something else caught his attention.

He seized the book and fell back into the canoe. The sudden loss of his closeness was like being released from a spell: I took a deep, fortifying breath, newly awake. What was I playing at? Everett may be innocently affectionate—he always was—but I was torturing myself. I'd made my choices. Made my deal with the Devil. And now I had to live with the consequences.

Ophelia, indeed. Singing in the water while it drowned me.

Everett held up the copy of *Twilight* I'd been rereading. "After all this time?"

I folded my arms and looked away. "Not tonight, Ever."

"No teasing," he promised. Then: "Though I did hear it got nominated for a Pulitzer. Something about the high-quality writing." He laughed. "Okay, no teasing after *that*. This is your replacement copy?"

I rolled my eyes but nodded. Thanks to my job, I'd been able to get my hands on it, plus the other books in the series. The original, I'd watched burn.

"Can I ask you a question?" His tone was serious enough to make me sit up. Pale hyacinths tumbled from my hair.

"Why have you always been so obsessed with it?"

I laughed—a low, tense sound. The irony of having this conversation now, after all these years and everything that happened. I decided, in a fit of pique, that if I was going to hurt tonight, I might as well go all the way. "Why do you think?" I fingered a fallen flower. "Because it's the ultimate in romance. Edward and Bella love each other so much he's willing to die for her, and she does die for him, in a way. She becomes a vampire so they can always be together."

"And you're sure that's love?" His eyes darkened. "Giving up your life for someone?"

This was the part I was waiting for. The knife twisted deep.

"I think Bella was better off dead than the girl she was before. Becoming a vampire let her protect herself and the people she loved." I was skirting too close to my own wound, but I couldn't help it. "There are some things that just have to be done, even if they're evil." And Ever was the only person I'd ever say that to.

It was remarkable, the change on his face. His skin seemed to glow, his eyes two black holes, sucking me in. "Ruth," he said, voice thick. "Are you saying you could love a monster?"

I looked at him. Really looked. At this friend I hadn't expected, whose life had turned out to be worth more to me than anything, even my place in Heaven. And my heart swelled with the strangest mix of hope and fear to have the truth so close to the surface. It would be easy right now to confess that *I* was the monster. I wanted to freeze the moment and live in it, stay in the possibility.

But of course I couldn't tell him what I'd done, the great sin he didn't even know was what really drove him away. I choked out a laugh and pressed a finger into my snakebite scar, willing the old pain to distract me. When I allowed myself to look again, I found Everett staring. "What?" My tone came out sharper than intended.

He cocked his head. "I'm not allowed to look at you?"

God forgive me for my weakness. "Only if you tell me what you see."

His slow unfurling smile was bittersweet. "The center of the world."

I exhaled. "Ever—"

He started to move. Holding my gaze, he slid on his knees across the boat. I startled back, shoulders rising against the bow, and he stopped. What shone in his eyes was my own hesitation, mirrored back. My own hope.

My own longing.

He raised a hand to touch my face.

He doesn't know. If he did, he would never touch you.

I turned my cheek. Ever's hand dropped.

"I'm tired," I said quietly. "Please take me home."

He was silent for so long that I closed my eyes. Then the boat rocked as he climbed back to the other end. I heard him pick up the oars, heard them slap the water.

"I'm sorry, Ruth." His voice was grave. "I promise, never again."

26

NOW

I'm lying on my couch watching the sheer white curtains twist in the wind, thinking about Herman Blanchard, the disinherited son outlived by his father, when I hear the sound of car tires crunching the dirt road, so fast it can only be Everett.

The screen door bangs behind me as I bound barefoot across the lawn. His convertible slides to a stop, dust flying, and he leaps out of the car.

"It's over." I fling my arms around him. "Renard's case is closed. We're free."

Ever folds me tightly against him. I press my face into his chest, breathing him in, feeling like I might sob from sheer relief. He cups my head, fingers catching in my hair, and rubs his other hand between my shoulder blades, the movement soothing. "What do you mean, we're free?"

I pull back. His thick hair stands high from the wind, a light sheen of sweat on his forehead. There's white gauze wrapped around his bicep where he got grazed by the drug dealer's bullet and something wild in his eyes. He hasn't raced here to celebrate.

"The sheriff came to see me at the library. After everything, they're ruling Renard's death an accident. No one told you?"

Ever's jaw tightens, but the look that flickers across his face isn't surprise. Why isn't he shocked?

"I don't understand," I say, still holding his waist. "Whether or not they investigated our tip, what would make them change their minds so radically?"

His fingers move down my spine. "Frankly, I don't care. I say let's just take the pardon. It's perfect, actually. I came here to—"

"Ever." If Sheriff Theriot hasn't gone to see him, he doesn't know the other half. "The sheriff was asking questions about you and Herman."

His brows knit together. "Herman Blanchard? What did he say?"

"Something about Herman being locked inside his garage, and then he asked if you ever had any involvement with the Blanchard family."

His eyes move over my shoulder into the distance. "I can't believe he had the gall to ask you that."

"Hey." I place my palms flat against his chest. "I've watched this town scapegoat people my whole life. I won't let them do it to you."

"Listen, Ruth. Forget about Herman. I came to tell you I'm leaving."

"No, you're not." My denial is reflexive. "What do you mean, you're leaving? We're free from Renard now. Whatever they throw at us with Herman, we'll figure it out. We can still have our summer."

I need our summers. I feed and live off them all year.

He places heavy hands on my shoulders. "I was preparing to leave anyway, and then I got an offer on the house. That miserable place, Ruth—someone actually wants to buy it. Can you believe it?" He shakes his head. "I was standing in the living room, imagining finally being done with it, and I thought: what if I ask her one last time to leave with me? What if this time, she says yes?" His fingers tighten on my shoulders. "So I'm here to ask. Beg, if you want. Grab a suitcase and let's just get in the car and leave. We can go anywhere."

Over Everett's head, a flock of birds comes screaming out of the trees. The earth tilts beneath my feet. "Why now? Why so urgent?"

He drops his hands. Without them, I feel I might tip over. "The time's right, is all. Come with me, Ruth. You always wanted to leave Bottom Springs. I never understood why you didn't."

First, it was the money. Then, a reason I'll never tell. The secret that lurks between us, keeping us marooned on different shores.

Ever searches my face. He must see my resistance, because his voice grows hoarse. "Why can't you, Ruth? For God's sake, just tell me why I left and you never followed."

It's knee-jerk, the need to avoid this question—that's the only reason I can think of for why I blurt out, "Barry asked me to marry him."

The news hits Everett like a wave: first, a pummel of shock, then the comedown of betrayal, a sort of sinking understanding. He swallows. "I see. And you said yes?"

"No. I don't know." Inside, alarms ring. What am I doing? "I haven't given him an answer."

"When?" He clears his throat. "Did he ask?"

"Days ago." Fear and adrenaline have muddied the waters of my mind since the day they pulled Fred's skull from the swamp, so time isn't clear. "Weeks, maybe?"

He holds his jaw so tight I think it'll shatter. "And you didn't think to tell me?"

"I did, but with everything happening..." My voice trails off.

He holds my eyes. "Ruth, are you sure you don't know your answer?"

It *is* strange that I've waited until now to tell Everett—even stranger that I'm still processing how I feel. It's like I'm groping my way through the dark, trying to understand my own heart. "Everyone expects me to, but the truth is, I don't know if I want to get married at all. Do you know what I picture when I think about marriage? Being trapped like Mary

Fortenot, or nameless like the fishing wives. I think of my own mother, and Ever—I can't be like that."

To my surprise, he scoffs. "That's not the kind of marriage you'd have."

"That's the only kind I know!" I press my hands to my neck, trying to suppress the heat welling, and turn from him. The late afternoon sun peeks over the roof of my house, extending soft beams like outstretched arms. It's easier to speak this way, facing the sun instead of him. "It's okay, really. I gave up on the idea of true love and soul mates a long time ago. Now the only kind of closeness I want is friendship. Like ours. That's enough."

His voice is sharp. "Of course it isn't."

I jerk like he's slapped me.

"Don't forget how well I know you, Ruth Cornier." Before I can protest, he's in front of me, the sun lighting his hair in a golden halo. "You've been in love with love your whole life. It's in all the books you read. It's all you used to talk about as a teenager. Of course you want it."

I wipe away the moisture in my eyes. "I was a fool. Fixating on it because I was lonely. But I know better now. Love isn't salvation; it's a curse. Feeling so much, wanting so much, not being in control of yourself. I closed that door and I'm better for it."

"You can't close it," he says gruffly. He reaches out, resting his fingers on my arm, not a demand but a plea. "It's who you are, and I need you—" He swallows hard. "I need you to believe it. My life used to be darkness, and then you came along, sunny Ruth with your big heart. If that part of you ever gets snuffed out, I swear to God, I don't know what I'll..."

He stops. The pain on his face is suddenly replaced by a gutted understanding. "What am I saying? You didn't shut the door. You just don't want to tell me you're going to say yes to Barry."

"Ever, that's not—"

"You're going to marry him." Ever's voice is full of conviction. "And grow old with him, and have his children." He cuts his eyes away and squares his jaw, trying to master himself. "You'll make a private world with him." He swallows hard and nods, as if it's already decided, a thing he can see clearly. "And I'll be the ghost who haunts you every summer."

I stand there in the grass watching him bear the pain of being left behind and think for the hundredth time that I should tell him why I don't deserve his friendship or his pain. "Ever." My voice snags. I'll do it, even if it means he hates me. It's on the tip of my tongue—

"No." He scrubs his hands over his face. "You don't have to placate me. I've always known this would happen. I just...got my head turned. Forgive me, and forget I asked." He starts toward his car.

"Stop."

Ever freezes midstride and turns, the look on his face hauntingly hopeful.

It's unfair of me to ask when it will change nothing. But it's been six years of wondering. Even now, as he skirts closer to saying *something*, I still don't know exactly what it is. I used to think maybe there was something growing between us different from our years of friendship...but then I committed my sin and he chose to leave. So I take a deep breath and ask, "What am I to you?"

The sun is in his eyes; he squints down at the grass. A smile curves his mouth—so sad I would give anything to retract the question. "It's funny. Since the day I found you in the swamp, I've been trying to answer that question. I thought once that you might be the answer to the only prayer I ever made. Or my conscience—my heart, beating outside my body. Sometimes..." He swallows. "I think you're a fistful of sand, and the tighter I clutch, the faster you spill. I don't know, Ruth. You're something I've never had a name for."

He doesn't know it, but once upon a time, I had the perfect name for him.

27

MAY, NINETEEN YEARS OLD

It's dead," Everett said, crouching to peer at the bird in the grass. It was beautiful and small: jewel-blue feathers and a snow-white belly, though the white was streaked with mud. A tree swallow. It lay there, one dark eye facing us. "Must've gotten attacked by something, or flown into a tree."

"No." I crouched beside it. "It's still alive." The way it lay, half-covered in dirt, made it look discarded. I willed it to live.

As if it heard my thoughts, the bird's head swiveled. It opened its small beak in a silent cry.

"See!" I squeezed Ever's arm.

"All right, all right. I think its wing's damaged, though." Gently, Ever lifted the bird and made a dark, cool basket of his T-shirt, placing the swallow inside. "Rescue's closed on Sundays, but we can go first thing in the morning." We'd pulled a lot of injured animals out of the swamp over the last year. Tenderhearted Mr. Wilkes who ran the makeshift clinic was probably the only other person in Bottom Springs who liked Ever. He looked at me, the bird cupped in his shirt. "Can you take her? I know you have the baptism, but I can't let my dad find her."

He didn't need to say more. For months I'd tried to talk to Everett about what his father had done to him but he refused to say a word, as if his silence could simply erase the January day I'd found him broken in his living room. If I tried to bring it up, he'd close down, change the subject, or get frustrated, making me swear not to tell anyone, especially my father or the cops. Maybe burying it was what he needed to survive, but I'd spent so much time since I'd found him imagining his father hurting him again that the scenes had started to bleed into my dreams. All I wanted to do was the one thing he'd expressly forbidden me to do: march into the sheriff's office and dispatch the deputies in to put Killian behind bars. It would be a horrible betrayal of Everett and his friendship, his agency, his trust in me, but wasn't his safety worth it? In this instance, didn't I know better than him?

These questions plagued me. So when I said, "Of course," the two simple words wavered, wanting to be so much more.

Back home, I took advantage of the fact that my parents were still down at the shore, where they were setting up for the afternoon's baptism, to sneak in the swallow. I'd learned from Everett and Mr. Wilkes what the bird needed, so I went right to my closet and pulled out an old boot box, shook out the contents, and stuffed it with towels, wrapping one around a hot-water bottle. After poking holes in the lid, I laid the swallow inside, taking care not to touch her more than necessary. It seemed counterintuitive to close her up in a box like a tomb, but Mr. Wilkes said birds needed it so they didn't go into shock. Too much stimulation could make her tiny heart give out from fright.

I heard the front door open sooner than expected and ran with the box as gently as I could. My parents wouldn't let me keep a dirty animal in the house—not to mention she was proof I'd been out in the swamp with Ever.

Heavy footsteps pounded up the stairs as I tucked the box into my closet. "Shh," I whispered. "Everything's going to be okay. Just hang on for one night."

"Ruth Sarah Cornier." My mother's sharp voice made me jump back from the closet, hitting my hip against the desk and knocking my book bag to the floor. The contents spilled everywhere.

She strode into the room. "If you're not dressed and ready—" Her eyes lasered on the mess: pens, a printed syllabus for LSU's History of Modern Philosophy course, and *Twilight*—bent, dog-eared, and splayed with the cover-up.

My mother looked at me. I found I couldn't say a word, in such shock that the moment I'd feared for so long was actually happening.

She bent and picked up the book. "What's this?"

My mouth opened but nothing came out. Seeing the book in her hand, it dawned on me for the first time that the cover of *Twilight*—pale hands holding out an apple—was meant to evoke Eve tempting Adam to sin. My stomach sank as my mother turned the book over and read the back. I was living a nightmare.

"This," she said slowly, "is that occult book I saw on the news. The girl who falls in love with a demon."

I placed a shaking hand on my desk, trying to steady myself. "It's just a book. Harmless." But even I didn't believe myself. It wasn't just a book. It was how my heart had discovered hope.

My mother stared at it. "This is how the Devil recruits young girls. It's brainwashing."

I braced for it: screaming, hitting, excoriation. I was the Devil's whore. An unrepentant sinner. She would shout for my father and he would bound up the stairs, push me to my knees, and beat me with the rattan cane until I sobbed my confessions.

But instead, my mother opened it and studied the title page. "'For

Ever and forever,'" she read, then looked up at me. "That doesn't sound harmless. It sounds like you signing your life away."

I flushed at her misreading. It was only a silly, idle scribble, based on that Tennyson poem Ever and I had recited to each other two years ago. "Mom—"

"This is going to make you want things." There was a creeping realization to her voice. "It's going to make you lustful and wanton."

I started to counter, then stopped. It wasn't entirely untrue.

She kept looking at that cover like it had hypnotized her. "You silly, silly girls." Her lip curled. "You're all so predictable. Wanting to light your lives on fire. I thought we'd raised you better."

"It's just a book," I repeated, and held out my hands, palms up. "I'm being rebaptized today, remember? I stayed in Bottom Springs and I go to church every Sunday and I've never caused you"—I paused—"much trouble."

She gave me the most incredulous look for a woman who was normally allergic to sarcasm and tossed the book on my bed. "Sit down," she said, gesturing to my mirror. "Vanity may be a sin, but there's no excuse for going to your baptism homely."

Moving cautiously, eyes on her, I edged to my vanity and sat in the pink padded chair.

She came behind me. Even though she'd just returned from the gulf, where Holy Fire Born Again held its baptisms, there wasn't a speck of sand on her. Her navy dress was beautiful, the fabric richer than we'd been able to afford back when I was young and the church was still growing. Her white-blond hair daggered straight to her shoulders, a stark contrast to mine, long and scarlet and tangled from the outdoors. But our blue eyes were twins. They met in the mirror.

"Over and over, you girls." She didn't look away as she took a fistful of my hair, seized the hairbrush, and dragged it through. When it caught on a tangle, she wrenched harder and I bit my lip. "Why do you always want so bad to fall in love?" Disdain hollowed the words *you girls*, as if she herself had never been such a creature. "Sickening, the lengths you'll go to. And always with the wrong boys." She ran the brush again, jerking my head. "It's like there's a switch in your brain once you hit a certain age, and you lose all reason. I was nothing like that when I was a girl. I never caused a lick of trouble. And look how I was rewarded." She raised her hand at my room. "Look at this house. My husband. My standing. Do you think it came easy?"

She paused and met my eyes. "If you think I'm blind to what's going on, you're wrong."

I blinked to clear the tears, being tender-headed. "You mean the book?"

She waved the brush. "The book, the boy. This *obsession*, Ruth. Why? What's in it for you?"

The question was remarkable: a singular event. She'd never asked me to explain myself before. Suddenly I wanted to answer with the truth. I thought of Bella, how she'd given up everything for Edward, no hesitation. The other girls at school, falling over boys at Starry Swamp, then sobbing over them in the girls' bathroom. Lila LeBlanc and her endless suitors, chasing their attention like she had a hole in her heart only they could fill. Beth Fortenot, always wanting boys she thought were bigger and better, trying so hard to escape herself. Why *did* we fall in love like lit matches dropped in kerosene?

The answer came to me easy as anything. And if I could've been honest with my mother, I would've said we loved like this, with an all-consuming passion, because our hearts had awakened to the truth of what we wanted for ourselves. The awakening itself was a miracle for those of us who had no map for love, who'd never once felt an emotion directed at ourselves as strong as the ones we gave to others. How do you draw a map of a place you've never been? *Twilight* had been my map. I thought of my love for Edward Cullen at fourteen. Yes. That was my heart's hunger showing its teeth.

Teeth. As if beckoned by his true name, Everett appeared in my mind, supplanting Edward.

"Well?" My mother smoothed my hair with cold fingers. "What do you have to say for yourself?"

Though I ached to tell her, I realized it might only be a trap. So I stayed quiet, hoping she'd read that as contrition.

But she wouldn't be dissuaded. She plucked a silver comb from the table. "Choosing obstinance. Well." She cleared her throat. "There was once another girl who was sullen and rebellious. Who didn't listen to her parents."

I was familiar with these cautionary tales. They all started the same way: *There was once a girl...* What followed was the same plot with different details: a girl who was headstrong and disobedient, whose great sin caused her life to end in tragic ruin. All these three-dimensional, living girls flattened into tales whispered by mothers to daughters. What did it feel like to become a warning? I imagined a great hand pressing me until I was paper thin, like Christ's wafer body at communion.

"She thought she was in love," my mother continued. "So even though he was older and refused to tell anyone they were dating, she gave herself to him. And do you know what happened? He left her pregnant and alone. Disgraced and untouchable."

This was by far the most familiar story. I bit the inside of my mouth, waiting as she scored the comb across my scalp, then said, "You can skip ahead. I've heard this one."

Our eyes met and held for a long time. Then she said softly, "I have one you haven't heard."

I couldn't look away.

"There was once a girl who came from an old, old family, so poor they had to live out in the swamp and kill with their bare hands to eat. Everyone in town looked down on them."

I was mesmerized by her eyes, focused on something far away. Already, this story felt different.

"As the girl grew up, she started coming into town. She was pretty enough to turn heads, and many men tried to court her. But she fell in love with the worst one. A dangerous man who made her big promises." My mother's hands tightened in my hair. "Everyone warned her he was masking his darkness while they were courting. But she ignored them and married him anyway. He bought her a pretty house right in town. And she became pregnant."

A faint echo of grief flitted across my mother's face. "Not long after that poor girl gave birth to their son, her husband came home miserably drunk and beat her to death in a fit of rage." She stroked my forehead. "She had the most luminous skin. The things he did to it." After a moment, her eyes refocused. "That's what can happen to you."

Luminous skin. Gave birth to a son. A drunk father. "It was Everett's mom," I breathed. "That's who you're talking about."

I wanted her to deny it. But she said, "It's a horrifying story. That's why I never told you."

In the thickness of my shock, I blinked at her. "But Ever's mom died giving birth to him."

She dropped the brush on the table. "That lie's probably the only mercy that boy's ever been given."

Entire belief systems reordered themselves in my head. "Then why didn't his father go to jail? You *knew* this happened and you let Everett live with him?"

"There was no police record," said my mother coldly. "The Duncans stayed to themselves, anyway. Didn't come to church. Had no community. Killian told everyone she died giving birth, and no one questioned him, not even her own family."

My mind whirred. "But if you knew, you could've saved him—"

"Hush," she hissed. "It's not our place to interfere with heathens. Besides, I'm sure that boy's as rotten inside as his daddy—and if he wasn't born that way, he is now. That's why you need to stay away. The Duncan line is darkness incarnate."

The words lashed out quick as a striking snake. "I thought Jesus preached kindness. Doesn't that make you a hypocrite?"

Her slap was so hard she nearly sent me off the chair. I caught myself against the vanity, cheek throbbing.

"How dare you? Do you want me to get your father?"

My ears rang. All I could think was: I had to tell Ever. This dark secret that had been kept from him, the real reason they called his father the Devil and avoided him at all costs. His whole life, he thought he'd killed his mother, had carried the weight of it. What would happen when he knew the truth?

That fierce anger filled me, the kind that begged me to defend him, the way he'd done for me in the swamp with Renard. I longed for the cool weight of a stone in my hand. But who would I turn it on—all of Bottom Springs? What could I actually do against people like my parents? Weak, meek Ruth Cornier.

My mother walked to the bed and seized *Twilight*. "Your rebaptism couldn't come at a better time. The Devil is hard at work inside you." She thrust the book at me. "Take this down to your father and show him what you've done."

The instincts seized me and I obeyed. And when my father commanded me to strike a match and set fire to the book, no matter how much it hurt, I didn't protest. I held the flame in the fireplace and let it drop. I thought of that girl: Ruth Cornier, the wisp. And as the pages blackened and curled, I imagined it was her who was burning.

"On this holy day," my father shouted, his voice triumphant, reaching across the waves to the congregation, who watched raptly from the shore. "We give thanks to the Lord for giving his life so we might have a path toward redemption!"

A wave crashed at my back, knocking me forward, the water warm and murky and high as my hip bone. My father seized a fistful of my hair and braced a hand against my back. The congregation swayed on their feet, anticipating.

"You are gathered here to witness the rebirth of Ruth Sarah Cornier," he yelled. "Today she recommits herself as God's servant. *This*, my friends, is how we defeat death. *This* is how we conquer that last great hurdle!"

They cheered. What a sight we must've been, my towering, golden-skinned father, holding me in the waves like a redheaded flame he would douse in the sea. He kept yelling, but I let his words fade out. My eyes drifted past the congregation to the blue sky above.

A flock of starlings was coming, hundreds of black birds pouring toward us like a dark wave. They danced in their murmuration, undulating like water, forming topography, twisting into spirals, mysterious messages I wished I could read. It was beautiful. Somehow, they knew how to do this, each of them born with an instinct for exactly where they were meant to be. They called to each other in a great cacophony and I imagined they were calling to me, asking where I was meant to go, what I wanted in this life.

In my heart, I knew the answer. It was the same as the answer to my mother's second question: *This all-encompassing love for all the wrong men—what's in it for you?* The truth was, I longed to kiss people like Edward Cullen, vampires and heartbreakers who could hurt me, kill me, men who walked the knife's edge of life, because what I really wanted—what I'd wanted from fourteen, even before I had the language to describe it—was to suck the marrow out of them and carry it myself. Forget puberty, forget growing up into a woman. I wanted to drink their threat, hold that volatile substance in my chest. Swallow their danger and become the danger myself. Vampire, viper; all that power, mine.

That was the thing everyone glossed over about Bella—why as I aged, I fell in love with her, I think, even more than him. Because all along, she knew she'd been born to be a vampire; it was only after Edward turned her, in her death and monstrosity, that she became her truest self. *That* was what I longed for, and no number of girls who died trying, no number of cautionary tales would ever stop me.

Because I wanted to be transformed. Same as all the people up there on the shore. Except baptism wasn't strong or quick enough for me. Love so violent it was a threat, a maelstrom—maybe that could do it. Maybe after it burned through me and I was transfigured, the world would look at *me* and be afraid. Wouldn't that be something? The prayer of every teenage girl.

A roar went up.

My father dragged me underwater.

28

NOW

I surface from my thoughts with a gasp as the organ music soars and the congregation rises to its feet.

"Earth to Ruth," says Barry, and yanks me up.

I grip the pew, unsteady like I've just emerged from somewhere deep. In front of us, the choir trails down ornate twin staircases to the stage in their red and white finery. Once Holy Fire Born Again was no more than a small, square building on an empty plot of land, its steeple the grandest thing about it—and even that, outmatched by the library. Over the years it's grown in every way: the building with renovations, the congregation filling this massive nave, and my father's reputation. After the choir sings their opening, he'll emerge on the balcony overlooking us, magisterial, an emissary from God. Like clockwork, the Holy Spirit will overtake someone, and they'll start speaking to him in tongues.

Barry pries one of my hands off the pew and squeezes it. "I was thinking we could have a short engagement. Get married right here in the fall. What do you think?"

I'd finally told him I needed more time to consider his proposal, and though he wasn't happy, he also hadn't let the answer stop him from planning. He seems to view our marriage as a foregone conclusion that I'll eventually catch up to.

I smile weakly. "Fall is nice."

A rare visitor appears in the aisle: Augustus Blanchard hobbles to his row up front, accompanied by a hovering usher. He's grown emaciated these last couple of years, no longer a commanding figure. He leans hard on his cane with every step.

"Looks awful," Barry whispers, leaning in. "That man hasn't been the same since Herman passed. That's what grief'll do to you, I guess. I'm worried reopening Herman's case is gonna make the old guy keel over."

I study Augustus's profile. His face, though hollowed, is as stern and unyielding as ever. I don't read grief in him.

"Barry," I say, and he straightens to attention. He's been fawning and attentive since I told him I needed time to think. Withholding my answer has given me more power over him than I've ever held—and unfortunately, I need to exploit it. "Who's inheriting the Blanchard fortune when Augustus dies?"

"Shoot." Barry raises his eyebrows. His hands are folded in front of him, his brown hair swept to the side, wearing a carefully ironed collared shirt. The spitting image of a good man. "That's the million-dollar question, ain't it? I got no clue. Just know it wasn't gonna go to Herman."

"Do you know if Mary Fortenot inherited Fortenot Fishing? She did, right, after Fred died, since she was his wife?"

He looks at me like I'm crazy. "She's a woman, Ruth. She don't know a thing about fishing. Course she didn't inherit it."

"Who did, then?"

Barry scratches his chin and eyes the choir, which has finished assembling. "I don't know who owns it, but Gerald Theriot runs it these days."

All around us, people start twisting in their seats to face the back of the church. Gasps go up, followed by fierce whispers. Barry and I turn to see what's caused the commotion, and my heart nearly falls out of my chest.

Everett stands at the back of the room, the massive double doors still swinging behind him. His hair is tousled from his convertible and he wears his usual black T-shirt, jeans, and heavy boots, an outfit that's tantamount to a crime here. He displays the gauze-wrapped bullet wound on his bicep like a badge of honor. As the entire congregation watches, he pats himself down, theatrically checking for flames—and, finding none, grins widely, showing off all his teeth. The volume of the whispers skyrockets as he swaggers down the aisle.

I meet his eyes and his grin grows. Then his gaze flicks down to where I hold Barry's hand and his smile falters for a second before it's back to full wattage. He winks and slides into the pew directly across from mine. Everyone sitting there scrambles away, a sight that would've been funny to teenage Ruth. But now that I'm older and know the consequences, it only brings me heartache.

He makes a show of sitting: dusting off his seat, then settling his tall body onto the cushioned pew, one leg crossed casually over the other. When the organ music stops, there's nothing to mask how savagely the whispers are flying. The Devil's son has appeared in church.

Catching his eye, I mouth, "What are you doing here?" It was a joke we used to make on lazy summer nights, lying on the dock: *Can you imagine if you just showed up to church one day, what they'd do?* He was never supposed to actually try it.

He smirks and shrugs, leaning back in the pew like it's a recliner. Dangerously reckless.

Only two days ago, he told me he was leaving Bottom Springs. I'm grateful he didn't, but this is the last place on earth I want to see him. The nerve, walking in here. "And for what?" I murmur.

"Provocation," says Barry, his narrowed eyes on Ever. "It's a thing they get off on."

"They?"

He settles back and drapes an arm over my shoulders. "Never mind. You'll know soon enough."

"What's that supposed to mean?"

My father strides onto the balcony and all talking stops. He stretches his arms out to encompass us, eyes sweeping his flock. They land on Everett.

Ever, for his part, turns and looks at me. My face burns, caught between them.

My father's expression remains impressively neutral. "Brothers and sisters in Christ," he calls, voice amplified by the microphone, "Praise Him!"

"Praise Him!" the whole congregation shouts. Far in the back corner, someone keeps chanting it, compelled by the Spirit. My father lifts his voice over it. "Today, I will tell you how the Lord shall avenge himself upon the souls of the sinners who've rejected His Wisdom and Light. Ours is a wrathful God, O brothers and sisters!"

The congregation hollers back, all eyes in the room on the Devil's son.

As soon as the congregation floods out of the church into the wide green lawn, I beeline to Ever.

"You need to leave," I hiss. "You're stirring up trouble. It's a ticking bomb."

He folds his hands behind his head like he's lying on a beach somewhere. "Maybe I don't care anymore."

"Ruth." Barry appears at my side. "Come now." He takes my elbow, pulling me away.

"Hello, Barrett," Ever says. "We were talking."

"Barry, hold on." I try to dig in my heels, but Barry grips me tighter and keeps moving.

"Hey." Ever's voice has lost its playful indifference. "Don't squeeze her like that."

People are turning to watch. The lawn is eerily quiet.

Barry leans in as he tugs me. "I don't want you seeing him anymore. Not in public or in private. Trust me, Ruth, something's brewing and you don't want to be near it. Now's not the time for childhood loyalties."

"You're holding me too tight." I try to wrestle my arm from him.

It seems Ever was lying to himself when he said he didn't care about anything anymore. When I whip my head over my shoulder, I find him striding purposefully after us.

Escalation is the last thing we need. Not outside of church in front of the whole town. I have to broker peace.

"Hey, Barrett!" Ever calls. "Why don't you let her walk on her own? She's capable."

Barry halts midstep and swings around. "Don't tell me how to treat my fiancée."

Ever's eyes jerk to me. "You said yes?"

Though he's asking me, Ever's question seems to strike Barry like an arrow to the chest. He drops my arm and thrusts his finger at Ever. The crowd's moved with us into the parking lot. We're surrounded by eyes.

"Just because your twisted brain has been obsessed with Ruth Cornier since high school don't mean you get her." Barry's heated. "It just means you're delusional."

"Stop," I beg, stepping between them. "There's no reason to get in an argument in the church parking lot. Let's just calm down and go our separate ways."

"You think you own her, don't you?" Unlike Barry's voice, Everett's is cool, his face an icy mask. "You think the reverend gave her to you as a trophy."

"He did!" Barry cries. "And it's my job to take care of her."

I turn incredulous eyes on him. "No one gave me to anyone."

Barry flushes redder. "You know what, Duncan?" He waves a hand. "It's past time we did somethin' 'bout you." He starts to turn, then jabs a finger in Ever's direction. "I *know* you, motherfucker. You act all high and mighty, but I know what you're really about. And soon they all will." He pushes through the crowd. I can only assume he's heading for my father.

"Ruth." Ever steps closer to me, his voice lowering. Despite the fact that we're ringed by spectators, the way he looks at me makes me feel, for a moment, like we're alone. "Come on." He says it impatiently, like he's waiting for me to catch up to something he's already realized. "You're choosing the path of least resistance again."

"The path of least *harm*."

"No." He shakes his head. "You know what? I think for all your ability to see inside these people, you're still theirs in the ways that matter."

Over his head, the great white steeple of Holy Fire Born Again rises like a needle. It's grown taller and taller over the years, closer and closer to God, and now it towers over us like a watchful eye. Beneath it, the gathered crowd tightens. The words *mob violence* slither through my mind. "Not here," I urge. "If you want to talk, let's go somewhere else."

Ever shakes his head. "You're falling at their feet like they want you to. Why? Because you're so determined to win back your place in Heaven?" He lowers his voice. "Do you really think what we did was so wrong?"

"Shut up," I hiss. He's treading on dangerous ground. "Why are you suddenly acting like the rules don't matter?"

"You think there's no rules for *me*?" His laugh is cutting. "Who's God really, huh, Ruth? Some ghost in the sky, or the men right here on earth who can do anything they want to us?"

"Don't talk like that." I give up and resort to Barry's tactic, gripping Ever by the arm and trying to muscle him away from the crowd. "I know what you think of church, but now's not the place or the time."

Ever looks at me like he's never seen me before. "Do you actually believe it?"

"Believe *what*?" All these eyes—it's like Barry's proposal, but worse. I'm nearly vibrating at the thought of one of these men catching the details of what Ever's saying. Their staring's already violent enough.

"Everything your father preaches. I always thought deep down you didn't believe it, but maybe I was wrong." Ever steps closer and taps two fingers against my temple. "Is he in there? Is this his?"

"Enough." I slap his hand away.

His eyes turn desperate, just like two nights ago, when he came to my house and asked me to leave with him. Why does he keep returning again and again to ask for things I can't give?

"Sometimes I think I know you better than any creature on earth, Ruth. Better than I know myself." His voice cracks and I cannot look away. "And then you side with them or refuse to fight for yourself, and I remember you've spent your whole life with that man, and I think, maybe she's a goner like the rest of them, and I just never wanted to see it."

"I'm *not* a goner." My eyes well against my will. Recklessly, self-destructively, Everett came to Holy Fire to pick a fight. And now he's doing it to me. Interrogating me in front of everyone, making me choose sides.

"You willing to do whatever it takes to get to Heaven?" His eyes burn. "Bend on your knees, wail in the streets?" He clutches my shoulders. "Tell me, Ruth, once and for all. I have to know who you belong to."

How dare he? The tears threaten to spill. "You *know*"—I choke on the words—"You know better than anyone I need to repent." Truthfully, he doesn't know the half of it.

Ever looks at me like I've stuck a knife in his gut. "Is *that* the lead weight tied to your feet? Is that why you won't ever leave—you're stuck here serving some kind of life sentence? For God's sake, Ruth, you don't have to repent like this."

"Of course you'd say that." Barry breaks back through the crowd, flanked by the sheriff and my father. All three of their faces are bloodred—livid. I realize Ever and I are talking so close we look like we're embracing, and step back.

"You killed them all, you sicko." Barry's voice soars. "Even your daddy. You're a goddamn psychopath."

The crowd explodes.

"Barry," the sheriff barks, shoving him back. "Stand down, Deputy."

"What's *wrong* with you, Barry?" I whirl to Ever. "I'm so sorry."

But he already senses it: Barry's words have inflamed the crowd. Any moment now, their shock and horror could ignite into violence. He starts backing away.

"It's not too late for you," he says, then turns and pushes through the crowd. People stumble away to let him through.

Heart pounding, I watch his car peel out of the parking lot, grateful he's escaping even if I never will. It was, after all, the price of my bargain.

29

AUGUST, NINETEEN YEARS OLD

I closed my eyes against the water and turned it up as hot as it would go, as hard as it would hit. Molten heat pummeled me from the showerhead, but I closed my eyes and bore it. I'd taken too many showers lately, driven by an impulse to get clean, though the scouring I craved was stronger than a shower could accomplish. I stood under the waterfall and imagined a great knife carving off my skin and muscle until it got to bone. That's when I'd be clean enough. When I was small and fragile again, unburdened of the monstrous layers I'd grown.

The heat finally grew too much. I turned off the shower, stepped out, and toweled off, twisting water out of my hair. I wrapped myself in my white robe and padded down the hall, opening my bedroom door.

Everett leaned against my desk. The window was open beside him, letting in sticky August air thick as honey and so humid rain would surely start any minute. His right arm was in a makeshift sling he'd made for himself. The large bruise that shadowed his right eye was finally starting to yellow, the cut slicing his lower lip scabbed and healing. I used to read books with heroes who got wounded in wars or in fights defending the woman they loved and pictured their bruises as romantic swipes of color. But I've since learned better. There was nothing romantic about what had happened to Ever. I was surprised he could still make it through my window.

I stopped midstep. "My parents are downstairs."

He cocked his head. Confused, probably, about my tone. I'd never minded him climbing in my room before. "I know," he said slowly, drawing out the words. "That's why I took the private route."

I shut the door quickly and cast my eyes to the carpet, folding my arms tightly over my chest, wishing I was wearing anything other than this thin, flimsy robe.

It hurt to look at him.

"What's wrong?" I could hear the frown in his voice.

"Nothing." Warm water beaded steadily down my back. "How's your arm?"

"It'll be okay."

"Your eye is looking better."

"I told you I'd be fine."

The words were a knife through my rib cage, whether he meant them to be or not. The message was clear: once again, I'd overreacted.

But I swallowed my protest. Everett was allowed to be rude these days. Because two weeks ago, he'd come home to find his father lying dead on the floor, a bottle of vodka next to him. Since then, Ever's life had consisted of a confusing maelstrom of end-of-life paperwork and tense interactions with the sheriff's office, the latter entirely my fault, though he didn't know that. Once, he'd told me he was glad I never walked on eggshells around him. But now I was doing worse than walking on eggshells. Facing him now required a magician's prowess, an immense sleight of hand to keep his attention where I wanted it and away from where I didn't. "Right," I acquiesced. "I forgot how fast you heal. Silly me."

His voice grew more concerned. "Ruth, if I did something..."

I glanced at him, then back down. Looking for too long was dangerous.

It was too soon, too raw. The hurt on his face, combined with the bruises and cuts—mixed with everything he'd been going through lately, losing his dad—could be my undoing. I cleared my throat. "Have the church folks stopped bothering you yet?"

Outside, thunder cracked—and just like that, rain began to fall, small drops sprinkling through the window. A breeze ruffled the curtains, cutting the oppressive heat.

Ever walked to the window and stuck out his uninjured hand, catching rain in his palm. "No. They're still coming by to tell me alcohol poisoning was what my dad deserved, and now he's most assuredly reigning in Hell. Pretty much every day someone comes by. I think it's the most visitors that house has ever had."

I walked to my dresser and pulled out a drawer. I needed to put clothes on—layers of sweaters, maybe, to build a barrier between us.

Ever's voice turned teasing. "They don't like it when I agree. Messes with their minds. It's pretty fun, actually. If your dad wants to send any more over..."

I stopped rooting in my drawer. "It's not funny. It's cruel."

"That's what's so funny about it." He drew his hand in from the window dripping rain and wiped it on his shirt, leaving a dark handprint. "The cruelest people we know are from church. Let that sink in."

I scoffed, turning back to the dresser drawer, and accidentally caught the knot tying my robe on the corner. Swiftly, the knot unwound and my robe fell open.

I drew a sharp breath, stomach plunging, and grabbed for the fabric, pinching the sides back together. I couldn't even look at him. The sheer humiliation. If he'd seen...

"Ruth."

Ever's voice was strangely low. That single word—my name in his deep, lilting tone—changed the temperature in the room. Charged the air.

I turned my head, knowing it was a bad idea.

The sight of him stilled me.

His dark eyes were intense, gaze unwavering, like a predator on a hunt, his muscles tensed. He took a slow, measured step toward me, as if he thought moving faster might send me running.

"What are you doing?" I whispered. My throat felt nearly closed.

He slowly lifted a hand, the same way he did to calm a scared animal. His eyes were trained on my face. "I'm coming closer." His soft voice found its way inside my chest.

"Why?" I breathed.

He stopped an inch away. Looked down at me with his hair falling over his forehead. I almost shook at our closeness.

Ever and I had always existed in a world of our own. We'd tried to be there for each other, as close as two friends could be. But what was happening now was different. Uncharted. I had no map for it.

"Can I?" he whispered. And though I didn't know what he was asking for, I dipped my head anyway.

Ever placed his hand over mine—then, slowly, with our eyes locked, lowered it to my side. The robe I clutched fell open, revealing a sliver of skin, the small curve of my breast.

I caught my breath.

He took my other hand and gently lowered it. The robe opened to my shoulders. His eyes took me in, drifting to the soft dip between my breasts. I had no idea what to do. My heart beat so fast I was sure he could see it under my skin.

Slowly—so slowly—he rested his fingertips against my bare stomach. A gentle touch, but each finger sparked a nerve. He skimmed his fingers higher, leaving goose bumps in their wake, until they came to rest between my breasts.

He pressed his hand flat, the warmth of his palm and his fingers spanning my chest. The unexpected rush of feeling made me close my eyes. I'd never been touched like this before.

"Your heart is racing," he whispered. "I can feel your blood pumping under your skin."

This, finally, was what Bella had felt in the meadow the moment before Edward kissed her. I took a deep inhale of Ever's woodsy scent and it was almost like I was there.

"Ruth," he said gently. "Look at me."

I opened my eyes. No amount of imagining could have prepared me for the beauty of his bruised face wearing that tender, urgent expression.

"I sold my dad's garage," he said thickly. "I have money now. Enough to leave Bottom Springs."

It was like he'd plunged a sword through my chest. "What?"

His eyes grew brighter, hopeful. "The garage—it sold immediately, for exactly what I asked. I have more goddamn money now than I ever expected. This is our shot to leave. We'll do it just like we said. I'll work, you'll go to school, we'll travel and read and be happy."

Somehow it hadn't occurred to me that Everett's father's death would finally give Ever what he needed to leave: freedom, money, and opportunity. How shameful, as an avid reader, that I hadn't predicted the textbook tragic irony: my fear that Ever would one day leave me had finally come true, and I'd been the very one to engineer it.

I took a step back and knotted my robe tightly. "I can't."

His face fell. "What? Why?"

Why? There was nothing on earth I wanted more than to go. Escaping was the dream that used to keep me going. It was also the possibility I'd sacrificed, the future I'd foreclosed, to strike my deal.

So no matter how mesmerized I was by his proximity, if Everett chose to leave, there could be no us in the way I'd only just allowed myself to begin to imagine.

"I don't get it." He took a step toward me, but I backed up and he stopped, hurt on his face. "This is what we've always talked about."

I'd have to lie. "I don't want it anymore." I crossed my arms. "I thought about it, and it doesn't make sense to leave. I'm happy here. I have a job and family. It was just talk, you know? Foolishness."

"Liar. Why are you acting like this?"

"It's not my fault you took it too seriously." Now I was the one plunging the sword.

His eyes widened. "Who *are* you right now? Seriously, who am I talking to, because it isn't Ruth Cornier."

"I don't—want—to—go," I said, raising my voice, parents downstairs be damned. "If you do, fine. But you can't drag me against my will."

I'd finally horrified him. His pleading expression closed up. "I would never do anything against your will."

We stood looking at each other for a long, tense moment, my hands clenched in the effort of keeping my true emotions off my face. Then Ever pressed his hand to his heart and twisted an invisible key—just a second, the briefest touch—but I knew what it meant. He was locking away this moment, never to be resurfaced. He turned to the window, swung a leg over the ledge, and vanished into the rain.

I stood there staring at the window but not seeing it. Then, like a dam cracking, the grief poured out. I sank to the floor and cried so hard it felt like I was breaking myself in half. And still, I couldn't get my body to express the true fullness of my grief. I was the architect of my own misery. No amount of sobbing was equal to the pain.

I was losing Ever. From this day forward, everything would change. He'd been more than my best friend—sometimes a person was bigger than that. Sometimes they were your freedom. The whole woods, the channel through which you first fell in love with the earth, felt at home in it. Sometimes a person *was* your home, the love you learned to grow for yourself, stored in another's body. Sometimes they were the way your body first learned what it wanted. Sometimes they were an awakening.

He'd been all of it, and now he was gone.

30

NOW

I slam Barry's car door as the sheriff's and my parents' cars come screeching to a halt.

"I don't have anything to say." I pull up my long dress and race across the lawn to my front door. I don't want to talk to Barry—not after what he pulled with Everett in the parking lot. And the sheriff and my parents are only here to harass me. I want to be alone in my small sanctuary, lock the door and pretend my house is hallowed ground.

"Ruth Sarah Cornier," my father booms, "you stop this instant."

Like a magic spell, I go rigid on the grass. So many years of obedience and it's like my body isn't fully mine. I remember Ever tapping my temple. *Is he in there? Is this his?*

All four of them—Barry, the sheriff, my mother, and my father—storm across the lawn in their pressed church clothes. The low heels and ironed button-ups are a disguise: no matter what they're wearing, they're an army, here to launch an assault. I steel my spine.

"You idiot." To my surprise, the sheriff shakes his head at Barry. "You tipped our hand. Now what if he skips town?"

"You can't blame the boy for getting excited," says my father. He's still in his white robe from church, the gold thread on the massive crosses adorning his shoulders catching in the sun. "The Duncan kid was being deliberately provocative."

"Tipped what hand?" I ask the sheriff, focused on using this ambush to at least learn whatever secret Barry referenced in his anger.

"He won't skip town." Barry says it bitterly, like a child unused to being criticized. "Ruth's still here."

I think of Ever's haste to leave Bottom Springs. Had he caught wind he was going to be scapegoated somehow? Is that why he was so eager to leave?

The sheriff clears his throat. "I don't think—"

"Someone tell me what's going on," I demand, taking everyone by surprise.

My mother's look is censorious. "Don't interrupt your elders."

I'm this close to screaming that I'm twenty-three years old and don't care about rules I never agreed to when the sheriff turns to my mother and says, "No, Ruth's right. It's time."

He mops his gleaming forehead. The mid-July afternoon heat is so thick it nearly ripples in the air. Sweat trickles down my back, but the last thing I'll do is invite these people into my house.

"The reason I came to question you the other day about Everett's connection to the Blanchards is because we're gathering evidence linking him to Herman Blanchard's death." Sheriff Theriot delivers the bombshell in a matter-of-fact voice. Even in his white church shirtsleeves, there's no mistaking he's the law. "We had a witness come forward, one of Herman's neighbors. Says two years ago, 'round the time Herman was found dead in his garage, her son—young boy, 'bout seven at the time—told his mother he saw the Low Man visit Herman. Said he spotted the man walkin' out of Herman's house, and when he saw the boy, the man put his finger to his lips to shush him and then ran away."

Goose bumps rise on my arms despite the heat.

"The woman didn't say anything until now because at first she thought her son was tellin' tall tales, and course Herman's death was ruled accidental. But with all the talk about the Low Man floatin' 'round Fred and Renard's deaths, she thought she better come talk. At first, I was ready to dismiss it as more occult hysteria."

"Then why are you telling me?" My voice is thick.

"Because I don't know 'bout no Low Man, but you know what I did realize? The creature's supposed to be pale and morose and good-lookin' enough to tempt a person. You know who fits that bill? Everett Duncan."

The sheriff glances at my father and they exchange portentous looks.

"Absolutely not," I said.

"Everett fits the description of a man a gas station attendant out in Forsythe recalls gettin' in a big fight with Fred Fortenot not too long before Fred went missin'."

That hits like a sledgehammer. Ever has never mentioned getting in a fight with Fred. It can't be true, then. It has to be someone else or something the sheriff invented to pin him.

Everyone watches me. They're waiting for me to break into tears, I realize. Gasp, scream, show some sign of horror. I make sure my face remains expressionless.

"We believe this explains why Everett didn't come back to town last summer. He knew the boy saw him outside Herman's house and he wanted to let the heat die down, make sure he wasn't gonna get caught."

"You have it all wrong," I say. "Everett is one of the best men I know."

"You're *still* defending him?" Barry's voice is incredulous.

"Told you she was obstinate." My mother's icy tone is the soundtrack of my childhood.

"Listen." The sheriff puts out his hands, placating. "Everett's going down for this, no two ways. But we need your help first. Why'd he come back this summer? What's he planning? You're his only friend. You have to know something."

To see me, I think, then feel naive. "He came back to sell his father's house," I say instead.

Barry shoots the sheriff a worried look. "He'll have no more ties here. He could slip away."

Exactly what I've been worried about.

"Ruth." The sheriff's voice grows grave. "We suspect Everett killed not only Herman, but Fred before that and his own father before Fred. We're waiting for money to exhume Killian's body and test it, since it wasn't done when he died. That's three murders we know of. Do you know what that makes him?"

The sun beats down on us—distorting the air, giving everyone auras. There are no bird calls, no frog croaks. The world is silent in this moment of anticipated dread.

The sheriff's voice is steady. "Ruth, your friend is a serial killer."

31

NOW

It's late when I meet Ever at the bar. There's no chance he'll be safe at the Blue Moon after the stunt he pulled at church, so I've asked him to meet me at the Alibi, a place I've heard mentioned in gossip. It's in a deserted part of Forsythe, nothing but trash tumbling down the street when I hurry across it. The only light comes from the red and blue bar signs.

But inside it's busier. I've noticed in Forsythe, people don't talk to each other much, maybe on account of it being a bigger town where everyone doesn't know each other's business. In the dim and moody Alibi, men sit alone, staring morosely over their beers, or in pairs at the bar, talking quietly. I spot Everett in a red booth and straighten my shoulders. I need to keep my wits about me tonight. It's not the time for emotion: it's time for logical thinking. Investigative Ruth, getting to the bottom of the sheriff's absurd accusations and finding a way to counter them.

"Got you this," Ever says when I walk up, sliding a glass of something so shockingly pink it can only be Boone's Farm across the table.

He wants me to sit across from him instead of next to him like usual. Okay. Taking the hint, I slide into the booth. "You assumed I'd need the hard stuff after what happened at church, looks like." I'm going for light to undercut the tension, a classic Everett move, but he doesn't smile. "Well, I'm just glad you agreed to meet me."

He looks away, jaw tightening, so I take the opportunity to study him. He's in a white T-shirt and blue jeans, innocent enough, though his sleeves are rolled up on account of the heat and it makes him look a little tough. The way he's sitting, arms folded over the table, shows off his pronounced muscles, his broad shoulders—and once again, like when he was wrenching open the safe in Earl's garage, I'm struck by his bulk and cut, things I stopped paying attention to when he became an extension of me. He's taken the gauze off his bullet wound: I can see the path the bullet took across his skin, red and angry. But even scarred and half-shadowed in the murky bar, I still see my Ever.

Of course, I know better than anyone you don't need to look like a killer to be one.

"Hey," yells Ever suddenly. Across the bar, two men stop playing pool. "Guy in the plaid's cheating."

"Fuck you," says the man in the plaid. He turns to his partner. "Am not."

Ever turns back to me as the man's partner starts pulling balls off the table and cursing loudly. He takes a sip of beer, a smile curving his mouth, and says, more to himself, "Just thought you'd like to know."

I frown at his strange mood. "I'm surprised you're still here. I'm happy about it, don't get me wrong, but it seemed like you were in a hurry to leave."

"Yeah, well." Ever drops his beer back on the table. "I guess I must be in the mood to torture myself." A new song comes on the jukebox and he yells without looking, "Someone turn it up!" I watch the lone other woman in the bar walk to the jukebox and turn the dial, eyeing Ever with intention.

Yesterday on my lawn, the sheriff had pleaded with me for help one last time before I fled into my house.

"We don't have enough evidence for a warrant yet," he'd said. "Which is why we haven't arrested him. We need a confession or some lead on evidence, a location where he stashes souvenirs, a tip on a weapon, something like that. You're the one he trusts. We need your help."

My father had turned to me with actual respect in his eyes and told me I had a chance to do something noble that would restore me to full righteousness in the eyes of the Lord. It was like he could see straight into my soul, the way he'd said, *No matter your past sins, it's a chance to repent.* I hadn't been able to look away from him. And it wasn't only the guilt that held me there—it was also that old impulse, the one I thought I'd outgrown, to be good in his eyes. To make him proud. To be loved.

It had taken muscular force to push the impulse down. I'd had to remind myself that I knew better than to trust them. If Ever was evil, I would've known by now. No two people in the world have been closer than us. I'm the one who keeps secrets, not him. So I'm here tonight to protect Ever. Warn him about the sheriff, tell him to get out of town. I open my mouth, and...

Nothing comes out.

He watches me expectantly. His face is truly so haunting—those flecks of color dancing in his eyes as hypnotic as the bands of color on a coral snake, rustling in warning under fall leaves. A memory comes back: that day at the dock when we were eighteen and I crouched in front of him in the sand, locking an invisible door in his chest, shutting away all the things better left unsaid.

All the things I didn't want to hear.

"Ever." I clear my throat. "Did you ever run into Fred Fortenot at a gas station?"

He barely looks at me—he's busy grinning at the woman who turned up the music, his white teeth dazzling in the low light. "I don't know,

Ruth." He turns, still wearing the Cheshire cat smile. "Bottom Springs is a small town. Chances are."

I try to sound casual. "You ever get in a fight with him?"

He rolls his empty bottle across the table, snatching it just before it falls to the floor. "You asked me here to talk about Fred?"

"Asshole," barks the man in plaid, knocking Ever's shoulder as he stalks past our table.

"Cheater," Ever calls back, and the man stops. He turns. His eyes are hard.

"Say that to my face."

Ever seems nearly giddy as he unfolds from the booth. "Gladly."

The man looks up at him, taking in his height and breadth, and clenches his jaw. "You know what? Not worth my time." He shoots me a dirty look and beelines out of the bar.

Ever sighs and drops back into the booth.

"Are you trying to start a fight?" I want to shake him. This is like his performance at Holy Fire: reckless, self-endangering. We've spent our friendship trying to take care of ourselves and each other, so I've never seen this side of him. He's like a stranger.

Is that why you haven't told him about the sheriff's accusation? Are you doubting him?

I push away the Boone's Farm.

"Let's say I am trying to start a fight." Ever's dark eyes glitter. "Everyone around here already thinks I'm a villain. Why not give them what they want?" He glances at the woman by the jukebox, dancing slow and sultry to the rock song, and shakes his head. "They want it so bad, after all. What have I got to lose?" He returns to me. "I've got nothing left to care about, anyway."

Hollowness empties my chest. Before I can answer, he leans in. "So, what's next? You going to ask if I've ever tampered with Herman

Blanchard's gas lines? Come on, Ruthie. Let's hear the next part of this very subtle interrogation."

I jerk back like he's slapped me, shame burning my cheeks, and then shove up out of the booth. "Whoever this person is I'm talking to, tell him I want my friend back."

Ever doesn't blink. "Funny. I'd like mine back, too."

We stare at each other, two faces mirroring anger, until I can't take it anymore. I leave him sitting in the booth, nearly kicking open the door to the bar on my way out. Let him keep drinking and fighting. Let him become his father for all I care.

Cloud cover means no stars tonight, so the outside world is dark and lonely. I'm unlocking my car when a deep voice calls, "Hey, Red. You're pretty cute."

Red. Like Renard used to call me. My hands freeze on the door handle. I look back and see a man standing in the parking lot near his driver's side door. He looks to be about my age, maybe a little younger, smiling and wearing a white baseball cap with LSU stitched into it. Back home from college for the summer, maybe.

I open the car door as fast as I can.

"What, no response?" The man's voice turns indignant. "That was a compliment."

Whisper-quiet, Everett appears at my side. I startle back. His eyes are locked on the man. A wicked smile spreads slowly across his face.

"Don't. Go back inside."

But Ever ignores me. In a flash, he's in front of the man, saying something so softly I can't hear it, and before I can yell for him to stop, the man in the baseball cap takes a swing.

It's the invitation Everett's been waiting for.

He ducks nimbly and catches the man in the face with his own fist, so hard he jerks the man's head back, sending him tumbling to the gravel, his baseball cap flying. Ever is good at this, well practiced at bar fights. People used to whisper about it, and I used to say it wasn't his fault, he wasn't asking for it.

What if I was wrong?

"Ever, *stop*," I yell, slamming my car door shut.

He shoves the man to the gravel, where he splays out. His arms go up, trying to shield his face; he's making some sort of incoherent noise of protest, something between a groan and a plea. Everett straddles him and pummels, blows that twist the man's face. His expression is vacant, like he's gone back to those nights with his father, locked in the past where I can't follow.

"Stop," I scream, and fling myself at him, catching his heavy arms and doing my best to wrench them back. "*Please*," I sob, and Ever stops, allowing me to pull him back. He staggers off the guy, breathing hard. The man lets out a sob and scrambles for his car.

"Who *are* you right now?" My voice is hoarse from yelling but no less stricken.

Everett wipes his mouth with a bloody hand, red pooling around his split knuckles. "I'm my father's son, Ruth. 'That which you are, you are.'"

A car engine roars and the man Ever beat peels out of the parking lot. His LSU baseball cap still lies overturned on the ground. Tears wet my cheeks. "Do you *want* to go to prison?"

Ever flings out his arms and takes a step backward. "Who cares what I want? I'm a dead man walking." He shoves his bloody hands in his pockets and turns away from me into the night.

As he leaves it hits me—this feeling. My heart like a hummingbird's, chills despite the heat, paralysis in my legs, rooting me to the gravel.

I'm scared of my friend.

And it's not the first time.

32

JUNE, NINETEEN YEARS OLD

The moon was bright enough to light my way around the back of Everett's house. I brushed aside a curtain of low-hanging branches, stepped over a section of rotted fence, and entered his backyard. It looked like the inside of a madman's mind: expansive, wild and unruly, the grass nearly up to my knees in some places, patches of mud in others, thorned branches grabbing at me like tentacled arms. The full moon shone on it all, lighting old beer bottles thick with film like a path to Ever's window. It was late, but I would knock anyway. This was too important to wait.

Today was his mother's birthday. When he'd told me earlier, almost shyly, I knew it was the first time he'd ever told anyone. It should've been a sacred moment. An outstretched hand, a show of trust.

Instead, it made me sick.

All day, I'd wrestled with the truth: I had to tell Ever how she really died. Since I couldn't get out of Bible study after work, I was left to sneak in the dark to his house the way he usually did to mine, crossing my fingers I wouldn't run into his father.

But before I could knock at Ever's window, movement in the farthest corner of the backyard, near the forest's edge, caught my eye. There—a flickering flame. A small bonfire. And was that—a figure, crouched low?

Even in the moonlight, it was far enough away that all I could see was a dark mass, vaguely human-shaped.

Ever?

As if in a trance, I moved toward the fire. Something shone in the grass. I stopped and squinted. It was a smooth white stone, glittering with tiny specks of minerals. There was something written on it, dark and barely discernible. I picked up the rock and turned it so it caught the light—there. A shape. Five curling spirals, their edges meeting in the center of the stone. Rust-red. Smelling faintly of iron.

The spirals were drawn in blood.

I dropped the stone and looked frantically around the grass. White rocks were everywhere, forming a giant circle around the bonfire, their surfaces gleaming with bloody spirals. What *was* this? What did it mean?

I looked up at the fire. There were two dark masses, not one. They seemed to be bent over something, their movements jerky, like wolves over a kill, tearing away flesh. Had I been wrong—were they animals? There was a strange smell as I moved closer, musky and putrid, the scent of the decaying animals we passed on our hikes.

Their dark movements against the orange-red crackling fire were hypnotizing. I drew forward like a woman under a spell. I needed to know what I was looking at.

I was close enough to peer. If I could only lean—

I stepped on a branch and it snapped with a loud crack.

The figures whirled at the noise, faces illuminated by the moonlight—

I screamed and stumbled back.

It was Ever and his father. They stared at me with vacant eyes, their faces smeared with blood, thick and dripping down their chins. There was blood everywhere, coating their hands, running up their arms. As they turned, they revealed what lay between them: a deer. Stomach split open, insides spilling out.

My eyes jumped to the blood around their mouths.

I was filled with an overwhelming sense of wrongness, what my father called the sense of sin. I begged my body to move, but my limbs were locked, terror turning me to stone.

The fire hissed and popped like a creature giving warning. Ever blinked, coming back to himself. "Ruth?"

Hearing my name in his hoarse voice unlocked me. I scrambled backward, slipping over the white stones and nearly falling in the grass. I righted myself, eyes locked on Everett's blood-soaked face—that terrible mask of gore and beauty—and a fear beyond rational thought filled me. The sight of them—demons feasting among the flames—triggered every warning I'd ever been given about Hell, every threat screamed by my father from his balcony. It was a holy terror that seized me. In that moment I ceased to be Ruth, the rational thinker, and became my father's creature, his weak-kneed acolyte, through and through.

I turned and took off through the yard.

"Wait!" Ever yelled.

I could've sworn I heard him getting to his feet. And the thought of him chasing me—strong Ever, impossibly fast—unleashed a new dimension of fear. I leapt over the rotted fence and streaked into the street, pumping my legs as fast as they would go.

It was midnight, his neighborhood was the hunting ground, and I was prey. That's what I felt, deep in my bones: I was the deer. Running to postpone the moment Ever's fingernails would rake across my back and I would fall, finally feeling his sharp canines deep in my neck. In that moment, in the height of my fear, it felt like some part of me had been waiting for it, secretly, since the moment I'd met him.

I ran like the Devil himself was behind me all the way home.

33

NOW

We keep the microfilm reader in the basement of the library, a place Nissa swears is haunted, though that's not a very Christian thing to say. It's dark and humid down here, no air conditioner and a single rickety light, but I'm willing to stay for as long as it takes. Like the sheriff, I need proof—except the evidence I'm searching for will show Everett's innocent and someone else is behind the deaths they'd like to pin on him. The case I need to build is diametrically opposed to the sheriff's, and it's half for Ever's sake, half for mine. An hour ago I searched "definition of a serial killer" on the computer, unable to help myself, and the results—the gruesome pictures and stories—made me sick. I can't get the memory of Ever beating the man outside the Alibi out of my head. The way he'd looked doing it, that grim satisfaction, those empty eyes. Like so many of the mug shots in the search results.

I load the reader with half a year's worth of issues of the *Bottom Springs Bugle*, the town's now-defunct newspaper, figuring that for thoroughness's sake I should go back to the beginning, which means 1999, the year Everett and I were born. I've just pulled the first issue up onscreen when I hear heavy creaking footsteps and labored breathing, the telltale sounds of Nissa willing herself to run down the stairs.

Sure enough, the next moment she bursts into the basement with wide eyes.

"I'm surprised you're down here," I say, leaning back in my chair. "What about the ghosts?"

She takes in the gloomy room, which we mostly use for storage these days, as the demand for microfilm is…not high. "Figured if I hustled fast enough, no ghosts could grab me." She side-eyes me and I can't help but laugh. I'd forgotten how much Nissa's presence is a balm.

"I'll make this quick," she says, and thrusts out a book. It's ancient, the cover threadbare. I have to squint at the tiny gold-embossed title: *Symbology of Euro-Descended Spiritual Philosophies, Vol. II*. Nissa's voice is charged with excitement. "I finally did it, Ruth. I found our symbol."

"You *did*?" I abandon the computer.

"This is one of the books I got shipped from the LSU archive. My old colleague had to go digging. Apparently, no one's checked out this baby for about fifteen years now, poor thing." Nissa pats the book, then starts flipping pages, her words coming a mile a minute. "Now, I think it's page 285… Yes, that's right."

"Nissa, you're a certified genius."

She waves the compliment away, but her cheeks tinge with pink. "Hush. There it is. In the section on French Catholicism—look."

It's right there in black-and-white: the same symbol Barry said had been carved over and over on the trees in the swamp. A circle between two crescent moons, their tips pointing in opposite directions.

"The book says that in some Madonna-worshipping sects that evolved out of French Catholicism—"

"Like Le Culte de la Lune," I interrupt.

"Exactly. In some of these, a circle topped by horns represents Lucifer and all the dark beings under his dominion."

"Wait, those aren't crescent moons?"

"Nope. They're curved horns, like the kind in old drawings of Satan. Adapted from goats and rams, apparently."

"So our symbol *is* a mark of evil?"

"No, see, here's the thing. *Our* symbol has horns on top but also on the bottom, facing down, and according to this, symbols facing down take on their opposite meaning."

I scrunch my nose. "Which means..."

Nissa's voice is practically jubilant. "Which means this symbol isn't supposed to *call forth* evil. It's supposed to get rid of it. Negate dark spirits, strip the Devil of power. It's an apotropaic mark."

"A what?"

"Apotropaic mark. They're found in every religion and culture the world over. Symbols people use to protect against bad spirits. You'll see them painted above houses, worn on necklaces, in grave sites, dating as far back as we can trace."

I blink at her. "So the symbol in the swamp, the one the whole town thinks is a mark of witchcraft meant to beckon the Low Man...is actually meant to protect us?"

"Exactly," she gushes, turning the page. "It was found on trees, right? All of them facing town. Just like this picture of a protection circle. Look."

There on the page is a scene I recognize: a black-and-white photo of a clearing. In the center is a small fire, and around that, a circle of white stones, each painted with our two-horned symbol.

"Is that a Le Culte de la Lune ritual?"

Nissa peers at the caption, then shrugs. "The book doesn't say which group it belongs to. Sorry. It just says 'protection circle found in the Southeastern United States.'"

It's our symbol from the swamp painted on the rocks, but otherwise so close to the scene I witnessed in Ever's backyard years ago that it can't be a coincidence. But he swore he wasn't responsible for the symbols in the swamp. Why would he lie about it, especially if he was only protecting the town?

Nissa slams the book shut. "Isn't this exciting? I'll tell you what. They'll probably give us honorary deputy badges. I'm gonna call my friend at LSU, see if she's got any more books like this." She pauses, her expression thoughtful. "And I guess it's time to tell the sheriff we've got a pagan vandal in our midst."

"But not one who's trying to hurt us," I murmur.

"No," she agrees. "Not at all."

That's exactly what Everett said to me all those years ago.

34

JUNE, NINETEEN YEARS OLD

The woods hummed with butterflies fluttering to wildflowers newly in bloom—tall, airy cleomes, perfect teacup marigolds, bright, spiky stalks of bee balm swaying in the sun—the very picture of summer beauty, and still my heart was cold as I followed Everett in. Staring at his back as we hiked to the mysterious thing he wanted to show me, all I could see was his face last night. That terrible mask of blood.

He was standing at the edge of my parents' lawn when I woke up this morning, as if he sensed he had to start over, win me back from the beginning. His tall frame and solemn face were the first things I saw when I peered out my window, exhausted from a night without sleep. I'd crept out of the house to meet him despite the potent mix of fear and embarrassment that still lingered because my curiosity was stronger. How would he possibly explain?

He'd studied me in silence for a long time before finally asking if I'd let him show me something. That's all he offered. Once again, it was curiosity that tipped the scales to bring me here, traipsing behind him through the morning mist into a corner of the woods where I'd never been before.

"This is it," Ever said, stopping to face a large, gnarled tree. "What I wanted to show you."

I stepped wordlessly around him. Not only was the tree thick and tall, but its weathered bark and knotted branches made it look old and wizened, like one of those ancient trees Old Man Jonas swore had stood in our forest for over a thousand years, bearing witness to a millennium of men. I felt an immediate reverence.

Smooth white stones were set around the tree in a small circle, decorated with the same five-spiraled symbol as last night. And carved into the tree was an alcove, a hollowed-out space with a thin ledge that must've been a beast to chisel. The ledge held two white candles, wax mostly melted. In the center of the alcove was a carved portrait of a woman. She had long hair, gentle eyes, and a small, knowing smile. At the base of the tree, wildflowers had been laid carefully between the roots. They were limp and browning, obviously put there some time ago, but I could still see some of the vivid blue of the swamp lilies.

"My shrine to Célestine Duncan," said Ever wistfully.

I stepped inside the circle of stones and ran my fingers over the roughly hewn lines of her face. "Célestine," I whispered. So that was his mother's name. A butterfly flapped close enough to brush my hair. The scent of flowers was so pungent here that I closed my eyes and took a deep breath, filling my lungs. Then I turned back to Ever. "I don't understand."

He dug his hands into his pockets. "My mom kept a room in the house where she sewed and knit and read poetry. She never got to go to high school, but she read a lot, like you do. She was smart and curious like you. My dad won't step foot in her room since she died. Which made it my refuge growing up."

I'd seen the room in Ever's house: the pressed flowers on the walls, the sewing machine, the illustration of the Virgin Mary.

"I spent a lot of time there as a kid, memorizing the poems she'd collected, teaching myself to use her sewing machine. Anything she liked, I wanted to learn. Trace her steps, I guess, to be close to her. I was pretty young when I found this wedged in her armchair." He pulled a small brown notebook out of his pocket, bound with a leather strap. "It's her diary. Well, half diary, half scribblings. Some grocery lists. My dad said she started carrying it when she got pregnant because she'd forget things. It's how I discovered her religion."

"Religion?" Everyone always said the Duncans never stepped foot in church.

"My dad called it 'swamp spiritualism.'" Ever cleared his throat. "It was a practice passed down from her parents, who were…self-imposed outcasts, I guess you'd call them. People who liked to live off the land, didn't really trust others."

That, I knew. Célestine's sheltered upbringing was what had made her dismiss the town gossip about how dangerous Killian Duncan was. I swallowed the sharp knowledge and said, "Living off the land. Like you do, with your hunting."

"Practical reasons aside, I figure it's my heritage. You know…" His voice grew quieter. "My mom wrote about being lonely. It's hard to picture her moving to Bottom Springs and falling in love with my dad, of all people. No one much talked to her after that. If I'd had the chance, I would've tried to be good company to her."

His eyes radiated a desire for me to believe him. "You would've been great company," I agreed, and he swallowed.

"I told my dad I'd found strange prayers and sketches in her diary and begged him to tell me about them. He offered to teach me what he knew."

"That doesn't sound like him."

A knowing smile curved Ever's lips, an echo of the one he'd carved for his mother. "No, it doesn't. But over time he became obsessed with doing her rituals. Nowadays it's the only time he acts like a real human being. I think she was the only person he ever truly loved."

There was a seed of grudging respect in his voice—maybe even a seed of love. How it had managed to take root in such inhospitable soil, after everything his father had done to him, I didn't know. Perhaps it was because Ever didn't know the worst of it. I needed to finish what I'd started last night and tell him the truth.

Ever stepped carefully over the stones and crouched low, picking up a wilted lily. He rolled a petal between his fingers. "It's a form of atonement, the rituals. As much as he's always blamed me for her death, I think part of him blames himself, too."

That was too much. "Ever..." I started, but he shook his head.

"Wait—what you saw last night. It's something my dad and I do every year on her birthday. I know it's strange and you probably think it's sacrilegious, but...it's one of her ceremonies." He dropped the lily and reached for the stones, brushing his fingers over the spirals. "The purpose is to show you're worthy of divine intervention. To do that, you give something in sacrifice. And if you're deemed worthy, the bridge between the living and the dead will open. It was in her notebook. She'd do it to commune with her parents, ask for advice." He held up the stone. "Five spirals. Five signs of worthiness. They all require giving something."

"There was so much blood," I whispered. "The two of you, bathed in it. It looked like..."

"I know." He smiled grimly. "There's a reason I never told you. Some of the rituals are a little...rough. You might be thinking everyone's right, and we're some kind of Devil-worshippers. But Ruth." He lowered himself all the way to his knees, eyes shining as he looked up at me. "It's harmless, I swear. Blood is natural, fire is natural. No one gets hurt."

"What about the deer?"

He raised an eyebrow. "I didn't realize you'd become a principled vegetarian."

"Did you eat it?"

"Not exactly."

"This is one of those details I'm going to need you to be exact about."

"I didn't eat it. I kind of...washed myself in its blood. To honor the sacrifice."

"It scared me," I admitted. "Seeing you the way other people make you out to be."

There was something fragile in his expression—in that moment he looked so much like a child. Except the Everett I remembered from elementary school had already been closed and guarded. This Everett was looking at me with precarious hope.

"I'm sorry," he said softly. "It's not that I actually believe I'm opening a bridge to the dead. But when I do her rituals, or come here to this shrine, I feel connected to her. They're the biggest pieces I have left. It's something she believed in, and I think she would've been happy to know we carried it forward. It feels like carrying her forward."

What I'd seen last night wasn't a demon, then. It was a boy, aching for his mother, going to any lengths to be close. What wouldn't I do for a person I loved?

The fear I'd felt—the whispers about Ever I'd allowed into my head—dissolved. I knelt so we were eye level and placed a hand on his shoulder. "I understand."

He brushed his cheek against my knuckles, his stubble lightly scratching. "You do?"

"Yes. But there's something I have to tell you."

"Listen to what she wrote," he insisted, rushing to open the little leather notebook. He thought I still had reservations. "It was her last entry. She said, 'I've had my troubles. Dark, dark days. But today, I'm happy knowing my Everett is coming soon. I didn't know love like this could exist. He's mine—the closest person in the world to me, this tiny baby I haven't even met yet. I hope all our lives, we'll be this close.'"

His mother's words stilled me. The sunshine found Ever through the branches, lighting his skin, making him look like an angel for once.

"It brings me peace," he said quietly, closing the book. "Knowing she was happy. Her spirit went gently, I think. Which means she's at rest."

My mother's voice echoed back: *That lie is probably the only mercy that boy's ever been given.*

A breeze ruffled Ever's hair. It carried the sweet scent of flowers. This was all he had: a pretty tree, a yearly ritual, a merciful lie. I couldn't tell him how she really died—not now or ever. It wouldn't bring his mother back, so what would the knowledge do other than wound him? No, I had to carry the horror alone so he could be spared. I'd always wanted to protect him—maybe this was how I was meant to do it.

Ever frowned at my silence, eyes tracking over my face. "What do you need to tell me?"

I took a deep breath. "Nothing after all."

35

NOW

Remembering the details of that day makes me all the more certain Everett's mother's "swamp spiritualism" can be traced back to Le Culte de la Lune—or whatever version of it survived in secret over the centuries, called Wicca or witchcraft depending on who you asked. It adds up: the symbols, the white stone circles, the illustration of the Virgin Mary hanging in Célestine's room. If I take Ever at his word that he's not the one who carved the symbols in the swamp—and remembering the way I'd judged him years ago, I'm keen to trust him now—that means someone else in Bottom Springs practices. Someone who's kept it hidden, only to go public now. But who and why, or does it even matter? Do the symbols in the swamp have anything to do with the murders, or are they connected only by happenstance, pieces of evidence discovered at the same time?

The more I learn, the more my list of questions grows.

All the more reason to take a page out of Nissa's book and research. I shake the mouse and wake the old dinosaur desktop, returning to the January 1999 issues of the *Bottom Springs Bugle*. Forcing myself to squint at the tiny print, I scroll through news of high school football games, a winter storm, the celebrated opening of the Rosethorn Café, and other quotidian happenings. It's not until I get to March that I find anything interesting: Célestine Duncan's obituary.

It's just two short lines. "Célestine Gabrielle Duncan, born in Trufayette Parish on June 9, 1974, passed away during childbirth on March 2, 1999. She is survived by her husband, Killian Duncan, and infant son, Everett Duncan."

Cold and nondescript, a woman's life reduced to less than a paragraph. And they printed the lie Killian must've fed them about how she died, no questions asked. My stomach turns. I keep scrolling, but there's no other mention of her.

But in a June issue, something new catches my eye: an article about my father titled "Young 'Reverend's' Fiery Speeches Court Controversy." I read aloud to the ghosts: "Bottom Springs native James Cornier, 25, has caused quite a stir in recent months with his radical, impassioned speeches against what he terms 'the malevolent influence of the occult' in Trufayette Parish. Mr. Cornier, who styles himself a 'born again' reverend despite his lack of formal religious training, claims God chose him to bring believers into the fold and eradicate a sinister network of occultists in Bottom Springs."

I blink at the screen for a second, then clear my throat and keep reading.

"His heated speeches about sin and corruption are delivered every weekend in a clearing near the entrance to Starry Swamp, where Mr. Cornier, under the influence of the Holy Spirit, has taken to speaking in tongues and even handling serpents, two of the five signs distinguishing God's true believers, according to a passage from the Book of Mark. While these controversial worship practices are most often associated with the Holiness movement and other forms of extreme evangelicalism, attendance at Mr. Cornier's rustic sermons has swelled to considerable numbers in recent months. And as his popularity grows, Mr. Cornier's words are having an impact: the 'reverend' is credited with driving out the Longbeaux family, longtime Bottom Springs residents accused by his followers of practicing witchcraft, as well as the Freeman family, whose home was vandalized twice with threatening graffiti before they relocated."

"Though Mr. Cornier's following is on the rise in Trufayette Parish, not all are impressed. Angela Links, spokesperson for the New Orleans chapter of the Anti-Defamation League, when sent a recording of one of Mr. Cornier's speeches, claimed any language inciting violence against particular peoples can be held liable for the resulting crimes. In particular, she flagged the parts of Mr. Cornier's speech that focused on a need to 'dispose of immoral women,' which she termed a thinly veiled threat."

"In defense of his methods, Mr. Cornier told the *Bugle*: 'It's time for real Christians to take our religion outside the walls of the church. True believers have been charged by God to bring our faith into every aspect of our lives. No more Sunday Christians. Our careers, our politics, our families, and our communities should all reflect Godly values. In this fallen world, ours must be a muscular faith. If not, like Sodom and Gomorrah, we will fall into ruin. I urge the people of Bottom Springs to eradicate the poisonous influences living among us. Our survival depends on it.'"

"Mr. Cornier does seem to be right that the fate of Bottom Springs is on the table. With dwindling attendance at Holy Fire Church compared to Mr. Cornier's growing flock, it seems the town has been overtaken by religious zealotry and evangelical fervor. This journalist, for one, would hate to see Bottom Springs become a place that drives out long-standing neighbors over feverish accusations. The soul of this town may indeed be in jeopardy."

I whistle softly. "You tell 'em..." I check the byline. "John Abraham."

Well, at least one person in history has had the stones to disagree with my father, even if he was a journalist I've never heard of at a now-defunct newspaper. I had no idea my father got his start like that, stoking a witch hunt, but I can't say I'm surprised. I search for more articles about him, but find none. In fact, as I pore through issues, searching for John Abraham's bylines, I notice the subjects of his articles turn to wedding announcements and social calendar coverage—no more religion, nothing hard hitting. Could my father have been powerful enough to shape the coverage?

I continue to scroll, reloading the reader twice with new film, but it's not until an issue dated nearly a year later that I find my father's name again. The article is the opposite of critical, celebrating Reverend James Cornier's ascendance to the pulpit of Holy Fire, made possible by the early retirement of the church's previous leader. To my surprise, I'm in the accompanying photo, a red-haired toddler in my mother's arms. She and my father stand in front of Holy Fire, renamed Holy Fire Born Again, a small and humble building with a parking lot paved with dirt. My mother's expression matches my father's: grim and haughty, chins held high, as if their inheritance of the church was a foregone conclusion. I can't help but wonder if the previous preacher actually retired or was forced out.

I groan into my hands. These glimpses of Cornier family history, while illuminating, have nothing to do with Fred's or Herman's murders. I need to focus. I rub my eyes and, with a weary sigh, start fresh on another roll of film.

Quickly, a new problem presents itself: as the years progress, the newspaper goes from scarce mentions of my father to an abundance. And not just him: I can trace the ascension of the Fortenot Fishing Company and Blanchard Hospital clearly through the issues, the *Bugle* turning chock-full of mentions of Fred Fortenot and the Blanchard family. The men I'm hunting are everywhere, making each page a labor to get through, and yet nothing I read gives any clue as to who might've wanted Herman dead or how Fred got involved with the Sons of Liberty, his likeliest killers. I find no evidence to support my favorite theory, that Herman got involved with the Sons of Liberty himself and they were also responsible for his death. It makes so much sense to me, though I can't tell if that's because I'm applying Occam's razor or I simply want a neat and tidy answer pointed away from Everett.

Hours slide by until I'm well past the library's closing time. It's hard to tell without windows or a reliable clock—the desktop's forever frozen at 1:14 p.m.—but I've stopped hearing footsteps from above, so Nissa must've gone home for the night. On-screen, black-and-white newspaper print bleeds one week into another until my vision swims. I close my eyes, lean back in my chair, and let out a sigh. The basement ghosts do not respond.

"Why," I wonder aloud, "did I think I could investigate two murders by myself? I work at a library and I'm being defeated by microfilm. Disgraceful."

I slump back over the keyboard and punch the forward key with more force than strictly necessary. I'm in July 2013 now, the last year the *Bugle* was in print, and the issues are preoccupied with the giant bicentennial celebration that took place that summer. I was fourteen at the time, so skimming through pictures of the parade and memorial dedication on Main Street triggers distant memories. I click to a spread of the town-wide barbecue on the shore and the day floods back: the smell of hot dogs burning, the crunch of hot sand under my feet, the glittering fireworks. I can remember my mother admonishing me to put down my book and join the other girls in the water, but I can't remember my father.

I click to the next page and find him glaring back at me. My gaze flicks to the other faces in the photograph, and my stomach drops in shock. Gathered in a close circle around my father on the beach are Killian

Duncan, drinking a beer, and Sheriff Theriot, shirtless and grinning, one arm slung over Fred Fortenot's shoulders. Fred's laughing behind mirrored sunglasses, and beside him is Augustus Blanchard in white linen, his disapproving gaze on Killian. Only my father seems aware their picture is being taken, and the look in his eyes is vicious. There's no one around them—they're set apart from the crowd as if they meant to be not noticed. I glance down at the photo credit: J. Abraham. My father's lone critic.

I reel back from the screen. There's no way to read their posture and expressions other than chummy, even intimate. But my father hated Killian Duncan. So did Sheriff Theriot and Fred Fortenot. What were these men doing together, and with Augustus Blanchard, of all people, presiding? I feel a distant sense of recognition, like a memory is struggling to surface. Is it possible I've seen them together before? Was Killian one of the men who used to come home with my father, high off some mysterious revelry, and I was just too young to remember?

I stare at the picture, tracing the image, and suddenly a small detail catches my eye. I zoom closer. There, on Sheriff Theriot's bare chest, near his rib cage—a small, dark tattoo. A circle with two sets of horns: one facing up, the other down.

It's unmistakable. The symbol from the swamp. Le Culte de la Lune's mark of protection.

"God Almighty," I whisper, though it's not God's language inked on the sheriff's skin. How is this possible? I drag the mouse slowly, forcing myself to focus and move methodically through the rest of the picture, scrutinizing the grainy image as if it will speak to me. There—the tips of the horns peek out from Killian's unbuttoned shirt. And there—the symbol's slender circle rests just above Fred's waistline, revealed by his lifted shirt as he laughs. I don't see tattoos on Augustus or my father, but they're both still wearing shirts. Could the symbol be hidden, waiting there, a thing I'd missed all my life?

And what does it mean that these men were bound together by it?

I print out a copy of the photograph on the basement's old, sputtering printer, then think twice and print four more. It can't be a coincidence that John Abraham, whoever he was, took a picture that clearly angered my father, published it, and then the newspaper was shuttered by the end of the year. In fact, no paper copies of the *Bugle* have survived. Only this microfilm, a technology so underused in the library that it would be easy to forget it existed. If someone did try to erase this photograph's existence—if they thought they'd gotten rid of it—better to have backups.

Sweeping up the warm pages, I'm about to head upstairs when I realize that in my haste, I skipped over the remaining photos in the issue. I force myself to sit back down and scroll to the end. There are so many faces I recognize: Old Man Jonas manning the barbecue; Mrs. Autin lying under an umbrella, clutching a bottle of sunscreen; a wide-framed picture of a huge crowd gathered near the docks, watching the fireworks. I search for my face but don't find it—it must've been after my parents forced me to go home. But there's thirteen-year-old Beth Fortenot at the outskirts of the crowd, wearing a rapt smile, holding hands with—

Barry Holt.

My Barry.

The sight punches me in the gut. If I was fourteen that summer, Barry was fifteen, not yet a football star but on his way. In the picture, he tosses back his swooped brown hair, grinning down at Beth with a matching secret smile.

They dated. Looking at the picture, there's no other reasonable conclusion. I'd never witnessed them together, and Barry had never told me. Then again, it's not like Fred Fortenot would've allowed it, so maybe that's why they kept quiet. Barry was exactly the kind of boy Beth longed for: popular, athletic, loved by everyone. Was he who she'd met out at Starry Swamp the night her father beat her?

Dear Lord. Was Barry...

No.

Nissa is right: the basement is full of ghosts—but not the kind I expected. It's where my certainty that I know anyone in this town has come to die.

I jab the computer's power button and bound up the stairs, my footsteps heavy. When I reach the top all I can think of is getting home and putting more pieces together. I whirl around the corner—

And run right into Coby, one of the Fortenot Fishing Wives, nearly knocking her over.

We both stagger back, arms pinwheeling. I only just manage to keep my pages from flying everywhere.

"I'm so sorry." Heat rushes to my face. "I didn't think anyone was here. We're supposed to be closed."

To my surprise, Coby clutches her purse to her chest, eyes finding the floor like she's afraid to meet my gaze. "I was just returning some books," she murmurs. "Forgot the hours. Silly me."

I watch, amazed, as she hustles to the door, unlocks it like an expert, and slips out.

"Oh!" booms a voice. "You still here?"

I whip around, my hand on my chest. "Nissa! You scared me half to death."

She chuckles, winding around an aisle before coming into view. "Look at us burning the midnight oil. We need a raise. Go tell your daddy."

"What are you doing here?" I glance at the door. "And what was that with Coby? She practically flew out of here."

Nissa puts a hand on her hip. "If I tell you, do you swear to keep it a secret?"

"Of course." I'm well versed in secrets. Like everyone else in this town.

She straightens a row of books. "You've probably noticed I make it my business to gather information—in whatever forms it comes. Certain people in this town know if they have news to share, they can drop by the library after hours."

I look around. The rows of books blink back innocently. "*That's* how you get your gossip? You use the library like an information speakeasy?"

"I give them a fair exchange," she insists. "Secrets for secrets. Everyone needs a whisper network. It's how we look out for each other. You know how people are always talkin' about Lila LeBlanc steppin' out on her man? We started that rumor. Keeps them distracted from the fact that she's been working on her AA out at the community college in Saint Lafitte."

"She has?"

"Studying to be a social worker. Says she's plannin' to leave her husband and move outta Bottom Springs as soon as she's through."

I blink, trying to process. "Her family will be furious." The LeBlancs had worked so hard to reestablish themselves at Holy Fire after Lila's fall from grace.

"Like I said, we protect our own. Especially from the closed-minded."

I remember Coby's swift exit and my heart leaps into my throat. "What did Coby tell you tonight?"

Nissa's face grows animated. "It's about Herman."

As I feared, the sheriff hasn't managed to keep a lid on Herman's case. "What about him?" I steel myself to hear the accusations against Everett repeated.

"There's rumors spreading he had *unnatural urges*." Nissa whispers the last two words, though we're the only two people here. "One of the fishing wives' kids, a girl from his old Bible study classes, started talking, sayin' he..." She swallowed. "Did inappropriate things. Things that don't bear repeatin'. When she was a *kid*, Ruth. And not just to her, either..." Nissa stops and shivers.

The goose bumps find me, too.

"So it's true," I whisper, thinking of my father's fury that day in the parking lot. Of Lila LeBlanc, allowed to step alone into Herman's car. Of what I'd wondered ever since. "All this time, that's why."

"You knew?"

"I...knew something was off," I say honestly. "I just didn't know what." I clear my throat, swallowing the unexpected emotion. "Why's this coming out now?"

Nissa's voice rises, her excitement palpable. "Because now we know how he really died."

Oh, no. She's about to say—

"Zola Miller, who used to live next door to Herman, you know the one—she's a nurse over at Blanchard, got all those Christmas decorations in her yard every year. Well, she's telling everyone that her son saw the Low Man leave Herman's house the night he died." Nissa's eyes shine. She blinks at me, waiting for my reaction. "Don't you understand? First Fred dies, and then the truth comes out that he was a bad man who was violent to his family. Now we have a witness who saw—"

"A *kid*—"

"A man fitting the Low Man's description leaving Herman's house, and it comes out that Herman was a—a—*pedophile*." She shakes her head, as if to rid herself of the word's malignance. "I'm not a superstitious person, Ruth. You know that. I'm a proponent of logic. But when both the Bible and the Bard say there are more things in Heaven and earth than we dreamt of, I've gotta admit there's something to this Low Man theory."

"You too?"

"Honey, it's too many bad men dying in a row to be a coincidence."

Her words freeze me. *Too many bad men dying in a row.*

"What's wrong?" Nissa presses a hand to my forehead. "You've gone paler than usual."

"I have to leave." I stagger back. "I'm sorry, Nissa. I have to go home."

"Okay, but be careful, hear? Coby said her part of town's up in arms over this news about the Low Man. People are scared. It might grow dangerous 'round here soon."

"Okay," I echo, barely registering what she's saying. I turn and grope my way to the front of the library.

"At least you have that good news, though, Miss Richie Rich," she calls to my back. "That should be enough to brighten your night."

I turn and frown. "What in the world are you talking about?"

Nissa searches my face, then draws her hands up to her generous hips and shakes her head. "As smart as you are, I swear you wouldn't know the sky was falling. And news about your own daddy, too."

"My father?"

"Augustus Blanchard died last night," she says. "It was the shame over Herman that finally did him in. Turns out he left his will in your daddy's care at the church. Augustus bequeathed all that Blanchard money to Holy Fire Born Again. Can you believe it?"

The world tilts under my feet.

"Only right, I guess." She clucks her tongue. "Leaving it to someone good and holy now the truth's come out about his wicked son."

I glance down at the printed pages now clutched tightly in my hand. "Nissa," I say hoarsely, my mind reeling. "Is there any way you could use your connections to track down a man named John Abraham?"

36

NOW

Thunder crashes around the house as I turn off the shower. I spent the morning thinking and digging in my garden, ripping out dead things, planting new flowers that will welcome the fall. Digging, digging, digging—roots and bulbs and bones and memories. The water has stripped the dirt from my skin, soil running in dark rivers down my legs, and now I finally feel clean in a way that reaches far beneath the surface.

I step out of the shower, ignoring my towel, and walk dripping into my bedroom, leaving a trail of footprints. The world rages outside my windows, the late-summer storm magnificent in its violence. Whistling wind and drumming rain move together in perfect synchrony, like a cataclysmic orchestra. Coastal Louisiana: a beautiful, otherworldly place; a land of deadly weather.

I lean over my quilted bedspread and reach for the long white dressing gown draped over my reading chair, the one Everett loves to make fun of. Fit for a Victorian maiden, he says, or else a Victorian ghost.

My room is small and muggy, half the shower's fault and half its perch on the second floor, where it collects the rising heat. The only relief I get comes from the wide bay windows that overlook the forest, the part the postman refuses to approach.

I slip on my gown and twist the hand cranks, opening the windows. Wind and rain whip inside, twisting the drapes. Outside, the tall trees shake fiercely, branches like arms clawing at the sky. I plant myself in the center of the windows and close my eyes, letting the wind lift my hair.

Four years ago, when I was still living in my parents' house, I came back from a shower and found Everett waiting in my bedroom. It started raining through the window, and then he asked me to leave with him. I refused, a decision that changed our relationship forever. A decision to keep my precious secret intact.

And now here I am again: in the rain, at the window, facing a pivotal decision. The past is resurging, breaking into the present, creating a second chance.

What will I do with it?

I lift my arms slowly, in supplication. The rain beats against my face, mixing cold with warm shower water. I open my eyes to the steel-gray sky. Clouds swirl confrontationally, as if challenging me to say out loud the truths I've spent all day digging up and piecing together in my garden.

Six years of friendship. Moments I've played back so many times. All the digs Ever used to make about what some people in this town got away with, how there should be justice. The anger he carried that I thought was just teenage rebelliousness—who could blame him? His burning hatred of town leadership. His questions on our canoe trip when we were twenty-one, probing Herman's oddness—the way I can see now, in retrospect, he'd danced around what he really wanted to know. How that day at the gulf when we were eighteen, he seemed to understand something I didn't about Fred. He's always known everyone's secrets, their sins. He even knew Renard's darkness before I did.

So many bad men dying in a row. All those men in the photograph, with their tattoos for protection—is this what they were afraid of?

Rough winds bang the windows. *Say it.*

I take a deep breath. Thunder explodes, shaking the house.

Is the person I know best actually a stranger?

I clench my fists.

A damned, cunning creature?

Reach deeper, the storm howls. *Retrieve the key, unlock the last door.*

And if he is, doesn't that make him exactly like...

Me?

The true Ruth. Buried in the corner of my garden, far beneath the blooming showpieces, a place I try never to unearth.

But now—wet hair streaming down my back, lightning cracking above the trees, the truth about Everett pressing—I make myself remember.

37

JULY, NINETEEN YEARS OLD

A knock sounded at the door. I sat straight up in bed. My parents were at an overnight church retreat, leaving me alone in the house, and it was far too late for visitors. Too late for me to even be awake with work in the morning, but I was lost in the pages of *Frankenstein*, amazed Mary Shelley had finished it, as the book's foreword claimed, "at the tender age of nineteen." (How strange to call it a tender age, as if we nineteen-year-old girls were soft and good to eat.)

The knock came again, feebler this time. My heart skipped as I crept out of bed, trying to imagine who it could be and what they could want in the dead of night. The moon barely shone through my window; the only sound was the chirp of crickets. Was it a parishioner looking for my father? Or someone—something—more sinister...

I pictured the beautiful, cruel face of the Low Man, come to claim my blood after all these years. But the Low Man crawled in through windows. Surely, he wouldn't knock...

I tiptoed downstairs, feeling like I was walking to my doom. Cracked the door with a timid "Hello?"—then threw it open.

Everett sank to his knees on the ground. His face was so bloody I could barely make out his eyes.

"Ever!" I fell and cupped his face. "Holy Father. What happened?"

"Fight," he rasped, sounding like he'd swallowed glass. "Bad one. I think my arm is broken."

His face was severely cut, his eyes almost swollen shut, clothes ripped across the chest and at the knees, hands and arms bloody. The way he was trying and failing to prop himself up, arms shaking—he looked near death. Fear knifed my heart.

"Stay right there." I leapt up. "I'm going to borrow the Fortenots' car and take you to the emergency room."

"No," he groaned. "I can't."

"Why in God's name can't you?"

"I just can't," he ground out. "They'll call the cops. Please, Ruth. Just bring me inside. I want to be near you."

I was beside myself. "If I don't take you to a doctor, you're going to die." With the volume of my voice, it was a wonder the Fortenots' lights hadn't come on.

He tried to lift his head to look at me. "No—"

"If you don't let me, I'll never speak to you again." Childish, but in my hysteria I wasn't above it. The last time his dad beat him had been horrible, and it was nothing compared to this. I didn't understand how he'd made it to my house—had he stumbled and crawled? "I'll stop being your friend," I warned. "You'll never see me again."

Ever's forehead dropped to the ground. "Ruth," he said weakly.

I crossed my arms, heart pounding. Silence stretched, wasting precious moments. *Please, God. Make him less stubborn.* I'd do anything to protect him.

Ever tried to curl into himself, then winced in pain. His eyes closed. "Please," he whispered. "I just want to be with you."

The words—and the sight of him trying to cradle himself—shattered my resolve.

"Come here." I swooped down. "Let me pull you up. Here, lean on me and try to stand."

Slowly, painstakingly, I got Ever to his feet. He leaned his full weight on me, and though my arms and legs trembled, I forced myself to remain upright. "Walk slowly," I urged. "That's it. One foot in front of the other."

Little by little, I got Ever into the house, up the stairs, and into my room. When he finally sank onto my bed, I collapsed on the floor, breathing heavy.

"Ruth," he whispered, "come closer."

I took a deep breath, gathering my resolve. "Since you won't let me take you to the hospital, you have to do what I say. I'm cleaning the blood off you and then you're going to rest. I'll stay awake and watch you. In the morning, we're going to Mr. Wilkes. If you won't let me treat you like a person, at least let me treat you like a broken bird."

A ghost of a smile curled Ever's bloody lips. "Okay, Ruthie."

Cleaning him with washcloths took a long time. I'd have to bleach them or throw them out before my parents returned; there was no way to explain the blood. I was weary tending his wounds, so I couldn't stop the tears from sliding down my face. *From his own father*, I kept thinking. *His own father*. Ever's right arm was surely broken. He'd hissed when I tried to touch it and kept it protectively at his side. But at least he'd relaxed at the gentle rub of the washcloth. His eyes closed, breath steadying. By the time I finished, I thought he was asleep until he murmured, "Lie next to me."

I took a deep breath, dropped the washcloths, and crawled in next to him. His cool hand found mine and squeezed. I studied his busted knuckles, then drew up the covers and pressed close to him, watching his chest rise and fall. In minutes, he was asleep.

That's when I started to sob. Great, silent, wrenching sobs, shaking with the effort of not waking him. His father was going to kill him. It was so obvious. I felt it in my bones. He'd gotten close tonight, walked right up to the line. The next time, he'd step over it, because that's how men like him worked. That's what happened to Ever's mom, and now the same fate was coming for Ever and he didn't even know. He didn't know because I hadn't told him what his father was truly capable of.

Possessive fury lit in me, filling me with living, breathing, combustible rage. It was one thing for people to hurt me. But not Ever. Not my kind, brilliant, sarcastic friend, the boy who'd saved me. I would do anything to keep him safe. But it was Ever himself who kept going back to his father, kept letting it happen, kept dismissing it. Why? He was drowning in pain and wouldn't pull himself out. The only way this could end was him black-and-blue and no longer breathing in the grave next to his mother.

The cold realization sank through me, putting out the fire of rage little by little, until every inch of my body was numb and calm. It was simple. Everett needed a life raft. I could be one. I could put myself between him and his father.

There was a way.

I climbed out of bed, taking care not to jostle him. Kissed Ever's cheek and put my hand above his nose to feel the shallow air he exhaled. Satisfied, I floated down the stairs, past the clock in the dining room with both hands up, pointing at midnight, like a compass confirming I was headed in the right direction. I shut the door and slipped into the night.

When I arrived at the Duncan house, it looked like Everett and Killian had gone to war. The garage was half-open, gallons of chemicals and tools everywhere. Shattered glass lay in the driveway, and there were divots in the grass, as if something had mauled it. The lights in the living room were on. The monster of this once-storybook castle was home.

I knocked.

Shuffling, loud grumbling, and then the door opened. Killian Duncan squinted at me. He was tall and lanky like Everett, with coal-black hair and pits of darkness for eyes, except in Killian's there were no redeeming flecks of light. His skin was strangely smooth and uncalloused for a man who owned a garage and spent his life stumbling drunk. Surprisingly ageless. I was cheered to see a dark bruise forming around his eye—at least Ever had managed that—until his lips pulled back against his sharp canines in an approximation of a smile. Then the normal clawing fear I felt around him returned.

"Shithead's not here." I could tell by his voice he was half-gone to the bottle. "Ran away to lick his wounds." He raised a brow. "Surprised he's not having you lick them for him."

He moved to close the door in my face, but I caught it with both hands. "Wait."

Mr. Duncan swayed, eyeing me curiously.

"Can I stay until he comes back?"

He studied me with his otherworldly eyes. After long enough that my hands turned clammy, he turned inside. "Wait for him in his room if you want. But only 'cause it'll piss off your daddy to know you were here." Mr. Duncan chuckled, then settled in his plaid armchair, unmuted the TV, and picked up his glass. Half-empty liters of Coke and Popov vodka rested on the table.

I shut the door quietly behind me, but it didn't matter—he had the volume up, lost to his football game. I walked behind him into the hallway, opened Ever's bedroom door...and then shut it, loud enough so he would hear. I crept back down the hall, peered around the corner, and watched.

It's one thing to kill a person in self-defense. One thing for your adrenaline to surge, flooding your body with chemicals, terror so potent it's an intoxicant, forcing you to act. It's another thing to wait and plot. To feel the icy burn of logic, the calm cool knitting of a plan. The patience it takes. The choice you're making. You don't just make it once. You make it again and again every minute you don't go home, don't give up, don't talk yourself out of it. Over and over, you're choosing. Which is the true nature of evil, fire or ice? The answer is ice. The cold, pragmatic calculation it takes to turn yourself into a predator.

I watched Mr. Duncan's every move. It was him or Ever, that much was obvious. But how to do it? I thought of the stone we'd used to kill Renard. A heavy object would be good, but messy. Same as a kitchen knife. Mr. Duncan was large and could overpower me. Anything that leaned on strength was a risk.

The minutes ticked by, the only sounds the game announcers and Mr. Duncan's occasional belching, the only movement the glass traveling to his lips and the sweat slipping down my back.

Finally, after what seemed like an hour of crouching, I closed my eyes. *Dear God,* I prayed, *He who smites his enemies and will return in a blaze of glory to take all heathens to Hell. Please help me bring this sinner to his knees.*

I opened my eyes and searched the room, waiting for an idea to jump out, a flash of inspiration. But I had nothing.

"Fucking Alabama," Mr. Duncan mumbled, and nearly tumbled out of his chair. He staggered in the direction of the bathroom.

This was my chance. Every nerve in my body sparked, begging for action. I thought of Everett lying broken in my bed. His dead mother's likeness carved into the tree. And that's when I realized: God hadn't helped either of them, and he wouldn't help me now.

I took a deep breath. There was only one choice.

Satan, I prayed. *Lord of Darkness. Help me get justice. Give me the tools.* I gritted my teeth. Seconds ticked by.

Suddenly, a light turned on in my mind, and I remembered the garage as I'd walked up. The door half-open, all those tools everywhere, those automotive chemicals...

Those chemicals.

I slipped out the door and flew to the garage, searching among the mess until I found the antifreeze, on its side in the corner. I snuck soundlessly back inside. Mr. Duncan was still in the bathroom. Hands shaking, I uncapped the gallon. The antifreeze glugged out bright orange and sweet-smelling. I didn't know how much to pour, so I let it run for a long time into his glass. Then I splashed in Coke to mask the taste and smell, guided by some foreign instinct, a stranger in my head.

The bathroom door opened, hinges groaning. He was coming. My last chance to make a different choice. If I left the glass here, there was no going back.

I remembered how it felt when Renard's weight lifted off me. That moment when I went from being crushed to sudden freedom, the ability to breathe again. Everett had thrown himself between us. It was a brave choice, with no going back.

I left the glass.

Mr. Duncan wiped his hands on his jeans and dropped ungracefully into his armchair. I watched from my hiding place, chewing my thumb.

He resumed the game and picked up the glass. I sank my teeth into my flesh as deep as they would go.

He drank. Long and deep, without flinching or studying the glass. He didn't even notice. The antifreeze must be too close to the taste of his drink, or he was simply too drunk to tell.

Minutes passed. He finished, then poured himself another drink. I waited and waited, but nothing happened. It hadn't worked. I hadn't poured enough. All of this was for nothing.

I closed my eyes one more time. *Please*, I prayed to the Devil. *You can have anything. My life, my freedom, in exchange for his. Please take this trade. Me for Ever. Please, for once, someone hear me.*

A crashing sound made my eyes fly open. Mr. Duncan jerked against his chair, his glass fallen on the carpet, dark liquid staining. His legs started shaking, rattling the table. He made a desperate gurgling sound and twisted off the chair, falling to the floor.

He was having a seizure. The poison was working. The Devil had taken my deal.

I stood, half of my face hidden behind the wall, watching as he spasmed. Eventually he wrenched up on his elbows and bent over, gagging violently, trying to throw up.

I emerged from the shadows and walked to him.

He felt my presence and twisted around, his bloodshot eyes widening in shock. "You," he choked. I'd never seen fear like this on anyone's face before. "I always knew it would be a Cornier," he rasped, saliva bubbling from one corner of his mouth. "But I never thought it would be you."

I froze, unmoored by his strange words.

"Please," he begged, reaching out his arms. "Have mercy. Call 911."

I looked at him. Past his pain and into his heart. And all I saw was sin.

"For Ever," I whispered, and stepped away.

For several minutes he struggled, legs and arms jerking, trying to crawl to me, but then he went still. His chest stopped rising and falling. The announcers on TV whooped at a touchdown. Killian's eyes were wide and unseeing.

I walked home as the first rays of dawn began to lighten the dark, a different person. So this was what it felt like to have your darkest prayer answered. To make a covenant with the Devil. I was a true killer now and would have to spend my life paying for it. I owed a debt.

I was back in bed lying next to Ever by the time he woke up. The moment his eyes opened and he looked at me, I knew.

I'd saved him.

I was a fallen woman.

It was worth it.

38

NOW

The wind carries me as I stride barefoot through the woods. Above me, the clouds crack open. Lightning lashes down in jagged strikes. I'm soaked, dressing gown clinging like a second skin, mud streaking my legs. The landscape I move through is surreal: in this storm my home has turned foreign, liminal, slipping back and forth between this world and a stranger one.

There's a charge in the air, a feeling like anything is possible.

Dark clouds swirl above the Duncan house, drenching it in rain. I pound on the front door. It swings open, as if I've been expected, and there he is. Twenty-three-year-old Everett Duncan, ageless like his father. Tall and dark; pale and beautiful. Since we were seventeen, his existence has made me feel like the real world might be more mysterious and exciting than I'd given it credit for, closer to the worlds inside my books.

His eyes widen as he takes me in, studying the long strings of hair dripping down my face. His eyes dip to my soaked white gown and then quickly jerk back up.

I finally catch my breath. "There's something I need to tell you."

He stares at me for the longest time, lingering over the pulse in my neck. Then he shakes his head. "No."

He turns and disappears into the house.

I follow him, leaving the door open. Wind rushes in. "You can't hide. We have to have it out."

He paces to the old chipped coffee table, pulling at his hair. The mist that's crept in with me is so thick it's already curling at the ends. "No, Ruth. Turn around and let's pretend you never came."

I stand firmly at the edge of the living room. "We have to have truth between us. It's time."

Ever strides to me. Presses two fingers to my chest and turns an invisible key. "Remember what you told me? It's better this way."

"The night your father almost killed you, when you showed up on my doorstep—"

"Don't," he begs.

"I went to your house while you were sleeping and poured antifreeze in your father's drink. I watched him die on the floor, right there." I point to the carpet in front of the TV. "I let everyone think he'd died of alcohol poisoning but it was me, Ever. I killed him so he wouldn't ever lay a hand on you again."

There. I've done the thing I once thought was impossible. I've confessed.

Ever drops his head in his hands. His shoulders shake.

"I know you hate me now," I say. "I know we can't be friends. But I thought maybe if I told you my secret, you'd tell me—"

"I already knew," he whispers.

I freeze. "What?"

Ever lifts his head. His eyes are weary. "I felt you leave and climb back into bed hours later. I left the antifreeze in the corner of the garage. That's where we always left it. A few days after he died, I found it tucked neatly on the shelf. Such a Ruth move, to put it away like that."

All this time. While I'd thought I was carrying a secret that would destroy us, he'd *known*. The things I'd sacrificed to keep it from him, to protect him from tying his life to the person who'd secretly killed his family. The things I'd done to *repent*. It feels like something fundamental has been ripped from me. "Then why aren't you furious? *Horrified* by me?"

He looks at me with such tender sadness. "How could I be furious when you only did it to protect me? When it was my fault, anyway?"

I can't process—I'm in too much shock. "Your fault?"

He paces to the other side of the room, only turning to look at me when his back is flat against the wall, like we need the distance for whatever he's about to say. His foot taps nervously. "The thing inside me. It got inside you, too."

This is it—we're circling his secret, I can feel it. "What thing inside you? The voice?"

Ever shakes his head. "If I tell you, I'll lose you. Don't you see why I've been so miserable? You're the only person I want to tell, and the last one I can."

This is why I've done the unthinkable and confessed I killed his father. To get his truth, I knew I had to offer mine first, one risk in exchange for another, both of us out on this terrifying limb. Now I steal his words: "Ever, I already know."

He looks at me cautiously. "You do?"

"There were so many clues once I knew to look." I steel myself, walking toward him slowly, praying he doesn't retreat. "If I'm honest, I've always known there was something different about you."

He doesn't move. Doesn't even blink as I inch closer, telling him what I've finally figured out. "You're too beautiful. Too pale and too cold. I can never feel your pulse. You run too fast. You've barely aged in six years. You sucked the copperhead venom from my leg. That night with the deer, all the blood in your mouth. The way you spend all your time outside, in the swamp. It's been staring me in the face all these years. You're not human."

Ever's voice comes out strangled. "What am I, then?"

I take a deep breath. All or nothing. "You're the Low Man."

His brow furrows. "*That's* what you think?"

I stop my progress. "Aren't you?"

"All these years, have you been waiting for me to tell you I'm some sort of supernatural creature?" His laugh is harsh and clipped. "Have you been hoping I'm fucking Edward Cullen?"

I can't speak.

He studies me. Then his voice softens. "My God. You have."

I can only press a hand to my chest. My emotions are too overwhelming, the certainty and thrill I'd felt just a moment ago transformed into shame and crushing disappointment. "But—your lack of a pulse."

"Of course I have a pulse." He holds up his wrist. "It's just faint. Maybe there's something wrong with me. I wouldn't know. I've never been to a doctor."

"That's *right*. You always refused to go to the hospital. There has to be a reason."

"I was an abused kid with zero money, Ruth. The last thing I could afford was a hospital visit and doctors who would ask questions I couldn't answer."

"But how fast you run and climb, how long you can hold your breath. It's not normal."

"I've spent my whole life outside."

"You won't step foot in the grocery store."

"I've been banned from the Piggly Wiggly since I got caught shoplifting peanut butter and bread when I was twelve."

"But..." My voice falters. "That time it looked like something bit you. The puncture wounds on your arm."

Ever looks down at the scar. "I *was* bitten. You might've noticed sharp teeth run in the family." He looks up at me. "What else?" he asks quietly. "Is that all?"

Humiliation floods me. He's right. At some point, I must've mapped Edward onto Everett, melding fiction and reality to create a friend who was larger than life, who was different in a way that could save me. I'd thought it made so much sense that Ever was the Low Man. It had clicked so fast that it was clear I *wanted* it to be true, that part of me has been waiting for him to reveal some last mysterious part of himself, a dangerous, romantic secret like Edward revealed to Bella.

What a fool I've been.

"I'm sorry to disappoint you, Ruth." Wind howls through the door, tossing Ever's hair, but his dark eyes stay fixed on me. "But that's not how it works. There are no heroic vampires or mystical swamp creatures. There's not even a God or a Devil. They're all fiction. There's no one out there making sure everyone gets what they deserve. It's just us. You and me. And I'm just a sick man. There's no secret that redeems me."

His jaw tightens. "I used to think it was a miracle you wanted to be my friend. This is why, isn't it? You were holding on to this fantasy, and I fit the bill." He jerks his head to the window. "God, Ruth. I didn't think it was possible to hurt any worse."

"Maybe I was holding on to a fantasy," I admit. The words come out rushed; I'm desperate for him to believe me. "Maybe I wanted my life to be different so badly I imagined you might be a way out. But you know what? I'm glad I did. Otherwise, I might've missed out on you. And it turns out I care about *you*, Ever. Who you really are. I promise."

"Ruth." I can hear his broken heart in his voice. "You have no idea who I really am."

I take a deep breath and touch his face, hoping he won't push me away. "Then tell me."

He looks at me like it's the last chance he'll get.

"Last Sunday when I walked into church."

I nod, heart pounding.

He swallows. "It wasn't the first time I've been inside Holy Fire."

39

NOW

I drop my hand.

"When I was young, maybe seven or eight, my father started taking me there at night."

"At night?"

"He would go to meet your father and the others, and they wanted cover. I was too young to understand what they were doing or why we didn't acknowledge the reverend when we passed him on the street. All I knew was I *hated* those nights. Church was a place of torment. My dad used to lock me in a room for hours while they met. No food, no water, not even a window." Ever looks down at his hands, clenched tight, and with effort, relaxes them. "At least at home, if things got bad, I could always escape outside. In there I was trapped. I couldn't get away from the crosses on the wall, all those bleeding bodies. Thorns and bones sticking out. I remember thinking those men looked as hungry as I felt. I had nightmares about them coming to life and climbing off the wall to eat me."

"Why didn't you ever tell me?"

He smiles ruefully. "One night I heard laughter outside the door. It swung open and Fred Fortenot was standing there. I didn't know him at the time. All I knew was he was drunk. Even that young, I knew the signs. Fred grabbed me and dragged me to your father's office, where they were all waiting."

Suddenly I'm the one who wants to beg Ever not to say whatever he's going to say next.

He must sense it, because his eyes soften. "They were performing some sort of ritual. I recognized the white circle on the floor and some of the symbols drawn around it from my mom's notebook. There were other symbols I'd never seen before."

Symbols and a white circle—what Ever's describing has to be connected to the men's tattoos.

"There were a dozen or so of them, and they were all drunk. Someone was in the back, near your dad's desk, holding a rattlesnake and singing." Ever's voice lowers. "Fred threw me in the middle of the circle and they started chanting at me. Then they took turns testing me."

"Testing?"

"Putting the rattlesnake in the circle with me to see if it struck. Forcing me to drink things that made me throw up. Beating me."

My voice comes out small. "My father did that?"

He shakes his head. "No. He watched. Fred, though. And plenty of the others. Some men I've never seen before or since. They were talking and laughing like they were all old pals. I didn't know what I was part of, if it was some strange religious ceremony or if I was just the entertainment."

I think back to those nights when the door to my parents' house would open and the living room would flood with drunk, laughing men. How I'd watch from an upstairs window while they smoked and yelled over each other among the hydrangeas. This must be what they were doing before they came to our house. Their mysterious revelry. *Daddy's social hour*.

I think I will be sick.

"I tried to fight back," Ever says, his tone carefully neutral, like he's trained himself. "But I was too young. I was so young I kept looking at my dad, thinking any minute he'd swoop in and save me. That's how naive I was."

"He didn't." My heart is full of horror. How could my father have stood there and watched a boy be beaten? How could any of them? If they were the same men who used to come pouring into my house, they were church elders, Godly men.

"No one saved me. Not that night or any of the others." Ever touches his chest. "One of the worst nights, Augustus held me down in the middle of the circle and burned his cigar into my chest. He said he was casting out devils. The scar was a lesson about what awaited me if I remained unsaved. That's how it always was with them—a mix of elements I recognized from my mom's notebook and other ramblings I didn't understand."

"Your scar," I whisper. The perfectly round burn I saw at the inlet when I'd pressured him into taking off his shirt. That's why he never undressed. He was ashamed of it.

"It went on for years. I didn't have anyone to tell, because everyone important was in that room. It only stopped when I got too big to go down easy. When I learned how to make them sorry to touch me." He takes a deep breath, looks at the carpet. "I was afraid to tell you."

I press a hand to his cheek, hot and flushed under his stubble. "Your father was a monster for letting it happen. They all were."

"You don't understand." Thunder rattles the house. Ever raises his eyes, and a chill goes down my spine. "I knew if I told you, you'd see they were right. It's inside me."

"What is?"

"Darkness. Whatever makes people a monster, whatever disease my father had. There were times growing up I thought I'd go crazy trying to keep it inside."

"Ever, you're starting to scare me. Keep *what* in?"

"The need to hurt people," he says quietly, his eyes fixed on me. "The urge to see them suffer."

I try to step back but he catches my hand, places it over his heart. "Listen to me. When we killed Renard, it unleashed something inside me. I liked killing him so much. I thought about it for weeks after, wishing I could do it again. I couldn't stop picturing the look on his face when he realized he wasn't going to win. I *savored* the blood."

I can barely breathe. The wind slams the door shut, locking us in.

His dark eyes trail over my face. "Growing up, I thought it was just me those men hurt, that I deserved it because I had these compulsions. It was enough to keep me in control. But when I saw Renard hurting you—*you,* of all people—and later, when you told me what Fred did to his wife and Beth, how afraid they were, when your dad didn't want you around Herman, but he let Lila go, it made me realize it wasn't just me. If I was sick, they were too."

"Ever, this sickness you're talking about—these violent urges. It's only natural to want to defend yourself."

He shakes his head. "You're not *listening,* Ruth."

The regret in his voice... "What did you do?" I whisper.

Our hands are still twined together on his chest. He squeezes mine tighter. "When I realized you killed my dad, and why, it was like some higher power showing me the answer. I thought: *Here's my solution.* I could feed the voice in my head, release the pressure valve, and at the same time punish people who deserved it, who'd never be stopped otherwise. So I gave myself permission. I went a little mad, Ruth."

"You killed them." I pull my hand from his chest, my words lancing the air. "Fred and Herman."

He doesn't need to answer. The look in his eyes is enough.

We stand there staring at each other. He and I have always been mirrors, reflecting our best parts back. We had to be, to have a shot at loving ourselves when no one else would. It was survival. Now I see my worst sins, the most gruesome parts of me, reflected. Two cold-blooded killers. Two damned souls.

So where is my remorse? Why don't I feel that old familiar guilt? My heart pounds and it's hard to breathe, but it's not from fear.

"This is who I am," he whispers. "And now you're the one who's horrified. You're the one who hates me."

"Tell me how it happened."

He blinks. "Okay," he says softly, watching me like he expects me to bolt any second. "Fred was the first. One night I was filling up at a gas station in Forsythe. He and Beth pulled up at one of the pumps, but they didn't see me. I watched him bully her like my dad used to bully me. He kept complaining she'd taken too long picking out a drink. He hit her so hard she fell against his truck. They were out in public, Ruth. It was like he had no fear. Like he knew he was untouchable."

A flash of lightning illuminates the window, making Ever's face glow. "My control snapped. I'd spent years fantasizing about it, and the compulsion just took over. I walked up and sucker punched him. He never saw it coming. He fought back, but not for long. When he realized I wasn't a boy anymore, that I was as strong as him, he forced Beth in his truck and drove away. It felt good, but it wasn't enough. He hadn't really paid. He wouldn't change. So that weekend when you were at the library, I followed him. When he went into the swamp to fish, I went too."

He takes a deep breath. "I beat him without mercy, the way he beat us. It was incredible." Ever's expression turns reverent as he remembers; his eyes are two dark pools, sucking me in. "The way his bones twisted, Ruth. His blood was all over me, sticky and salty. I was the one in charge." He closes his eyes, savoring. "I had to wash his blood off in the water. And when I was done, I threw him in for the gators like we did to Renard. I knew I needed to cover my tracks. So I snuck to his boat, drove it into the gulf, and swam back, hoping they'd think he got lost at sea. It was the best I could think of at the time. Sloppy, I know, but it worked for a while."

A coldness has stolen over me. "Fred went missing three years ago, when we were twenty. You did it when you came back to visit me that summer."

He hesitates, then nods. "The next summer I got smarter. With Herman, I made it look like an accident. It was easier to be detached with him, since he wasn't one of the men from those nights at church. But he was still a predator who needed to be stopped. What you told me confirmed it. So I disabled the garage door to lock him in. Made it look like a gas leak. It worked flawlessly until a boy spotted me when I was leaving."

"That's why you didn't come back last summer," I whisper. "You were afraid of getting caught." The sheriff was right. I'd cried myself to sleep for ages, thinking it had to do with me. I take a step back.

"I thought it would be better if I laid low." He doesn't stop me. "In truth, I shouldn't have come back."

So many pieces are fitting together. "Augustus died two nights ago. Was that you?"

He looks at me like he regrets what he's going to say. "I did plan to kill him. But scrutiny was too high after the sheriff found Fred's skull. I hate that Augustus died naturally. He robbed me of the chance to give him a matching scar. The coward must've known I was coming."

"You came back to Bottom Springs this summer to kill him." One by one, he was going after all the men in the photograph. I take another step away. "Not for me."

"Come on, Ruth. It's complicated." Ever starts to step toward me, then halts, forcing himself to give me space. "But I did lie to you, and I'm sorry. You defended me even though everything Barry and the sheriff said is true." His voice turns bitter. "I'm a freak and a sicko. A monster."

More than that. Herman, Fred, Renard. He was a serial killer.

"Why didn't you leave the minute I told you the sheriff found a skull?" I ask. "You could've disappeared and saved yourself all this heartache."

"And leave you to suffer alone? Never."

"But once we knew it was Fred's skull and I was safe—"

"But you weren't. With the sheriff dredging the swamp, I knew it would only be a matter of time before they found something pointing to Renard. I couldn't leave you to face that on your own. I needed a plan to keep you out of prison, and I found one." He takes a deep breath. "Besides..."

"What?"

"I thought if I made sure you couldn't get caught for Renard, I could convince you to finally leave Bottom Springs."

"You risked getting caught to stick around for me. Why would you endanger yourself like that?"

"I told you. It's complicated."

I turn from him to look out the window. I'm trying to process, but it's so much, requiring a rewrite of my entire life. My father's capacity for cruelness, the truth about the men in my house, Ever knowing I poisoned his dad, committing matching sins. I'm still searching for the emotions I'm supposed to feel, the terror and fury, but I'm strangely numb. I keep circling an unavoidable truth. I test it by saying it out loud. "If you're sick, then I'm sick, too."

Ever shakes his head. "Like hell. You did what you did to protect me. And you know what? The world's better off without my father. I'm glad he's dead. How's that for sick?"

"What you did to Fred and Herman protected a lot more people." I think of Mrs. Fortenot and Beth, who didn't even wait around for Fred's memorial to escape Bottom Springs. Lila and all the other kids who might be haunted because of Herman. It will never happen to another kid. Ever's long-ago jab comes back: *It's funny what you can see for other people that you can't see for yourself.*

And just like that, it all comes together. All the years of my life spent on the outside, tiptoeing in the background of classrooms and the church and my own house, all the philosophy and history I've read, all the love stories—every book, in fact. Every quiet rebellion, every time a fire stoked in my heart when something wasn't right, every harsh word I bore witness to, every cruelty, every strike of the rattan cane, every night I cried myself to sleep, thinking life should be different. Each thought and feeling was a brick placed one right after the other, building a bridge to a new place, a new way of thinking that might've been impossible if not for those twenty-three years of pain. Now I know why my heart isn't pounding in fear or regret.

I gather myself to my fullest. Everett stills. "Here's how I see it. Fred and Herman. Your dad and Renard. Those weren't crimes."

"What?" His dark eyes scan my face.

"Killing them wasn't the crime, Ever. It was the justice."

"That's not what the sheriff would say. Or your father."

"Who cares about their paper-thin morals and self-serving laws?" My chest expands as I breathe deeply. What I'm about to say is my mightiest rebellion yet. "The kings get to make the rules, but that doesn't make them right. All your life they've treated you like something unnatural and outside them. You know why my father is so powerful? Not because he's wise or good. Because he has the ability to point to someone and cast them out of the Kingdom of Heaven."

Cast them out of goodness, out of community. That's how he'd gotten his start, after all. The foundation of his power was fear and exclusion, not holiness.

"Why should we have to love and obey a world that doesn't love us back?" My voice rises above the pounding rain. "Renard treated me like

I was less than a person when he tried to rape me. And all those men told you that you were less every time they abused you. To them, we're not people the way they are. We're lower creatures. Animals. Beasts. You know what I say to that? Okay, then! I'm done trying to change their minds." I swallow past the lump in my throat. "Twenty-three years of trying to persuade them, to make them love us, has gotten us nowhere. I accept it—we're not human. So why should we be bound by human laws?"

Ever stands transfixed.

"Who would defend us if we didn't defend ourselves? Who would've *ever* stopped Fred and Herman and Renard if not you? Your father, if not me? Their rules don't apply to us, Ever. We didn't ask for it, we didn't *want* it, but they forced us to become a law unto ourselves."

How ironic that Augustus was the one who'd laid it out for me when I was a child. It had taken me this long to understand what he'd told me was a confession. Laws, religion, civil society—they were just veneers, constructions put in place by the powerful to tame us animals, impose control. Over so many years we'd forgotten, treating the constructions like they were part of nature. But nature doesn't know good or evil. All nature knows is survival. How terrifying and freeing that right and wrong aren't laws in stone but navigational instincts, like the kind of instinct a swallow feels for its place in a murmuration, like what guides geese north on a dark and starless night. My father, Augustus, the sheriff, all those men—they haven't done anything holy. They simply wrested control over Bottom Springs like so many conquerors before them.

"Listen to you, Ruth." Ever shakes his head. "I take back all my teasing about your fake college syllabus."

"Don't make light."

"I'm not. You're wasted here. You almost sound like a pastor, the way you talk." He clears his throat. "But I know what you're doing. You're trying to justify my crimes."

"They *are* justified. Sometimes what's right isn't the same as what's lawful or holy. I'm done feeling guilty for what I've done. And I'm not afraid of you, either."

He takes a step away from me. "That's because I've been corrupting you since high school. And that's not some Christian bullshit I'm spouting. That's science; that's in books. Influence is a contagion." His voice is bitter. "If you stick with me, I'll ruin you like Barry said. He's right and it *kills* me, but you're better off without me. That's why I'm going away for good."

"You can't."

"It's already in motion. The house will sell and you'll get everything. It's all in my will. You'll have freedom and power, however you want to spend it." He swallows. "Here with Barry if you wish."

"That's why you went to Durham to see Sam—to make a will? Ever, that would mean..." I freeze as I realize what he's been planning. "No."

"We both know what's coming. I'll be lucky if I get the electric chair, and Gerald and those fishing boys don't tear me up first."

"That's not—"

He shakes his head. "Don't look at me like that, Ruth. 'Your two great eyes will slay me suddenly.'"

"No more Chaucer. I told you to stop teasing."

He lifts his gaze. "Come on. You and I both know I was never teasing."

My protest dies on my tongue. The next lines of the poem slip back to me as easily as if we were eighteen again, and he'd whispered them in my ear. "'Straight through my heart, the wound is quick and keen.'"

I look at him and the longing on his face steals my breath. His eyes are burning, one hand pressed to his chest—over his heart or his scar, I don't know. "Ever—"

He pushes past me, throws open the door, and rushes out into the rain.

40

NOW

I seize the hem of my dressing gown and run after him. Every nightmare I've ever had about the Duncan house, this haunted place filled with evil spirits, has come to life. The forest is wild and howling: tree branches twist violently, whipping into my path like malevolent creatures bent on keeping me out.

"Ever," I yell. "Stop!" But the thunder drowns my voice. The storm's still raging; it's the kind they pull boats off the water and board up windows for. Ever's headed through the trees in the direction of the swamp. If he makes it there, I'll lose him.

"Ever!" My lungs burn. I slip in mud and barely keep upright. Brilliant white lightning daggers into a clearing just ahead of him.

"Please," I shout, and, like magic, he stills. I keep running even as he turns and strides in my direction.

"Go back inside," he yells. He's soaked as I am, his black T-shirt clinging to his chest, his biceps, his black jeans to his thighs. He shoves dripping hair off his forehead. "It's too dangerous."

"You've never infantilized me before." I struggle to catch my breath. "Don't start now."

Rain begins to pour so thick I can barely see past him. It creates an eerie sense of seclusion, just the two of us in a bubble of space and time and tempest.

Ever yells to be heard over the wind. "Why are you following me?"

"You can't just say that and leave."

"You have a fiancé."

Even though we're standing in the pouring rain, heat radiates from me. "Don't try to turn this around. And he's not my fiancé—I never said yes."

"You said no to me when we were nineteen and I asked you to leave Bottom Springs, remember? You practically shoved me away. And then you said no again just days ago. Remember that night on the canoe, when I tried to touch you and you were so frightened you practically dove off the boat?" Ever's eyes search mine. "You've always been clear about where you stood and that's okay, that's good. I respect it and I promised to never overstep. So let me keep my promise."

I have to restrain myself from shaking him. "I said no because of what I *did*. I thought you'd hate me if you found out. I thought you'd feel betrayed. I was trying to protect you and punish myself."

I take a step closer, but he throws out a hand to stop me, like I'm dangerous. "I know what you want, Ruth." His chest heaves. "And it's not fair."

"What do I want?"

"You want one last confession. But you already know the answer."

I shake my head. Water runs down my temple. "No, I don't."

Ever tips his head up to the clouds. When he looks at me again, his eyes have changed. The flecks of light are dancing. "*Of course* you know." Thunder booms. "You're too-smart, too-good Ruth Cornier. The girl who watches everyone and reads every book and thinks she's keeping it a secret. So kind she gives people the things she wants for herself. Hair you can see coming a mile away, bright as the sunset." His voice grows thick. "Daughter of the man I hate almost as much my own father." Ever presses the heels of his hands into his eyes. "I should've stayed away from you after the swamp."

"Maybe you should've," I yell, furious at him for even suggesting it.

He strides to me without warning. I suck in a breath, resisting the urge to back up. He pushes his fingers through my hair. Grips the strands so I have to look up at him.

"Ruth."

"But you didn't," I say softly. "You didn't stay away."

A moment of stillness, my hair taut in his hand. Then, roughly, Ever shakes his head.

"Why didn't you tell me?" I whisper.

His hand slides from my hair to my cheek, his palm icy against my skin. "I told you so many times."

I swallow thickly. My heart beats too fast. "Other people's poems don't count."

He looks me in the eyes. "I love you, Ruth. Of course I love you. It's the only thing that's ever redeemed me."

This—standing in the howling wind and driving rain, the whole world turned upside down—is the place I've been searching for, the place for which I'd had no map. Everything between us is bared—we are new and raw and standing on a cliff's edge. *This* is what I'd hoped love would be. *This* is what I've waited for. Something unlocks in my heart. Wheels turn; transcendence floods my veins, transforming me from the inside out, turning me into something different, something more, than I was only a moment ago. Everett Duncan loves me.

His voice is tortured. "That's why I have to leave before the sheriff gets his evidence and catches up to me. If he does, I'll fry. And I can't have you going down with me."

I shake my head.

"Ruth—"

"I love you, too, Ever. I always have."

He takes a deep breath and closes his eyes, as if looking at me is too much. Drops of rain hit his forehead and fall down his cheeks. "I can't tell you—how that makes me..." His voice falters. "I'm not a good man, Ruth."

"I love you anyway." With his eyes closed, I trace a finger over his cheekbones, his nose, his brow—this profile I've marveled at. "We're the same."

"You're not a monster," he says roughly.

"No," I agree. "We're not monsters. We're the sane ones."

I think of the poor frightened child I'd been in church, searching for love and acceptance, doing my best to repeat *You will be saved. You must be good. Be good and be spared the lake of fire.* How deep the wound must've been for me to carry it for so long.

But Everett loves me. And I'm no longer a child. I will not be afraid. "The truth is," I say, "I love you more for having killed them. Let the sheriff come. We'll fry together."

Like a perfect moment in a dream, Ever seizes my face and kisses me. Lightning flashes—real or imagined, I can't tell. His warm, insistent mouth is all I'm aware of. The pulsing feeling from years ago when I lay in the grass and he put his mouth on my wound comes back tenfold, making me shudder, making me feel like every part of my body is meant to be touched. He pulls me flush against him, his thumb on the pulse pumping at the hollow of my throat, and I've never known such need, such hunger. I've never known how good it could feel to be in my body. What one human being could do to another.

Ever picks me up, clutching me to his chest, and takes off for the tree line. "Better in here," he murmurs, right before we slip into the darkness. He lays me on the forest floor and kneels beside me, eyes dark and reverent. Pulls my damp gown down my shoulders so my chest is bare. Goose bumps flood my skin. My heart races, chest rising and falling quickly, nervously. But when I look up, I see nothing but his beautiful face bent over me, and above it a shield of trees, and above that the endless roiling sky.

He sinks down, captures my breast in his mouth, and skims it with his tongue. Slowly, he sinks his teeth in.

I gasp and arch up off the ground, like I'm possessed, like he's bewitched me. He grips my hips and skims his sharp teeth lower. Torture, pleasure, need.

Maybe I was destined for this: self-immolation in the rain. Our story is darker, messier, than the love stories I read as a kid. It began messy and I know, down here in the leaves with Everett's mouth sending me, that it will end messy. But this is what I wanted before I even had the language for it: the kind of love that can look at ugliness, complexity, the unvarnished truth, and not flinch. A love that peels back the layers. Forget God. This is the love that will save me.

As the storm rages, as the trees shake, I learn, over and over, what my beastly body can do.

41

NOW

I can tell Everett's gone before I open my eyes, so I don't. Instead I lie on the ground, feeling the warm sun on my face, listening to birds chirp and tree branches swish in the breeze. When I finally do look, I find a bright morning, strikingly peaceful in the wake of last night's storm. Two sprigs of heal-all rest where Ever's body did, and beside them are the words *My house, tonight* written in the dirt. I pick up the flowers, fingering the cone-shaped heads and delicate purple petals, running them like silk over my skin. They're used to make a healing salve, according to Mr. Wilkes. To put broken things to mend.

I place them on my chest and let my eyes drift shut. Ever loves me. I'm not alone, and never will be.

My eyes fly open at the sound of twigs snapping. To my right, tall bushes shake. There's something large in them. My adrenaline spikes. More shaking—branches cracking—

A narrow-snouted black bear pushes out of the bushes. I gasp, then slap my hand over my mouth, terrified to have made a sound.

It towers above me, black fur studded with motes of dust that glisten in the sun. It lowers its head and our eyes lock. The bear's eyes are surprisingly beautiful, amber ringed with black. My body is rigid, immobile—except for my heart, which pounds so hard I can barely breathe around it.

All those warnings my mother gave me about the creatures in the deep woods, how they could sneak up on you, lash out, and kill. Inhuman, with no capacity for reason or logic, only an instinct to hurt. I look at the bear's claws, long as my fingers and thick with mud. The potency of my fear makes my vision hazy.

It creeps closer. Even my pulse freezes.

The bear lowers its head to the side where Ever laid and sniffs. I stifle a sob, squeezing my eyes closed, as its soft nose brushes my waist.

Then it stops.

I crack open an eye. The bear lets out a breathy sigh that smells of musk and, strangely, berries. It rubs the flat of its head against my stomach and—too fast for me to scream—opens its yellowed jaws and snatches one of the flowers off my chest, chomping it back in a single gulp. It eyes me again, then turns and shuffles away.

I lie still. Long after I've stopped hearing it move, my body remains frozen. Finally, a bird chirps high and searching through the trees, and when it's answered by another, I burst into tears.

Before I know it, I'm laughing and weeping. My body shakes, first with disbelief, then joy. Squirrels scamper in the trees above my head and I rock with delight. A bee swoops low about its business, an ant crawls up my arm, and I'm gasping, wiping away tears.

The truth breaks wide open. I belong here on this good green earth. I'm part of it. Not a sinner or a saint—just another creature. Mud and pollen and teeth and sinew. If there is a God, some higher power, it's here in these woods. In the beautiful strangeness of being a human, an animal wandering the world with soul-deep yearning. I belong here, and nothing can take that away from me.

I climb to my feet, put on my muddy dressing gown, and start for home.

42

NOW

I'm nearing my porch when the screen door bangs open and Barry bursts out of my house.

"Ruth," he calls, then stops short at the sight of me.

"What are you doing here?" He must've parked his truck in the back where I wouldn't see, but how he got inside when I've never given him a key is a mystery. My arms spike with goose bumps.

"I came to warn you." Barry's resplendent this morning in his deputy uniform, his metal badge and swooped brown hair gleaming. Though he's older than me, I suspect he'll always look like this, like a boy. And such a good one, too. A Boy Scout officer, upholder of all the rules. He squints as I step onto the staircase. "What happened to you?"

I look down. I'm wearing nothing but my dressing gown, of course, which is caked in dried mud, with matching streaks along my skin. My hair forms a wild, tangled nest, twisted with leaves. I must look like I clawed my way out of a grave. "I was in the woods," I say simply.

Barry's hazel eyes widen—then narrow. "With him?"

"Yes." There's no point denying it. But even though I'm taking pains to appear nonchalant, I don't climb any higher up the steps. I don't know how Barry will take this.

"Shit—I mean—*Christ*," Barry growls, frustrated at his inability to swear in my presence. "Please tell me you got evidence. A confession—*something*."

"I told you I wasn't doing that."

Barry presses his hands to his mouth and roughly exhales. "You mean to tell me you've come home lookin' like that from the woods, where you were with a *serial killer*, and you don't even..." A light comes on in his eyes. "Why you barely dressed, Ruth? Why do you look like you been tumblin' round in the grass? You are my fiancé, recall?"

"I don't recall giving you an answer," I say, cool on the outside, but I swallow a lump. "Let me remedy that now. Thank you for the offer, but I decline."

"You—*what*?" From the look on his face, Barry never imagined declining was an option.

"I'm saying no," I repeat, and steel myself for his pleading.

But instead, his eyes scour me. An ugly look transforms his face—half disgust, half vindication. "You laid with him."

My heartbeat picks up, but I try not to show it. "Please leave my porch, Barry. I need to clean up."

He moves in front of the screen to block my path. "Ruth, tell me plain. Are you still pure?"

"Leave," I repeat, eyeing the gun at his waist, the width of his arms.

"You really did it. You ruined yourself." He sounds almost awed. "God Almighty, I was right all along. He's got some kind of sick hold over you. I know you, Ruth, and you are not a natural-born whore. Not with the great James Cornier as your father. This is *his* fault."

If only being a whore was the worst of it, I think, and almost smile. Suddenly I understand why Ever constantly makes light of things. It's a brace against the fear. And it's enough to rally me.

"Tell me, Barry." I grip one of the porch columns for support. "How well did you know Beth Fortenot?"

The question floors him. I can tell by the way his mouth drops open a little, even if the next moment he's feigning disinterest.

"We were friends in school," he says stiffly. "Why?"

"What with the sheriff asking so many questions about Fred lately, it's dredged up a lot of memories. I got to thinking about what happened to her."

He swallows. "What do you mean?"

"You know—how in high school, Beth had this boy she was crazy about, who she would've done anything for, and he went and knocked her up."

He shifts. The porch creaks under his feet.

"And her daddy forced her to get an abortion against her will. Not to speak ill of the dead, but can you believe it? Fred Fortenot would've sworn up and down it was a mortal sin, except, I guess, for his girl. What gets me is, Beth never gave up the name of the boy who got her pregnant. And he never stepped up to defend her. My guess is he thought poor Beth wasn't worth risking his golden reputation."

Barry's eyes lift to mine. His face has gone from flushed to white.

"I know it was you. I found a picture of you and Beth in an old issue of the *Bugle*. There's no mistaking what you two were."

"That's impossible," he chokes. "You couldn't have."

How ironic: Barry the deputy is folding under pressure. "Did you love her?" I ask, and before he can answer, I add, "I don't know which is worse—if you did and still left her to the wolves, or if you never loved her and let her fall on her sword for you anyway. Which makes you more of a coward?"

"She was trying to trap me," he bursts out, punching the porch column I'm holding so it shakes. "She wasn't like you in high school, Ruth. She was willing to give it up. And if she was sleeping with me, who else was she sleeping with? Girls like that—loose girls—you never know. I wasn't going to have my whole life derailed by some jersey chaser who can't keep her legs shut. My momma, the church, everyone woulda known. You know what town is like. It woulda been over for me."

There it is.

I laugh. "Yes, Barry, I know what this town is like. Your hypocrisy is remarkable." But something else he said is sticking with me. "And what do you mean, I couldn't have seen a picture of you in the *Bugle*?"

"Because your own daddy promised they're gone," he hisses, like this is definitive proof he's in the right. "He told me it was just one mistake with Beth, and no one would know."

"Did he say he was destroying the old *Bugle* issues?"

"No—what? I don't know." Barry shakes his head. "He just said there wouldn't be any proof, no witnesses or pictures, so everything would be okay. Why do you care?"

"Barry," I say, unable to keep the excitement out of my voice. I take a step closer. He eyes me warily. "Did you know my father, Killian Duncan, the sheriff, Fred, and Augustus were all secret friends with matching tattoos?" Barry *had* claimed my father was grooming him to be his successor. Maybe he knows something.

He shakes his head at me. "What are you on about?"

"It's the same design as that symbol you found in the swamp. Have you seen a tattoo like that on the sheriff?"

He looks at me for a long time before he says, "You really are going insane. Just like your momma warned. She kept tryin' to tell us there was somethin' wrong with you ever since you said no to the sheriff, but I wasn't hearin' it. She said they put you on medicine for it. Is that true?" Barry puts his hands up in surrender and inches closer. His eyes have gone soft. "It's okay if it is. You don't have to be ashamed. Maybe what happened is, you stopped taking your medicine. And all we need to do is get you help, and everythin's gonna be okay."

"There's nothing wrong with me." But of course, as soon I say it, the old demon is back, panic clawing up my throat.

Barry's watching, his eyes keen. "That's what I said at first: 'There ain't nothin' wrong with Ruth, Mrs. Cornier, with all due respect.' But now I see it explains everythin'. Why you hung around Everett in the first place and won't give him up, why you're so antisocial and stubborn." He speaks soothingly, as if to a child. "But we'll fix you. Your parents'll take you to Blanchard."

"To commit me?" The panic is starting to win.

"Just come with me, Ruth. It's for the best. Blanchard's your daddy's place now, so they'll treat you right, keep it hushed. They'll do whatever he asks."

"No. I have to go." I shoulder past Barry to my door.

"You think I'm a fool?" He grabs my arm and yanks me so hard I rebound to him with a gasp. "You've made a habit of slipping past me. But no more, girl. I came for you and I'm leavin' with you."

"As a deputy, you should know this is assault." I pull my arm back, but Barry's stronger than me. I can't break his grasp.

"Where exactly do you think you're goin'?" Wrestling with me has finally mussed Barry's perfect hair—it hangs over his forehead, covering one eye, making him look unhinged. "The entire town's up in arms. That's what I came to warn you about. They think the Low Man murdered everyone and is gonna kill more people if we don't stop him. All those damn Fishing Company boys, all them fools from church. They're in Main Street, practically riotin'. Sheriff can't control 'em. We're 'bout to call in reinforcements from the next parish."

"They're rioting?" For a moment I forget to fight him, lost in the image of Main Street flooded with angry townspeople outside my father's or the sheriff's control.

"But you and I both know the truth. There's no supernatural creature."

Barry shakes me so hard I think he'll dislocate my arm. "See, I had Everett figured from the beginning. That all-black freak-show look, never talkin', always drawin' weird symbols in his notebooks. Just look at his father, the way he beat on him. I bet you anything that's what made him snap. That's who he killed first, you know—his daddy. Gave him a taste for it and now he can't stop. That's why he moves around all the time. Slips 'round like a ghost so he can kill all over Louisiana." Barry has the audacity to soften his voice. "He's gonna hurt others if we don't stop him, Ruth. We need you to help."

"Get your hands off me."

Barry seizes my shoulders and pushes me down the stairs. "We're goin' to the hospital. Once you get right, you'll see your so-called friend's a predator." My feet hit the grass and I stumble, but Barry's grip on me keeps me upright. "I'm gonna keep you safe, Ruth. You'll thank me later."

For the first time in my life, my panic becomes a gift. It fills me with such powerful frantic energy that I'm able to twist and yank my arm free from Barry's grasp. I slap him across the face with all my might.

Barry's head swivels with the force of the blow. He drops my arms and staggers back, almost tripping into the staircase. He blinks up at me, incredulous, one hand finding the sharp red mark I've made across his cheek.

"You think I'm at risk from *Ever*?" My voice booms across the lawn. I swell to my full height, letting my fear become a source of intensity, of might. Barry watches me, transfixed. "You think I need you to swoop in and shield me, take me to the hospital and chain me up for my own good? Listen to me, Barry, and listen well: *I* am the one you aren't safe from. You better hurry up and run from *me*."

I don't know where it comes from. But I hold his gaze without flinching, chest heaving, until—to my shock—Barry scrambles up and runs.

43

NOW

When I finally step into my house, the phone is ringing, loud and shrill. No one ever calls on the landline except for telemarketers. Covered in dried mud and still shaking from my standoff with Barry, the last thing I want to do is make forced conversation. I sink to the living room floor, back against the couch, and let it ring. Finally, the noise cuts off as the answering machine picks up.

"Hello, Miss Cornier?" warbles a thin voice from the speaker. "This is Mr. Johnathan Abraham giving you another call. I dialed you yesterday at the request of your friend Mrs. Nissa Guidry and left a message but never heard back. She gave me the impression you wished to speak with me rather urgently—"

I leap from the floor so fast I nearly trip over my dressing gown and lunge for the phone, yanking it off the receiver. "Mr. Abraham? Are you still there?"

"Why, yes." He sounds startled. In addition to the reediness of his voice, which suggests Mr. Abraham is older, there's an oddly formal cadence to his words. I've noticed it's the way well-educated Southern men sometimes speak when they have a chip on their shoulder and need the world to know they are, in fact, well educated. "Is this Miss Ruth Cornier?"

"It is." I'm still a little out of breath. This is *the* John Abraham, the old *Bugle* journalist, manifested out of the ether, or perhaps just the telephone book. Either way, Nissa has worked some magic to locate him this quickly. "Thank you for calling."

"I'll be honest with you." His voice turns wry. "Receiving a call out of the blue that Reverend Cornier's daughter wished to speak with me certainly piqued my interest. My history with your daddy goes back."

"That's what I wanted to talk to you about." I twist the phone cord around my fingers. "Mr. Abraham, I know you used to live in Bottom Springs and work for the *Bugle*. I read some of your old stories."

"Yes, I did. Before Augustus Blanchard and your daddy ran me out of town. So imagine my surprise to find myself talking to a Cornier on the phone."

My heart rate picked up. "I found your earliest articles about my father, before he worked at Holy Fire—"

"Oh, he didn't like those," interrupted Mr. Abraham. I could feel his bottled frustration through the phone line. "Back then he was so green. This young whippersnapper who popped up out of nowhere and starting riling people up. I was a seasoned reporter—I'd come down to Bottom Springs from New Orleans after twenty-two years at the *Times-Picayune* looking for a slower life. My health wasn't great at the time, on account of a lot of stress that wasn't good for my heart. When the owner of the *Bugle* offered me a job, I thought, why not go down South? I could whip the old paper into shape, maybe turn it into an award-winning local outfit, leave my mark that way. And then I met your daddy. At first, I thought he didn't stand a chance against me." Mr. Abraham's laugh is tinged with bitterness.

"What happened?"

"Turns out people liked what he was peddling more than what I was. Liked his nightmares and fairy tales better than the truth."

"I'm guessing you're not particularly...religious?"

Mr. Abraham remains silent for a beat, then asks, "And exactly how straight and narrow are you, Miss Nosing Around in Her Daddy's Business?"

Point taken. I clear my throat. "So, you found yourself butting heads..."

"Somehow he got the *Bugle's* owner to forbid me from covering him, which irked me to all hell. Goes against every journalistic principle. But the owner was a businessman, not a journalist—owned a chain of papers all over the state—and he didn't want the trouble. So for a while I was muzzled."

"What changed?"

Mr. Abraham sighs. "Look, Miss Cornier. I've been waiting a long time to talk about what transpired down in Bottom Springs, but no one was ever interested in asking. Most people wanted me to shut up and not rock the boat. So I'm certainly willing to play your source, but before I spill, I have a question for you."

"Okay."

"Why?"

I blinked. "What?"

"Why am I talking to you? What's got you dredging up the past, peering down the dark rabbit holes in your own father's life?"

I weigh my options for a moment before deciding that a man like John Abraham, who prizes the truth, requires honesty. "I'll tell you plain, Mr. Abraham. I recently learned my father, Augustus, and a small group of other leaders in town were involved in some despicable behavior years ago, and I'm trying to get to the bottom of it. I want to know the truth about what they've done and who they are. I think Bottom Springs deserves it. And now, with Augustus dead and Blanchard Hospital passing to my father—"

Mr. Abraham nearly gasps. "Augustus is dead?"

"It happened just a few days ago. He died in his sleep and left everything to my dad."

"Sweet Jesus," Mr. Abraham whispers. "Those sons of bitches got away with it."

"Please, tell me what you mean. I saw the photos you took from the bicentennial. The ones you published right before the *Bugle* got shut down."

"How? All the old issues were destroyed."

"No they weren't. We kept them on microfilm at the library."

At this, Mr. Abraham chuckles. "Good old Mrs. Dupre! I knew she had some fire in her, the old bat."

"The picture," I repeat. "Of my dad and the others at the beach, where you can see their tattoos."

"Your daddy hated those pictures. Especially the ones I didn't print that showed his own little witch-mark."

I press my shoulders hard against the wall. "Wait a second. Are you saying my father has a tattoo? I only saw them on three of the men."

Mr. Abraham's voice goes flat. "They all have them. The whole cabal."

In all my life, I've rarely witnessed my father without a pressed, buttoned dress shirt on. I'd always assumed his formality, the care with which he covered himself, was evidence of his godliness, or even an insecurity, some shame over his large, broad body. The humanness of it had actually endeared him to me. But now I know the real reason he's kept his skin out of sight: the great Reverend James Cornier, the man whose fame and power has been built in opposition to the occult, wears an occult symbol on his chest.

With my back to the wall, I slide all the way down to the floor. "Is that why the *Bugle* got shut down?" My voice is low. "Because you published that picture? I know it was your last issue. Did my father have something to do with it?"

"It wasn't the pictures," says Mr. Abraham. "The pictures were only a nuisance. I'm guessing what drove Augustus Blanchard to acquire the *Bugle* for well over market price and then promptly dismantle it was something he deemed much more dangerous." He waited a moment. "My investigation into Blanchard Hospital."

Beneath my surprise, a white-hot spark of interest flares. "On what grounds?"

"This is your scoop," Mr. Abraham promises, lowering his voice like we're meeting in a dark alley with enemies in the shadows. "After I was told not to go after the promising young reverend, I had a bit of an ax to grind. So I started poking around—in his dealings, his friends' dealings, you name it. Whatever they touched, I studied. I was hungry and itching for a story no one could suppress, to show those bastards even they didn't have power over the truth. As part of that, I FOIA-ed—sorry, requested—all the publicly available files I could get on Blanchard Hospital. It turned into a little hobbyhorse, me digging around in those files every day after work. Eventually I noticed something in Blanchard's purchase orders that struck me."

"What was it?"

"They were ordering massive amounts of painkillers. Mostly Schedule II opioids like oxycodone and hydrocodone. Back then those things were still considered miracle drugs, but there were some cracks beginning to show, some stories swirling around about how addictive they were, over and beyond anything else. And Blanchard was ordering—we're talking hundreds of thousands of these pills a year, and their orders increased every year, all the way up to half a million the last year I had records for. When I checked the number of patients they typically saw in a year, the numbers didn't match up. Even if they prescribed those opioids to every person who came in for a runny nose, the amount would still be excessive."

Painkillers—the goods the Sons of Liberty stole from the hospital and trafficked around the state. Maybe Blanchard was ordering massive amounts because the Sons were stealing them...but if so, if the thefts were affecting the hospital's bottom line, why hadn't anyone ever alerted the sheriff?

"I started researching pill mills." A new enthusiasm brightened Mr. Abraham's voice, and in it, I caught a glimpse of the tenacious reporter he'd been all those years ago. "You ever heard of those? It happens when the good guys turn dirty—the doctors and hospitals themselves. I found out about them from some old colleagues who started working for the AP—they said the FBI had started quietly investigating a few pharmacies and pain clinics in other states after they discovered they were selling opioids to drug traffickers to hawk on the black market."

"My God," I whisper, because I know where this is going.

"The conclusion I came to was that Blanchard Hospital was running the same sort of operation, except the one thing I could never figure out was who they were handing their pills off to. I did everything by the book—gathered evidence, was meticulous in my research. I even got a doctor from Blanchard to agree to go on the record with his suspicions. Do you know how hard that was? I was going to publish the story and take down Augustus. And then, right before my big interview, Augustus swooped in and bought the *Bugle* and shut it down. After that, for some *mysterious* reason, the doctor wouldn't talk."

"Augustus found out what you were planning? How?"

"I have no idea. But I was furious. Behind his old Southern aristocrat veneer, Augustus Blanchard was a rat bastard who deserved to be exposed. I was going to take my story somewhere else, try to get it published in the *Times-Picayune* as a freelancer, but then one morning I walked outside to collect my mail and found these strange symbols carved above my door."

Here they were—symbols again. "What kind?"

"They looked almost like your daddy's tattoo, except the ones on my door had only a single set of horns."

I remembered what Nissa had said about apotropaic marks: the two-horned symbol in the woods and tattooed on the men was a protective mark because it inverted something dangerous, and thus warded it off. So, without the inversion… "Someone put the mark of the beast on your door."

"I figured it wasn't good," Mr. Abraham said dryly. "I knew about your daddy's history, running off people he didn't like by accusing them of being Devil-worshippers. So I knew the symbols were a warning, and I knew who from. I decided it might be best to leave town and lie low for a little while. Sadly, a little while turned into years. Until this phone call."

I straighten my back against the wall. "Thank you so much for telling me, Mr. Abraham. I know you took a risk. And I'm…well, I'm sorry for what my father and Augustus did to you."

"It's what powerful people do. Don't get me wrong—that's not an excuse. I'm not excusing them. But I've had a lifetime to think, and what I've observed is that power is a parasite. It wriggles inside you and takes over so all you can think about is how to get more of it and cut down anyone in your way. For that reason you can't trust anyone with a lick of it." Before I can think too long about this, he adds, "But something tells me if the reverend's own daughter wants to know the truth, my work might finally go to good use. So maybe all isn't lost."

"It's not," I promise. "The work you did won't be in vain."

John Abraham whistles, low and short. "If you would've told me that one day James Cornier would be felled by his own damn kid, I never would've believed you. Sometimes the world really is a strange and wonderful place."

"I have to go," I tell him. Because finally, all the disparate threads I've uncovered since the trapper first pulled Fred's skull out of the swamp have woven together, and now I can see the God's-eye view. And there's only one place to go. "Thank you so much, Mr. Abraham."

"All right, kid," he says. "You go raise some hell."

44

NOW

Instead of the rioters Barry promised, Main Street is a ghost town. Not a soul on the sidewalks, shops locked and dark, even the Piggly Wiggly. I find the emptiness unsettling, stronger proof that something big and terrible is underway. Or maybe it's that I'm on my way to do something big and terrible, a confrontation twenty-three years in the making.

By the time I make it to my parents' house, my hands are shaking. I stop at the edge of their lawn and study the place like Ever must have done all those mornings he waited for me. From this angle, you can see straight into my old room, pink curtains hanging slightly askew from getting caught so many times on Ever's shoes when he climbed in. I remember when the house was just a two-story clapboard. Like Holy Fire Born Again, it's swollen over the years, new wings added, columns and windows, metamorphosing into the hulking manor it is now, sprawled triumphantly across the lawn. With the added cupola on top, it mirrors Holy Fire's steeple, two buildings competing in their reach for God.

But it's not God my father has been reaching for all these years. At the thought, my composure breaks, and I bend over to clutch a stone flowerpot, trying to catch my breath. My adrenaline is sending my heart rate through the roof, my instincts begging me to turn and flee instead of going in. This grand house is where I learned to be afraid, learned to be a wisp. The mere sight of it slumps my spine.

But I'm armed with the truth, and I will no longer be afraid. I force myself upright and make it to the door. It creaks open to a foyer full of people buzzing around, carrying things like posterboard, water bottles, and wooden stakes. As I push my way inside, they eye me warily, as if they know something I don't; as if this is their house, not mine.

There's no one in town, but a small army here. What is my father planning?

"Ruth." His unmistakable baritone reverberates through the house. I turn to find him descending the staircase, a smile on his face. "To what do we owe the pleasure?"

I crane my head. The great Reverend Cornier is always on high, like the sun. Even here at home in August, he wears his stiff button-down, slacks, and shiny loafers. The only hint of disorder is the chest hair that curls from the top of his collar, as if he is too virile to be contained. His mane of dark hair gleams with oil.

A feeling of disassociation seeps through me. How could any part of me have come from him?

My father's smile widens, revealing large, square teeth. Perhaps he thinks I've come to beg forgiveness, pledge myself to his side in whatever war he's preparing for.

"We need to talk," I say. I don't lower my eyes like I would've when I was a girl and afraid to hold his gaze.

He studies me for a moment. Whatever he sees makes him clear his throat. "Friends and neighbors, will you look at this? The prodigal daughter has returned."

Everyone around us—his faithful flock—laughs.

"Go on now," he grins, waving them away. "Head on down to the church. Our work can continue there."

I don't budge as people I've known all my life file past me, staring like I'm some sort of salacious curiosity. When the door finally shuts, the sound echoes. My father and I stare at each other.

"Well." He grips both sides of the staircase. "Talk."

I've been imagining this from the moment Barry fled my house. As I stood in the shower washing the mud off, on the walk through the ghostly town square. I know I must remain calm and composed. I cannot allow him to wound me, make me panic and lose control.

"I know what you did," I say.

"Let me guess." He steps languidly down the last stairs. "You're here to complain about my treatment of your friend—is that it? The Devil will have far worse punishments waiting for him in Hell."

I ignore him, press forward. "It took me too long to see it, especially since I was so close. But I see now, Dad. You're the missing ingredient. It's been you from the beginning."

"I can't imagine what you're talking about." He stands a foot away in the gleaming white foyer, towering above me. "And frankly, I don't have time to guess. It's a big day." His small, satisfied smile reappears. "You'll find out soon enough."

This is meant to be an interrogation, but he's not complying. "Do you deny being friends with Killian Duncan?"

"Killian?" My mother emerges from the kitchen, wiping her hands on her apron. Her blond hair lays in a perfect bob, the ends brushing the Louisiana pearls she wears whenever company's over. "Why would you accuse your father of such a thing?"

I slide the folded paper out of my dress. "Explain this, then." I step forward, holding it so they can both see John Abraham's damning photograph.

My mother squints. "What does this prove? Killian Duncan was a degenerate in need of counsel. Your father was probably shepherding him. That's his obligation."

"Where'd you find this?" The reverend's voice is quiet and controlled, but red patches have appeared on his neck. A telltale sign of anger.

"You may have destroyed all the physical copies, but you forgot about the microfilm." I take a deep breath. "Pity you were too busy banning books from the library to spare a moment to learn how it works." My heart hammers with adrenaline. I have no idea where this bravado is coming from.

"I did no such thing. And I won't stand here listening to vile accusations from my own daughter." He rips the paper out of my hand and tears it. The pieces fall like ashes to the floor.

"I told you." My mother takes a step toward me. She and my father have always had this habit of edging closer to me as they talk when I'm in trouble, as if they are large cats hunting me. "First she refused to believe the sheriff and sided with a killer. Now she's making up lies about you. She needs an intervention."

"*Look* at this!" Using their closeness as an advantage, I seize my father's shirt and tear it open with both hands. Buttons fly as his chest is revealed. And there it is, above his heart: the tattoo. Just as John Abraham promised.

My mother gasps in outrage. I jab my finger at his chest. "You see? Your mighty reverend has a pagan symbol on his skin."

My father's face is beet red. "How *dare* you?" he seethes, trying to pull the halves of his shirt together and button what's left.

I stare at my mother, waiting for her shock and indignation. But her gaze remains cold.

"Do you think," she says, each word sharp enough to cut, "that I don't know my own husband's body?"

Her words chill me. Why did I assume she didn't know? It's one thing to hide a tattoo from your child, but your wife? The implications flood me. My holier-than-thou mother is in on it.

I step back, looking between them. "I know you carved the wards in the trees. You, Augustus, Fred, and the sheriff, who had to pretend he'd never seen them before." It was the only thing that made sense—outside of Ever, they were the only people who knew about the symbols, believed in them.

"That's absurd," my mother snaps. "His tattoo is private, from an ancient biblical language. It means chosen by God."

My father and I stare at each other. I can practically feel the heat emanating from him. He lied to her. And what a lie.

"I know it was you," I say softly.

"James?" My mother looks at him. For once, she sounds unsure.

He clutches his shirt tighter and twists away from us. "It was a *precaution*," he growls, striding into the dark-paneled living room. As if he can run from me.

"You were scared of the Low Man," I say, quick on his heels. Moments ago, they were cornering me. But now, the tables have turned.

He circles his armchair and stops, using it as a barrier between us. I've never seen him so disheveled. "The Devil takes many names and many faces. We were protecting ourselves."

His confession causes warm satisfaction to seep through me. I was *right*. "How did you even find out about the Le Culte de la Lune?"

"You're speaking gibberish."

"The symbol, Dad. The one on your chest, on the trees. You and I both know it's not really from the Bible. How'd you find it?"

He stares at me but says nothing. Only clenches his jaw.

"It was Célestine Duncan, wasn't it? You stole it from her."

"Célestine?" my mother echoes. "Killian's wife?"

"She was a witch," he spits out. "Her whole family were witches. That's why they hid in the swamp. They were an abomination."

"And yet you took from them." I push aside his hypocrisy to focus on the more urgent question. “Why did you think you needed protecting from a beast that hunts wicked men, Dad?”

He clutches the top of the armchair and glares. And it’s this stony silence that I’ve been waiting for. After twenty-three years listening to him preach, it’s my turn to talk.

45

NOW

I pieced it all together." I stand directly in front of his armchair, not giving him an inch. "Fred's secret dock. The sheriff turning a blind eye to the Sons of Liberty. Why you're inheriting the Blanchard empire."

"What's she talking about?" my mother asks.

I refuse to drop his gaze. "You holy men are the real drug kingpins of south Louisiana."

"*Excuse* me?" She takes a step forward and lifts her hand as if to slap me but wavers when she glances at my father, still as a statue, red as murder.

"All these years," I say, ignoring her and giving voice to what had finally occurred to me the moment John Abraham shared his suspicions. "All the money that flowed to us and Holy Fire. Our home improvements, the church renovations, our new cars, Mom's dresses. The hospital's growth. The wild success of the Fortenot Fishing Company. None of that came from God's blessing, did it? It came from good old earthly crime."

"You have no idea what you're talking about," my mother snipes. "Tithing's up, thanks to your father."

He's kept her in the dark.

"This slander is dangerous." My father's voice is a snarl, low and vicious. "Think about what you're doing, who you're betraying. What does God say righteous men should do to liars and traitors?"

A threat already. He's feeling cornered.

I stand taller. "I *do* know what I'm doing. Maybe you never saw it, Dad, but I have a brain. Or maybe you did see it, and that's why you and Mom tried so hard to make me think I couldn't trust my own mind." The accusations of hysteria, the doctors, the pills—I'd almost fallen for it. "I know Blanchard Hospital supplies opioids to the Sons. I found proof of the connection in Jebediah Ray's basement."

My father startles at the mention of Jebediah.

"And your old friend John Abraham told me he'd suspected it before he got run out of town. Only," I say, brushing the leather of his armchair, "he didn't know who Augustus had struck a deal with. But I do. Blanchard supplied the painkillers. Then Killian and his drug runners in the Sons of Liberty sold them all over Louisiana."

"Tell her she's insane." My mother's eyes are round and disbelieving. "Tell her she's hallucinating."

"You're insane," my father agrees.

I shake my head. "Fred was a runner, too. He brought the drugs across state lines in his boats, disguised as Fortenot Fishing cargo. The sheriff covered things up when you needed him to, and everyone got their cut. The perfect plan. A whole drug empire down here in little ol' Bottom Springs, where no one would suspect. How long has it been working for you, Dad?"

"Stop it!" He sweeps his massive arm and knocks the lamp off the side table, shattering it, in warning. My mother jumps back.

"It explains everything," I press, walking around the armchair, stepping over the sharp pieces. "That's why Gerard Theriot took over Fred's business. You needed to keep those ships running or the Sons wouldn't have been happy. They were already looking to switch suppliers, weren't they? Augustus was getting old and you probably kept the Sons on a tight leash. They've been shopping for new alliances." Hence that rival gang from up north at Jebediah's compound—a fruitless attempt to strike a truce.

My father looks at me incredulously. "How could you possibly know that?"

"James," my mother breathes, "it isn't true."

"Who better to take over the Fishing Company than the sheriff's nephew? He was already complaining about having to run Fred's illegal cargo. You let him in on your secret and solved two problems in one—no more employee mutiny and the drugs kept flowing. Same as Herman Blanchard—you let him have free rein in your church because you needed to keep his father happy."

My mother squares her shoulders. "We had no idea about Herman's sickness. We never would've allowed that poison in our church."

My father's look is murderous.

I smile. "See, Dad? I am smart. Are you proud? You wouldn't have gotten anywhere without the pills from Blanchard Hospital, so you had to keep Augustus happy and protect his son from scandal, all while lining yourself up to inherit when Augustus died. That's why you tolerated Killian, too, even though you hated him. He was the connection to the Sons you needed. Maybe he's even the one who brought them in, helped you mastermind it. When did it start? I know you were holding meetings at night in your office when I was a kid. What were you doing—planning drug runs? Figuring out how to expand your territory, manipulate the Sons? Is that why you started saying prayers to dark gods in those white stone circles? Were you begging for success?"

His eyes widen. "You couldn't possibly know—"

"Ever told me about the circles. Did you know your God wouldn't listen?"

"It was *Killian,*" he snaps. "Killian and his guilt. After Célestine died he was obsessed with her rituals. Trying to piece her back together after he tore her apart. He performed one the night before Jebediah and the Sons were supposed to take down one of our rivals in New Orleans. We were expanding our territory. It was risky, dangerous, but I saw a path. And the ambush worked. Tom and Fred were convinced it was because of Killian's ritual. So the next time we had a shipment going out, he did it again. He brought a rabbit into my office, slit its throat right there on the floor. A bloody sacrifice. And it worked." My father shakes his head, as if he's still mystified. "That's when I realized what shapeshifters our God and Lucifer are. They were speaking to me anew through this paganism. The Queen Mother and the Low Man—just different names for the same powers."

"When you beat Everett, was it part of a ritual?"

"Ruth, stop," my mother gasps.

"Did you need a sacrifice, and thought, why not this little boy? He was as powerless as a rabbit, after all."

My mother whips to my father. "This has crossed a line. Tell her to stop talking."

"Everett was *weak,*" my father spits out. "He came from a corrupt family. We taught him his place early. It was a mercy."

His words pierce my heart. "Everything you did to protect yourself from the Low Man tells me you knew all along what you were doing was wrong."

"James—" my mother starts.

"*Enough,* Adele. Jesus Christ, *enough.*" He whirls to her, and she blinks in shock. "What is a wife's role?"

"I—"

"*Answer* me. Does she question her husband, or is she his faithful lieutenant?"

I can see her pride warring with her sense of duty. Finally, she lowers her eyes. "His lieutenant."

"Then be silent." He spins to me and I take an instinctive step back. "And you. Listen to me. All I've ever done was be the leader this town needed. *I* made it a God-fearing place. *I* grew Holy Fire. *I've* drawn in people from Forsythe, Port Sulphur, Houma, all over the state. And to do it—to serve the Lord—I needed money. Earthly power. Everything I've done was to expand the Kingdom of Heaven."

"To expand *your* kingdom."

"Of course it's mine," he shouts, seizing the armchair and shaking it. "My kingdom and God's kingdom are one and the same. I am the *way*, child. God came to me in a vision when I was younger than you and gave me this mission. And what are the laws of men compared to the will of God?"

"That's what all of this has been about? The apotheosis of James Cornier?"

He hits the wall with his fist; a photograph falls to the floor and cracks. "That's how He's worked His will on earth since the beginning. He calls some of us to be his emissaries. And there are always doubters. Their fate is to burn with the rest of the nonbelievers."

I stare at him, watching his chest heave. "You don't get to pretend that it's God who wants you to be powerful."

"God speaks to me—"

"Did He tell you to do nothing while Everett was beaten? Look the other way while Fred hurt his daughter? Let Lila drive off with Herman? Did God tell you to do all of those things?"

My father rolls his neck, as if I'm trying his patience. "The end justifies the means, Ruth. That's a thing you'll learn as you get older. Sometimes regretful things happen on the path to greater good. And you should be grateful to me. I've shielded and protected you your entire life."

It echoes back, the memory of him pulling me away from Herman.

He's right—I alone was protected. Compared to Everett, Lila, Beth, and who knows who else, I've been as cosseted as a princess. A deep sense of debt wells inside me. "I never asked you to do that."

"You didn't have to. You're my daughter. Everett and Beth were bad seeds, anyway. You have to take a firm hand with children like that. And when it came to Herman, well, the most important thing was keeping the town on the right path to prosperity. I had to focus on the bigger picture."

"The bigger picture is you're killing people with opioids. At best, making them sick. How could that possibly be part of God's plan?"

"We're all sick, Ruth." My father delivers the words like he's back on his balcony, preaching. "We're all born sinners, in need of redemption. But not all of us are destined to be saved. That was never God's plan, to let everyone into Heaven. It's some men's fate to fill the bowels of Hell. Look around our country and you can see it. A great sickness sucking the marrow out of once-great towns. The whole nation falling to atheism and immorality. But not here. In Bottom Springs, we're protected. Their wickedness can't hurt us. On the contrary, it fuels our growth, the beauty of our parks, the might of our businesses. Why shouldn't addicts' and sinners' bad choices enrich us? Let them be good for something."

"How can you—"

"Like you," he says, as if I haven't spoken. "You never obeyed—not in your heart. You claim you've grown into a God-fearing woman, but inside you're still the same sad and silly teenage girl. 'Pay attention to me, Daddy, but don't punish me when I've done wrong.' Here you are again, in my house, taking my time, demanding I explain myself. Well, there are bigger things than you and your feelings, Ruth. It's time to grow up."

The way he's looking at me; the way he spit out *teenage girl* like it's the most pathetic thing a person could be. And maybe he's right. Maybe I froze at seventeen and am still carrying around my tender girl-heart. Because I feel ashamed at the very suggestion that I'm needy. Pitiable.

And that shame triggers an avalanche. It all comes back: shame, shame, shame. Over the intensity of my feelings, over *Twilight*, over wanting contemptible things like love and magic, over my desire for affection, over the ugliness my mere presence seems to bring out in people.

What is it about us teenage girls that claws so deeply under people's skin? We're reviled and desired in equal measure; cringed at, laughed at, then lunged at. The sheer effort people like my father and my teachers have spent trying to control us. So many dress codes and rigid rules and unspoken ones we have taken on the mantel of policing ourselves, looking in the mirror and wincing at our reflections, drawing our own blood first, before others can. I think my father wants me to erase myself the way everyone who opposed him erased themselves while he was rising to power. Perhaps he's doing the same thing to me he did with the occult. Perhaps deep down, like with the swamp spiritualism, he recognizes I could be a threat and must be taken off the map.

"You want me to feel ashamed." I can't help the tears that have formed in my eyes. I simply brush them away. "You know what, Dad? Let's say deep down, I *am* still a teenage girl. I think you want me to feel bad about that because you have a teenage girl inside you, too, and you're embarrassed. Everything you hate—my hunger, my softness, my need—you can't look me without seeing those parts of yourself, and you're terrified they make you weak. But I know they're strengths. I'm choosing to be proud. Which means you can't control me anymore."

"It's God's control you should be worried about." My father closes the distance between us and takes my hands. His skin is fever-hot. "Come to church tonight and repent in front of the whole town. Admit how you've been wrong and be redeemed. This doesn't have to be who you are anymore. Come to the light."

I don't remove my hands. Somewhere inside me is still a little girl who desperately wants his touch. "Why will the whole town be there?"

He looks so much like a cunning lion with his dark mane, lips stretching into a smile. "They think the Low Man is our murderer. And they believe Everett is the Low Man. They're going to hang him."

Fear freezes my heart. "Who told them to do that?"

His smile widens. "The sheriff and I have an obligation to punish sinners. You refused to give us the evidence we needed to imprison Everett, so we're improvising. Come with us, Ruth. Choose your family."

"And if I don't?"

He squeezes my hands so hard I wince. "Then I won't shield you any longer." I try to wrest my hands away, but he only grips them tighter.

"Let go," I say, sinking at the pain. But his eyes burn. I look to my mother, desperate, but she's shriveled into nothing.

Here, in the living room where I used to kneel at his feet, praying he'd stroke my hair; where I once watched my favorite book burn, wishing it was me, I finally understand the greatest pain of all. It's the moment you realize the family who raised you—the people who witnessed you in every moment of tender vulnerability growing up, who saw your small scraped knees, your spilled tears, your young eyes wide in wonder—don't love you back. At least not the same way. Your love is, and will always be, unrequited. Maybe I'd been a masochist for holding on to hope for so long, or maybe it was only human, the resilience of that tiny flicker in my heart. Either way, kneeling on the floor of their house, the flame is finally snuffed. Loneliness and despair wash over me.

But as my father begins to lecture about repenting, sweat shining on his face, I remember Everett. The person who is more than a person. Who is the shield I once fashioned for myself, a reminder that the world is bigger than this house, and now, the difference between being destroyed and walking away.

My father looks down at me when I stop fighting his grip, my face expressionless. His lecture falters. Silence stretches until I ask one last question. One final interrogation. "Dad, did you ever love me?"

Pain flickers over my mother's face. But he frowns. "When you refuse God, what do you give me to love?"

There. All this time, I've been the one chaining myself. I rise to my feet and leave. As hard and simple as that.

46

NOW

Tears cloud my vision as I press my palm to the sun-warmed wall of the library, so I hardly register the bright blur before it barrels into me.

"Ruth!" Nissa envelopes me in softness and her clean citrus scent. We've never hugged before—and any other day, this display would cause me awkward consternation. But today's different. I close my eyes and let myself be held.

"I was beside myself." She pulls back to study me. "You didn't show up for work, so I went to your house and you weren't there. I thought for sure they'd gotten you."

"The rioters?"

"They're more than that." Nissa squeezes my shoulders. "I know I said I found the Low Man theory compelling, but it isn't a theory anymore—it's a manhunt. They've got guns and knives, Ruth, and they're searching for your friend to kill him. They think he's the Low Man—an actual beast, a demon. I thought I knew these people, that they were salt-of-the-earth folk with good heads on their shoulders, but it's like some switch's flipped. Even Old Man Jonas is walking around with a fishing spear like a pitchfork."

This is worse than Barry or my father described. "Where'd you last see them?"

She shakes her sorrowfully. "On their way to Everett's house."

That's where I'm supposed to meet him. If they find him first—

"I have to go," I say, and start to pull out of her arms, but Nissa tugs me back.

"Listen." In her tangerine blouse, dark eyes searching my face, she radiates warmth and concern. "I've always tried not to act like your big sister. I figured you had enough people in your life tellin' you what to do. But I need you safe, you hear?"

"I'll try my best, Nissa. I promise. And thank you for finding John Abraham. It really helped."

She smiles sadly. "I was a young woman once. I know what it's like to be torn in different directions. To try to understand what *you* think is right and wrong, what *you* care about, who *you* are, when everyone's trying to sell you their version. It's a rite of passage as old as time. The only way through it is to trust yourself, okay? Choose your own path."

"Okay," I say softly. Something occurs to me. "You aren't going to Holy Fire tonight, are you?"

"For the town meeting?" she scoffs. "You couldn't pay me enough. Elijah and I are staying home and boardin' up the windows."

"Good."

She narrows her eyes. "Why are you asking?"

This time I squeeze her shoulders. "Because I need you safe, too."

"Why does it feel like you're saying goodbye to me?"

I give in to my desire and lay my head back on her shoulder. "Thank you for being such a good friend."

"Oh, honey." Nissa strokes my hair. "Don't thank me. Loving you's easy."

The bullet holes are the first thing I see when the Duncan house comes into view. They form a cluster in the front door, then sweep across the house in big sawdusted blasts, like someone let loose with a shotgun. Next is the graffiti, in dripping red: *Murderer. Demon. God Hates You. Rot in Hell.* The windows are all shattered—even the stained-glass pane is now a mess of jagged edges. The fence is busted, the garage door smashed in like the lid of an aluminum can. Catastrophic damage.

I race to the garage door and yank it up, finding the garage in ruins, chemicals dumped across the concrete, but no Ever. I sprint out and try the front door. Locked. I pound. "Everett!" With no answer, I fling myself into the lawn, round the corner of the house—

And halt right before impaling myself on a knife.

"Ruth—I didn't know it was you." Ever drops the knife and seizes me. "Are you okay?"

"Am *I* okay? What happened?"

He falls into the grass beside the knife, drawing his knees up. He looks exhausted. "I went to hide my car in the woods. When I came back, it looked like this." He looks up at me and tries to smile. "Think the buyer's still going to want it with a few extra holes?"

"The entire town is after you, Ever. This is as bad as it gets."

He shifts in the grass, trying to appear nonchalant, but he's biting his lip. "How are you..." He clears his throat. "After last night?"

There's a manhunt after him, and this is what he's nervous about? I crouch and take his hands, ignoring his busted knuckles. "It was perfect. Everything *Twilight* promised."

Ever groans. I grin. "I knew you'd like that."

He yanks me into his lap and cups my face, eyes on my mouth. He tugs my bottom lip between his teeth and then kisses me, his tongue playful, teasing. I chase his mouth and stop his teasing, finding a rhythm that grows more and more intense, until I'm fisting my hands in his shirt, dragging my knuckles across the bare skin of his stomach. He is safety, comfort. It's us against the world.

We pull apart, breathing heavily. I rest my forehead against his and whisper: "I figured out what our dads were doing those nights at Holy Fire."

"You did?"

Secure in his lap, forehead to forehead, I tell him everything. When I'm done, his expression hasn't changed.

"You knew."

"I suspected." His cool fingers grip my waist. "I wasn't sure."

"All along?"

"No. Only recently."

I study him, feeling my heart rate pick up. "There's one last thing I don't understand."

"Yeah?"

"I know why my dad worked with yours. He wanted Killian's connection to the Sons. But why would your dad agree to help mine when he hated him?"

I recognize Ever's brand of quiet: calculating.

"There's something your dad said to me." I take a deep breath. "Before he died."

Ever's jaw tightens. "What was it?"

"When he saw me, he said, 'I always knew it would be a Cornier, but I never thought it would be you.' Do you know why he'd say that?"

I don't like the way Ever looks down at his hands, or the way his mouth forms a tight line. "There's one last thing I haven't told you."

I go rigid in his arms. "I thought we were done with secrets."

"I know. Just—" He looks up at me through his lashes. "Promise you won't run."

I dig my fingernails into the dirt to ground myself. "Tell me."

He sighs. "A few months ago, I was drinking in a bar in Trouville when Jebediah Ray walked in. I'd seen him once or twice a long time ago when he came by the garage to talk business with my dad, but it had been long enough I wasn't sure he'd recognize me. He did, though. Took one look at me and came over. Said he'd know Killian's boy anywhere. I didn't know what to make of it—why he was in Trouville or at my bar without his entourage. But we got to drinking. Hours later, when we were deep in our cups, do you know what he turned to me and said?"

I wait. Afraid, yet mesmerized.

"He told me he was trying to get right with God. Make amends. And he wanted to tell me he was sorry for what happened to my momma. That it had been real hard to watch what my daddy did to her that night. It was one of his regrets."

Dread spills through my veins.

"My heart broke the minute I understood what he meant. But I played it cool. Asked him questions. He said he and my dad grew up together. Used to drink together and stir up trouble, even after they got married. But Jebediah said after I was born, my dad changed. He started going on and on about witchcraft every time he got drunk. Asking Jebediah if he believed in demons and dark magic, that sort of thing. He was obsessed, like a dog with a bone."

"One night they got so drunk they could barely see straight and stumbled to my parents' house. They found my mom in the backyard in her prayer circle. And my dad went berserk. Started screaming that he knew she was a witch. No matter how hard she tried to talk him down, he was convinced, said the reverend warned him she needed to convert, otherwise she was gonna sacrifice our entire family to the

Devil. She was too dangerous to live. When she wouldn't agree to it, he beat her to death."

"Ever—"

"Jebediah said as soon as my dad finished, he burst into tears and started yelling *no, no, no*. He wanted to take it back. He said that's why my dad turned into such a nasty son of a bitch. His regret ate him up."

I'm afraid to touch him, even though I want to. Ever's eyes are incandescent with anger. "I'm so sorry," I say instead. "It's an understatement to say it's horrible, and she didn't deserve it."

"All my life, Ruth, I thought my mom's death was my fault. I blamed myself, accepted the hate my father gave me, didn't even fight back half the time. But *he's* the one who killed her." Our eyes lock. "Because your dad told him to."

I take a deep breath.

"And after my dad confessed, yours used it as leverage. Blackmailed him into working together."

As much as I hate it, it makes sense. *That's* how my mother had known how Célestine really died. Because Killian had spilled to my father, who'd used his guilt as a weapon. With that, the final puzzle piece falls into place. "You didn't just come back this summer for Augustus. You came to kill my dad."

Ever doesn't flinch. "My dad may have beat her, but yours pulled the strings. He's just as guilty."

We stare at each other, our parents' sins hanging like stones around our necks. "You wanted to frame Sons of Liberty for Renard's murder to get back at Jebediah for not intervening with your mom. That's why you were so adamant about avoiding him at the biker bar. You knew he'd recognize you if he saw us."

"It was a good plan to take the heat off us," Ever insists, "regardless of the other motives."

"Because either the sheriff would actually go after Jebediah, or, if they were working together like you suspected, he'd bury Renard's case. Either way, you'd win."

"*We'd* win."

I scramble away from him. "You *are* the Count of Monte Cristo. All of this, from that first day in the swamp with Renard, has been part of an elaborate revenge plot." I'm almost dizzy thinking back. "When I handed you the rock...when you killed him...I didn't know what I was putting myself in the middle of."

Ever's eyes flash. He jumps to his feet. "I didn't know we'd kill him, either. All I knew was you were hurting, and I could help. The rest of them? Fine—part of it *was* revenge. And you know what? It was sweet. But it was also about justice. Protection. The fact that people are in danger so long as these men are alive."

My mind races. "You stayed in Bottom Springs even after you knew the sheriff suspected you because you thought you could still find a way to kill my dad."

Tension ripples between us. "Yes."

We stare at each other. "The thing I don't get is..." I swallow the lump in my throat. "Where do I fit in?"

"Ruth, it's all for you," Ever says, and kicks the wall of his ruined house. Somewhere inside, glass shatters. "Coming, going. Hurting, protecting. I'm always thinking of you, revolving around you. Everything else about my life was forced on me, but you're what I chose for myself."

What I chose. So close to what Nissa said: *Choose your own path*. And suddenly I know what I want. I'm the ultimate hypocrite, but I say it anyway: "Don't kill him."

"Ruth—"

"I know my father's terrible, but—"

"I know he's terrible, *but*. Trust me." Ever spits in the grass. "As the son of an addict, I'm familiar with that song."

"Please." I don't know what compels me—whatever sliver of love remains for my father, maybe, or some sliver of grace. I fall to my knees in the grass. "Don't."

To my surprise, Ever pulls me up. "You don't have to beg. I want you more than any revenge. I won't touch him if you don't want me to. But we need to leave now, before they come back."

Run away with Ever and leave my father to his kingdom. Leave my mother, Nissa and her husband, Lila, the Fortenot Fishing wives, all of the town to their fate.

I take a deep breath and shake my head. I don't want my father dead, but I also don't want that.

Ever blows out a breath. "You've got to be kidding me."

"Do you remember when we burned Renard's necklace in the fire?" I watch him. I need him to understand.

"To see if the gold melted," he says reluctantly. "If he cared as much as he claimed."

"I need to do that to my father."

"Why?"

"I need to know who he is in his heart. If there's anything redeemable."

A look of understanding dawns. "You want proof he's worth leaving alive. A test."

The Bible talks endlessly about parental sacrifice: God sacrificing Jesus, Abraham sacrificing Isaac. Tests of love and devotion. But what about what children sacrifice? What about the courage it takes to right our parents' wrongs, course correct the mess they've left us?

I seize Ever's hands. "I have an idea. But if we do it, there's no trying to insist we're innocent. We'll go down as villains. Only you and I will ever know the truth."

When he blows out a breath, I know I have him. "What do you need from me?"

"To call Sam Landry, steal one more thing, and run for your life."

"You remember I'm not actually the Low Man, right?"

"I know. But Bottom Springs wants a beast." I place my hands on Everett's knife-sharp cheekbones, remembering the power I once gave him and taking it back, swallowing it, drinking his threat, holding the volatile substance in my chest. All that danger, all that potential, mine. "So I'm going to give them one."

47

NOW

Night falls pitch-black. Against it, the stars have never been clearer, out in full force to witness what Ever and I have planned, our shot at infamy. It's so velvety dark that on the walk to Holy Fire, we can see the torches blazing from a quarter mile away. The chanting doesn't hit until later, but when it does, the sound of those familiar voices roaring for blood makes me reach for Ever's hand.

People I've known my whole life, who watched me play as a child, fill the lawn around the church. They hold torches and pistols, shotguns, kitchen knives. I catch sight of Old Man Jonas with his fishing spear like Nissa warned. The chanting comes and goes, but when it swells, I catch the words, "Send him back to Hell."

Ever lets go of my hand and slinks away silently, on his first mission. When he returns, he finds me crouched behind a truck in the parking lot, holding my breath. He hands me a packet of papers and I exhale.

"I was right?"

"Just like you said." He takes his place beside me and studies the crowd. "Look at them. They've finally taken off their masks. They're animals."

"They're scared," I whisper. I can feel it in the air.

Suddenly the crowd parts to let my father through. He's flanked by the sheriff, Barry, and Deputy Roy McClaren. Their eyes scan the crowd, hands resting near their guns. Sweet old Roy looks nervous and uncomfortable, but a small smirk curls Barry's mouth. This must be exactly what he hoped for.

"My good people," my father bellows. "Our home has been poisoned by evil." His deep voice rings across the lawn, causing all to fall silent. "We've grown too Godly. Too powerful in our faith. We've drawn an ancient enemy out of the dark. The Low Man has risen on a mission from the Devil. One by one, he'll butcher us until none are left."

The crowd buzzes.

"How convenient," Ever whispers.

My father raises his arms and silence falls. "In the face of true evil, God commands us to act in his stead and carry out his holy punishments."

The townspeople shout, raising their guns and torches.

"We must cast this demon back to Hell," my father shouts, and as the crowd clamors, he turns and sweeps back into the church, disappearing through the double doors. The sheriff takes over, shepherding townsfolk. Are they planning to march through town in search of Everett? It doesn't matter. Nothing they plan will come to pass.

I lean my head against Ever's shoulder. "Are you ready?"

His stubble rubs my forehead as he nods. "Are you?"

I pat the papers in my dress and raise the branch we picked up on our walk. "I have everything I need."

Someone bellows. Ever and I glance sharply at the crowd. A large, brawny man standing with Gerald Theriot—one of his fishing crew—raises his shotgun, pumping it. The men around him cheer.

"You don't have to do this," Ever says quietly. "It doesn't have to be you."

"Of course it does." I'm the one who was shielded. I owe a debt. My father is my angel to bear. "Now remember, I need you to fly."

"I know." Ever cups my face. "I'll see you when this is over."

"I'll be there," I promise. He kisses my forehead and straightens to his full height.

As Ever strides toward the crowd, I watch him transform, exorcising his fear. His back straightens, he shakes out his arms, rolls his neck. He's so well versed at walking into viper's nests, into no-win situations. He's been doing it all his life. I hate that I've asked it of him, pray it's the last time.

He strides out of the dark into the ring of light cast by the crowd's torches. The reaction is instantaneous. Screams and gasps puncture the air as hundreds of people turn in a rippling wave.

"You want me?" Ever shouts, throwing out his arms. "Well, I'm right here."

Now run, I beg. *Straight into the woods.*

"It's him," Barry roars, and mercifully Ever takes that as his cue to whip around and run in the direction of the trees. People stumble into each other, random gunfire thundering, shots hitting the ground near Ever's feet. Torches are dropped and stomped, and then in a massive swell the crowd charges after him, Barry and the sheriff in the lead.

I have no time to waste. As soon as the crowd clears, I head for the church with my branch in hand, only stopping to bend and seize one of the torches with embers still smoldering. I breathe life into it like Ever taught me, and when the flame is tall again, I kick open the double doors.

I know where my father will be: his favorite place on earth. Where he reigns on high.

The doors to the nave are open. A small crowd of women gathers around my mother onstage. I recognize Mrs. Autin the tailor, Julie Broussard the fishing wife, and Mrs. Anderson, my mother's haughty doppelgänger, among them. Above them on the balcony, where I knew he'd be, stands my father.

"Did anyone else hear gunshots?" Julie asks, at the same time my father booms, "Bring in the crowd!"

I close the nave doors with a boom and shove the branch between the handles so the doors can't open. A gasp sounds behind me. When I turn around, every person in the large, ornate space is gaping at me.

"Ruth." My father's voice echoes down. His eyes are fixed on my torch. "You came to repent."

"No." My voice is loud and clear. "I'm here so you can."

"What's the meaning of this?" Mrs. Anderson hisses to my mother, but my mother's face is stony.

"Someone get the sheriff," the reverend commands. But when one of the fishing wives darts toward me and the door, I point my torch at her.

"Stay back." The woman halts. "The sheriff's gone. They all are. There's no one here but us."

"Adele," Mrs. Autin says, her voice soft and confused. "It's only Ruth. Your daughter."

My mother and I lock eyes. "That's not my daughter," she says. "I don't know what that is."

So be it. I point my torch up at the balcony. "That justice you've always feared, Dad. It's here."

Surprise drains the color out of his face. The severity of his reaction is more than I expected. He seems suddenly, truly, afraid. "It's you?" he asks, voice wavering. "You're the Low Man?"

"Yes, Dad. I'm the beast you made."

The people onstage crowd closer, looking at each other in alarm. "What about Everett Duncan?" Julie cries.

"James, get hold of yourself," my mother barks. "This is no time to lose your head."

He's terrified—but it's not because of me. It's decades of his own guilt and paranoia catching up to him. I am his telltale heart, walking before him. I stride to the velvet wall hangings, deep purple and stitched with gold crosses, and hold up my torch. "I'm going to ask you a question. If you answer honestly, I'll let someone leave. If you don't, this church will burn."

"You're holding us hostage?" Mrs. Autin twists her head to my father. "Your daughter's gone mad, Reverend! Stop her!"

He remains rigid, watching me.

"First question's easy. Did you help distribute drugs with the sheriff, Fred Fortenot, Augustus Blanchard, and the Sons of Liberty? Is everything in this church—all these fine things—the spoils of your crimes?" I draw the torch closer to the velvet. "Was this bought with drug money?"

"Don't listen to her," my mother shouts. I can hear her panic, her fear that the town she's lorded over for so many years will know the truth. "She's gone mad, like Mrs. Autin said."

But Julie's eyes gleam, and I know she's thinking of Fred and his secret dock. They'll believe me when this is all over. I must trust it.

My father is now red-faced, scanning the people below. "I did no such thing."

I tip the torch to the velvet hanging, and then its neighbor. The flames catch quick, racing up the wall.

"Bad start." I walk to the pews and point at the cushioned seats. "Try again. Did you allow Fred Fortenot to beat his daughter, Beth, without intervention, yes or no?"

"Quiet!" he roars, gripping the balustrade. "She's been sent by the Devil to confuse us."

"Liar," I call, and set the pews on fire. The cloth seats catch as quickly as the velvet, flames crawling down the rows. Smoke billows from the wall.

I move closer to the stage. The small group staggers back, Mrs. Autin clinging to Julie.

"All you need to do," I yell to my father, "is choose these people over your ego." *Don't melt in the fire,* I beg. *Show me what you're made of.*

"Reverend," one of the fishing wives calls, "help us."

"Did you allow Herman Blanchard to teach children for decades even though you knew he was a predator? Did you sacrifice kids for the sake of your own power, yes or no?"

Mrs. Anderson gasps, turning to my mother in disgust. Oh, yes—however this ends, word will spread. He'll never be free of it.

"She lies," my father yells. "Don't fall into her trap."

I light more pews on fire. Sweat beads my skin. The fire from the velvet hangings is traveling across the wall, slowly consuming the textile art they've hung, and the pews behind me are ablaze. Smoke stings my eyes.

I climb onstage to the podium and my hostages cower in the corner. There's no escaping it: I am the villain. But this justice will be worth it.

I point my torch at the sumptuous red cloth hanging from the podium. Holy Fire Born Again is embroidered in gold thread. "Did you tell Killian Duncan his wife was a witch, and if she wouldn't come to church, she was too dangerous to live?"

"No!" he yells.

"Did that lead him to kill her?" Sweat slides down my face. "Was she the first person you killed, or were there others before her?"

"Be silent!" he screams, and I light the podium on fire.

"Please," Julie begs. "Let us go." I realize she's talking to me, not my father. "Spare us. We did nothing wrong."

The fire encroaches, eating up the pews. Soon it will block the path to the door. Even worse is the thickening smoke, which poisons the air. Mrs. Autin won't stop coughing.

I know they're scared and hurting, but I need these people to stay. They're my witnesses. Without them, I have little leverage. Besides, I'm the villain, aren't I? The beast, the Low Man. Their discomfort should mean little to me. They're collateral damage.

But I can't do it that way.

I growl and sweep down the aisle past the growing flames, scalded by the heat licking my arms and legs. I can smell my hair burning, but I push through to the doors, grip the large branch wedged in the handles, and tug with all my might. It wrenches free and I tumble back. "Leave!" I yell, and race for the stairs to the balcony.

I'm not even halfway up them before I hear the doors to the nave swing open and crack against the wall. Everyone has escaped—except my mother.

She's climbing over the pews toward me.

I leap up the rest of the stairs and run down the narrow path to the balcony. My father has sequestered himself in the corner farthest from me. He holds up a gold cross, as if I am truly a demon. "Back, beast!"

"One last question," I say, breathing heavily, and pull my last and greatest weapon from my dress: the papers Ever stole from my father's safe while everyone was chanting. The document Sam Landry counseled us on, in exchange for a long-ago kindness. The last will and testament of Augustus Lear Blanchard.

The look on my father's face when he see what I hold... He transforms. "Ruth." So much fear packed into the word. "Please." He lowers the cross. From king to beggar.

My mother rushes up behind us, but before she gets close, my father shouts, "Don't touch her! She has the will."

My mother halts. "*How?*"

"Everett," my father answers grimly. "I was right. He's the one who stole money from my safe."

I hold the will tantalizingly close to the flame. My parents' eyes track it. "I'm sure you know this, Dad, but if you destroy the only copy of a will, it's like it never existed. Samuel Landry told us that. You remember Sam, don't you? The boy who got into Duke, who you told everyone not to support? Well, he says without this, lawyers will have to rely on earlier versions of Augustus's will, which I'm guessing name Herman as his heir. But Herman's not alive anymore, so...I guess the state will be in charge of all that money. Maybe there are some distant Blanchard cousins they can track down."

He shivers despite the heat from the fire below. "This has gone beyond rebellion. Give me the will."

"Like I said. One more question." I look at him. At my mother. I'd planned to ask how he'd convinced Augustus to name him as his heir, thinking to expose his machinations to our witnesses. But they're gone now. It's just the three of us. So I take a deep breath and ask something different. "When you struck me as a child. Or when I tried to get you to hug me and you wouldn't. When you locked me in my room for days and told me not to talk. Did you know what you were doing?" I swallow. "Did you mean for it to hurt?"

My father's eyes flick from the will to my face, weighing.

"Yes," my mother says, gripping the balustrade. "I knew."

Slowly, my father nods.

I read it in their eyes: with the will on the line, they're finally telling the truth.

"Thank you," I say, and light the will on fire.

"No," my father roars, lunging at me. I twist away, bending over the balustrade to hold the will out of his reach. He knocks the torch from my hand and it rolls to my mother, who stomps the flame. My father wraps a massive hand around my throat.

"Stop," I wheeze, but he's squeezing my neck too tight. I can barely get the word out.

"James, *enough*." My mother claws at his hand, trying to pull it away, but he elbows her.

"Give me the will," he seethes, our faces inches apart. Heat radiates from him, as blistering as any fire. "You have *no idea* what I've done for it. This is my life's work. Quick, girl."

"No," I manage to rasp, before he squeezes my neck so tight that my vision goes black and the whole church disappears. I'm back on a warm June day in the swamp with the birds singing, frogs croaking. Renard's hands are around my throat, his body crushing mine.

Panic clutches me. I need Ever—I need saving.

You will be saved. You must be good.

But there's no one out there making sure people get mercy or justice. It's just us.

It's just me on this ledge. In this world.

I use the only weapon I have, touching the burning will to my father's shoulder and lighting his shirt. He jumps back in horror, trying to extinguish the fire, but it spreads across his back where he can't reach. My mother leaps at him, striking the flames. I clutch my aching throat and suck in air. "Good riddance," I whisper, and my desperate father meets my eyes.

I let go of the will.

"No," he screams, and dives over the balustrade.

His heels leave the floor. For a single, suspended moment, I watch as my father realizes he's leapt too high, too far, and his muscles seize, as if he can claw back his momentum. No miracle intervenes. His untethered body tumbles after the will. He lands facedown with a crack on the stage. The smoking remains of the will rest by his outstretched hand.

My mother's scream rends the air.

I stare at his unmoving body. In the paralysis of shock, I feel no panic. Only numbness. "Now we know," I whisper.

My mother sobs, clutching the bars of the balustrade. I unpeel her fingers and lift her, dragging her limp, despondent body down the stairs and through the towering arch of fire.

We walk out the double doors of the church with raw, burned skin, her pale hair smoking, my white dress gray with ash. My mother wrestles out of my arms the instant we hit cool air and falls to her knees in the grass. Behind us, a fiery beam falls and crashes. Holy Fire Born Again is coming down. The flames are climbing to the roof, reaching for that glorious, needle-tipped spire.

Be good, he always said. *And be spared the lake of fire.*

I walk away and let it burn.

48

NOW

The tree-ringed highway is quiet as a tomb as I wait in the dark. Everett was supposed to be here by now. There are a million things that could've gone wrong. I'm willing myself not to think about them, not to imagine the sheriff or Barry catching ahold of Ever. As if refusing to admit the possibility can somehow keep it from happening.

Tires squeal. Headlights appear through the trees. Suddenly a convertible charges out of the woods, kicking up dust and swerving onto the highway.

I leap to my feet, heart swelling, as it skids to a stop on the side of the road. Everett, hair slicked back with sweat, grins at me from the driver's seat. "Thank God," we both say. I choke back a laugh as I climb into the passenger side.

The minute I slam the door, Ever jams the gas and guns down the road.

"It worked," I yell over the wind, giddy with the thrill of victory. "You escaped."

He twines his fingers between mine over the gearshift, one hand on the wheel. "They stopped chasing me to run back to the church." He eyes me, an incredulous laugh bubbling. "I heard them shouting that it was burning down."

Tall trees whip by. "He's dead, Ever. His body's in that fire."

The look in his eyes as he squeezes my hand is tender. "I'm sorry. I really am. I know how you must feel."

I'm probably the only person alive who would believe him. Wind lifts my hair. "He wasn't who I hoped." I close my eyes. "At least we're getting out."

"We're getting *out*," Ever shouts, and his jubilance takes me by surprise, makes me laugh. He pulls my hand to his chest. "This is it, Ruth. My dream since we were seventeen."

I bite my lip—then scream, at the top of my lungs, "We're free!"

He reaches his fingers into my hair. "Tell me I can have you forever."

I press my hand over his. "You'll have me and I'll have you."

Nothing could've prepared me for the sudden joy of being unencumbered, without limits, speeding down the road. I lean my head against the headrest as we sail, taking in the inky sky, the diamond stars, the towering trees. Yes, my father is dead; yes, the church is burning; yes, we are criminals; but the world has never been so beautiful. I've never felt so at peace.

"We're going to Texas," Ever yells, his dark curls a halo in the wind. "No more Louisiana."

Into the West. I drape my arm over the convertible door and let it surf the wind. "I'll go to school."

"And I'll open a garage." He kisses the back of my hand. "We'll explore during the day and read at night and—"

"Be happy," I finish.

"And be happy."

We drive for hours. The steady dark lulls me into a dream state. Pieces of the last few days flutter through my mind: kissing Ever in the storm. Kneeling before my father. Burning the church. Barry's shock when I told him he should run. The look on Barry's face. The things he told me...

"Hey, look." Ever points to a lone gas station up ahead, barely more than a sign and two pumps. "We need more gas." We pull into it and refuel, Ever leaning against the convertible while the gasoline chugs.

Barry said he had Everett all figured out, and almost everything he claimed had turned out to be true...

The gas clicks off. After a minute, Ever opens the door and drops back into the driver's seat.

I turn to him. There's one lamp in this gas station and it's flickering, turning his face from light to dark, dark to light. "Ever. I have a question. Why'd you never settle in one place?"

He smiles. His sharp canines glint. "Oh, I don't know."

"Barry guessed it's because you kill people everywhere you live. Not just men from Bottom Springs. But it's Barry, so..."

For a long time, Everett doesn't answer. Finally, he rests his hands on the steering wheel and eyes me. His words are as taut as the rope on a noose. "There are a lot of bad men in the world, Ruth."

A bead of sweat rolls down my neck.

"A lot of men whose punishments will never come unless someone takes it into their own hands."

"I see."

Barry was right.

"Are you afraid now?" he whispers. In the flickering light, I can't read his face. But it doesn't matter. It's my heart on the scale, not his. The chains are tilting back and forth, asking, *Who are you?*

If this scene were a painting in my father's office, it might be called *The Final Corruption of Ruth Cornier*. In one of my mother's cautionary tales, this would be the moment she leaned in and whispered, *And the girl signed her soul away*. If we were in one of the books I loved, those literary classics, it would be the moment the reader knew I was doomed.

I cover Ever's hands on the steering wheel. "How about this. We go to school and work and read and be happy. And sometimes, when the time is right, we'll take care of the people who need it." My voice is low. "We'll be a law unto ourselves."

His eyes shine back. "Two Low Men, prowling the dark."

"Bonnie and Clyde," I whisper, and he seizes and kisses me.

The scale tips.

I taste the sweet heat of his mouth, feel our teeth scrape together, losing myself until I hear something faint in the distant, something that tugs at me. I shake Everett, and he pulls away. We twist in our seats and stare behind us.

That's when my mind makes sense of the sound.

Sirens.

"Start the car," I urge. "Hurry."

Ever's ahead of me, twisting the key and revving the engine until it roars. We race backward, swerve in a giant V, and launch forward. The sirens grow a decibel louder. I turn to watch the road, heart thundering.

"It won't be for us," Ever murmurs, his eyes on the rearview. "It's a coincidence."

Red and blue lights appear in the murky distance. "Drive faster."

He jams the gas, fingers clutching the steering wheel so hard they turn red. The arrow on his odometer is shaking, hitting the max. At this speed, the wind brings tears to my eyes, but I can still see the lights grow bigger, loom closer.

"We're almost to the border," Ever shouts, pointing in the distance. "There'll be a bridge, and on the other side's Texas. We'll lose them."

My hair, my dress—the wind whips them up like sails. The cars are close enough now that I can see they're a caravan. I can just make out the Trufayette Parish Sheriff's logo on the car in the lead. Sheriff Theriot's found us. He must've recruited cops from the next parish like Barry warned. There are too many.

"They're gaining on us!" I can barely hear myself over the thunder of the tires.

"Shit," Ever swears.

A loud voice booms toward us. "Everett Duncan and Ruth Cornier, pull over immediately."

"It's the sheriff." Even with the sound system distorting his voice, I recognize him.

"You're wanted on counts of murder and arson. Do not resist arrest."

"Faster," I chant, "faster, faster." But I know Ever's gunning it.

And there it is, like a mirage: Heaven appearing around the bend. Lights dot an arched bridge. Ever grips my hand. "See?" he shouts. "It's going to be okay."

It has to be. They cannot win.

The bridge shudders and splits in two. The halves begin to rise. The sheriff's voice echoes again: "Do not attempt to cross state lines. We're raising the bridge."

"God Almighty," I breathe.

Ever jerks my hand. "What do we do?"

"I don't know." I'm terrified of what's ahead and behind. I can't think straight.

"Ruth, what should we *do*?"

What should we do, what should we do?

What we've always done.

I shake Ever's hand. "Never give in, remember? Never give ourselves over. That's what we promised."

He tightens his jaw and stares at the rising bridge. "Then I'll drive fast. We'll soar and we'll make it."

"We'll make it," I echo. The pavement is sliding beneath us, but we'll transform into birds and fly away. I always knew that's how I'd escape—as a scarlet Ruth-bird.

Gunshots explode into the asphalt, ricocheting rocks that sting my cheeks, my forehead. We're racing so fast.

"Ready?" Ever roars, and we clutch each other's hands as our tires leave the bridge.

Then we're weightless. Soaring. Suspended above the rushing river, the nose of the convertible pointed at the other half of the bridge. We can make it. I feel it in my bones.

I push against gravity and turn my head to Everett. His eyes are fixed on me, alive and brimming with love. The whole world shimmers: the stars above, the waves below, the metal bridge ahead, receding faster than I expected.

It's dizzying, the sound of the cop cars screeching to a halt behind us, the sheriff's horrified voice, the wind, our height—but at the center is Ever, still and calm. And sometimes a person is more than a person. Sometimes they're a lifeline. Your ticket out, not just of a house or a town but an invisible prison whose bars are in your mind. Sometimes they're a key in the exact shape of the lock that cages you.

"I love you," he shouts, or I think he does. The wind eats his words. But the way he's looking at me—God Almighty, the way he looks…

The nose of the car dips, pointing at the black water, but there's still time, still a chance. If only we could stay here in this moment, suspended, reaching for our freedom. If only I could ask for one miracle, to stop time here and now and never meet what happens next, never know if it was worth it, whether we will get our futures.

"I love you, too," I yell, but I don't know if he hears.

Dear God, I pray. *Dear Devil, dear whoever's listening. I beg you: no more forward motion, no more physics, no more consequences.*

The dark water reaches for us.

Give us this moment forever.

Ever kisses my hand. His eyes are full of stars.

Give us a world where we can be happy. If you've ever loved us, if any part of this was right, stop us here and now.

Below us, the bridge—

Read on for a look at another novel by Ashley Winstead,

In My Dreams I Hold a Knife

1

Now

Your body has a knowing. Like an antenna, attuned to tremors in the air, or a dowsing rod, tracing things so deeply buried you have no language for them yet. The Saturday it arrived, I woke taut as a guitar string. All day I felt a hum of something straightening my spine, something I didn't recognize as anticipation until the moment my key slid into the mailbox, turned the lock, and there it was. With all the pomp and circumstance you could count on Duquette University to deliver: a thick, creamy envelope, stamped with the blood-red emblem of Blackwell Tower in wax along the seam. The moment I pulled it out, my hands began to tremble. I'd waited a long time, and it was finally here.

As if in a dream, I crossed the marble floor of my building and entered the elevator, faintly aware of other people, stops on other floors, until finally we reached eighteen. Inside my apartment, I locked the door, kicked my shoes to the corner, and tossed my keys on the counter. Against my rules, I dropped onto my ivory couch in workout clothes, my spandex tights still damp with sweat.

I slid my finger under the flap and tugged, slitting the envelope, ignoring the small bite of the paper against my skin. The heavy invitation sprang out, the words bold and raised. *You are formally invited to Duquette*

University Homecoming, October 5–7. A sketch of Blackwell Tower in red ink, so tall the top of the spire nearly broke into the words. *We look forward to welcoming you back for reunion weekend, a beloved Duquette tradition. Enclosed please find your invitation to the Class of 2009 ten-year reunion party. Come relive your Duquette days and celebrate your many successes—and those of your classmates—since leaving Crimson Campus.*

A small red invitation slid out of the envelope when I shook it. I laid it next to the larger one in a line on the coffee table, smoothing my fingers over the embossed letters, tapping the sharp right angles of each corner. My breath hitched, lungs working like I was back on the stationary bike. *Duquette Homecoming.* I couldn't pinpoint when it had become an obsession—gradually, perhaps, as my plan grew, solidified into a richly detailed vision.

I looked at the banner hanging over my dining table, spelling out C-O-N-G-R-A-T-U-L-A-T-I-O-N-S-! I'd left it there since my party two weeks ago, celebrating my promotion—the youngest woman ever named partner at consulting giant Coldwell & Company New York. There'd even been a short write-up about it in the *Daily News*, taking a feminist angle about young female corporate climbers. I had the piece hanging on my fridge—removed when friends came over—and six more copies stuffed into my desk drawer. The seventh I'd mailed to my mother in Virginia.

That victory, perfectly timed ahead of this. I sprang from the couch to the bathroom, leaving the curtains open to look over the city. I was an Upper East Side girl now; I had been an East House girl in college. I liked the continuity of it, how my life was still connected to who I'd been back then. *Come relive your Duquette days,* the invitation said. As I stood in front of the bathroom mirror, the words acted like a spell. I closed my eyes and remembered.

Walking across campus, under soaring Gothic towers, the dramatic architecture softened by magnolia trees, their thick curved branches, waxy leaves, and white blooms so dizzyingly perfumed they could pull you in, close enough to touch, before you blinked and realized you'd wandered off the sidewalk. College: a freedom so profound the joy of it didn't wear off the entire four years.

The brick walls of East House, still the picture in my head when I thought of home, though I'd lived there only a year. And the Phi Delt house at midnight, music thundering behind closed doors, strobe lights flashing through the windows, students dressed for one of the theme parties Mint was always dreaming up. The spark in my stomach every time I walked up the stone steps, eyes rimmed in black liner, arm laced through Caro's. The whole of it intoxicating, even before the red cups came out.

Four years of living life like it was some kind of fauvist painting, days soaked in vivid colors, emotions thick as gesso. Like it was some kind of play, the highs dramatic cliff tops, the lows dark valleys. Our ensemble cast as stars, ever since the fall of freshman year, when we'd won our notoriety and our nickname. The East House Seven. Mint, Caro, Frankie, Coop, Heather, Jack, and me.

The people responsible for the best days of my life, and the worst.

But even at our worst, no one could have predicted that one of us would never make it out of college. Another, accused of murdering her. The rest of us, spun adrift. East House Seven no longer an honor but an accusation, splashed across headlines.

I opened my eyes to the bathroom mirror. For a second, eighteen-year-old Jessica Miller looked back at me, virgin hair undyed and in need of the kind of haircut that didn't exist in Norfolk, Virginia. Bony-elbowed with the skinniness of a teenager, wearing one of those pleated skirts, painted nails. Desperate to be seen.

A flash, and then she was gone. In her place stood thirty-two-year-old Jessica, red-faced and sweaty, yes, but polished in every way a New York consultant's salary could manage: blonder, whiter-teethed, smoother-skinned, leaner and more muscled.

I studied myself the way I'd done my whole life, searching for what others saw when they looked at me.

I wanted them to see perfection. I ached for it in the deep, dark core of me: to be so good I left other people in the dust. It wasn't an endearing thing to admit, so I'd never told anyone, save a therapist, once. She'd asked if I thought it was possible to be perfect, and I'd amended that I didn't need to be perfect, per se, as long as I was the best.

An even less endearing confession: sometimes—rarely, but *sometimes*—I felt I was perfect, or at least close.

Sometimes I stood in front of the bathroom mirror, like now, slowly brushing my hair, examining the straight line of my nose, the pronounced curves of my cheekbones, thinking: *You are beautiful, Jessica Miller*. Sometimes, when I thought of myself like a spreadsheet, all my assets tallied, I was filled with pride at how objectively good I'd become. At thirty-two, career on the rise, summa cum laude degree from Duquette, Kappa sorority alum, salutatorian of Lake Granville High. An enviable list of past boyfriends, student loans *finally* paid off, my own apartment in the most prestigious city in the world, a full closet and a fuller passport, high SAT scores. Any way you sliced it, I was *good*. Top percentile of human beings, you could say, in terms of success.

But no matter how much I tried to cling to the shining jewels of my accomplishments, it never took long before my shadow list surfaced. Everything I'd ever failed at, every second place, every rejection, *mounting, mounting, mounting*, until the suspicion became unbearable, and the hairbrush clattered to the sink. In the mirror, a new vision. The blond hair and white teeth and expensive cycling tights, all pathetic attempts to cover the truth: that I, Jessica Miller, was utterly mediocre and had been my entire life.

No matter how I tried to deny it, the shadow list would whisper: *You only became a consultant out of desperation, when the path you wanted was ripped away. Kappa, salutatorian? Always second best. Your SAT scores, not as high as you were hoping.* It said I was as ordinary and unoriginal as my name promised: *Jessica*, the most common girl's name the year I was born; *Miller*, one of the most common surnames in America for the last hundred years. The whole world awash in Jessica Millers, a dime a dozen.

I never could tell which story was right—Exceptional Jessica, or Mediocre Jessica. My life was a narrative I couldn't parse, full of conflicting evidence.

I picked the brush out of the sink and placed it carefully on the bathroom counter, then thought better, picking it up and ripping a nest of blond hair from the bristles. I balled the hair in my fingers, feeling the strands tear.

This was why Homecoming was so important. No part of my life looked like I'd imagined during college. Every dream, every plan, had been crushed. In the ten years since I'd graduated, I'd worked tirelessly to recover: to be beautiful, successful, fascinating. To create the version of myself I'd always wanted people to see. Had it worked? If I could go back to Duquette and reveal myself to the people whose opinions mattered most, I would read the truth in their eyes. And then I'd know, once and for all, who I really was.

I would go to Homecoming, and walk the familiar halls, talk to the familiar people, insert New Jessica into Old Jessica's story, and see how things changed.

I closed my eyes and called up the vision, by now so familiar it was like I'd already lived it. Walking into the Class of 2009 party, everyone gathered in cocktail finery. All eyes turning to me, conversations halting, music cutting out, champagne flutes lowering to get a better look. Parting the sea of former students, hearing them whisper: *Is that Jessica Miller? She looks incredible. Now that I think about it, I guess she always was the most beautiful girl in school,* and *Did you know she's the youngest-ever female partner at Coldwell New York? I heard she's being featured in* Forbes. *I guess she always was a genius. Wonder why I never paid attention.*

And finally, arriving at my destination: where I always gravitated, no matter the miles or the years. The people who pulled me into their orbit. Mint, Caro, Frankie, Coop. Except this time, no Heather or Jack. This time, Courtney would be there, since she'd reinserted herself so unavoidably. But it would be okay, because this time, I would be the star. Caro would gasp when she saw me, and Frankie would say that even though he ran with models, I was still the prettiest girl he'd ever seen. Courtney would turn green with envy, too embarrassed by how successful I was, how much money I made, to talk about her ridiculous career as a fitness influencer. Mint would drop Courtney's hand like it was on fire, unable to take his eyes off me, and Coop...Coop...

That's where I lost the thread every time.

It was a ridiculous vision. I knew that, but it didn't stop me from wanting it. And thirty-two-year-old Jessica Miller lived by a lesson college Jessica had only started to learn: if you wanted something bad enough, you did anything to get it. Yes, I'd go back and relive my Duquette days, like the invitation said, but this time, I'd do it better. I would be Exceptional Jessica. Show them they'd been wrong not to see it before. Homecoming would be my triumph.

I released the ball of hair into the trash. Even tangled, the highlights were pretty against the Q-tips and wads of white tissue paper.

But in a flash, a vision of torn blond hair, sticky and red, matted against white sheets. I shook my head, pushing away the glitch.

I would show them all. And then I would finally rid myself of that dark suspicion, that insidious whisper—the one that said I'd done it all wrong, made the worst possible mistakes, ever since the day East House first loomed into view through my parents' cracked windshield.

At long last, I was going back.

2

Now

The night before I left for Homecoming, I met Jack for a drink. In the weeks since the invite arrived, my excitement had been tempered with guilt, knowing Jack had gotten one, too, but couldn't go back, not in a million years. Traveling across the city to his favorite bar—a quiet, unpretentious dive—was small penance for all the things I'd never be able to atone for. Chief among them, the fact that my whole life hadn't come crashing down around me when I was twenty-two, like his.

I slid into the booth across from him. He tipped his whiskey and smiled. "Hello, friend. I take it you're Duquette-bound?"

We never talked about college. I took a deep breath and folded my hands on the table. "I fly out tomorrow."

"You know..." Jack smiled down at his glass. "I really miss that place. All the gargoyles, and the stained glass, and the flying buttresses." He lifted his eyes back to me. "So pretentious, especially for North Carolina, but so beautiful, you know?"

I studied him. Out of all of us, Jack wasn't the most changed—that was probably Frankie, maybe Mint—but he'd certainly aged more than ten years warranted. He wore his hair long, tucked behind his ears, and he'd covered his baby face with a beard, like a mask. There were premature wrinkles in the corners of his eyes. He was still handsome, but not in the way of the past, that clean-cut handsomeness you'd expect out of a youth-group leader, the boy in the neighborhood you wouldn't think twice about letting babysit.

"I wonder how campus has changed." Jack wore a dreamy smile. "You think the Frothy Monkey coffee shop is still there?"

"I don't know." The affection in his voice slayed me. My gaze dropped to my hands.

"Hey." Jack's tone changed, and I looked up, catching his eyes. Brown, long-lashed, and as earnest as always. How he'd managed to preserve that, I'd never know. "I hope you're not feeling weird on my account. I want you to have fun. I'll be waiting to hear about it as soon as you get back. Do me a favor and check on the Monkey, okay? Heather and I used to go there every Sun—" He cut himself off, but at least his voice didn't catch like it used to. He was getting better. It had been years since he'd called me in the middle of one of his panic attacks, his voice high as a child's, telling me over and over, *I can't stop seeing her body*.

"Of course I'll go." One of the bar's two waitresses, the extra-surly one, slid a glass of wine in front of me and left without comment. "Thanks," I called to her back, sipping and doing my best not to wince while Jack was watching. My usual order was the bar's most expensive glass of red, but that wasn't saying much.

I forced myself to swallow. "What else should I report back on?"

He straightened, excited, and for a second, he looked eighteen again. "Oh man, what do I want to know? Okay, first, I want all the details about Caro and Coop—how did he pop the question, when's the date, what's she wearing?" Jack barreled on, neatly sidestepping the fact that he wasn't invited to the wedding. "Do you think they hooked up in college and kept it a secret from the rest of us? *Ask* her. I want the dirt. Who would've pictured the two of them together? It's so unexpected."

I tipped my glass back and lifted my finger for another, though I knew the waitress hated when I did that. "Mm-hmm," I said, swallowing. "Sure."

Jack grinned. "I need the *full* report on what Coop looks like now. I need to know how many tattoos he has, if he's still rocking that *Outsiders* vibe, if he cut his hair." He tugged a strand of his own hair. "What do you think... Did I get close to the way Coop used to wear it?"

Death by a million paper cuts. "It's very *zero fucks* meets Ponyboy. Classic Coop. Um, what about Caro, anything?"

His gaze turned thoughtful. "I guess I just want to know she's happy. I don't know... Caro never really changes. You talk about her the most, anyway."

He was right. Caro looked and acted exactly the same now as she did then. She still texted me regularly, albeit not every five minutes, like in college. In fact, the only thing that had really changed about Caro was the addition of Coop.

"You have to tell me if Mint still looks like a movie star," Jack said, "or if his hairline is finally receding like his dad's. God, I don't know whether I want you to say he's even more handsome, or his hair is falling out, 'cause that would serve him right. I can't believe he left law school to rescue the family business. There was always something off about his family, right? His dad, or was it his mom? I remember that one time senior year, when Mint lost it—" Jack stopped midsentence, eyes widening. "Oh *crap*, I'm sorry. I'm an idiot."

And there it was. Pity, even from Jack. Because I'd lost Mint, the person who used to make me valuable just by association. And even though no one had been there to witness the breakup, to see how deep the blow had struck, it seemed everyone could sense it anyway.

"First of all," I said, trading the waitress my empty glass for a full one, "that was a long time ago, and I literally could not care less. I'm actually looking forward to seeing Mint. And Courtney. I'm sure they're very happy together." I blinked away a vision of my laptop, shattered against the wall, screen still stuttering on a picture of their wedding. "Second, *crap*? I find it adorable you still don't curse. Once a Boy Scout, always a Boy Scout. Hey," I continued, "did you know Frankie just bought one of Mint's houses?"

Knife, twist. Tit for tat.

"Really?" Jack shrugged, playing nonchalant, but his Adam's apple rose and fell as he swallowed hard. "Good for him. I guess he's getting everything he wanted." He tossed his hair, another stolen Coopism. "Whatever... Everyone in the world sees Frankie every Sunday. Not hard to tell how he's doing. What I really want is for you to come back and tell me Courtney's into new age crystals and meditation, or she does physical therapy with retired racehorses. Something charitable and unexpected."

I almost snorted my wine. "*Courtney?* If she's even one iota less a mean girl, I will consider that immense personal growth."

Jack rolled his eyes. "I said it was my *hope*, not my expectation, Miss Literally-Could-Not-Care-Less."

"Ha."

"You know, I always felt bad for her. Underneath the designer clothes and bitchiness, Courtney seemed like an insecure little girl, desperate to be liked." He gasped, lifting a hand to his chest. "Will you look at that... I *cursed*. Soak it in, 'cause it's not happening again. The Baptist guilt hangover is already setting in."

I shook my head, trying to keep the smile on my face, but inside my heart was breaking.

"Jess." Jack laid his hand over mine. "I really do want you to have fun. For both of us."

Fun. I was going back for so much more than that. I cleared my throat.

"After I give you my report on everyone, my reward is that I finally get to meet Will."

Jack withdrew his hand. "Maybe. You know I like to keep things... separate."

Jack had never introduced me to his boyfriend. Not once in the years since we'd been friends again, which was itself a strange story. When Jack was accused of murdering Heather our senior year, in the few months before he left campus for good, the other students crossed the street wherever he walked, sure down to their bones they were looking at a killer. If he entered a room, everyone stiffened and fled.

But not me. My limbs had remained relaxed, limber, fluid around him—no escalating heartbeat, no tremor in the hands—despite the police's nearly airtight case.

It wasn't a logical reaction. Jack was Heather's boyfriend, the person most likely to kill her, according to statistics. The scissors crusted with Heather's blood—used to stab her, over and over—were found in his dorm room. Witnesses saw Jack and Heather screaming at each other hours before her body was found. The evidence was damning.

But in the end, the police weren't able to convict Jack. In some ways, it didn't matter. He was a murderer in everyone's eyes.

Everyone except for me.

Slowly, inch by inch, my body's knowing filtered into my brain. One night, a year or so after I moved to New York City, I woke in a cold sweat, sitting up rigid as a board in my tiny rented bedroom, filled to the brim with a single conviction: Jack was innocent.

It took me another three months to reach out to him. He was also living in the city, trying to disappear. I'd told him I thought he was innocent, and from that day forward, I'd been one of his few friends. I was his only friend from college, where, until Heather died, he'd been popular. Student body president. Phi Delt treasurer. Duquette University Volunteer of the Year.

To this day, I hadn't told anyone I still saw Jack. He was my secret. One of them, at least.

Looking at him now, radiating kindness, filled me with anger. Jack was undeniably *good*, so easy to read. The fact that so many believed he was capable of brutal violence was baffling. I'd met dangerous people—*truly* dangerous people—and seen the violence in their eyes, heard it brimming in their voices. Jack wasn't like that.

So I understood why he wanted to shield the new people in his life from his past, the horror of the accusation that remained unresolved, despite the dropped charges. It's not like he could ever truly hide it from someone, not with the internet, or the fact that his whole life, he was doomed to menial jobs that wouldn't fire him after a startling Google search. *Or* the fact that he barely spoke to his family anymore. Though, to be fair, that was because of more than Heather, because of their southernness, their Baptistness, their rigidness…

I understood why Jack would want to draw a solid, impenetrable line between *now* and *then*. But still, it was hard to wrap my mind around, because the past was still so much with me. I lived with the constant unfolding of memories, past scenes still rolling, still playing out. I heard my friends' voices in my head, kept our conversations alive, even if for years now it had just been me talking, one-sided, saying, *Just you wait*.

A thrill lifted the small hairs on my arms. Tomorrow, there'd be no more waiting.

Jack sighed. "Thanks for coming to see me before you left. You know, I'm glad you never changed. Seriously. Ten years, and same old Jess."

I nearly dropped my glass. "What are you talking about?" I waved at myself. "This dress is Rodarte. Look at this hair, these nails. I've been in *Page Six*. I've been to Europe, like, *eight times*. I'm totally different now."

Jack laughed as if I was joking and rose from his seat, leaning forward to kiss my forehead. "Never stop being a sweetheart, okay? You're one of the good ones."

I didn't want to be a sweetheart. How uninteresting, how pathetic. But I did want to be one of the good ones, which sounded like an exclusive club. I didn't know how to respond. At least Jack had given me what I'd come here looking for, besides the penance: his blessing. Now I could go to Duquette guilt-free. For that, I held my tongue as he tugged his coat over his shoulders.

He stepped away from the table, then turned back, and there was something in his eyes—worry? Fear? I couldn't quite pin it. "One more thing. I've been getting these letters—"

"Please don't tell me it's the Jesus freaks again, saying you're going to burn in hell for all eternity."

Jack winced. "No. Kind of the opposite." He looked down at me, at my raised brows. "You know what, it's not important. It might not mean anything in the end." He squared his shoulders. "Put your wine on my tab. Clara never makes me pay."

He squeezed my shoulder and took off, winding around the bar's motley collection of chairs. He paused by the door and looked over his shoulder. "Just... When you get to Duquette, say hi to Eric Shelby for me." Then he was out the door, on the sidewalk, carried away by a sea of people.

This time, I actually did spit out my wine. *Eric Shelby*—Heather's younger brother? Eric had been a freshman when we were seniors. I'd never forget the look on his face when he came flying around the corner the day they found Heather, saw the crowd gathered outside our dorm room, scanned it for his sister's face, didn't find her...

The last time I'd seen Eric and Jack in the same place, it was outside the library ten years ago. A crowd had gathered around them. Eric was screaming at Jack that he was a murderer, that he was going to pay for what he'd done to his sister, that even though the cops had let him go, Eric wouldn't stop until he found out the truth. Jack's face had gone white as a ghost's, but he hadn't walked away. He'd stood there taking it with fists clenched as Eric screamed, his friends trying to hold him back by his scrawny, flailing arms. If there was anyone alive who hated Jack Carroll more than Eric Shelby, I didn't know them.

So why the hell would Jack tell me to say hi to him?

READING GROUP GUIDE

1. How does reading *Twilight* alter Ruth's worldview? Do you think that was a positive or negative change for her? What books have had lasting effects on your perspective?

2. Ruth observes that "even if you hate your family, you still inherit from them." What does she mean? What is her inheritance from her parents?

3. Everett argues that pain is how you know you're alive. Why does he believe this? How is that belief dangerous throughout the book?

4. What did the incident with Beth Fortenot teach Ruth about her parents—her father in particular? How does Reverend Cornier uphold and enforce his faith throughout the book?

5. How do the different characters in the book define justice? Whose definition did you find the most compelling?

6. What did you make of Everett's overt desire to protect Ruth in the first half of the book? What are Ruth's thoughts about it?

7. Ruth struggles with the idea of people being all bad or all good. How do the events of the book change her thinking about morality? Which of her decisions best reflects her evolving viewpoint?

8. How would you characterize Ruth's mother? What does she gain from her obedience and what does it cost her?

9. How is the idea of community used as a weapon throughout the book?

10. Everett challenges Ruth by saying he needs to know whom she belongs to. How would you answer that question at the end of the book?

11. In your opinion, did Everett and Ruth succeed in their unlikely escape? If they were to survive, do you think they could create the life they were dreaming of?

A CONVERSATION WITH THE AUTHOR

Ruth and Everett's loyalty transcends their definitions of morality. What was most challenging about balancing these competing beliefs?

I would say Ruth and Everett's loyalty to each other *is* their definition of morality. In Bottom Springs, the dominant morality is set forth by Holy Fire Baptist Church. What the church says is good and moral—and by extension what Reverend Cornier says, as Holy Fire's emissary—is the definition the whole town accepts and lives by. They have to or else face severe ostracization or worse.

What Ruth and Everett model with their resistance is what often happens when morality regimes like Holy Fire's fundamentalist Christian one clash with what people feel in their hearts to be fair, just, and kind. When what people are told is right doesn't fit what they're experiencing in daily life, or fit their instincts for justice, they usually have two choices: either live in a state of cognitive dissonance (much to their psychological peril, like in the case of Ruth's mother) or develop "countermoralities": privately held definitions of what's right and wrong that exist apart from the dominant model. When enough people hold private countermoralities, you have the seeds of social change. You can see this throughout history: for example, society's growing conviction that many forms of discrimination against women, while considered morally, socially, and legally acceptable for much of human existence, are actually at odds with values of fairness and paved the way for gains in women's rights. The way Ruth and Everett reject Bottom Springs's morality and develop their own, based on what the two of them privately understand to be good (loyalty, kindness, making sure people are held accountable for their harms), is a microcosm of the way people have evolved moral consciousness for all time.

And we love these kinds of stories. We love "antiheroes," or "moral outlaws." There's a long tradition in art, and especially literature, of protagonists who act in defiance of prevailing laws or moral rules for reasons we can empathize with, reasons that even make them *right*. I suspect we're drawn to these kinds of moral outlaw characters because deep down, we're all a little more morally relativistic than we might admit. And I think we understand intrinsically what Ruth learns—that what's right isn't always what's legal or holy—and we chafe at the ways our legal and moral systems sometimes fail to match our internal moral compasses. We like to watch antiheroes respond to systems they don't agree with because we're interested in seeing what paths are open to us.

Of course, I wanted to really challenge my readers with this book. Because there's a big difference between, say, Luke Skywalker breaking the legal and moral rules of the authoritarian Galactic Empire and true antiheroes like Tony Soprano and Walter White breaking laws and hurting people to get ahead. I suspect most people who read this book will feel sympathy for Ruth and Everett's definition of morality over Holy Fire's. But I wanted to see how far I could push readers' allegiance by making them guilty of extremely violent and ruthless crimes. Will readers accept these acts, which they would normally categorize as morally reprehensible, as good or neutral because they understand why Ruth and Everett did it? If so, what does that say about us? Do we believe our individual moral compasses are more important than society's laws? And if so, how far are we willing to let people like Everett push that?

One last thing I'll say is that with the inclusion of *Twilight* as an important text to Ruth and with Everett as a kind of Edward figure for her, I wanted to make the case that popular media aimed at young women (like *Twilight*), which is so routinely dismissed and denigrated, actually falls into the canon of antihero/moral outlaw narratives, which are typically afforded more prestige. That is to say, I think part of the draw of books like *Twilight* is that the dark, brooding love interest exists at the very edge of, or outside, society and morality. I suspect part of readers' desire for an Edward Cullen–esque figure, much like Ruth's desire, is that being loved by him guarantees an escape from the confines of normal society and traditional morality, a life lived in defiance of law, social convention, and what most people would consider right and wrong. And since those systems are things that have never served young women, it's no wonder they're longing to escape.

When Ever first mentions his intrusive and violent thoughts, Ruth makes him promise to never speak of them again. How did she think she was helping? What effect did she actually have?

Ruth and Everett are two sides of the same coin. Oppressed by the same system, Ruth becomes the ultimate good girl, learning to play by the rules. What playing by the rules means as a young woman in a fundamentalist society is disappearing—suppressing her independent will, intellect, and desires and becoming a wisp. Ruth earns an A+ in obedience. Everett, on the other hand, is a failure. Where Ruth falls in line, Everett disrupts. He's the kid who's always in trouble, the one who won't play by the rules, and therefore he suffers the consequences of social ostracization and physical and psychological punishments.

During the scene at the docks, Ruth isn't yet able to see that Everett's way might actually be the better way to respond to oppression. (She'll decide it is later in the book.) At this point, she thinks she can help him by teaching him how to fall in line. She knows whatever Everett's trying to confess to her, it's something that will get him in trouble, and so she thinks if she can just teach him to do what she does—suppress his thoughts and feelings—she'll save him from punishment and heartache. But what's clear to the reader is that Everett is coming to her for a safe space, for help confronting his intrusive thoughts, and repressing them is only going to be unhealthy in the long run (and boy is it!). Believing that she's acting as Everett's friend, Ruth is in reality acting as an envoy of the town, reinforcing their message that Everett is unnatural and needs to change. Ruth's growth arc in the book is one in which she comes to recognize how unhealthy playing by the rules of an oppressive system is and instead embraces causing trouble as an act of justice and moral good.

The Fortenot Fishing wives are well informed but easily overlooked. Why was it important for Ruth to see the power they can wield, even though it doesn't change her own trajectory?

The Fortenot Fishing wives and Nissa Guidry, Ruth's beloved colleague at the library, represent a different way of responding to oppression. Rather than confront it head-on as Ruth does when, for example, she shows up at church to declare her father's sins before burning the place down, the fishing wives and Nissa operate under the radar. Their acts of defiance are quiet and (they hope) undetectable, such as how they keep track of what the men in town are up to through their whisper network, speculate and warn about possible wrongdoing, and protect and shield each other through rumor campaigns and misdirection.

Ruth ultimately doesn't choose this way of responding because she feels the sins of her father and the other town leaders deserve more radical forms of accountability, and on a pragmatic note, she doesn't have a husband or family to protect. But it's important for Ruth to see that she's not alone in chafing against Holy Fire and the harsh rules that govern people's lives in Bottom Springs. And she's not alone in rebelling against it. Truthfully, very few people in real life respond to oppression the way Ruth does, by trying to burn down the system. Most of us quietly rebel like the fishing wives and Nissa, doing what we can in our own ways to make things right and protect the people we care about. It was important to me to show that there are multiple ways of resisting.

Ruth, faced with her father's power and entrenchment, realizes that "what's right isn't the same as what's lawful or holy." How should we define justice without the external measures of law or scripture?

Wow, this is *the* question, isn't it? I mean, this is one of the questions humanity has been debating since we developed the capacity for abstract thinking and conceived of a thing called "justice." One of the things I was most interested in exploring through this book—this murder mystery full of crimes—is the question of what makes something a crime in the first place and whether that legal designation ("crime") is as seamlessly connected to our idea of justice, and thus to a moral system, as we'd like to believe. If it is, whose moral system is the one we all live by? Because certainly, not all humans share the same beliefs. In fact, we've been arguing about how to define moral good, and thus justice (and thereby form our laws in response), since way before Immanuel Kant and Jeremy Bentham ever came along, even if their ideas about duty/intention and greatest good, respectively, have come to dominate moral thinking in many Western cultures.

Readers are probably familiar with the phrase "History is written by the winners," which of course means that our history, and thus how we understand the world, has been unduly influenced by the perspectives of those in power. *Midnight* is a piece of crime fiction that I hope asks: Is justice also written by the winners? That is, is what's considered just determined by who's in power? Is what's right something we feel intrinsically in our hearts, captured by those little moral compasses we're said to have, or is it an understanding we inherit from whichever people or ideologies happen to be on top? Certainly, if you look at history, what's considered just and morally right has changed over time, not to mention differs by culture. What if these concepts are more arbitrary then we would like to believe? Doesn't that mean they deserve to be consistently challenged to make sure they still hold up? And what do we do with troublemakers, the people who challenge them?

Bottom Springs is haunted not only by the specter of the Low Man but by a moral system that has arisen out of the ultraconservative, patriarchal, fire-and-brimstone teachings of the Holy Fire Church. Everyone in town knows the rules of how they should feel and behave. The church's definition of morality is so concrete and loudly advertised, it might as well as be law. (Ruth's awareness of it is so strong that she actually feels as if these rules are surveilling her the way a policeman would.)

And *yet*, despite the well-understood, commonly agreed-upon moral and legal system governing Bottom Springs, it turns out no one actually believes in it. The leaders of the town are the best example. Ruth's father, despite being a spokesperson for the church, has his own private definition of morality: whatever makes him powerful, as God's agent on earth, is what's moral and good, and whatever obstructs his ascendence is immoral and bad. (Readers who are cynics about organized religion might argue that the reverend's definition isn't actually a departure from how the church has acted throughout history.)

For Reverend Cornier, what's just and what's legal are clearly not the same thing. That's why he can run his drug ring without believing he deserves to be punished. And think about how quickly the idea of lawfulness falls apart when the townspeople feel threatened by Everett, who they believe is the Low Man. These formerly peaceful shop owners and fishermen take up torches and guns, ready to kill without trial in order to protect themselves. The townspeople are also clearly comfortable separating what's legal from what's just. What's remarkable about Ruth and Everett may just be that they learned this lesson at an early age when they killed Renard Michaels. In some ways, the lesson was a gift because it forced them to think critically about all accepted wisdom from that point forward.

Let's say readers are comfortable accepting that crimes aren't always immoral or unjust actions. And let's say we can agree that acting in accordance with moral good is more important than acting lawfully. This is where things get messy. Because at this point you have to ask: Okay, then, what makes something morally good? Who gets to define it? Religions like Holy Fire certainly offer their versions. On the secular side, we'll circle back to Kant and Bentham, who tried to define moral good. Kant said that any action committed with the *intention* of respecting another person's humanity and dignity is morally good, regardless of the consequences. For Bentham, the utilitarian, it's all about the outcome: Did an action produce the best possible good for the greatest number of people, regardless of the intent or even the action? If so, then it's morally good. Ironically, even though Everett and Ruth are the book's most prolific and deadly criminals, their actions are the most morally good according to both Kantian and utilitarian theories.

It's probably obvious by this point, but I think of justice as more personal than many people may want it to be. And I wanted to write a crime novel that wrestled with the difficulty of justice and moral good as concepts. I love books that challenge readers, whether it's asking them to root for characters that commit awful actions or hate characters that are the heroes on paper. I think that challenge opens room for reflection.

What I specifically hope readers will reflect on is the possibility that a person can act unlawfully or even in ways that seem immoral at first, but when understood in full context, the morality of their actions becomes clear. Or perhaps they possess a moral vision that's different from the status quo but may be where the status quo needs to evolve to. An obvious example is activists who exist at the edge of what's legally or morally acceptable—people who defy laws to protest actions they deem immoral or skirt the lines of what's considered morally acceptable to challenge that very system of morality. I would not claim that Ruth and Everett are some great moral change agents, but sometimes a story has the power to open a reader's mind and help them look at what's happening in the world in a fresh light. And I suppose I'd love it if readers finished *Midnight* and then tried to understand other people's definitions of justice before judging their actions.

The ending of the book is ambiguous. Why was it important to you to leave Ruth and Ever's escape unlikely but plausible?

It was important to me to leave Ruth and Everett's fate in the reader's hands. Here's why. At the end of the book, as their car is sailing through the air, Ruth pleads to "God or the Devil or whoever's listening" to take mercy on her. That "whoever's listening" is important to me because it holds space for all that's unknown in the world, all that's still a mystery about the purpose and meaning of human life. It shows the freedom of mind Ruth has achieved, on one hand, that she's acknowledging there could be a possible listener outside of the Christian God she's grown up believing in. But more than that, it shows her desperation. She's hoping that someone or something *is* in charge and that they'll take notice of her, have mercy on her. She'll take anyone or anything at this point.

The fervent desire that Ruth has for there to be someone out there and for there to be more to this world and our lives than we can see, is actually the central desire that drives every character in the book. It's the thing Ruth has most in common with her fellow townspeople. While they're looking for higher meaning and transcendence through Holy Fire Baptist, Ruth is searching for a path everywhere (through romance, through religion, through books). So, in her final plea, Ruth is putting voice to the search that has animated her throughout the story. Are you out there, she asks, and if you are, will you save me?

What Ruth can't know is that there *is* someone listening: the reader. The reader becomes the person she's pleading with. We're the ones who get to decide whether to forgive her, to find the good in what she's done, to weigh her and find her worthy or not, and thus imagine that she clears the bridge (or not). In that moment, the reader becomes God. What do you think Ruth and Everett deserve?

Your books all reckon with narratives that govern women's lives. What do you hope readers will take away from your characters' responses to and rejections of these narratives?

I love the distinction here about narratives. Because you could say I write books about *institutions* and *people* that govern women's lives: schools, religions, governments, husbands, cult leaders, the criminal justice system, parents, the list goes on. In my books, many of these actors exercise really egregious control over women by physically or legally coercing them. And I'm interested in exploring that form of control and how to resist it, certainly. But what I'm most interested in are, as this question puts it, the *narratives* women are told or tell themselves that exert maybe a slipperier but no less powerful control.

In each of my thrillers (and honestly in my romance novels too, but that's a discussion for another day), you might say the chief antagonists my characters face are actually narratives: stories they've heard or tell themselves about who they are and how incapable they are of change, about their weaknesses, their inferiority, their inherent lack of value. Stories about how women are supposed to feel and think and behave.

These are stories my characters have deeply internalized, and their lives and possibilities are foreclosed by them.

Coming to recognize and resist these narratives is a big part of Ruth's arc in *Midnight*. One question I anticipate readers asking is: *Why doesn't Ruth just leave?* Readers might even feel frustrated by her for this reason. Why doesn't she just pack up and drive out of town and never see her parents or Bottom Springs again—what's stopping her?

Well. A lot, actually. At different points in the book Ruth describes being held in an invisible prison, its bars in her mind, and being tethered to her parents and the town by invisible chains that she herself helps keep fastened. These invisible forms of bondage are the narratives Ruth has been fed since she was born about her weakness, her lack of capacity for change, the inferior quality of her mind, her low place in the world, and what makes her valuable and lovable (namely, how obedient and submissive she is). They've set up shop in her mind and even if she knows she shouldn't, some deep down part of her believes them.

That's the hard thing about these identity-shaping narratives: even when you know intellectually that you should reject them, the actual doing is difficult because the narratives have shaped you. Sadly, they're part of you, they're home, and it takes monumental work to disentangle yourself. This is the kind of work characters like Ruth model. As someone who has done a lot of work to disentangle myself from harmful narratives that were keeping me small and afraid, I take great joy in writing female characters who liberate themselves and, furthermore, do so in ways both quiet and quotidian and wild, earth-shattering, and bombastic. I hope what readers take away are possible paths they might try, too.

ACKNOWLEDGMENTS

My name may be on the cover, but this book is the result of a community of talented people. I want to start by thanking my publishing colleagues from the bottom of my heart for what they've done for me as a person this year, outside of any book. I suffered a hard loss while writing *Midnight,* and my grief became a lead weight that would've sunk me without the help of the people listed below, a group who lifted me up and helped me breathe. They didn't have to do it—the kindness and care I received exceeded any professional obligation—but I will never, ever forget that they did.

To my Sourcebooks family: I adore you. Emily Luedloff, you are the ultimate pleasure to work with and so good at what you do. Thanks a million for everything you've done to support my books. (I wish we lived closer so we could be IRL buddies!) Ashlyn Keil, every email from you is good news—thank you for all you do to get me off my couch and into the world. To the inimitable Diane Dannenfeldt, thank you for lending me your sharp, incisive brain and thank you for your patience with my insistence on using the word "breathed." Jessica Thelander and Laura Boren, thank you for making the inside of my books so very beautiful. Kelly Lawler, Erin Fitzsimmons, and Stephanie Rocha—wow. Thank you for creating the cover of my dreams and for being such considerate and patient partners. Findlay McCarthy, thank you for engaging with my work so thoughtfully and beautifully and coming up with incredible questions—you make me feel seen. Dominique Raccah, thank you for my career! It's an honor to be published by you. Molly Waxman, thank you for lending me your PR and marketing genius. Every time, it's an honor.

Cristina Arreola, I'm the luckiest for getting to work with you on three books now. You are brilliant, innovative, and a master of the strategic pivot. A total star. On top of that, your kindness and generosity this last year has meant more than I can say. I, for one, look forward to the day when you simply rule over the entire book world. I'm willing it into being.

Shana Drehs, you are a dream editor. I'm so grateful for your insights, storytelling instincts, and intuitive understanding of how to strengthen plots and characters. Most of all, I'm grateful to have found such a wonderful publishing partner and friend.

Julia McDowell and the rest of the HarperCollins Canada team, what a joy it is to work with you! You are some of my favorite people in publishing. Thank you for believing in my books and helping get them in the hands of Canadian readers.

Melissa Edwards, this book wouldn't be half as twisty without your brilliant contributions—thank you for those early plot brainstorms. Even more, thank you for being my ambitious champion on Mondays, Wednesdays, and Fridays and my level-headed gut checker on Tuesdays and Thursdays. You're the greatest, and there's no one else I'd rather do this with.

Addison Duffy, thank you for everything we can't talk about yet. I'm lucky to work with you.

A huge thanks to the amazing booksellers who've become friends: John McDougall, McKenna Jordan, Rebecca Minnock, Sally Woods, Barbara Peters, Julie Swearingen, Sterling Miller, and many more. A special shout-out to Murder by the Book for basically letting me take up residency and Poisoned Pen Bookstore for being so welcoming and such a mecca for readers and authors alike.

To my beloved Bookstagram community: I see you out there spreading joy and love and thoughtful conversations about art, and I appreciate you so much. You are the kindest, most supportive friends a person could ask for. Talk about keeping me afloat during hard times. Gare (@gareindeed-reads) and Chip (@booksovrbros), I'll never be able to thank either of you enough for being such rocks on top of amazing friends. I am in awe of both of your creative talents. Dennis (@scaredstraightreads), thank you for the above and beyond support on *The Last Housewife* and for being so kind when my life blew up and I had to change our plans last minute. You're one of my absolute favorites, and I hope I never have to attend a thriller conference without you (because obviously it would be 1000% less fun).

Huge, huge thanks especially to Abby (@crimebythebook), Emily (@emilybookedup), Elodie (@elosreadingcorner), the incredible Jordy (@jordysbookclub), Katie (@katieloybythebook), Jamie (@beautyandthebook), Kayla (@kayreadwhat), Nikki (@poetry.and.plot.twists), Jill (@romanticizedreads), Bailey (@hardcoverbooklover), Heather (@booksbyheath), Chelsea (@thrillerbookbabe), Yolanda (@readmorethrillers), Kori (@thrillbythepage_), Tonya (@blondethriller-booklover), Olivia (@oliviadaywrites), Rachel (@bellvillefl), Krissy (@books_and_biceps9155), Thomas (@readwiththomas), Erin (@the_boozy_baking_bibliophile), Lauren (@girlsgoalsandgongshows), Nikki (@nikkihrose), Ashley (@ashleyspivey), Natalie (@booknerdalie), Andrew (@romantichorror), Marisha (@marishareadsalot), Phil (@philsbookcorner), Yenny (@readswithyenny), Amanda (@read-ergirlie), Alice (@bookslover_16), Meghna (@read_between_the_lines_._), Robyn (@robyn_reads1), Carrie (@carriereadsthem_all), Ally (@allysbookshoparoundthecorner), Erin (@thrillofthepage), Brei (@sweethoneyandbrei), Mallory (@mallorylbates), Dani and Brit

(@bookshelfbesties), and Jessica (@bookish.fit.nurse_jess). Each of you have touched my heart and brought me joy, and for that I'm so grateful.

To the incredible authors who've welcomed me into the book community and supported me in ways big and small, I will never stop being grateful for your talent, generosity, humor, and kindness. Huge thanks to Vanessa Lillie, Danielle Girard (Vanessa and Danielle, I will never forget how kind you were to me this year), Mary Kubica, Samantha Downing, Layne Fargo, Megan Collins, Kristen Bird, Alison Wisdom, Amy Gentry, May Cobb, Julie Clark, Stacy Willingham, Amanda Jayatissa, Vera Kurian, Lyssa Smith, Ruby Barrett, Yasmin Angoe, Jennifer Hillier, Hannah Mary McKinnon, Hank Ryan, Clare Macintosh, Sandra Brown, Andi Bartz, Lynn Painter, Abby Jimenez, Meredith Schorr, Kimberly Belle, Heather Gudenkauf, Kaira Rouda, Samantha Bailey, Jaime Lynn Hendricks, Rosie Danan, Rachel Lynn Solomon, Ava Wilder, Trish Doller, Kate Bromley, Mazey Eddings, Jen Devon, Kate Spencer, and Lauren Nossett. I will forever be a fangirl to all of you.

Russell, you are so special to me. Thank you for a lifetime of love, care, and devotion. Since you first opened that Mary Oliver collection and read "Wild Geese" to me, intuiting that I'd understand why it moved you, you've shaped me as a person and an artist. It seems at every pivotal point in my life, I've come to you and you've steered me in a direction that allowed me to grow more fully myself, more comfortable in my own skin. What heroics did I perform in a past life to receive the gift of spending this one with you? I love you madly.

Diana and Terry Sobey, thank you for being incredible parents to Alex and to me—I'm so lucky to have you as my in-laws.

Mom, Ryan, Amanda, Celeste, Ezra, Taylor, Catherine, Mallory, and Alex: thank you for being the best parts of my life. Dad, some feelings are too big even for a book. So I'll simply say: I've never wished heaven existed more than I do now. I will love and miss you forever.

ABOUT THE AUTHOR

Photo © Luis Noble

Ashley Winstead writes about power, ambition, and love across wildly different genres. She received her BA in English, creative writing, and art history from Vanderbilt University and her PhD in English from Southern Methodist University. She lives in Houston, TX, with her husband and two cats. Find out more at ashleywinstead.com.